Praise for *Damas*

"[An] exciting spy thriller." —*Washington Post*

"[David McCloskey] captures the places and people—and most of all, the sickening feeling in the gut—of this war that shattered poor Syria while America mostly watched. . . . This isn't just a realistic spy novel, it's real life."
—David Ignatius, columnist for the *Washington Post* and author of *The Paladin*

"The power of this book is that it tells this devastating story through the eyes of those who suffered and survived because of love, the human relationship, and the power of what makes life worth living."
—Leon E. Panetta, former director of the CIA and former secretary of defense

"A sweeping spy thriller packed with true to life tradecraft. There's no doubt that McCloskey is a CIA veteran."
—Karen Cleveland, *New York Times* best-selling author of *Need to Know*

"I've never known a writer as good at the spy novel as John le Carré, but McCloskey approaches."
—Nick Kristof, former *New York Times* columnist

"From an exfiltration gone awry to a stunning endgame, *Damascus Station* takes the reader on a breathtaking journey in war-torn Syria."
—Dan Hoffman, former Chief of CIA Middle East Operations and three-time Chief of Station

"An extremely effective modern espionage novel. . . . [A] dazzling debut."
—Neil Nyren, *Booktrib*

"Riveting . . . a swift dive into the lethal, nebulous world of CIA operations in the Middle East. . . . [A] breathless ride."—Peter Eisner, *SpyTalk*

"Truly one of the finest entries into the modern spy thriller genre. In a field groaning with ludicrous plots, absurd characters, and laughable 'espionage,' McCloskey—a former CIA analyst—has crafted a book that goes back to the roots of what makes a spy thriller great, the spying."
—Joshua Huminski, *Diplomatic Courier*

"Simply intoxicating. A vortex of love, loyalty, murder, and damn good espionage."
—Don Hepburn, former CIA Chief of Station

"An uncommonly gripping first novel. . . . *Damascus Station* combines an insider's account of tradecraft . . . with compassion for the Syrian people, outrage at the Assad regime, and an up-to-the-minute old-fashioned love story."
—John Wilson, *First Things*

"*Damascus Station* is an exceptionally well-crafted novel of espionage, tradecraft and Syria at the onset of the Civil War. . . . [The book] serves as a tutorial on tradecraft for those on the outside."
—Robert Richer, *Cipher Brief*

"[An] exhilarating debut. . . . McCloskey portrays the brutal inner functioning of the Assad regime, as well as the CIA's occasional ineptitude, while detailing such elements of spy craft as avoiding tails, maximizing dead drops, and operating safe houses."
—*Publishers Weekly*

DAMASCUS STATION

DAMASCUS STATION

a novel

DAVID McCLOSKEY

W. W. NORTON & COMPANY
Independent Publishers Since 1923

Printed in the United States of America
First published as a Norton paperback 2022

For information about permission to reproduce selections from this book, write to Permissions, W. W. Norton & Company, Inc., 500 Fifth Avenue, New York, NY 10110

For information about special discounts for bulk purchases, please contact W. W. Norton Special Sales at specialsales@wwnorton.com or 800-233-4830

Damascus map by World Sites Atlas
Damascus street data © OpenStreetMap contributors (openstreetmap.org)

Manufacturing by Lakeside Book Company
Book design by Beth Steidle
Production manager: Beth Steidle

Library of Congress Cataloging-in-Publication Data

Names: McCloskey, David, author.
Title: Damascus Station : a novel / David McCloskey.
Description: First edition. | New York, N.Y. : W. W. Norton & Company, [2021]
Identifiers: LCCN 2021025200 | ISBN 9780393881042 (hardcover) | ISBN 9780393881059 (epub)
Subjects: LCSH: United States. Central Intelligence Agency—Fiction. | Syria—History—Civil War, 2011– —Fiction. | GSAFD: Spy stories. | Romantic suspense fiction. | LCGFT: Spy fiction. | Thrillers (Fiction) | Romance fiction. | Novels.
Classification: LCC PS3613.C35845 D36 2021 | DDC 813/.6—dc23
LC record available at https://lccn.loc.gov/2021025200

ISBN 978-1-324-03613-5 pbk.

W. W. Norton & Company, Inc., 500 Fifth Avenue, New York, N.Y. 10110
www.wwnorton.com

W. W. Norton & Company Ltd., 15 Carlisle Street, London W1D 3BS

1 2 3 4 5 6 7 8 9 0

For Abby, my love and co-conspirator
And for Syria and her people, for a future brighter than the past

Damascus has seen all that has ever occurred on earth, and still she lives. She has looked upon the dry bones of a thousand empires, and will see the tombs of a thousand more before she dies.

—MARK TWAIN,
THE INNOCENTS ABROAD, 1869

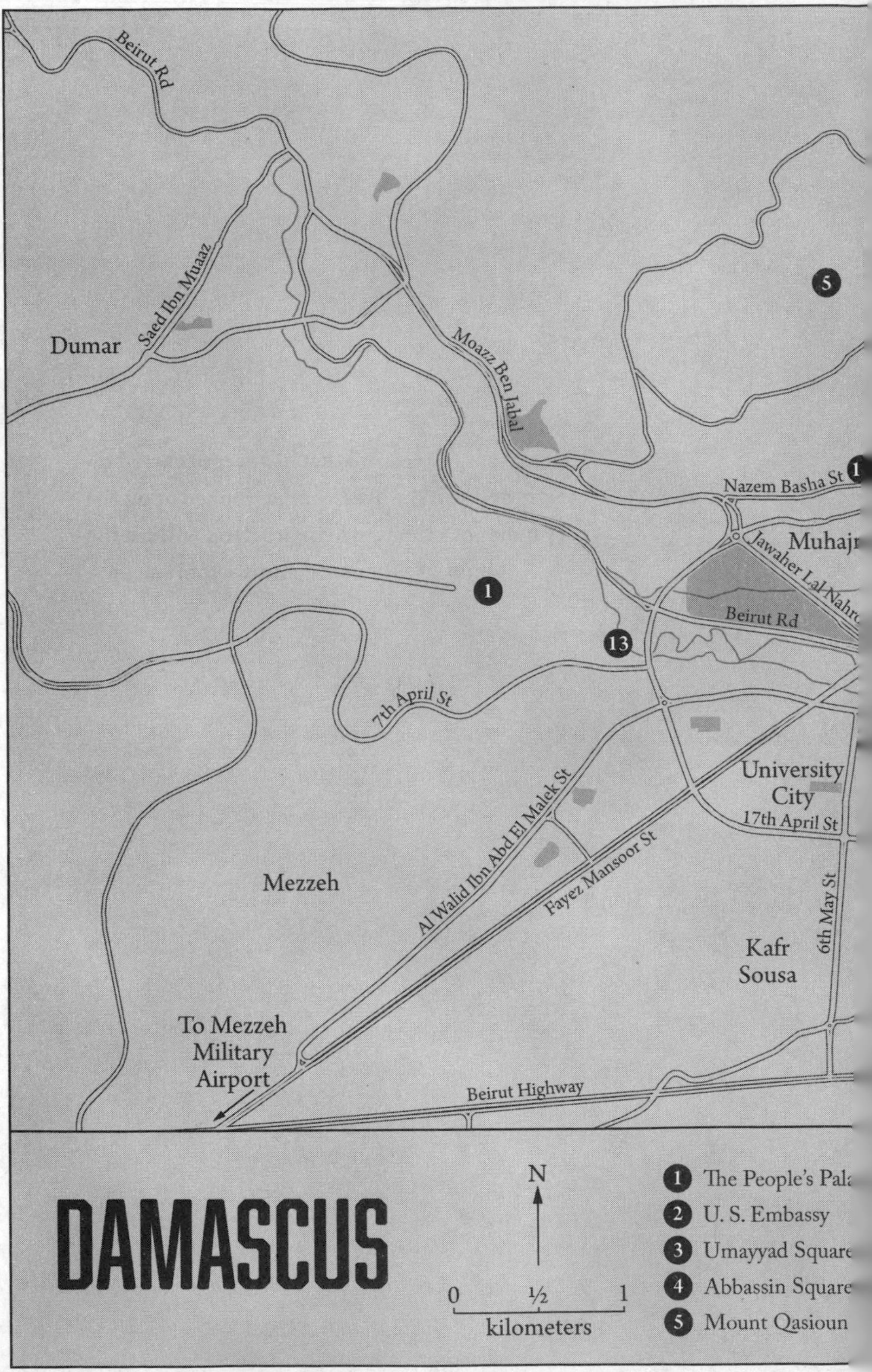

Beirut Rd

Saed Ibn Muaaz

Dumar

Moazz Ben Jabal

5

Nazem Basha St 1

Muhajr

Jawaher Lal Nahr

1

Beirut Rd

13

7th April St

Al Walid Ibn Abd El Malek St

University City

17th April St

Fayez Mansoor St

Mezzeh

6th May St

Kafr Sousa

To Mezzeh Military Airport

Beirut Highway

DAMASCUS

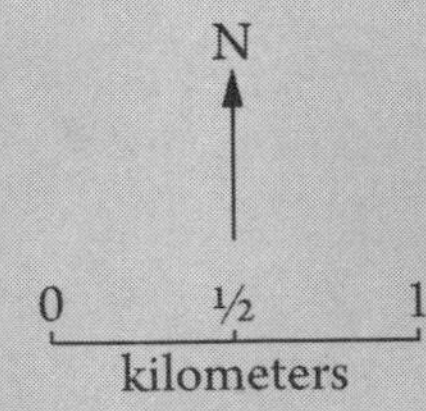

1 The People's Pala
2 U. S. Embassy
3 Umayyad Squar
4 Abbassin Square
5 Mount Qasioun

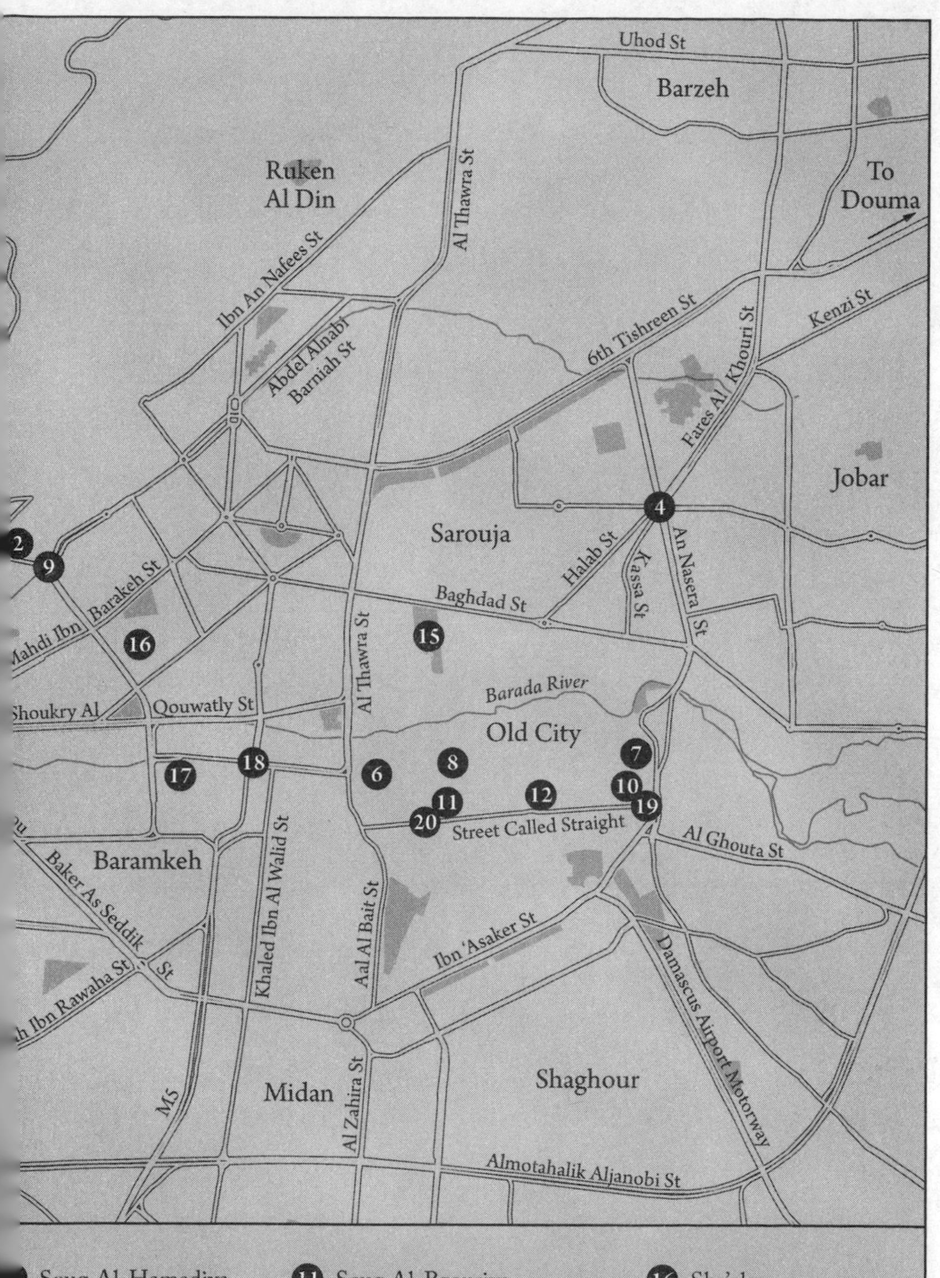

Souq Al-Hamadiya
Ananias Chapel
Umayyad Mosque
Al Rawda Square
Bab Touma

11 Souq Al-Bzouriye
12 Mariamite Cathedral
13 Art House Restaurant
14 Presidential Residence
15 Dahdah Cemetery

16 Sha'alan
17 Damascus University
18 Hijaz Square
19 Bab Sharqi
20 Souq Midhat Basha

PART I

Murders

1

THE EARLY YEARS OF THE SYRIAN UPRISING

Eight hours into his surveillance detection route Sam's grip on the steering wheel loosened and his pulse began to slow. He'd made three stops in and around Damascus and executed the planned turns on the SDR, each time scanning for watchers, his eyes darting between the mirrors. At each stop he'd lingered, trying to draw out opposition surveillance. The heat burned through the windshield and the air conditioner struggled to keep up. His back hurt, and his shoulders felt permanently hunched over. He hit traffic and idled the car in an intersection mercifully shaded by palm and pine. Sam drummed his fingers on the wheel and checked the mirrors as the light lingered red, comparing each vehicle to a mental catalog of the cars he had seen earlier in the day. The light turned green. A *mukhabarat* officer in a leather jacket marched into the road with his hand up and gestured for the first car in line to stay in place. A car behind him honked. Another *mukhabarat* officer now dragged into the road a sawhorse emblazoned with stickers of President Bashar al-Assad and waved the first car forward. Someone yelled that it was a checkpoint.

Though it was the sixth of the day, Sam's heartbeat picked up again. Nonofficial cover meant everything was on the line. There would be no diplomatic immunity if he was caught. There would be no trade. He would disappear into a basement prison. If you weren't twitchy driving in a hostile country with no lifeline, you were probably a sociopath.

He slid the passport from his breast pocket and placed it on the dashboard. The document was Canadian, dark blue (tourist), and included a picture of a man named James Hansen. The photo was Sam's, as was the birthday. He'd collected the document from the Canadian Security Intelligence Service on a slushy spring day in Ottawa after touring the office spaces of the recently established yet nonexistent Orion Real Estate Investments, LLC. The cover was fully backstopped—humans would answer the phones and respond to emails—the Canadians only too happy to participate in exchange for a seat at the debriefing table once KOMODO was safe at Langley. For even friendly intelligence services do not share, they trade.

KOMODO was one of the most productive assets in Damascus Station's stable. Middle-aged, lonely, a little creepy according to the ops cables, he was a mid-level scientist in Syria's Scientific Studies and Research Center, the SSRC, the organization responsible for Assad's chemical weapons. The NSA believed that the Syrians had breached KOMODO's covert communications system, and so over the course of a frenetic day Langley had built an exfiltration plan that involved Sam driving into Syria under commercial cover to get the asset out. CIA had also decided to bring home Val Owens, KOMODO's handling officer. Sam and Val had served together in Iraq, her first tour, his third. They'd become close, like family. Val was a friend, an asset's life was on the line, and when he thought of those two things his heart rate picked up again as a soldier waved him forward.

A young soldier with hard eyes and a wispy mustache approached the driver's window and asked for documents. Sam held eye contact for a respectful second, then gave him the passport—already turned to the page with the ninety-day Syrian visa—and stared out the windshield toward the highway. The soldier flipped through the book, scanned around as if questioning whether to call his supervisor, then squinted at Sam.

"Why in Syria?" he said in heavily accented English.

"Business," Sam said in Arabic.

The soldier nodded to one of his approaching comrades, their eyes nervously searching the parked cars and buildings. The regime controlled this part of the city, but rebels and jihadis sometimes hit the checkpoints. Suicide bombings, rocket-propelled grenades, the run-and-gun tactics like he'd seen during his tour in Baghdad—all of it was increasingly common in Damascus. The soldier set his jaw and smacked the passport into his own open palm.

"Open the trunk," he told Sam.

Sam pressed the button to open the rear hatch. Another soldier opened the back and removed Sam's suitcase, thunking it onto the pavement.

"Is it locked?" the soldier said.

"No," Sam said. He heard unzippering and the muffled sound of clothes being tossed back into the car.

"Why is nothing folded?" the other soldier asked.

"Because I have already been through several checkpoints today," Sam said.

"Rental?" the first soldier said, smacking the driver's door with the butt of his AK-47.

Sam nodded.

"Papers."

Sam opened the glove compartment and handed the soldier a set of papers indicating the car belonged to Rainbow Rentals of Amman, Jordan. As the soldier reviewed the papers, Sam shoved from his mind the image of an Amman Station mechanic using a mannequin precisely matching KOMODO's height and weight (five-foot-five, 145 pounds) to illustrate how to fold a human into the specially fabricated trunk compartment.

The soldier handed back the papers. "What type of business, Mr. Hansen?"

"Real estate investment. Villas out here, maybe some homes in the Old City."

"The villas are cheap now."

"Yes." Sam smiled. "Yes, they are."

"The suitcase is fine," said the man behind the car.

The soldier handed back the passport and grunted. "Move along."

Clear of the checkpoint, he nosed the car onto the M1 highway and toward the Old City as the *maghrib*, the sunset call to prayer, rang from the muezzins of the mosques. The evening traffic was light. Syrians now rushed indoors at nightfall to avoid the mortars lobbed between the regime and the rebels.

As the sun dipped below the horizon behind him, his body now agreed with what his mind had already concluded: He was black. Free of surveillance. For a moment, he felt relief. Then the second-guessing began, an SDR ritual for every CIA case officer since the first training-wheels run at the Farm. This was the bitch of the Mission. The cold fact that you could never be sure, that it was always easier to abort when covered than to commit the operational act knowing you could be wrong.

So he let the questions flow.

Had he been made by the black Lexus with the scuffed passenger door in Yafour? Had he seen the dusty yellow cab now trailing him just after his second stop, at the tacky villa with the hourglass-shaped pool? Had the glint from an apartment building window during the last checkpoint been a fixed surveillance post? Sam popped a tab of spearmint gum in his mouth. He chewed slowly, staring through the weather-beaten windshield as Damascus neared. Vehicular SDRs made it maddeningly difficult to spot repeats. He wanted to get out onto the street but had no reason for the move. Suburban Damascus was now a war zone and Sam was James Hansen, real estate investor. James Hansen would not make random stops in a war zone. James Hansen would hustle to his rented house in the Old City and bed down for the night before returning to Amman.

He stopped the Land Cruiser two blocks from the safe house. He slapped a yellowed atlas on the roof and pretended to scour the winding alleys for his ultimate destination. This was the final chance to abort. Sam took in a deep breath and felt the cool night air on his skin. The hairs on his neck did not stand. He did not feel watched. He looked around, picking up the atlas like an idiot tourist in one last attempt to search for watchers in the night. He looked down the correct road and tossed the atlas into the passenger's seat.

He pulled the Land Cruiser outside a house just off Bab Touma. The Canadians had picked an ideal location on the Old City's outer rim: the ARCHIMEDES safe house had easy access to the winding alleys and narrow roads of the city center—perfect for surveillance detection—as well as the wider roads encircling it, making it accessible by car. The house was a three-story Ottoman-era palace that sprawled for what Sam judged was half a city block. Garages were uncommon in Damascus and considered unsightly in a grand old house like this. To achieve the functionality without sacrificing aesthetic, this owner—a Canadian support asset—had fashioned an elaborate door that appeared to be one of the home's street-facing exterior walls.

Sam pressed a button tucked beside a gas lantern on the northern wall. It opened with a creak and he backed the car into the garage. Despite the villa's size, the corridor set behind the garage was tight. At its end, the marble floor spilled into a set of double doors fifteen feet high, with iron latticework wrought into Quranic phrases forming dozens of intricate panes. Sam opened the doors into the inner courtyard. A fountain gurgled in its center, ringed by small clusters of orange and lemon trees. Unseen rooks squawked warnings as he entered. To the east a mortar volley kicked up, and he flinched instinctively before backing inside the hallway and closing the doors.

The Canadians had included a floor plan in the liaison traffic, so he had no trouble navigating the winding hallways to reach the kitchen. In a musty cabinet he found the items he'd requested: a pack of high-calorie granola bars, a baggie with ten two-milligram Xanax pills, a portable oxygen concentrator, a CamelBak hydration pack, and adult diapers. He filled the CamelBak with water and removed one diaper from the pack. He put everything into a black satchel and zippered it shut.

Returning to the garage, he opened the Land Cruiser's rear hatch. He slid open the compartment tucked into the rear seats beneath the trunk space by turning a series of hidden dials in the precise order demonstrated in Amman. Sam ran his hand along the compartment's thin lining. It was black silicon, transported from a Langley basement to Amman Station via diplomatic pouch and designed to absorb heat, rendering warm objects underneath invisible to infrared sensors. He tossed the satchel inside, wishing that CIA could tuck cyanide pills in these go-bags like the Russians did for their assets. A CIA asset caught in Syria could expect months of interrogation and torture. If Sam were in KOMODO's shoes he'd want the pill.

TO WORK OUT THE STRESS Sam did rounds of push-ups and sit-ups for thirty minutes. When he'd finished, he took a hot shower. Val was fifteen minutes late. He didn't need to check clocks or watches any-more. Training at the Farm had seen to that.

He changed into a fresh white shirt and light gray suit and returned to the kitchen to see if he could find coffee. He located an old press coated in dust, along with an electric tea kettle and a tin of ground coffee. He didn't check the expiration date because he didn't care. He needed the caffeine.

Sam steeped the coffee, let the cup cool, then drank it in three gulps. He filled a second cup, gazing at the escaping steam. He called a memorized phone number and asked for an update on the Dubai acquisition. The voice on the other end, a Syrian support asset who did not know the true meaning of any of the prearranged codes, told Sam that the transaction was on hold. Sam asked him to confirm.

"It is on hold, Mr. Hansen."

Sam finished the second cup of coffee in two gulps and shattered the empty mug on the floor.

THE PROSPECT OF KOMODO'S IMMINENT arrest and the deteriorating security situation in Syria meant CIA had to forgo the usual exfiltration playbook: spirit the asset between safe houses for weeks, let the heat simmer down, then smuggle them over the border. KOMODO had been under surveillance for weeks. All three would leave Syria from the safe house.

Sam lay on the bed in his suit, heart stampeding from the caffeine and the adrenaline. If the *mukhabarat* had snatched up KOMODO, they'd come for Val next. And all he could do was wait for Val. It was, more than anything, a business of waiting. The waiting, though, created a sharp edge that made him want to drink half a handle of whiskey or take a couple of KOMODO's Xanax pills. Some officers tried to numb the edge with booze or drugs or women. It always led to the gutter, dismissal from the service, or worse. They'd found one of his Farm classmates—an officer under non-official cover, a NOC operating in Belarus—hanging from an exposed rafter in his Minsk apartment, pills and syringes and empty vodka bottles littering the floor.

The Mission could wear on you.

It was almost two in the morning. He heard a door creak somewhere in the house, then footfalls in a hallway.

He found Val in the kitchen, one foot tapping the floor, a shaky hand scooping coffee into the press. She spilled a spoonful of grounds and slammed her hands on the counter.

"Fuck, fuck, fuck," she yelled. "Three windows. He missed three pickup windows."

Her taut frame swelled as she sucked in deep breaths, trying to calm herself. She flipped on the kettle and slid onto the floor, back against the cabinets. Sam sat down next to her. Both were silent as the kettle bubbled to life. She was sinewy and lean, very much the way he remembered her in Baghdad, but she'd let her blond hair grow out well past the shoulders. He put his arm around her. She slumped her head on his shoulder.

After a few minutes he stood and retrieved a red satchel from the Land Cruiser's compartment. Returning to the kitchen, he tossed it to Val. It contained a Canadian passport that, like Sam's, bore her own picture and a false name. She examined the disguises—wig, eyeglasses, foam gut to add twenty pounds—all bespoke to match the picture. "Dude, I look terrible as an overweight brunette," she said.

"I know. That's why I picked it."

She smiled, then her face darkened. "We need to give him a few more hours to make the emergency signal. Then, if he's still a no-show, we leave."

THEY SAT ON THE KITCHEN floor waiting for a signal that KOMODO had reappeared, for daylight, for the *mukhabarat* to kick in the door. They each took turns keeping watch while the other slept, but neither managed sleep, and both now rubbed raw eyes as a metallic screech rang from the street. The protester working the megaphone yelled, *Selmiyyeh, selmiyyeh*—Peaceful, peaceful—and the crowd's murmurs reverberated inside the house.

"Friday protests starting," Sam said.

"Abbassin Square is just a few blocks north," she said groggily. "The big opposition committees and Facebook pages called for a demonstration today. They want to camp out until the regime falls. They are starting early today, though. We should leave soon."

Sam now looked out one of the windows at the large crowd pouring through the street below.

"This is going to be the biggest protest so far in Damascus," she said. "Could be bloody." Val sat back down and folded her arms on the table. "I think he's gone."

"Probably," Sam said as he stood. "But we talk about anything other than this busted op right now. We should go."

She was opening her mouth to speak when the rooks squawked outside and the hairs on Sam's neck shot up straight. Her mouth closed and Sam could see in Val's widening eyes that she sensed the same disturbance.

Selmiyyeh, selmiyyeh.

They both stood. Sam's chair creaked against the floor in the sticky silence.

Selmiyyeh, selmiyyeh. The home's ancient door groaned as it splintered from its hinges.

2

ONLY AS A LITTLE GIRL HAD MARIAM SEEN CROWDS SO large in Syria. Pressed shoulder-to-shoulder with the protesters, she approached Abbassin Square with the chanting mass. They carried homemade signs, many had painted their faces, and some carried coolers as if preparing for a picnic. A burly man on her left lugged a folding chair and a small green, white, and black tristar flag, the symbol of the rebellion. Each time one of the protest leaders cried out on the megaphone, the man raised the flag above his head. A woman on Mariam's right led a small girl by the hand, FREEDOM emblazoned on her little pink T-shirt. Mariam held the girl's eyes as they moved quickly past. The girl flashed a V with her fingers before disappearing into the crowd. The square pulsed with energy, but Mariam felt only rising fear. She worked in the Palace, so she knew the government would not let this fester for long. In the meantime, she had work to do.

From the square, a megaphone shrieked, *Selmiyyeh, selmiyyeh.*

At Abbassin's southern rim Mariam saw that the square—really a traffic circle—had disappeared beneath the crowd. A mass of heads, shoulders, flags, and banners replaced the roads and pavement. She was here to protect Razan, her beloved cousin. Careless, carefree. Simple to follow. Draped in the flag of rebellion, probably a little high, Razan marched to Abbassin under cardboard signs demanding freedom, the end of the emergency law, and new elections. All reasonable. All treasonous, legally speaking. Mariam knew this and pressed on, fighting the urge to yell for her cousin to return home. Avoid the square, the protest. Let's go get drunk. Like the old days. Razan kept marching into the heart of the square, toward a stage fashioned with scraps of wood and furniture borrowed from the homes of those friendly to the opposition. Mariam scanned for *mukhabarat* officers and set herself sufficiently away from the stage so she could claim to be an innocent passerby. *I went out for pastries and only observed the traitorous demonstration, Officer,* she shamefully practiced the words in silence. Always have a story for the *mukhabarat* donkeys, Razan liked to say.

Mariam stopped at a sweets shop just inside the square. The crowd's sound was deafening now, a kind of revelry she'd never heard in Syria. Large gatherings had only been permitted for the staged, compulsory rallies the old President, the current President's father, had held in the stadium just off the square. She had been a little girl immersed in the crowd, reciting a chant declaring him to be the country's premier pharmacist. "Syria's gallant knight!" the government officials had urged them to sing. "The Lion of Damascus!" Is he really a good pharmacist, the President? Mariam had asked her father afterward, old enough to understand one asked such questions in private, if ever. He'd just smiled, stroked her hair, looked around uneasily, and whispered in her ear: He is a good liar, *habibti*.

Two handsome, wiry boys took the stage. They demanded the President resign as the crowd cheered in approval. She saw a *mukhabarat* man in a leather jacket filming the masses. One of probably hundreds of such men. The crowd's size, initially a comfort, now filled her with dread. Her eyes darted back to her cousin at the foot of the stage. A faceless protester handed Razan a megaphone. Mariam began to move. Time to rip this *bint mbarih,* this naïve bitch, from the stage before she gets herself killed.

As she stepped forward, a shadow appeared on the ground in front of her, like ink spilled into the dust.

Stopping, Mariam looked up and saw a man in black on the sweets shop roof. He had a scarf pulled over his nose and mouth and he held a large gun. He placed a hand to his head as if listening to an earpiece radio. He looked across the road to another rooftop, where a similarly clad man was mounting a gun on a tripod. One of the young men held a megaphone and cried for President Assad—her boss, technically—to legalize new political parties. But Mariam stayed behind the sweets shop. A sign passed in front of her: FREEDOM STARTS AT BIRTH. IN SYRIA IT STARTS AT DEATH. She saw a young couple kissing in the crowd, a pudgy woman with impossibly heavy breasts dancing in front of a sign that read ASSAD WAKE UP, YOUR TIME IS UP.

Mariam watched her cousin mount the stage with the megaphone. The crowd cheered. She looked up and could no longer see the men on the rooftops. Razan wore painted-on jeans and a T-shirt embroidered with the tristar flag. She raised a defiant hand, demanded freedom, declared that the people wanted the fall of the regime. Her cousin said, *Selmiyyeh, selmiyyeh*, and the crowd echoed.

"He is a butcher, a tyrant," Razan shrieked. "Assad must step down, he must resign."

And now Mariam really tried to move—it seemed like her muscles were firing—but instead found herself hugging the wall of the sweets shop and soon felt the wind of *mukhabarat* foot soldiers rushing past. The insanity of what Razan had just screamed took hold and Mariam felt like she was outside herself, watching her own body scream a string of profanities at her stupid, brave cousin.

She saw a *mukhabarat* plant in the crowd whisper into his radio. Then a gunshot. Another. Another. One of the wiry boys on the stage collapsed in puffs of red and pink. Mariam plastered herself against the wall, her back cold though the stone was very hot. The air fell silent and banners began to collapse as people fled.

Then the *mukhabarat* guns began riddling the crowd, the shots sporadic and hesitant before settling into a rhythm as the shooters worked up the courage. A young woman in a white hijab held up her arms to block blows from a club. A *mukhabarat* man swung his club into another man's head once, twice, three times until it opened. The man tried to stand, but his legs folded and the *mukhabarat* man pushed him down and swung his club again.

"Move, move, move," Mariam yelled uselessly at Razan. But her cousin could not hear and would not have listened anyhow.

"Freedom," Razan screamed. "Freedom! Freedom!"

Now the rooftop guns roared to life, the high-caliber bullets tearing through flesh and the signs and flags. Something sprayed on Mariam's face and she looked downward, blinking, cursing her cousin, as she wiped it from her eyes. It was blood, but she did not know where it had come from. She felt her head, her legs, her chest. Everything was intact. The crowd fled past as the gunfire rattled. Razan defiantly commanded the stage, clutching the megaphone as the crowd stampeded like wildebeests.

A beefy *mukhabarat* man hopped onstage waving his club.

"Freedom," Mariam heard her cousin scream through the megaphone. "We want freedom." Then Razan set down the megaphone as the man approached. Her cousin looked into the sky, toward Qasioun Mountain, and closed her eyes. Then he brought down the club on Razan's head.

3

"SAM, I DON'T FIT," VAL HAD HISSED TO HIM. "I DON'T fit, man. KOMODO's a midget and I'm six fucking feet tall." Sam had had his hand on one of her hips, pushing down as Val tried to bend her legs into the Land Cruiser's clandestine compartment. She cursed and winced as he folded her limbs like origami. He heard yelling in the house, the footsteps drawing close. They yelled her name as they cleared the rooms. They had come for her.

She gave that desperate laugh, the one he recognized from Baghdad that said, *This has all gone to shit*. She swung herself out of the compartment. He had a sick feeling about this, and asked again if she wanted to risk it, knowing the answer. "Maybe we just take you in the front seat?"

"You heard what they're yelling in there, no way, man. I've got the dip passport. I've got immunity. I'll be fine. You're the one who's screwed if we get caught."

He nodded. He'd had to offer, but both were professionals and knew what had to be done. He kissed her on the cheek. She smiled thinly and pressed the button on the wall. The garage door slowly creaked open.

Drinks back home in a few weeks, she said, and went back inside the safe house.

[INAUDIBLE VOICES AND THE SOUND of papers shuffling]

Is this on? [Muffled response, noises]

Better? Okay. This is the second joint counterintelligence and security interview of Samuel Joseph, GS-12 operations officer, upon his return from Damascus. We are presently in Amman Station. It is the twenty-sixth of March, one p.m. local time. Reference draft cable 2345 for the first half of Mr. Joseph's statement describing the exfiltration operation in Syria.

Interviewing officers Tim McManus from Counterintelligence and Lloyd—

[Coughing] *Hand me . . . thanks.* [Unknown sounds]

Lloyd Craig from Security. We'll run through a set of questions based on our understanding of the operation.

Q. *Please state your name for the record.*

A. *Samuel Joseph.*

Q. *Valerie Owens told you the asset, KOMODO, missed three pickup windows?*

A. *We discussed this earlier, Tim. Yes. She said he missed all three.*

Q. *And the SDR was one-way? She was going to leave Syria with you?*

A. *Tim, I feel like we're going backwards.*

[Shuffling papers, inaudible conversation]

Q. *She didn't talk about the SDR once she'd arrived at the safe house?*

A. *No.*

Q. *Is that unusual?*

A. *Not if it was successful. If Val thought she was covered, she wouldn't have completed the SDR. She would have aborted and gone home.*

Q. *How do you know this?*

A. *I served with her before, in Baghdad. Shit, Lloyd, we've—*

Q. *Sam, we gotta go through the questions. Headquarters sent more an hour ago.*

A. *Fine. Fine. Val was an exceptional case officer. We got our denied-*

area ops certs together. If she came to the safe house, she thought she was black.

Q. *You knew her well?*

A. *Yes. We were close.*

[Hushed voices, coughing]

A. *Just ask.*

Q. *It's—uh—* [Coughing]

A. *Just ask, Tim.*

Q. *Were you at any point romantically involved with Ms. Owens?*

A. *No.*

Q. *Thanks. And you did not personally detect surveillance at any time while you were in Syria?*

A. *No.*

Q. [Sound of paper shuffling] *This is a floor plan of the safe house. Can you point and tell us where they breached the entrances?*

A. *They came in the front door. Here. They used a battering ram, I think. They also broke through at least one of the windows along the street. Here. Based on how quickly they got to the garage, I'd say a couple must have jumped one of the walls into the courtyard, but I'm not certain. They were swarming in. We ran for the car. Through this hallway, then out into the courtyard. That's when I think I heard a few of them coming over the walls. We made it to the garage, and—*

Q. *Hold on, Sam, the headquarters folks had a specific question here.* [Papers shuffling] *Why not just drive away together with her in the front seat and bring her back home?*

A. *Val and I both speak Arabic fluently. We heard the* mukhabarat *team yelling the same phrase over and over as they cleared rooms: She's not here. They used her name. They were coming for her, not me. We couldn't risk being seen together.*

Q. *So then you try the Land Cruiser's hidden compartment?*

A. *Yes. She didn't fit.*

Q. *What did you do then?*

A. *We made a decision. She stays and takes the heat because she has diplomatic immunity. They'll ask her questions, PNG her, then she comes home.*

Q. *And if you're caught—*

A. *If I'm caught, I disappear forever into a Syrian dungeon owing to the tourist Canadian passport. It's the right operational call and any Peer Review Board will back it up.*

Q. *We're not disputing that, Sam. So, your suitcase is already in the car. What next?*

A. *She opens the garage door and I drive off and head for the border.*

Q. *The* mukhabarat *don't see you?*

A. *They must not have known the house had a garage or an exit on that side. As far as I know they never even saw the car.*

Q. *You mentioned to Chief of Station Amman that you heard something as you drove off?*

A. *Yes.*

Q. *Can you tell us what you heard?*

A. *Val screaming.*

SAM CLICKED STOP ON THE computer audio. Noticing his fingers drumming on the table, he folded his hands in his lap. Then he stared at the wall as Val's scream rolled through his mind. Unlike those of most of his counterparts in the Directorate of Operations, C/NE Division Ed Bradley's "Me Wall" was bare. On the back bookshelf sat a few gifts from special friends, including a half-folded Aussie digger hat and Khalid Sheikh Mohammed's AK-47. But perched on a shelf was Bradley's pride and joy—a neutralized missile system gifted for leading the Stinger Program against the Soviets in Afghanistan. Rumor had it the launcher had not been properly decommissioned. A visitor had once pulled the trigger, lighting it up like a Christmas tree. Downrange at Bradley's office table sat Procter, Chief of Station Damascus, back at Langley to deal with the fallout from Val Owens's capture.

Sam would decide after this first meeting that Artemis Aphrodite

Procter, born to a father obsessed with Greek mythology, hewed to the spirit of her first name more than the middle.

Procter was many things, and one of them was short. She barely scratched five feet. Her black hair, exploding into curls as if she were plugged into an electrical socket, contrasted with her pale, freckled skin. Everything strained and stretched with muscle. Even under the blouse, Sam saw the outlines of the toned arms and the spread of her shoulders. Sam remembered what one of her case officers in Moscow had told him: "She's a frazzled Energizer Bunny, man. They don't call her he Proctologist for nothing. She's intense. And if you slow down, she'll eat you alive." The officer had also told Sam about an ops plan he'd designed that Procter had called "dogshit" in a cable. "She literally sent that cable back to Russia House front office," he had said, "and you know what, she was right. I learned a lot from her."

Procter picked at her teeth. Bradley gripped Sam on the shoulder and collected a coffee thermos from his desk and sat down at the table. He was six-foot-two, a former linebacker at the University of Texas who had struggled—and eventually given up on—shaking the Lone Star drawl of his youth. The raw physical presence masked a finely tuned intuition for people and the savvy of an operational pro. But Bradley now shuttled between Middle Eastern crises, impatient political masters, and pompous overseers in Congress. His face bore the stress.

"The scream," Procter said, breaking the silence. "What kind was it?"

"Pain. They beat the shit out of her."

He looked away from the wall toward Procter. "Any leads?"

"One, actually," said Procter. "Came in last night. We picked up an intercept that a *mukhabarat* agency called the Security Office recently arrested an American. Uncorroborated so far, but it seems credible."

"I've never heard of the Security Office," Sam said.

"Honestly we hadn't, either," Procter said. "But we did some research and found a couple mentions in stolen documents from late last year. Assad apparently wanted someone to keep tabs on the rest of the *mukhabarat,* so he put a general, Ali Hassan, in charge and vested him with a ton of power inside the Palace. Guy is a real son of the regime. His brother is Rustum Hassan, commander of the Republican Guard."

"It would be good news if the Syrians had her," Bradley said. "We can at least press them government-to-government."

"We've warned Assad through back channels that we will hold the regime accountable if anything happens," Procter said. "But they continue to deny that she is in custody. The White House and the douchebags on the Hill might be fine leaving our people in prison for weeks at a time, but I'm not. If I find Ali Hassan's phone number, I'm calling him directly, Ed. Send him a message."

"We're not threatening them at all?" Sam asked. He fingered the knot of his tie, unconsciously loosening it. "That's crap. She's being held illegally."

Bradley shot him a glare. "POTUS has a broader Syria policy to manage that extends beyond one of us, Sam. She has the dip passport. We will get her back soon."

"And until then we'll just keep warning them over and over without imposing consequences?" Sam said.

Bradley shrugged and poured more coffee from his thermos. "I agree with you, but it is the White House's policy right now. We wait. We will get her back, it will just take time. The Syrians would have to be nuts to do anything other than put her in a cell and ask polite questions. Eventually they will turn her loose. And yes, Artemis, if NSA can find us his number, we should have a conversation with General Hassan."

Bradley looked at the wall clock. "I gotta run to catch a car in a few minutes. A full afternoon of grilling down on the Hill."

"SSCI?" Sam asked Bradley, pronouncing the acronym for the Senate Select Committee on Intelligence, appropriately, as *Sissy*.

"Yep. The Sissies themselves," Bradley said, clenching and pumping his right fist. "Questions about Val."

Sam shook hands with Procter and the Chief left. Sam dawdled, examining the Stinger launcher as Bradley packed up his lock bag for the Hill briefing.

"I've heard she's a little nuts," Sam said.

"Procter?"

"Yeah."

"She's something. By the way, you got dinner plans tonight?"

"I have a whole rotisserie chicken and a six-pack of beer in my otherwise empty fridge," Sam said.

"Good. Bring the beer. Come out to the farm for dinner with me and Angela tonight? I've got something for you."

"What's that?"

"A distraction."

SAM FOUGHT RUSH-HOUR TRAFFIC ON 267 and the Greenway for nearly two hours to reach the Bradley farm, an exhausting experience on par with his drive through wartime Damascus.

He pulled into the farmhouse's gravel drive. The foothills of the Blue Ridge prickled the horizon, the sunset an orange ribbon receding behind them. Three horses chewed grass along the stone fence, and as he got out of the car he remembered he'd forgotten the beer. He was weighing whether to head to a store when Angela Bradley opened the front door. "Hey, Sam!" She greeted him with a hug and showed him into the kitchen. "Ed's down in the Box"—her name for the Sensitive Compartmented Information Facility, or SCIF, in the basement, which allowed him to take work calls and read cable traffic from home. Angela hated the Box. One of her conditions upon Ed taking the Near East Division job had been the horse farm on the rural edge of suburban Washington. It added an hour to Bradley's commute, but when he had resisted, she said simply: "I don't give a shit, Ed."

Without asking, she opened a Coors Light and slid it across the counter to Sam. Then she opened one for herself, popped onto the counter like a schoolgirl, and started the interrogation.

"How is the family?"

"Good, everyone's good."

"Girlfriends?"

"None now."

"I see. Too bad for you. Where next?"

"Powers that be working it out."

"Ed needs to make a goddamn decision, huh?"

"Yes ma'am."

Interrogation complete, Angela nodded, though at and for what Sam had no idea. She wiped her hands on a rag and announced that they were having steaks. The cast-iron pan soon sizzled and two fresh Coors were cracked open when they heard Ed's footsteps on the stairs.

Angela tossed Ed a beer with one hand and flipped the meat with the other. He opened his mouth to speak, but Angela stopped him.

"Listen, boys, you know the rules," Angela said. "I get thirty minutes without any shop talk."

"Yes, ma'am," said Sam, his best attempt at mimicking her drawl.

She gave a middle finger in return.

AS IT TURNED OUT, SHE got forty-five.

Then Sam and Ed cleared the table, cleaned the dishes, and, as was their custom, took six beers in a Styrofoam cooler onto the back deck. Mosquitoes whined around the porchlights.

They each drank half a can in silence. Then it was on to war stories from Cairo, the do-you-remembers of old friends drinking together.

Angela cracked open the screen door as Sam finished another beer. "I'm going to bed. Sam, you sleeping here tonight?"

"You mind?" he said.

"Course not," Ed said. "We can caravan in tomorrow."

"I figured," Angela said. "You take the room next to the Box. Sheets and all that in the closet downstairs. Night, dear." She planted a kiss on Bradley's forehead and disappeared into the house.

Sam pulled the tab off his empty beer can and stared out at the shadowed mountains. He grabbed the final round from the cooler and tossed a can to Ed.

"I've got an errand I need you to run," Bradley finally said. "Might cheer you up from this ugliness with Val."

"What's up?"

"Warm-pitch recruitment attempt in Paris. A Syrian Palace delegation is meeting with a few of the exiled oppositionists. Since Syrian government officials don't leave Damascus much anymore, it's worth a shot. You are the perfect candidate: a top recruiter in NE Division, fluent Arabic, you've recruited Syrians before. There are a number of Syrian officials traveling; you'll need to determine the right one to pitch." Sam knew before Bradley opened his mouth that he would say yes to whatever was proposed. But he wanted to sit in the warm buzz that had settled over his body, so he asked needless questions, all of which he knew the answers to already.

"Paris Station not interested?"

"We're trying to keep the French out of this, so we don't want to use local talent they may know about."

"You never send me nice places. This will be a welcome change from the usual hellholes. Can I bring the BANDITOs? They know Paris and we'll need countersurveillance."

BANDITO was the cryptonym for the Kassab triplets: Elias, Yusuf, and Rami. All were CIA support assets. The brothers were Syrian-American dual citizens hailing from a wealthy Christian family that owned car dealerships throughout Syria and Lebanon. The family lived mostly in Beirut and Istanbul, preferring to manage the dealerships remotely. Sam had struck up a close friendship with the brothers, which eventually transformed into recruitment during his Istanbul tour. They secured cars, safe houses, and conducted basic surveillance for Beirut Station. Sam occasionally read the cable traffic and learned that they'd each passed a polygraph.

"Yes, bring them." Bradley paused to swat at a mosquito. "And I've also taken the liberty of sequestering a few analyst resources for your use. They can get you up to speed on Syria and help prep for the pitch. Look, I'm gonna hit the sack—it's been six days and I'm still jet-lagged from my Cairo trip." Bradley stood and was about to open the door to the house when he stopped and looked back at Sam.

"Give the op some serious thought, okay? A Palace official would be a big fish. We're basically flying blind inside Syria right now."

"Of course," Sam said. "And Ed, one more thing." Bradley turned his head, still holding the door ajar. "My next tour. I have a proposal."

"Yes?" Bradley said, closing the door to turn and face Sam.

"How about Damascus?"

Bradley smiled weakly and looked out to the mountains.

"You need good people there," Sam continued. "It's a hardship post now, no families. I don't have that complication. I can help out there. I can help you and Procter."

"Is this a revenge play or something? Get back at the Syrians for Val?"

"You tell me where else I could be more helpful. You said it yourself. We're flying blind in Syria. My Levantine Arabic is pretty good, you don't have to send me to language school in Rosslyn for a year, I'm ready now. Plus, if I put one of these Syrians in harness coming out of Paris I can work the case inside Damascus."

"Procter is a hard-ass," Bradley said.

"So?"

Bradley shrugged. "So, it could be miserable if you guys don't get along."

"There's a civil war burning," Sam said. "It's not gonna be an easy one, Procter aside."

Bradley smirked.

"Not joking, Ed. I want the post. And I never ask you for anything."

"Fine. Done. Damascus it is. We'll set it in motion tomorrow." Bradley swung open the creaky swing door and disappeared into the house. Sam went to the fridge for another beer. He cracked it open on the porch and closed his eyes. Val's scream again passed through his mind before it drifted off into the warm night air.

THE NEXT DAY SAM WALKED to the analysts' spaces in the New Headquarters Building—a box of steel and glass facing the concrete of Original Headquarters. The Front Office Conference Room's centerpiece was a faux-wood table ringed by government-issue swivel chairs: some new and ergonomic, while others' creaks and moans suggested they had been procured during the Carter administration. On the wall hung four clocks showing the time in D.C., Rabat, Tel Aviv, Baghdad—the rough boundaries of the Middle East and North Africa analytics shop. Each clock was amusingly between four and seven minutes slow. The interior wall was a scattershot of random awards and plaques, many quite dated ("Meritorious Unit Citation—Camp David Accords," "Team Chief of the Year—Erin Yazgall"), others weeny-ish and incomprehensible to the visiting operator ("World Intelligence Review Article of the Month —James Debman").

Two analysts sat inside, bickering. They stood to greet Sam as he entered the room.

Zelda Zaydan was skinny and had a shoulder-length bob of jet-black hair. Her nose was beaky and Romanesque and she wore an ill-fitting black pantsuit with a pink scarf.

James Debman, on the other hand, was a butterball who wore a short-sleeved white dress shirt and garish orange bow tie. He offered a clammy hand to Sam, who had no choice but to accept, and beckoned him to sit. Zelda slid a giant stack of papers and binders across the table. "This is our team's production over the past six months, you should read it," Debman said. He sat back, picking at the flaking plastic cover securing the blue badge hanging around his neck. Zelda eyed him, then said: "We know you've done a bunch of tours in the Middle East but never Syria. What is most helpful to cover?"

"The typical briefing you give to case officers," Sam said. He knew the country at a high level, mostly from his time in Iraq, but hadn't paid much attention to the CIA analysis so far.

Debman's eyes flickered with excitement. He slid his prepared talking points aside, mumbling *overcoordinated* and *watered down* in Zelda's direction. He coughed, took a drink of water from a large bottle, and cracked his knuckles.

"Our story begins in 1930."

Zelda rolled her eyes.

THIS WAS THE BIRTH YEAR of Hafez al-Assad, the current President's father, and it was, Sam thought, a bit too early in the chronology.

Zelda agreed. "Goddammit, Debman, you always do this," she said, her voice rising. "Let's start with the war. The relevant stuff.

"Here's the thing," she said, wiping a forelock of hair from her face. "Syria prior to the war had become a brittle thing. Sure, it was stable"—Debman supplied air quotes as Zelda said the word—"but the state itself had hollowed. They don't have oil, so Assad can't grease the skids and pay off the population with cash. The patronage that did exist went to a smaller number of people, mostly members of the Assad family. This pissed people off. All the telecom operators are owned by the President's cousin, for example. Big drought in the north and east that brought more than a million people west, to slums outside the big cities. Destabilizing. Security forces are brutal, absolutely ubiquitous: you need their approval to add a second story onto your house, to get married. Mundane stuff. Pissed everyone off."

"Quotidian brutality," Debman said. "Absolutely banal." Zelda looked as though she wanted to strangle him with the chain holding his badge. Sam would have been satisfied with the orange bow tie.

Someone opened the door to the conference room, then ducked back out. "Where was I?" Zelda said. "Oh yeah." She took a drink of water. "Tunisia and Egypt happen. Some Syrians think, Why not us? Kindling is bone-dry, we just need a spark. A few smallish protests occur in Damascus. Nothing. We get one in the south, random place called Daraa. Visited it once. Not a happy town. *Mukhabarat* tortures a few kids. Boom. Protest, killings, funerals, killings. Rinse and repeat. Protests blossom in other cities. It becomes a nationwide movement. Demonstrations get big, like really big. Tens of thousands one Friday in Hama. Satellite images are crazy. And the regime, they have no clue what to do. I mean, think about it. You could just go in guns blazing, mowing down the protesters. Like his old man did in Hama back in '82, leveled most of the city to suppress a rebellion."

"More than ten thousand dead, but no one can really agree on the number," Debman added, making a distasteful slicing motion across his neck.

Zelda wrinkled her forehead. "What the hell, Debman? Behave yourself. Anyway, the regime does not do this. They waffle instead. They were restrained in some ways early on, despite all the press coverage saying the opposite. They give half-hearted political concessions that please no one. Sometimes they shoot protesters on purpose, sometimes it's an accident, sometimes they don't shoot at all and allow the protests. Then finally the regime shifted to a scorched-earth military campaign because they ran out of options. Kill them all."

"Confusing, Sam, it was confusing," said Debman, wiping his glasses on his shirt. "The regime eventually burned its bridges. No way back, fight on." He took another drink and wiped his mouth with his hand.

"Now, what did this accomplish?" Zelda said rhetorically. Debman started to answer; she cut him off with a wave of her hand. "First, it did not suppress the opposition. It strengthened it, particularly the more radical Islamist and jihadi elements. The violence helped them make the case that they needed weapons to counter the regime. Second, it polarized the country along sectarian and ethnic lines. In general, it swung the minority groups—Christian, Alawi, Druze—toward the regime. The Sunni Arab majority against. The Assad family is Alawi, remember. Syria is really diverse, Sam. Christians and Alawis, for example, are each like ten percent of the total population. The regime has done a good job binding most of the minority groups—and many of the well-off Sunni Arabs, to be honest—into it. They don't have other options. Third, it turned the government into a big, radicalized militia all its own."

"Except instead of worshipping Allah, it worships Bashar," Debman said.

"Huge chasm between the communities that support the opposition and the pro-regime side," Zelda said.

Debman chuckled. "Yeah, for example, regime side has electricity and food, opposition doesn't."

"Policy makers are really interested in a few of Syria's institutions,"

Zelda said. "First, the Palace. It's effectively Bashar's personal office, includes his senior advisers and liaisons to all the big government agencies. For example, he just set up this thing called the Security Office to run his most sensitive *mukhabarat* errands. Ali Hassan is in charge. Bashar runs the country from the Palace. Second is the Republican Guard. Syria's paramount military force, run by General Rustum Hassan, Ali's brother. Rustum is the pointy tip of the military spear and acts as Bashar's enforcing hand inside the Scientific Studies and Research Center, the SSRC. They've consolidated and centralized control because the institutions of state are weakening. Defections, rebel assassination campaigns. It's all taking a toll."

"So where do you see the fight going?" Sam asked.

Zelda stood now, hands behind her back, gazing out the window.

"The regime stands," Zelda said. "Because it is a deeper thing than the Assad family, its Alawi community, or even its repressive apparatus. It so deeply co-opted the nation and the organs of state that it was stronger than we all thought. It has the resources, the loyalty, and the ruthlessness to do so. And as for what is coming. The protests, the hope, all that is gone. Shot to pieces. Negotiations are window dressing because there is no chance for a settlement. Both sides believe they must win."

"And both sides believe they can," said Debman. "The jihadists, who drive the rebellion on the ground, and the Assadists, the militia masquerading as a government. The bystanders, the people trying to get by, keeping their heads down, are faced with that choice."

Someone else poked their head in and said in a squeaky, insistent voice that they had the room, you guys are already five minutes late.

"It's a fight to the death," Zelda said as they gathered the binders. "It's the Octagon."

THAT AFTERNOON ZELDA HELPED SAM run bio searches and conduct research on the Syrians traveling to Paris with the Palace delegation.

Trace results from the Syria Desk Staff Operations Officer came back late that night. Sam and Zelda ate hot dogs from the Hormel vending machine in the Original Headquarters Building. The CIA was the only place Sam had ever seen a hot dog vending machine. He'd always wanted to take a picture, but cameras were not allowed in the building.

Seated next to Zelda in the analyst cube farm, Sam took a bite of the hot dog and read the results for one of the officials, Mariam Haddad.

1. TRACE RESULTS (1 OF 2): REF SUBJECT SYRIAN NATIONAL IS PALACE POLITICAL COUNSELOR REPORTING TO PRESIDENTIAL ADVISER BOUTHAINA NAJJAR. REF A COLLATERAL INDICATES SUBJECT IS 32 YEARS OLD AND SYRIAN CHRISTIAN. REF B COLLATERAL INDICATES REGULAR CONTACT WITH SENIOR PALACE OFFICIALS, INCLUDING PRESIDENT ASSAD, AND COUNSELOR JAMIL ATIYAH.

2. TRACE RESULTS (2 OF 2): REF C INDICATES SUBJECT'S MOTHER WAS CHARGE D'AFFAIRES IN PARIS BEFORE RETIREMENT. SUBJECT'S FATHER, MAJOR GENERAL GEORGES HADDAD, COMMANDS THE SYRIAN ARMY III CORPS, CURRENTLY IN ALEPPO. REF D INDICATES SUBJECT'S PATERNAL UNCLE DAOUD HADDAD IS COLONEL IN SSRC BRANCH 450.

3. COUNTERINTELLIGENCE DIVISION SUPPORTS DEVELOPMENTAL CONTACT WITH SUBJECT PENDING NEAR EAST DIVISION CONCURRENCE.

"Well connected," Sam said.

"A real daughter of the regime," Zelda said, chewing a pen. "You need a family like that to get a job in the Palace."

Sam swung around in his chair to face the analyst.

"Mariam could be interesting," he said. "Mid-level officials typically have great access and are less invested in the regime. Plus, if she can even casually elicit information from her uncle we could tap into the chemical weapons program. Can you pull up the REF reports?"

Zelda nodded and started scrubbing the CIA's galaxy of intelligence databases. All housed a mixture of overlapping and exclusive reporting like a shotgun blast of Venn diagrams. She pressed her face toward the screen as she typed.

"Found something," she said after a few minutes. Sam swiveled behind her to look. It was a stolen *mukhabarat* report describing a protest in Damascus. Sam checked the date. March 25. The day they took Val. The report said the *mukhabarat* arrested a young woman named Razan Haddad. He stopped reading.

"It's a common last name," he said. "Like Smith."

"I know, but check out the bottom of the report. A comment from the author."

Sam read: *Prisoner released following formal request traced back to Political Security officer attached to III Corps.*

"Mariam's father's unit."

"Yep. Can't think of a good reason anyone else fighting in Aleppo would call a *mukhabarat* detachment in Damascus pleading for someone's release."

"Arrested family members are good fuel for recruitment," Sam said. "I ran a guy in Saudi whose brother had been tortured. He kept his mouth shut but spied for us for more than fifteen years. Silent revenge."

He finished the hot dog. "We found our girl."

4

MARIAM STARED AT THE PICTURE OF FATIMAH WAEL clipped to the yellowed folder resting on the table. The *mukhabarat* photo, taken at the start of Fatimah's last imprisonment, was now frayed. She ran her fingertips along its edges and met Fatimah's haunted eyes. The eyes usually looked dead in these *mukhabarat* albums. But Fatimah bore the gaze of a woman who had taken a lifetime of beatings and still stood. Mariam put the photo aside and again reviewed the dossier contents as her boss spoke on the phone.

The first page: a summary of Fatimah's arrests. Most fell under the decades-old emergency law, which gave the state expansive authority to prosecute vague crimes, including "Sedition" (Translation: participation in peaceful protest) and "Nefarious Cooperation with a Foreign Power" (Translation: political discussions with the French ambassador to Damascus). The file was at least five inches thick. It included every report filed on Fatimah dating back to the early 1990s, when, as a twenty-two-year-old, she unwisely submitted an article to a newspaper calling for the elder Assad's resignation. Five years in prison from 2003 to 2008. Charge: Sedition. Now Fatimah was an exile, shuttling between France and Italy. A brave Syrian woman leading the foreign opposition, well respected by many of the fighting groups on the ground. A constant thorn in Assad's side.

Mariam put down the file as her boss, the political counselor to the President, Bouthaina Najjar, ended her phone call. Bouthaina had placed Mariam in charge of the negotiations with foreign-based oppositionists, namely the National Council, the umbrella group claiming to represent the fighters on the ground. Mariam's goal was simple: persuade them to renounce the Islamist fighters now leading the civil war, denounce their fellow exiles, then come home, where safety and pardon would be granted in exchange for silence. It was Mariam's most important assignment yet, and it promised to be a stepping-stone to greater things.

Bouthaina joined Mariam at the table, opened her own file on Fatimah, and, as she always did when concentrating, began nibbling on her Gucci eyeglasses. "So, Mariam, what do you think about Fatimah? What angle should we take in Paris?"

Mariam smoothed her beige skirt and pulled a report from the file. "The Iranian signals intelligence covering Fatimah's Paris apartment and the Tuscan villa were superb," Mariam said. "And they make it clear she misses Syria. She is living well abroad, but Damascus is home. She will want to negotiate." Mariam took a sip of coffee. "But the price should be high."

She rifled through the stack of reports. Her thumb stopped on one she'd dog-eared the night before, cross-legged on her bed in a long T-shirt, preparing for this discussion. She'd been on her fourth cup of coffee.

"Here it is. Three reports from opposition sources: Paris, Rome, Istanbul. All allege corruption and misuse of funds. Here is an amusing one." She slid it across to Bouthaina, who put on her eyeglasses to read.

"It is a bill the National Council tried to submit to the French Foreign Ministry for a block of rooms at the Hotel Bristol. A delegation arrived from Istanbul."

"Only the best," Bouthaina said, clicking her tongue.

"The rooms were twelve hundred euros per night. Everyone appears to have required their own."

"Of course." Bouthaina smirked as she bit off the horn of a croissant.

"The French rejected the bill, so the council will eat the cost. There are a dozen other examples, and you can read in the reports that the profligate spending is leading to fissures among some of the senior leaders. Fatimah among them. She despises the waste."

"How can these fools think they are making a difference?" Bouthaina said. "We are fighting terrorists. These idiots party in Paris."

Mariam slid a memo toward Bouthaina. "My proposal: safe passage back to Damascus in exchange for a public description of the rebels as terrorists and silence upon her return."

"She'll refuse you at first. She is stubborn."

Mariam respected Fatimah for it. We'd be sisters in another life, she thought, in a world that does not exist.

"I agree. But Fatimah is the linchpin of the National Council. If she departs, it will collapse. If she does not cooperate, we should deploy less pleasant methods." Mariam slid another paper across the table. A single sheet. The one that had made her queasy as she typed on her bed.

"This is the list of Fatimah's relatives still inside Syria, ordered by those closest to her. If she does not agree to our terms, I propose that we start the arrests at the top until she agrees. I will give her this list in Paris."

Bouthaina smiled, savoring the combat. "Approved. I agree the arm-twisting will be necessary, unfortunately." She removed her glasses and set them on the table. Bouthaina looked toward the door to confirm it was closed.

"You should know before we go to Paris," Bouthaina continued, "that one of my sources in Jamil Atiyah's office has told me that the old pedophile is conspiring against us. He wants our trip to fail."

Jamil Atiyah was another Palace counselor to the President. He and Bouthaina despised each other and had been engaged in a running turf battle for influence inside the Palace. Atiyah's predilection for underage girls, typically procured on diplomatic trips to East Asia, was well known. But this had not yet been sufficient to oust him. Bouthaina still sought the appropriate bureaucratic weaponry.

"What do you think he is planning?" Mariam asked. Atiyah had targeted others in her office to instill fear and throw Bouthaina off balance. Adnan, a clerical aide, had once spent three nights in the hospital after a visit from Atiyah's thugs.

"I do not know. Just be careful," Bouthaina said. "He is a clever and savage old bastard."

MARIAM HADDAD'S FAMILY BELIEVED most of all in throwing parties. With a cousin at long last engaged, the family had an excuse. They rented out the inner courtyard of an upscale restaurant in Damascus's Christian Quarter, once an Ottoman mansion.

Tables were spread in the marble courtyard around the fountain. A waiter glided past Mariam carrying a bottle of champagne buried in ice. Mariam had chosen a tight silken black dress for the occasion, and she felt both beautiful and powerful as she slipped across the courtyard to her mother and planted a kiss on a cheek clotted with makeup. She instinctively scanned for her absent father and brother. A difficult habit to break. They were artillery officers in Aleppo, and they had been absent for close to six months. It's Stalingrad in Syria, her brother had said during a phone call. Mariam accepted a glass of champagne from a waiter and spoke with her mother about nothing: clothes, shopping, her cousin's drab fiancée.

No expense had been spared. Stuffed grape leaves, tabbouleh, za'atar, and baba ghanoush were wheeled out and devoured just as quickly by the clan. There were courses of dawood basha—Syrian meatballs—kibbe, kebabs of all types, fried white fish covered in chilies, stews with leeks and tomatoes and okra, and trays of desserts from a renowned pastry chef in Souq Al-Hamadiya. A band played in a corner of the light-strung courtyard.

Mariam's uncle Daoud held court at one of the larger tables. Mariam had just finished an awkward dance with a very drunk cousin when he waved Mariam over.

"We all miss your father and brother," Daoud said. "I had to say it, we don't have to talk about it anymore. We will see them soon."

Mariam nodded and smiled, weak and thin. "Thank you, Uncle."

Uncle Daoud twirled champagne in a full glass and held it up to gaze into the bubbles.

"How is Razan?" he asked.

"She is doing better. She is not meaning to ignore you, Uncle, she just—"

Daoud raised his hand. "I understand she does not want to be seen in public. But tell her to call her father."

"I will, Uncle. She is just sad. She is healing. She is embarrassed."

"She is angry," he finished. "As am I." He pushed the champagne glass aside. "I wish she had come tonight, regardless. Thank you for letting her stay with you, Mariam. It means a great deal. She loves you. And with Mona gone—" He stopped himself. The mention of Aunt Mona's name was still difficult, though she'd been dead for more than ten years.

"I just mean that, with an empty house and a father consumed by work, it's not a good place for her. I know she appreciates being in your apartment."

"We were always close, like sisters."

"I know. Your father and I were lucky to have daughters two months apart."

Mariam wanted to change the subject, but Uncle Daoud needed to speak. Mariam flagged a waiter and asked for whiskey. The waiter's eyebrows arched in surprise. He shuffled off.

"Tell her we're continuing to search for the *mukhabarat* thug who did it. We have leads, but we do not have a name yet," Uncle Daoud said.

"I will. It means a lot to her that you and Father are searching."

He nodded. The waiter returned with a glass of whiskey. Mariam took his champagne flute, dumped the champagne, and replaced it with some of the liquor. He smiled.

"You were always one of us, Mariam, since you were little." He took a sip. "A member of the war councils." He looked up as a couple swung through the dance floor, groups of onlookers hollering and whistling.

"Your father and I took our positions to protect *this*," he said, hand sweeping out toward the mobbed courtyard. "To keep a big, Christian family safe in Syria. Look at what we've done. Your father in the military, in Aleppo. Me . . ." He gave a weak smile as he trailed off.

They never spoke of Daoud's work. The Scientific Studies and Research Center, Branch 450. Chemical weapons security and transport.

Daoud took more whiskey. "Our family did what was asked. We are loyal, silent, and complacent in exchange for safety. We are model Syrians. The regime broke its end of the deal. Look what happened to Razan. And we have no recourse. We are trapped." He took a drink. Something glinted through Daoud's eyes, like he knew he'd overshared. He looked off toward the dancing.

"Razan has always been rebellious, Uncle," Mariam said, hating herself for the words, as if her fiery cousin had deserved it. "She will come around."

He nodded toward the dance floor. "Shall we?"

MARIAM ARRIVED AT HER APARTMENT near dawn to find Razan still awake, sprawled on the couch in rumpled silk pajamas watching an Al Jazeera anchor interview Fatimah Wael. Mariam turned off the television and slid her cousin's legs aside to sit down beside her. An empty bottle of white wine sat on the table.

"You smell nice," Razan said, her left eye glued to the darkened television screen. The right one was still bandaged. Like a pirate, Razan had said in one of her lighter moments. The blow to her face had cratered her eye. It still had not flickered on. The doctors did not know if it ever would.

"Your father misses you," Mariam said. "For God's sake, call him back. It's not his fault."

"I know. Was it fun tonight?"

"Yes." Mariam told her about the family, the restaurant, the dancing. Razan's eye made her feel guilty for all of it.

"Why are you hiding from him?" Mariam asked.

"From Papa?"

"Yes."

"I don't know."

"Do you hate me, too? Mariam asked. "I work in the Palace. I am no better than your father."

Razan pulled into a ball. She looked down. "I don't hate either of you."

A tear rolled from her left eye. She pawed at it. "I hate the man who did this. I hate our prison." She slumped into Mariam's shoulder, feathering her fingers on the skin below her bandage. She sniffled. "The doctor says I'm not supposed to cry. It slows the healing."

MARIAM LEFT RAZAN ON THE couch and went into her bedroom, leaving the lights off. She slid from her dress and stood next to the bed in her underwear. She breathed heavily, clenching her fingers into fists, releasing, repeating.

She started with the front kicks, jumping to switch sides, moving quicker now, taking the rage inside and sweeping it away with each strike. She could hear the air crack as she moved, feel the sweaty moisture beading on her back and brow. She dropped to the floor for push-ups, stretching and straining her arms until the muscles burned. She stood and shifted to palm strikes, imagining the blows crushing the nose of Razan's *mukhabarat* assailant. Faster, Mariam, faster, her Krav Maga instructor had said in Paris all those years ago, do not stop. Move.

5

GENERAL ALI HASSAN WAS WELL ACQUAINTED WITH death, having killed his own mother his first hours in the world and many others in the four decades since. And now, in the high heat of Syria's civil war, he again courted death as he worked a blade under the skin of CIA spy Marwan Ghazali's left thumb. The man screamed as Ali removed the knife, wiped it with a rag, and returned it to his shirt pocket.

"Inconsistencies cannot be tolerated," Ali said, taking a seat in front of the prisoner. "I explained this to you."

Ghazali sat nude, bound to a rickety chair beside a table. Floodlights glared behind him. Colonel Saleh Kanaan, one of Ali's lieutenants, fanned several pieces of paper out on the table for effect. Ali already knew what they said.

"On the third draft, Marwan, you said you met your CIA handler, Valerie Owens, only in Damascus," Ali said. He reached for another paper and slid it to the prisoner, who tried blinking at it but could only seem to focus on the ruins of his thumb.

"I will read it for you," Ali said. "On your fourth testimonial, you mention a meeting with Owens in Abu Dhabi." He flipped to another page. "But on your fifth draft the Abu Dhabi meeting is gone. Just Damascus."

Ali lit a cigarette and leaned back in his chair. "Now, please tell me: What happened in Abu Dhabi?"

"I made a mistake," Ghazali pleaded. "I had not slept in days, I was delirious. I explained this to your man." Ghazali motioned to Kanaan. His teeth clattered in the cold.

"You are lying," Ali said, dragging his chair closer. "Tell me the truth and we can avoid more trouble. What happened in Abu Dhabi?"

Ghazali hung his head and began whimpering. "I never met anyone there."

Ali sighed. He had been a criminal investigator before he joined the *mukhabarat*. He had investigated murders, robberies, and, once, a gruesome crucifixion that he could still see on the back side of his eyes. Physical pain alone was not the most effective way to elicit the truth: best to wear down a spy over months of isolation and constant testimonial. Eventually the disoriented prisoner would lose the will or the ability to maintain their cover and they would break. Then they would reveal everything.

But there had to be consequences when a prisoner lied. It was one of his rules.

Ali removed the knife from his shirt pocket. Ghazali screamed.

ALI RINSED OFF HIS SHIRT and cleaned the blade in one of the basement's bathroom sinks. He dried it and slipped it back into his breast pocket, then lit another Marlboro. Smoke hung in the unventilated room as he wrung out the shirt.

As he'd expected, Ghazali had met Owens once in Abu Dhabi. He had provided stolen documents at the meeting.

Ali stubbed out the cigarette and walked upstairs to his office, eyes slitting against the morning light seeping through the windows. He wandered to the window to watch a Syrian fighter jet, a MiG purchased from the Russians, wind through the predawn and drop its payload on a rebel-held suburb. The glass panes shuddered, and smoke poured over the rubble of what used to be apartment buildings.

He lit another cigarette and looked up at the portrait of President Bashar al-Assad hanging above his door. Every bureaucrat and security official had one.

Ali was slightly framed but with a tube of belly fat, the fruit of nearly two decades of late nights and the residual stress of criminal investigations, intelligence work, and, now, civil war. A helmet of black hair was smoothed backward over a skull set with intense eyes, a nose bent rightward at the halfway mark, and a sharp jawline. A textured scar wound up the left side of his neck and ended at the bottom of his cheek. Sometimes it itched.

He looked down at the maze of concrete berms outside the ten-story building. A flaking sign read SYRIAN ARAB REPUBLIC MINISTRY OF AGRICULTURE AND AGRARIAN REFORM. A lie, but it was not intentional. It was just that no one had bothered to take it down.

The building now housed the Security Office, an intelligence agency attached to the Presidential Palace. It was one of Syria's many security services. By Ali's count, there were seventeen different security organizations in wartime Syria. The world of the secret police—the *mukhabarat*, as these institutions were collectively known—was a byzantine jumble of overlapping agencies, competing egos, and unseen patronage networks. Even senior officials like Ali had difficulty understanding the boundaries and jurisdictions that separated them. The President, like his father, had purposely fashioned it that way—the easier to play each institution off the other. But as the civil war burned and the rebels, the *irhabiun*, the terrorists, became entrenched, the President established the Security Office to carry out the government's most sensitive spy hunting. He put Ali in charge of it.

Ali put out the cigarette and checked his watch. It was time to speak with Valerie Owens. He took his pack of Marlboros and descended back into the basement.

THE SECURITY OFFICE'S BASEMENT WAS filled with dank rooms, stacks of filing cabinets, and boxes brimming with agricultural studies from the 1970s. Ali and his team had converted the space into a warren of cells and interrogation rooms. It had been soundproofed, wired with cameras and microphones, and outfitted with concrete-slab beds and toilet buckets. Several of the floors had been tiled and fitted with small drains to collect the residue from interrogations.

Kanaan opened the cell door and Ali walked in. Owens lay on her slab passing the time staring at the ceiling. She still wore a bandage on her head to cover the fractures from the violence during her arrest. He had provided direct orders that she was not to be harmed, and in a rage had suspended the idiot officer who struck her.

Ali sat by Owens's feet. They spoke in Arabic.

"General, I asked you not to smoke in here."

"Of course, Ms. Owens," Ali said, stubbing it out on the floor. Then, smiling, he lit another and expelled the first drag in a cloud over her slab bed. She scowled. "I wanted to ask again about how you communicated with Marwan Ghazali here in Damascus." He reviewed her eyes to check for a flicker of recognition and instead saw hatred. This one was well trained. Two weeks of cold and discomfort, and she'd provided nothing of value.

Owens sat up and ran her hands through her blond hair, matted and greasy from her stay in the cell. The end of the slab where her hair had been was shiny with oil. "We've covered this before, General. I do not know this Marwan Ghazali. I am a second—"

"Yes, yes," Ali said. "A second secretary at the U.S. Embassy. I know. Shall I perhaps play again the surveillance footage of your car—with your diplomatic plates—driving past the location Ghazali told us had been arranged for his exfiltration? Maybe we watch it again, Ms. Owens?"

Valerie stood and stretched her lithe frame. Skinnier now, he could see as her shirt hiked up to expose her lower ribs.

"We've been over the tape, General," she said. "I was running errands. I've shown you the stores I visited on your nice maps. Now please let me speak with the embassy. My detention here is illegal."

Ali ignored this request, just as he had done every day for the past two weeks. "Ghazali has told us many things. In fact, we just learned about a meeting in Abu Dhabi. Quite interesting, the documents Ghazali stole. But, Ms. Owens, what I really want to know about are his communication methods with you. Was there a device? Maybe if you tell me about the device and where it is, I will let you call the embassy? A reasonable offer, no?"

Owens lay back down on the slab bed. "I do not know a Marwan Ghazali. I am a U.S. diplomat, a second secretary—"

Ali cut her off with a wave and stood, closing the door behind him and leaving her in darkness.

IT WAS TEN O'CLOCK WHEN Ali's driver left him outside his apartment. The twins were asleep. Layla was reclined on the sofa reading and drinking wine. Following their custom, she asked no questions about his day, and he offered nothing in return. He poured himself a steep glass and sat down beside her feet, which he began rubbing. She put the book down and shut her eyes.

"What did you and the boys do today?" he said.

"Shut up and just keep rubbing," she said.

He complied, nurturing his well-honed instinct to follow orders.

After several minutes Ali had earned her answer: "We got groceries—the lines were horrendous and there was very little meat this week, by the way—then played around here. Fine day. Ah . . . a bit lighter." She winced as he worked a pressure point near her right heel.

He looked down the couch. Her black hair was tossed over the armrest, the open silken robe exposing her legs, and her toenails were freshly painted. His hand was slowly sliding up the exposed skin of her right leg when the apartment phone rang. Anyone who was worth answering knew to call his mobile, so he ignored the call and retreated to focus on Layla's feet, her hand having playfully blocked his northward advances.

Then they heard a rap at the door. First one, then a rapid succession, followed by the sound of shouting in the hallway. At the door he saw through the peephole Mrs. Ghraoui, widow, next-door neighbor, and sole occupant of Apartment 46. Her hair was flung wildly about and her caky makeup was furrowed with tearstains. Ali motioned to Layla, who answered and ushered the woman inside. "He's gone, he's gone, he's gone, they took him, took him somewhere," was all she would say for the first several minutes. It took a cup of tea for Mrs. Ghraoui to finally get it out: her son had been arrested at a government checkpoint. Maybe yesterday, maybe the day before, she did not know. She had just now heard from a nephew on the police force, who saw the name on a list of recent arrests in Damascus. The Republican Guard had him, and that was all she knew.

Ali yearned for another cigarette as she sobbed. Even without any details, he knew that the boy would follow a common path through the system. First, he would be taken to an improvised detention center and accused of treason. Second, a rough interrogation, with the pain increasing as time spun into an infinite loop. Third, when the confession had been extracted, he would be packed off to Saydnaya, tortured for sport, then executed by hanging. They dumped the dead in mass graves outside the prison. Several backhoe operators had been permanently assigned from the Housing Ministry to support the grave-digging work.

Of course, there were two possible off-ramps. Either the detainee had the good fortune to encounter one of the few *mukhabarat* officers who was an actual criminal investigator capable of evaluating the evidence, or they knew someone with *wasta*, influence, who could vouch for them. This was why she had come. She understood Ali was a general and she certainly knew his brother, Rustum, was the powerful commander of the Republican Guard.

"Can you help, General?" she said. "I just want to know where he is." She rubbed her eyes, smearing makeup onto her cheeks and nose.

Ali did not know why the boy had been arrested, but he could guess. His government-issued ID card would show that he had been born in a village north of Homs currently controlled by a rebel emir who claimed the town as his caliphate. Mix that with alcohol, or an aggressive Republican Guard lieutenant, and suddenly you were moving through the detention pipeline.

Not that Ali much cared why the boy had been taken. Ali had known him since he was five. He had played with the twins. He was no jihadist, criminal, or insurgent. Ali had also seen the inside of the makeshift prison his brother Rustum had built at the stadium: the wafer-thin bodies scrunching close to the barbed fencing, the faceless symphony of groans echoing through basement pipes, the antiseptic smell of the room—drain cut into the center and clogged with shapeless matter. He had been there before, to recover his doctor's battered son. But even he was not so powerful that he could just waltz in and take the boy. He had been forced to submit to Rustum, which was its own torture. Eventually he'd been allowed to take the boy, whom he found chained to a drainpipe in a pool of stale blood. That night, Ali drank himself to sleep.

He nodded at her. "I will find him. Wait at home until I call you."

She nodded, then glanced at Layla, who looked very tired. Ali thought she might ask to stay the night, but thankfully she stood to go, and Layla walked her out. Ali trotted to the living room, snatched his pack of Marlboros, and lit another, debating whether he could wait until morning to call Rustum. He decided to act. They could move the boy at any time, and he would be lost. He dialed the number. Three rings, then a voice that said: "Hello, little brother."

Ali bit the inside of his mouth. "Big brother, how are you?"

"Finishing paperwork. What do you want?"

"You have a boy in custody. I'd like to check on him."

Rustum loudly shuffled papers to register his agitation. "Not again, Ali. You must let the judicial system work things out, we can't be intervening in every case."

Ah yes, the same system that leashed my doctor's son to a prison drainpipe for joining a Facebook group critical of the government? Ali wanted to say, but he bit his tongue. For to say what he thought would end the conversation and doom the boy. He chose his words carefully. "The detainee comes from a good family," Ali said. "Layla and I know him well. I vouch for him."

"You think too much like a detective," Rustum said with exasperation. "A blanket of fear keeps things stable, and your detective work puts holes in that blanket. But, fine. I'm tired and it's late. What's his name?"

"Thank you, big brother. His name is Ghraoui."

"I'll call you back with the location in a few minutes and make the necessary arrangements." A pause, the sound of shuffling papers. "Oh, and Ali? Has the traitor or the CIA woman given up a device yet?"

There had been endless questioning about the device Marwan Ghazali used to communicate with Valerie Owens. Ghazali had confessed that he had communicated with the CIA through secret websites. Ali knew that was true because it was how they'd caught him, after getting some help from his Iranian technical advisers. He also knew why Rustum wanted a CIA device because the Iranian Ministry of Intelligence and Security technical lead had explained it to them both. The Persians believed they might be able to use a device to deploy a cyberweapon, not unlike Israel's Stuxnet virus, onto one of the CIA's satellite platforms. It could enable Damascus and Tehran to read covert communications and identify additional spies.

"Ghazali's story has not changed on this point about the website."

"How hard have you pressed?"

"Darkness, cold, starvation, cutting, he hasn't changed his story, big brother," Ali said. "The answer is disappointing, but the man is not lying. I am certain."

"What has the CIA officer said?" Rustum asked.

"She still denies she is CIA. She has given nothing of value."

"We should be rougher with her."

"President's orders, big brother. We keep the American out of it. Just questions for now. Nothing physical."

"I'm working to change that, little brother. I would like a proper questioning for them both, the CIA woman and Ghazali. It is overdue."

Ali scratched at his scar and opened the refrigerator for a snack. He saw a bag of carrots, and for the first time since returning home he thought of Marwan Ghazali's left thumb and the risk he was taking holding a CIA officer at the President's request. Empty-handed, he closed the refrigerator door.

"Why the sudden interest in finding more spies, big brother?" Ali said.

"You ask too many questions, Ali. Always a detective, never a soldier."

"It's *my* job to find the spies. What is going on, Rustum?" Ali asked again.

"This life is full of unanswerable questions," Rustum said. "I will find the boy." He hung up.

Layla emerged from the living room. "Are you going out tonight?"

He nodded. She gave him a kiss on the cheek, picked up her book, and vanished into the bedroom.

THE NEIGHBOR BOY WAS IN an old warehouse that had recently been converted into a holding center. Ali's arrival was expected, thanks to Rustum, and the captain in charge of the facility immediately escorted him to the boy's cell. An unspeakable smell escaped from the room as the captain opened the rusting door. As the guard stepped back, Ali looked into the room on the anguished eyes of what must have been seventy-five men crammed into a space the size of his living room. The officer called for the boy, and the mass of men shifted here and there until a bloodied youth limped forward. Ali nodded to the officer. "I'll have my guards bring him out while we take care of the paperwork," the officer said coldly, then closed the door.

In the captain's office, Ali looked over the paperwork. He had been beaten and, according to the captain on duty, "examined."

"What is the charge?" Ali asked the captain after he'd finished signing the paperwork.

"Anti-government sentiment."

"What does that mean, Captain?"

The captain put his hands behind his back. "He was disrespectful to one of our officers."

"I see," said Ali. "Had he been drinking?"

"Yes."

"Were you planning to release him after you taught him a lesson?" Ali said.

The captain said nothing.

"What did you examine?" Ali asked. "And why?"

"We completed a full-body examination to ensure he did not possess a weapon." The captain gave a thin smile. "As a precaution."

A Republican Guard colonel emerged from a back room holding the boy by the shoulder. His face was blue-black and reddened from tears. The smell of feces instantly filled the room.

"He shit his pants during the examination," the colonel said with a shrug.

The colonel gestured to the boy's puffy face as if unveiling a painting and yanked his collar to meet his eyes. "If we see you again, you'll never get out. Understand?"

The boy nodded.

"He's all yours," the colonel said, tossing him toward Ali. He crumpled onto the floor.

Ali drove the boy back to the apartment building. They kept the car windows open to dilute the smell of excrement. They did not speak until he parked the car on the sidewalk. There were no other spots available.

"Say that you were robbed and beaten," Ali said. "They took your wallet. Never go back to the place where they took you."

The boy nodded, staring at the floor. The system had claimed another. "I won't tell anyone about this," Ali said.

The boy sank his head onto the dashboard and cried.

RUSTUM AND BASIL MAHKLUF, HIS brother's favorite lieutenant, arrived at the Security Office early the next morning carrying papers embossed with the President's wax *quraysh* hawk seal. Ali scanned the document and tossed the papers onto his desk after finishing the first few lines. *"By presidential decree under the powers vested by the Emergency Law of 1963, the investigation into the traitor Marwan Ghazali will hereby and immediately be transferred from the Security Office to the Republican Guard . . ."* Ali pushed more papers aside, sat down at the table, and lit a cigarette without offering one to his guests.

Basil, Rustum's executioner—the little brother Ali was not and never would be—pulled up a chair next to Ali. Basil was wiry and his skin was ashy and pale. A swoop of thinning hair sat in opposition to his thick Saddam Hussein mustache, which he frequently and, Ali believed, unconsciously slathered with his tongue. His feet were gargantuan, out of all proportion to the rest of his body. But Basil was distinct for two features: the dishwater eyes and his low, scratchy voice. The former seemed the perfect reflection of a soulless inner void. The latter, the result of a shredded trachea courtesy of the Muslim Brotherhood during the last rebellion, in the winter of 1982.

Rustum entrusted Basil with his most sensitive tasks. Basil officially managed the Republican Guard's Missile and Rocket Directorate. He was responsible for every strategic weapon in Assad's arsenal.

Ali had also read the psychological reports on Basil drafted by the Republican Guard doctors. He'd had Kanaan steal them from Records. *He is prone to fugues, Commander*, the psychologist had written after one of Basil's visits. *There are periods in which he disassociates from his environment, perhaps reliving traumatic events. He speaks frequently of Hama, as though he is still there. Sometimes he speaks of himself in the third person. He calls himself a Comanche, Commander. A Native American tribe, apparently. He says this word in English during our visits.*

Basil had earned the nickname Comanche during the winter in Hama. Ali had heard the stories, as had everyone else in the regime.

"Basil," Ali said. "I'm glad to see you're able to take some time away from managing our missile and rocket forces for a minor interrogation. You truly are a renaissance man."

"The personal touch is important to me," said Basil in his growl. He did not even crack a sardonic smile.

"Did you bring a transport van, or should I arrange one for the prisoner?" Ali said.

Rustum stood at the window, smiling. "We thought we'd do it here."

"And make sure the room has a drain in the middle," Basil said. "I don't want to leave you with a mess."

"Big brother, this is not—"

Rustum raised his hand. "I am in charge of this investigation now, little brother. Put Ghazali in the large interrogation room and ensure Basil has what he needs."

"And bring in Valerie Owens," Basil said. "I have questions for her as well." He licked his mustache.

6

A JET-LAGGED SAM DROVE TO PARIS STATION DIRECTLY from Charles de Gaulle after a sleepless night in an economy-class middle seat—in-flight entertainment: nonfunctioning—sandwiched between a hefty Montanan and a toddler who had found it amusing to poke his arm throughout the flight. The taxi dropped him at the embassy, a cream-colored mansion standing in a leafy corner of the Place de la Concorde. Even at the early hour, Sam had to wait in line to flash his badge and black passport. He wanted nothing more than a hot shower and a morning nap in his hotel room, but he had to log on to the Agency network to see if any overnight cables had arrived on the Haddad recruitment operation.

A Station support officer met Sam as he cleared the line and escorted him up a four-flight, winding marble staircase. He put his phone in one of the cubbies and followed her inside the Station vault as she punched the code and the door clicked open.

"Windows, huh?" he said looking around the spacious room.

"In Europe our Stations have windows. We also have good coffee." She gestured to the kitchenette. He grabbed a TDY—temporary duty—pack, jammed it into a computer, and began reading the cables. There was, thankfully, confirmation that the BANDITO surveillance team had arrived in Paris. They would meet him this afternoon to begin the dry runs. He reviewed maps showing the hotel housing the Syrian delegation and the likely routes they would take. He again studied the one picture of Mariam Haddad that the CIA possessed. It had been snapped for her Palace identification badge before the entire digital directory had been copied by a CIA document thief. He sat for a moment, transfixed by the picture.

"That," said a voice behind him, "is quite the developmental."

Sam swiveled around to see Peter Shipley, the Paris Station Chief, smiling. He had never met the Chief, but knew him by reputation and his friendship with Ed Bradley. Shipley had been Chief in Kabul in the early days of the war in Afghanistan and had saved the Afghan President from an assassination attempt during one of their meetings. As with many case officers, Shipley's marriage fell apart, and his wife, French by birth, had left for Paris with the kids. He'd asked for the job to be near the family and try to set things right.

"Good to see you, Chief," Sam said, shaking his hand. He noted with approval that Shipley drank his coffee black.

"That the Syrian case you're working here?"

"It—she—is. Palace official. Mariam Haddad. Odds are low. I don't think we've recruited a Syrian in about two years."

"But we take our shots, don't we?" Shipley nodded toward his office. "There is news from Damascus. NSA found Ali Hassan's office landline."

"When?"

"Last night. Bradley just approved the op. Procter's making the call here in a few minutes. She asked that you sit in."

Inside the Chief's office, Sam looked out the window onto the Place de la Concorde as Shipley dialed. Procter's distinctive voice answered. "Peter? He with you?" Shipley and Procter knew each other from Afghanistan.

"He is indeed, Artemis. Fresh off a plane and looking like it." Shipley motioned for Sam to sit at the table and handed him a single piece of paper. It was a printed ops cable from the NSA to Damascus Station containing the phone number.

"It's just before lunch here in Damascus, so we'll try to catch him now," Procter said. "I've got one of the Station's comms officers to monkey around with the call's origin. If Hassan's got caller ID it will look like another Palace number is calling. We'll use some of those freaky robots so my voice sounds like a dude. Sam, you jump in if I screw up the Arabic. We'll all sound the same, right, Stapp?

"Yes, Chief," said Stapp, the comms officer. "We've essentially set this up as a conference call, but any speaking from our side will go out through a modulator. It will sound like a low male voice."

"Draft script is attached to the cable," Procter said.

"Artemis, there is no attachment on this cable," Shipley said. "What script are you talking about?"

The phone had started ringing. Procter fell silent and did not answer.

The phone rang five times. "General Ali Hassan," said a voice in Arabic.

"Listen up, General," Procter said in the same language. "You get one warning."

A MAN COULD NOT SUCCEED inside the Syrian regime without paranoia. Even the most well-adjusted, seemingly relaxed bureaucrats had it. That gnawing fear that a rival would supplant them. That a knock would come in the night. That their wives and children would be threatened. Ali did not consider himself overly paranoid for recording most of his conversations on the office phone. It was a matter of prudence and self-protection, even though he knew that Air Force intelligence had the phone monitored, a fact he had discovered, ironically, because his own organization had bugged several of their lines. A half second into the phone conversation, as soon as he'd heard that low robotic voice, Ali had turned on the recorder.

Ali had studied English for a few months in Moscow. Not under the best tutors, he would be the first to admit, but he'd developed a familiarity with the language and considered himself proficient. The call he had just received—been subjected to, really—had been conducted primarily in Arabic, but at a few points had detoured into a street English that he did not understand. Kanaan had studied at the University of North Dakota in the nineties, when the peace negotiations between Syria and Israel had created some measure of goodwill between the Syrian and American governments. Kanaan's family had taken advantage and packed him off to study in America. He returned speaking fluently, albeit with an inexplicable lilt that was nothing like the American accents Ali had heard.

Ali pressed stop on the recorder and turned away from the table to sneeze. Kanaan sat across the table. Ali lit a cigarette and walked to the window. Kanaan had been slightly amused listening to the call, but now he stared into the middle distance as he worked through the implications. Ali looked out the window, burning down the cigarette in silence. A helicopter operated above Douma. He watched something, probably a barrel bomb, drop from its hulk to the ground. He turned away.

"Rewind it," Ali said. "I want to hear it again."

BG ALI HASSAN: *Who is this?*

UNKNOWN CALLER: *Doesn't matter. We know you are holding Valerie Owens. We want her released today and returned to the American Embassy.*

BG ALI HASSAN: *Who is this?*

UNKNOWN CALLER: *Already told you, it doesn't matter. And let me be clear: We know you have her inside the Security Office, General. We hold you responsible for her safety.*

[Sound of a cigarette lighter clicking]

UNKNOWN CALLER: *Hello?*

BG ALI HASSAN: *I do not know a Valerie Owens. You are CIA?*

UNKNOWN CALLER: *I thought you'd say that, douchebag.*

"Pause it," Ali said. He looked at Kanaan, who swallowed hard.

"What was the English word spoken at the end?"

Kanaan's eyes narrowed in contemplation. "It is vulgar American slang for a man who is an idiot but does not know it."

"Why is it a bag?"

"The first part of the word is a reference to feminine products."

"Put into a bag?"

"Yes."

Ali frowned. "Start it again."

BG ALI HASSAN: *This is the CIA, yes? I will be reporting this call to the President.*

UNKNOWN CALLER: *We hold you personally responsible, General, understand? Release her now.*

BG ALI HASSAN: *I told you I do not know what you are talking about. Goodbye."*

UNKNOWN CALLER: *Don't you hang up.* [Inaudible muttering and yelling] *You are responsible. And if she is harmed I am going to personally deal with you, Ali. If you touch a single hair on her head I will remove your nut sack and feed it to you. I will—*

[BG Ali Hassan ends call]

"The last bit there," Ali said. "I suspect it is all in English because this person became very angry. I understand that they told me not to hang up, but I missed the rest. They were speaking very quickly."

Kanaan summarized.

"My own balls? This is what they said?"

Kanaan nodded.

"And the part about her hair?"

"It is an expression that means if we hurt her even a little bit they will punish us. If we touch a hair on her head." Kanaan pulled at a tuft of his own for emphasis.

Ali frowned again, stood to collect another Marlboro from the desk, and lit it facing the window. "Thank you, that's all for now."

Kanaan stopped in the doorway. "General, an aide from your brother's office called and asked when the final report on the CIA woman would be finished. He said your brother is expecting his copy today."

Ali nodded. "Let me read it one more time. Wait here."

He picked up the brief report he had drafted for the President describing the events that had taken place in his interrogation chamber two days earlier. He and Rustum had come to blows over who should draft it. The Comanche had put a knife against Kanaan's throat and made the choice simple. "You write it, little brother," Rustum had said. Ali opened the manila folder and read it again. He set it down and looked at the second page, which included the photograph.

He waved Kanaan over and handed him the folder. "Make copies, then submit them. We keep the originals." Kanaan did so and returned the packet to Ali's office.

Picking up the folder, Ali descended the stairs into the basement. He lit a cigarette as he moved through the darkness toward a particular filing cabinet. Ali kept a safe in his office, as did every senior official in the regime, but this was typically the first thing taken in a political or anticorruption raid. His home could also be ransacked, and he did not have the foreign access to manage a Swiss bank account, at least not yet. For now, he used the agricultural filing cabinets as his safe-deposit box. It was into the folder he now opened, labeled "Lake Assad Water Level, Reports and Analysis, 1988–1992," that he placed the picture, nestling it next to the videotape of the interrogation. He shut the filing cabinet.

Back in his office, Ali lit another cigarette as he called home. He checked his watch. "*Habibti*, have you and the boys eaten yet?"

IN THE APARTMENT ALI TOSSED Sami into the nest of pillows on the bed. The boy shrieked joyfully as he flew through the air. Then Ali howled like a wolf and chased Bassam out of the bedroom into the living room. He caught him near the kitchen, where Layla was preparing a late dinner. Snatching him up, Ali pressed his lips into his stomach and pretended to blow bubbles. The boy giggled and then Ali felt Sami clutch his legs as he mounted his shoes to join Ali as he walked. They collapsed into the couch. Sticky hands covered his eyes, and Sami said: "Who is it, Papa, who is it?" Ali tousled Sami's hair before swinging him around to his front and tickling his big toddler belly. The boy collapsed into the sofa, squealing in delight. Ali chased Bassam into the boys' bedroom and, capturing him, swung him over a shoulder to return the boy to the couch with his twin brother. The boys jumped together on the couch and Ali joined Layla in the kitchen to help finish the meal.

"It is a nice surprise to have you home early," she said. He stopped in the doorway and did not answer as he watched her cut peppers. She sliced cleanly but forcefully, driving the knife blade into the cutting board. She chopped quickly, working through a long orange pepper, setting the slices aside, and moving on to a green one. Hack, hack, hack on the wood. She slid more pepper slices onto the boys' plates, then scooped hummus alongside.

"I will make you some, before you go back to the office." She took another orange pepper from the package and began slicing. She severed the stem with a final smack of the blade and set the knife aside with a flourish.

Ali steadied himself on the doorframe and smiled at Layla. She handed him two plates. He put them on the kitchen table, then collected two of the little *Toy Story* cups and began filling them with water. Layla hugged him from behind as he stood at the sink. "I'm glad you're home," she said. He felt her hair gently gliding over his shoulder as she kissed his neck.

If you touch a single hair on her head . . .

Water ran down shaky fingers as the first cup overflowed. He swore softly, dumped some of the water, and dried his hands.

"Are you okay?" Layla said.

"Of course, *habibti.*" He turned to kiss her on the forehead.

Then he turned to the living room. "Boys, dinner is ready," he called out.

PART II

Recruitment

7

THE COUNTERSURVEILLANCE OPERATION ON MARIAM Haddad had taken shape over two days of planning in the living room of a Paris Station safe house near the Place des Vosges in the trendy Marais district. Sam, accustomed to grimier NE Division real estate, was surprised to find that it was an elegant pied-à-terre set behind a thick wooden door on the fifth floor of a creamy stone building. The windows opened onto the square below. The view was all roofs and chimneys: a canopy of slates, ambers, and ochers. But now the elegant living room was littered with maps, satellite imagery, pizza boxes, and discarded cartons of Chinese food.

At night they drove the routes and rehearsed the dance of trading places as choreographer, the person on the surveillance team who would keep eyes on Mariam. The BANDITOs—the Kassab triplets—had earned their cryptonym on the streets of Beirut running similar ops to determine if Hizballah was watching the CIA Station's assets. But the French had not invested in surveillance cameras like the Brits. And budget cuts in the French security services, according to one report Sam had read, had led to wholesale cancellations of domestic surveillance for anything other than counterterrorism concerns. The odds of the French embarrassing them on the streets were low. "Really, Sam, c'mon," Rami said. "This op, Paris, the whole thing is like a nice vacation." The trio had been hunched over a satellite image of the streets around the Syrian delegation's hotel, each delicately blowing on a carton of Peking duck. Sam laughed.

"What's so funny?" Rami had said. All three brothers looked up at Sam.

"You guys may not look much like brothers," Sam said. "But you've got the same tics."

"Triplets running surveillance, you nuts, Sam?" Bradley had said when he heard Sam wanted to recruit them. "Whole point of a surveillance op is to avoid getting spotted, not to have three chances to spot the same guy." Sam included pictures in his next cable to make the point. Rami: squatty and jowly. Yusuf: long and lean. Elias: right in the middle.

Rami took a bite of the duck and rolled his eyes.

"Anyways," Sam said. "Might be a vacation for you guys, but I'm the one who has to warm-pitch a Syrian woman on the street." The pitch—warm, not cold, because the CIA had background information on Haddad—was arguably the toughest and most uncertain recruitment act in the trade. Sam would approach her on the street and, in a matter of seconds, attempt to convince her to meet him in a discreet location. CIA could never be certain how the target would respond. A case officer Sam knew in Istanbul had been pushed down a flight of stairs after pitching a Russian GRU official at the top of the metro. Always pitch 'em on flat ground, he had said.

Sam stood over the map and pointed at a stone staircase on the banks of the Seine, a few blocks from Mariam's hotel. One of the brothers had circled it with a red marker. "Let's not do it here."

MORNING BROUGHT BRILLIANT SPRINGTIME LIGHT and the monotony of the waiting, the first, essential, and most mind-numbing act of any surveillance operation. Sam had already downed two coffees and was a little jittery from the caffeine when the hotel's double doors swung open and Mariam Haddad emerged onto the street just off the Rue de Rivoli, which was brimming with luxury shops, breezy awninged cafés, and high-end boutiques.

"She's out," Sam said into the encrypted earpiece radio. From the bakery across the street, he finished his third cup of coffee and took the last bite of a pain au chocolat.

He left a stack of small coins on the table and stood up. It was time to begin the dance. Would the Syrians stick close to her, bumper-lock her all day, just to check? Would the boys at La Piscine, the DGSE, the French external service, try to recruit her? A day of watching, of beating the pavement, would provide an early answer.

"Copy," said the Kassab triplets in unison, from their positions scattered around the neighborhood's arteries, the team positioned to pick her up whichever way she'd ventured.

"She's in athletic gear, looks like a morning run," Sam said. "We got lucky."

A run would almost certainly occur along a route unknown to all but Mariam herself. This meant that any opposing surveillance teams would be forced to rely heavily on mobile assets—people, cars, motorcycles—trailing Mariam, dropping clues for Sam and the BANDITOs. The fixed positions—parked cars, prearranged cameras, people at cafés—would be tricky for Sam and his team to detect on foreign ground. Mobile teams would move. The movement could be spotted.

She stood on the sidewalk outside the hotel stretching, taking in the spring air.

She still resembled the single stolen photo CIA possessed. And, as he had with the photo, Sam looked for a beat longer than was professionally necessary. She had chestnut hair that descended halfway down her back, well-defined cheekbones, and a rounded, natural nose. She must have passed on the plastic surgery common among so many upper-class Syrian women.

She tied her hair up into a ponytail and looked around, as if debating her route.

A young businessman walking past broke Parisian custom and

smiled at her, and she responded with an easy, toothy smile that brought out the dimples in her cheeks.

She ran toward the Tuileries at a steady clip.

"Your direction, Rami," Sam said. "South on Castiglione." He went to collect the Vespa rental he had parked on the sidewalk.

"Copy. Heading to intersection." Rami would mark her path and either follow or lead Sam or one of his brothers in the right direction. They had to follow but not spook her, which meant constantly rotating roles so their presence remained undetected.

Sam drove the Vespa until he reached the Place de la Concorde, where he would take up Rami's position. He motored past Concorde's obelisk centerpiece and hit a red light near the bridge just before the Seine.

"She's, uh, not the typical surveillance target, Sam," Rami said. "She's more, what's the word . . ."

"Beautiful?" Sam said. Yusuf chuckled over the radio.

"I was going to say buxom," Rami said.

"Just like the target we watched in Istanbul," Sam said. "Except in this case it's a woman, not a Saudi general, and she appears well below three hundred pounds. Consider yourselves lucky."

"She's cutting through the garden toward the river," Rami said into the radio, huffing. "There is a younger guy, maybe six feet tall, black athletic shirt and shorts, running behind her. Probably nothing. But he looks Levantine."

"Copy," said everyone.

"Rami, I'm stuck at a light outside of Concorde," Sam said. "Can you get far enough into the garden to see which way she turns when she hits the river?"

"Yes," Rami said, breathing heavy. Sam waited a beat. "She's heading your way. That dude turned with her. About twenty yards back."

One turn. Nothing to worry about yet. Countersurveillance required time. Two hours of watching would be inconclusive. But ten, twelve, a full day—then you knew, usually. The light held red. He popped a piece of gum into his mouth. The watching made him fidgety. Five cars in front lay the pedestrian crossing. Sam saw Mariam run through quickly. The male runner kept his eyes locked on her.

Something felt off. Sam banked right to follow the river tucked below. He lost sight of Mariam from the road. He heard the horn from one of the Bateaux Mouches riverboats. A flock of pigeons dispersed overhead as he swept along.

Sam wanted a closer look at the other runner, whose presence now tingled his neck. The sensation was an old friend since the Farm, the signal that watchers lurked nearby. It required skill for a solo tail to maintain a clandestine presence for a long period of time. Even those untrained in surveillance and countersurveillance tended to notice, eventually. And the French DGSE—they wouldn't use an obvious guy like this for the ground team. Sam accelerated the bike, pulling it onto the sidewalk when he reached the next stone staircase that descended to the riverside walkway.

"I'm going to follow on foot." He ran down the stairwell, arriving at the bottom forty yards behind the man tailing Mariam. Sam ran behind him. Now he could watch for details: pace, line of sight, subtle signals to a hidden team like working an ear-fitted radio, as Sam now was. Mariam's pace accelerated. She had a motor. Sam's jeans and T-shirt were starting to cling to his sweaty body, and he knew he would not be able to jog unnoticed for long.

"Guy's tracking with her," Sam said. "I'm going up to the road. I'll keep running from there. Yusuf, you take them if I get spread out."

"Copy."

Sam ascended a stone staircase at the next bridge into a leafy park littered with glass bottles and cigarettes. He jogged along the river, dodging idle clumps of pedestrians, strollers, and the Parisian dog walkers, leashes crisscrossing the path like trip wire. An old man walking a pudgy bulldog gasped as Sam jumped over the leash.

When he reached the Alma Bridge, he thought he had the answer: the black-clad runner ascended the steps behind Mariam, reached the top, and exchanged words with another young man wearing workout gear. The fresh runner, this one in baggy red shorts, took off behind her, tracing her path.

"She's covered, guys," Sam said. "The runner just passed the baton to a fresh set of legs."

NOW CERTAIN THAT MARIAM WAS COVERED, Sam and the BANDITOs set about discovering their identity. They backed off Mariam and focused on what they soon determined was a three-man team. All Syrian or Lebanese, the BANDITOs agreed. The two younger men, both athletic, and a third, an older heavyset man—"Definitely Syrian," Elias said, "he's got that *mukhabarat* look, the troglodyte sensibility, the throwback mustache"—who revealed himself by communicating with Red Shorts through a clunky hand signal from a bookstore window.

The Syrian watchers tracked Mariam until she returned to her hotel, then reappeared to follow her on a shopping trip to Les Galeries Lafayette. At no point did they attempt to detect or draw out surveillance.

The watch continued until she joined her Palace comrades for a dinner on Saint Honoré. Later, with Mariam safely snug in her hotel room, Sam and the BANDITOs decamped to debrief at the Marais safe house. To this elegance Yusuf brought two Pizza Hut pepperoni pizzas and twelve bottles of cheap French beer.

Sam scowled. "What the hell, man, we're in the food capital of the world and you insist that we eat this crap? Two days of nothing but lousy takeout."

Yusuf shrugged. "We watch, we eat Pizza Hut."

"If it ain't broken," Elias said.

They set the pizza on the coffee table—purchased at the flea market by a Paris Station support asset with an eye for vintage chic—and realized the safe house did not have a bottle opener. By tradition they did not drink during the planning phase of an operation, and had not noticed the oversight until now.

"Unbelievable," Sam said.

No one had a cigarette lighter, so Sam got a chef's knife from the kitchen and tried to pry the caps loose. The blade broke almost immediately. They only chipped the table a little bit as they placed the lip of the cap on the table and smacked it down against the wood, snapping it off. Sam brushed aside the teak fragments and took a long swig of beer.

"French stringers?" Rami said as they arrived on topic.

"Feels unlikely," Sam said. "The French aren't this sloppy. It's the Syrians."

Sam ripped off a slice of pizza and lifted it to his mouth, only to realize the crust was still linked to the pie by a foot-long cord of cheese. "Are you kidding me with this food? This is the best you guys can do?"

THE SYRIAN TEAM COMPLICATED THE operation. Sam had to pitch her privately, and it could not be on the street. He could try to exploit a gap in the Syrian surveillance team's coverage, but it would be risky. If they saw her speaking with an American on the street, even casually, they might ask follow-up questions. He could put her in danger. No, he needed a few minutes with Mariam in a place where it would be normal to speak briefly with an American.

So Sam went to Paris Station to read operational SIGINT—signals intelligence—and rebuild the plan. A techie named Lisa who was on loan from NSA helped compile the relevant recordings: a few calls from Bouthaina Najjar to an as-yet-unidentified lover—"Probably want to skip those, though," she said, flushing red, "a bit graphic"—and a recorded call between Mariam and her father. Sam found he enjoyed listening to her singsong Arabic and laugh. When the conversation turned to the battle in Aleppo (NSA comment: "Georges Haddad's III Corps has been stationed in Aleppo since October") Mariam's voice tightened and her father grew quiet and evasive. "Turn it off," Sam said gruffly. "They can have the moment."

The techie clicked stop.

"Anything on the delegation's schedule?" Sam asked.

"One thing," she said. She wheeled around to her computer and pulled up a short NSA report dated six days earlier. It was an intercepted conversation between the French ambassador to Damascus and the French deputy foreign minister. In it, the ambassador explained that despite the public relations optics, it would be helpful to the foreign minister's rapport with Bouthaina if a social event were held sometime during her visit. The deputy foreign minister agreed as long as he did not have to attend. It would be important to have multiple foreign partners represented, particularly the Americans, the ambassador concluded, before hanging up abruptly.

Sam picked up the paper and made for Peter Shipley's office. He loitered outside as the Chief concluded a tense phone call with his ex-wife about his son's math test. Not the best time to poke the bear, but Sam had no choice. The diplomatic event would be his best chance to pitch Mariam. Hearing Shipley put down the receiver on his open line, Sam knocked on the door. Shipley waved him in and put on a pair of reading glasses to review the report. After a few seconds, he flipped the paper onto the desk. "Goddammit." He leaned back in his chair and thumbed at his left suspender. "The Ambo keeps this shit from us all the time. You're certain she's covered?"

"Yes."

He nodded. "Step outside for a second, this will be unpleasant."

Sam sat on a fuzzy green couch outside the office for three minutes while Shipley called the U.S. ambassador to France: pharmaceutical executive, gold-plated political donor, hoarder of useful information. The details were hard to make out, but the tones were not. The screaming started at the tail end of minute one, hit crescendo halfway through the second, and simmered into a hissy conversation through the third. It ended with the ceremonious slamming of a secure telephone into a desk and the unambiguous utterance of the word "motherfucker" from the Chief of Station Paris.

When he opened the door, his face was still red with rage, but Sam caught a wry smirk breaking through Shipley's scowl.

"I got you an invite. Tomorrow night. Palais Louis Philippe. Eight p.m. Wear something nice."

MOST RECRUITMENTS TOOK MONTHS, OR even years. The skills that separated the recruiters, a rare breed, from the rest of the case officer cadre was that they could spot people with the right access, build a relationship, then successfully pitch them to work for CIA. Sam had done it fifteen times in his ten years in the service, the most of anyone in his Farm class by a long shot. He knew people, understood how they worked, and could read them. He had yakked it up with Saudi princes, Egyptian *mukhabarat*, itinerant gamblers in Vegas, the union boys at the flour mill back home in Minnesota. Agent recruitment was his sport.

The Farm prescribed a three-part outline for public, official encounters like this: strike up a conversation, elicit as much information on the target as possible (without raising suspicion), arrange a follow-up in a more private setting. It would come down to chemistry. Sam had one evening to start the process. If they had a bond, she might agree to meet the next day. If they didn't, it would be over.

Patridge, one of the State Political Counselors, showed their invitations outside a palatial building a few blocks from the Foreign Ministry building at the Quai d'Orsay. Twenty or so protesters gathered outside, flapping tristar Syrian rebel flags and holding motley signs. A crew of gendarmes idled on the sidewalk, radios crackling with static, machine guns pointed into the pavement. At the massive door, a tuxedoed attendant ushered them inside with a sweep of his arm. Patridge disappeared to mingle without saying a word.

The room was decorated in the style of a corporatist cocktail party: cavernous, wood-paneled, chandeliered, two bars, and a table for hors' d'oeuvres. Sam foraged a small plate of spiced chicken and sidled up to one of the high tops, alone, to take the room's pulse. One chicken skewer in, he saw that nations were clumped together, mostly speaking to themselves. He fiddled with his tie.

He first noticed her trying to escape from conversation with a squat diplomat, whose home, Sam could tell, lay somewhere east of the Iron Curtain. He watched, smiling, at Mariam's subtle but growing discomfort as she planned her flight from the conversation. Her eyes moved about, looking for help.

Then they met his.

The look she threw to Sam was universal: *I need a bailout*. Now was the time to take the shot. Walking over, he gave her a warm hug and in fluent Arabic asked how she had been. He was relieved when she held the embrace and told the diplomat she had to catch up with her friend. Scowling, he stomped off.

The image of Mariam in that dress would linger in Sam's mind. Silky and bright red, almost matching her lipstick, it cinched above her hips before flowing to the floor. Her hair was up, revealing much of her back.

"Sam Joseph," he whispered as they took up residence at a high-top table, still pretending to be old friends as the glaring Slav nursed his wounds across the room with a new drink. They accepted champagne from a passing waiter.

"Mariam Haddad," she whispered back. She smiled and looked at Sam. "American?"

He nodded, holding her gaze.

"Your Arabic is excellent."

"Thanks. Lots of practice. How do you know Igor over there?"

"Who? Oh. His name is Nikolay, I think. Bulgarian."

"Oh, uh, yeah, Igor was just a general way to . . . Never mind. Yes, Nikolay."

"I just met him tonight, unfortunately. Thanks for the rescue, by the way." She had switched to a near-flawless English.

"Of course," Sam said. "Now he's targeting one of my friends. She deserves it, though." Mariam laughed as they watched Nikolay beeline for Patridge.

"Your English is perfect, by the way," he said. "Where did you learn?"

A waiter strolled by with a platter of crackers topped with a mysterious gray meat. Sam waved him off.

"Lessons here when I was young," she said. "My mother was a diplomat. She took advantage of the Paris posting and helped me learn French and English. And also how to fight." She gave a menacing smile and took a sip of champagne.

He took a sip of champagne, reading her body language and considering whether the fighting comment was in jest.

She rearranged the dress. "I'm serious," she said.

He thought she was. "Your mother wanted you to learn self-defense?"

"Of course. My mother savors scandal, so she recommended Krav Maga."

He smiled, now not sure if she was sarcastic. She could tell.

"What better way to get in the head of the Zionists than to beat them at their own games?" She joked. "Know thine enemy."

He laughed. Mariam gave a wry smile but it disappeared as a mustachioed Syrian in a suit at least two sizes too small approached the table, reminding her gruffly that all interactions with Americans must be reported. He evidently did not know that Sam spoke Arabic, because he made several derogatory remarks pointing in his direction. Sam figured him for the *mukhabarat* goon who kept tabs on the embassy staff, and just smiled at him stupidly.

She gave an exaggerated eye roll. "Of course I know, Mohannad," she said in Arabic as if Sam could not understand. "I'll file the report in the morning. For God's sake, go bother someone else." She turned away. His face clenched and he walked off, glaring at Sam.

They sipped champagne silently until Mohannad reached the bar and began wolfing down crackers, still looking at them. Then she turned to Sam. "Mohannad is very suspicious and he enjoys writing reports," she said in English.

"Maybe we could continue our discussion tomorrow evening over a drink?" he said. He'd already scouted a small bar near the Sorbonne.

She took a sip of champagne, holding his eyes. "Where?" she said.

"How about Au Torchon? Latin Quarter. You name the time."

"Eight-thirty? We have meetings until seven."

"That's perfect. See you then."

She clinked an empty glass to his and walked off. He caught himself staring as she left and then downed the last pull of champagne. There was a lot to unpack: the initial cartoon of the sensual, olive-skinned desert princess melting into the English-speaking, Krav Maga–practicing diplomat and eventually arriving downstream to the capable professional who had the courage to uproot Mohannad. Also, that dress.

"More champagne, monsieur?" A waiter intruded on the thought. Turning him down, he scanned for one last look at Mariam but had no luck.

On his way out he smiled at Patridge, still trapped in conversation by the girthy Bulgarian.

8

THE NEXT MORNING SAM, PROCTER, AND BRADLEY joined a secure video-teleconference to debate the wisdom of meeting for a drink with Mariam if the Syrian team continued to blanket her. "A quick conversation at a party," Procter said. "That's fine. Security goon from the embassy writes it up, she says an American cornered her, no biggie. But a second meet? Puts you on the *mukhabarat*'s radar."

"Agreed. Make sure she's clean before you meet with her," Bradley decreed.

Sam, free of surveillance duty, now sipped coffee a block from Au Torchon, listening to the BANDITOs chatter as they continued their vigil.

"She's clean so far, Sam," Yusuf said. "I've got the cab's tail."

"I'll go to the restaurant," Sam said as he set aside his coffee.

"Copy."

He'd chosen Au Torchon because it had a back room and three possible exits. The BANDITOs would watch from the outside. Sam would ditch the encrypted radio earpiece and instead monitor a throwaway phone, which the BANDITOs would contact if the Syrian team approached the restaurant.

He went to the back room and found a small table in the corner. Two French college students sat on the other side of the room, leaning in close. An elderly couple shuffled in behind him.

Sam removed the earpiece—assets found them off-putting—and sent a text message to the BANDITOs: *At restaurant. Switching to phone.*

The reply from Elias: *Five minutes out. Still black.*

Sam pretended to scan the menu as he considered the task. Paris Station had highlighted SIGINT with the Syrian delegation's travel itinerary: they planned to stay in Paris for another four days. He could continue developing the case in Damascus, but it would be more complicated. Time was short.

Rami: *Arriving. Black.*

Those dimples greeted Sam as Mariam entered the back room. She wore dark jeans, gray suede heels, and a breezy white top. Her hair was parted slightly left of center and fell down either shoulder. "Well, hello," she said playfully.

Sam, who wore a blue suit and white oxford—he ditched the tie—stood to greet her. "You've escaped your friend, I see," he said.

"Sometimes he lets me out of the dungeon, and other times I leave without telling him," she said. "I filed a scandalous report on you this morning, so he was happy."

Sam smiled, curious what was actually in the report. "A glass of wine?"

They sat and she snatched the menu. "Yes, but I will order. You strike me as a . . . a . . . how do you say it in English?"

"A beer guy?"

"A man of simple taste."

"That works."

She grinned, then flagged the waiter, asked him a few questions in flawless French, and placed an order off the wine list.

The waiter returned with two glasses of a red from a village called Gigondas. "I visited with my mother. A lifetime ago," Mariam said. She sipped the wine and nodded to the waiter, who disappeared.

"How long did you live in Paris?" Sam asked in Arabic.

"Two years. I was sixteen when we arrived, eighteen when we left. I went back home to go to college. My father insisted I attend Damascus University."

She would expect questions about work, he knew. Banter about the conflict in Syria, the discussions with the opposition. He did not want to talk about any of that, not with her, not now. He needed to fuel the recruitment by building the connection, by getting her talking about herself.

"What do you love most about Paris?" he asked.

She took a sip of wine. "The freedom," she said, fingers running along the stem of the glass.

"Tell me about it."

She smiled and took another sip.

"When I first arrived, I was sixteen and I'd never been out of Syria. It was May. I remember leaving our apartment. I walked along the Seine in the sunshine. I could feel lightness in the air. It's hard to describe. It was like someone had been pressing a hand into your chest, not hard, but enough to make you feel the pressure. I'd carried it my entire life, but in Paris the hand came off and I remember closing my eyes and just breathing. And then I was running, coat flapping, tears streaming down my cheeks." She laughed.

Sam smiled. "Everyone must have thought you were nuts."

She snorted, the same sound from the NSA recordings.

"I bought cigarettes. Once darkness came I was outside Sacré-Coeur, on Montmartre, looking at the city lights below. I smoked and watched the twinkling sea."

"Breathing?" He smiled.

She snorted again. "Every chance I could. Expecting the hand to return, but it didn't. The world was light. And then from nowhere a woman sidled up. She was young, very thin, dirty blond hair cut short and these beautiful wide cheekbones and milky skin. She asked for a light. I lit her cigarette and she sat and we stared down the hill. She told me she'd run away from home. I asked why. She told me she had to be free. That now she was. She looked into my eyes and asked if I was free. I didn't know, I said. She finished her cigarette and left."

Sam took a sip of wine. "Do you want anything to eat?" he asked.

"No, I'm fine, thanks. So, I've just told you a story about me. Tell me something about you. Something fun. Not a chronology. A story." She leaned back in her chair and smirked as she twirled the wineglass on the table. "Tell me a crazy story, Sam."

The elderly couple across the room, now seated on the same side of a four-seat table, had begun kissing. He motioned toward them. Watching, Mariam suppressed a laugh as she turned back to face Sam. *So sweet,* she mouthed in Arabic. "Won't get you out of the story, though."

He laughed. "Fine. I grew up in Minnesota, it's a state in the northern part of the country. Small town called Shermans Corner. Farm, flour mill, very working-class. I'm twenty, maybe, when some guys from the mill invite me to a poker game. And I clean up."

"You are good at cards?"

"I became obsessive. I read everything I could, I watched poker tournaments on TV and covered up the spot on the screen where they show the hand, to guess what the players had. I kept winning and finally one of the guys comes to me with a proposition: poker tournament, pretty high stakes, down at an Indian casino out of town. Five thousand bucks to enter, two hundred and fifty grand for the winner. He asked, if a few of the guys chipped in, would I play? I would take twenty-five percent of the winnings."

"Let me guess, you won?"

"I did. Sixty-two thousand dollars. As we drove home I looked around the car, all these guys going home to their wives and kids and the mill, and I thought: This is a ticket out. They dropped me at home, I went upstairs, packed a duffel bag, jumped in my car, drove down to Minneapolis, and bought a ticket for Vegas. I stayed. My mother was furious."

"I would be, too, if my son just left. So let me guess, you went to Vegas and won millions and decided you did not need more money, why not do something incredible, like join the State Department and travel the world?"

He laughed. "I wish. I did well to start. I found the right games, I played it safe, generally. If I felt myself losing control, I would walk away. I became even more obsessed with the game, kind of OCD. Soon I'm up to almost one hundred and fifty thousand and it gets in my head. I joined a big-time, high-stakes private game. I put down everything."

"What happened?"

"I lost. I remember doing the math: three years' salary at the mill evaporated. As I'm shuffling out, the host, this guy named Max, tells me to stop. I turn around and he asks why I play. And I shrug and say: To win. I'm sure I gave him some punk attitude. I asked him why he cared. He said he didn't. But he knew I was either lying or mistaken. He'd seen it during the game, in my eyes. Just winning won't be enough for you, Sam. You need more."

"What did he mean?" Mariam asked.

"We walk to a window. He had a place in the Bellagio, a big casino on the Strip. He said I could have it all. I could earn back the money in a couple months, drive the Aston Martin, get the place in L.A., Tahoe, wherever. He told me he'd wrestled with it. Vegas had carved him up, left him hollow. He asked if I wanted to make a contribution. I had no idea what he was talking about. But I said yes. Something resonated with me. This emptiness I'd felt in Minnesota and now in Vegas, like I was adrift from anything that really mattered."

"That, or the fact you had just lost over one hundred thousand dollars," Mariam said with a smile.

Sam laughed. "There was that, too. But in either case, this guy, it turns out, helped find people for the State Department. And here I am."

"Very unconventional," she said, as if she knew some of the facts were false. Sam finished his wine. She leaned closer. "Thank you for telling me," she said.

She ordered another bottle and Sam said he'd just told her about the craziest thing he'd ever done. "What's your thing?"

"Aren't you going to ask me about Syria, about the discussions with the opposition?" she said with a laugh. "Don't you have reports to write for Washington?"

"My question is more interesting," he said.

Her face darkened as she took a generous sip of wine. "Fine. Once, I went to a protest."

"I knew you were a rebel." Sam was joking but noticed now her fingers fidgeting on the table around the base of her wineglass. "I'm sorry," he said. "I didn't mean to trivialize it. We can talk about something else."

She considered this for a moment and took another sip of wine. "No, it's all right. It's just that I haven't told anyone about it."

And there it was, a secret. His mind photographed the moment, as it had for every asset he'd recruited. Once a developmental offers a secret about themselves, he knew, they eventually provide one belonging to their government.

"What happened?" Sam pressed gently.

"I have a lovely, impetuous cousin named Razan," Mariam said. "We are almost the same age. We are like sisters. Razan had a friend in one of the opposition's coordinating committees, the *tansiqiyas,* in Damascus. They organized protests. The Haddads are a big, well-known Damascene Christian family. And Christians have largely sat on the sidelines of the uprising, hoping it will end. The protest organizers said it would be helpful if Razan attended. It would demonstrate Christian solidarity with the opposition. Razan told me about it, that's how close we are. Even though I work in the Palace, she told me."

"And you followed her there?"

Mariam nodded, calculating her words, still keeping a wall up with this American. "I did."

Mariam finished her wine, refilled her glass, looked him directly in the eye to deliver a message. "I went to keep her safe, not because I supported it."

"Okay," he said quietly.

Mariam reviewed his face as if confirming the message had been received. Sam examined the eyes, the body language, those hips shifting in the chair. He could intuit the tension but wanted her to offer it first. He stayed silent, creating space.

"They gave Razan a megaphone. She made unfortunate public statements criticizing the President. I watched from outside the crowd like a spectator."

"What did the *mukhabarat* do?"

"They stopped her, of course. Someone swung a club into her right eye. They dragged her away, beat her, arrested her. She stayed in prison for a few days. My father secured her release. She was lucky. But she still can't see from that eye."

"What did you do?"

"I did nothing."

Sam placed his hand on the table, fingers outstretched, inviting. She put her hand on his, warm and delicate and smooth. She gave him a weak, dimpled smile, a thank-you for letting the story end there.

Sam tried to remind himself that this was a developmental meeting, not a date, and that certain boundaries had to be respected. One of them was to avoid physical contact, he knew, looking at the hands on the table. A case officer could use physical attraction as an influencing mechanism but under no circumstances could they indulge the asset or themselves. This, he knew, was indulgence.

"I should probably get back to the hotel," Mariam said, withdrawing her hand.

"How much longer are you in Paris?"

"A few days, until the end of the week."

"Can I see you again?" As soon as the words came out, he wondered why he'd said it that way, like it would be a date.

She looked like she wanted to say yes, but instead she said: "I'm not sure it's a good idea. I will be very busy. And you are, well, American." She looked at his hand on the table, and her eyes darted away.

Respect the first no, he knew. The good recruits are not coerced. Let them choose.

"I understand," he said. He took the pen inside the leather flap holding the bill and wrote a phone number down on a napkin. "This is my number," he said. "I'd love to continue our conversation. To see you again. I'll be here for the rest of the week. Personal time." He slid the paper across the table. She looked at it, debating, then slipped it into her handbag.

The back room had emptied, the French couples long gone.

Mariam left an imprint of red lipstick on his right cheek before she left. She tried wiping it off and held up stained fingers, toothy mischief stretching across her face. "I didn't get all of it."

He laughed and pulled her in for a hug. She leaned back and took him in before saying a quick good night and disappearing into the cloudy evening.

9

MARIAM AWOKE THE NEXT MORNING AND THOUGHT OF his outstretched hand inviting hers onto the table. Why had she told him those things? She still could not fathom why she'd opened herself so fully to a strange diplomat. And an American, at that. She thought of the phone number written on the napkin, now folded in her wallet behind a credit card. She shuddered. She should rip it to shreds and flush the pieces down the toilet. She knew this. Still, she had not. It did not make sense, but there it was.

She got up and worked through the Krav motions until she could no longer move. Slick with sweat, she showered, tossed on a robe, and ordered macchiato and brioche to the room. She stared into the cup and her brain began posing the simple questions, the ones that tortured. Who are you? Why are you doing this? Why have you come to Paris to threaten Fatimah Wael?

She didn't answer, though. Instead, she went to the closet, put on a black pencil skirt, a flowing cream blouse, black heels, and a simple string of Mikimoto pearls, a gift from her mother. She tied her hair up and applied her red lipstick in the mirror. She appraised her look: elegant, simple, the opposite of the *mukhabarat* knuckle-draggers who normally threatened Fatimah. I am the young face of the new Syria, Fatimah. Come join me and renounce the rebellion. Come home. Or you will be destroyed.

Mariam went downstairs to find Bouthaina eating breakfast in the dining room off the lobby. Her security detail lounged at the table behind like jungle cats. Bouthaina had a notebook open on the table and her phone out, her fingers sending frenzied text messages. "Mariam, my dear, I won't be able to join you this morning with Fatimah. And in fact I may need to cut my trip short. Drama in Damascus." She sent another text message. Mariam saw a phone call from an unknown number flash on the screen.

"Shit," Bouthaina mumbled. "Take the meeting and we can regroup later." She looked at another text message. "Shit."

AN EMBASSY DRIVER COLLECTED MARIAM from the hotel at eight. It had rained in the early morning and the Parisian streets were now slick with oily pools so the morning dog walkers wore high boots. Waiters at the passing cafés were toweling down the chairs. They drove to the embassy to retrieve Mariam's bureaucratic weaponry: paper, files, names.

Outside the embassy the driver cut through a gaggle of protesters. One held a sign that said DR. DEATH over Assad's picture. Mariam took a deep breath as they entered the gates. Protesters banged on the hood and windows as the car crawled along. A young Syrian man pointed at Mariam through the window. "You are the butcher's slave," he said. He plastered a homemade poster against the window. On it were pictures of dead bodies: some in rubble, others lined up in *kaffans,* the burial shrouds. The man pointed at Mariam again. She looked past him, at a picture of a dead woman who resembled someone from a night in a long-ago Syria.

IN THEIR THIRD YEAR AT Damascus University, Mariam and Razan drank.

They also shopped, lunched, partied, danced, dated, groomed, smoked, gossiped, consumed, ignored. Times were heady for sons and daughters of the regime. Bashar had recently ascended to the presidency following his father's death. The papers spoke of change: after all, the old president had ruled for thirty years. Political salons opened in the homes of several geriatric oppositionists. Western politicians came to Damascus. Bashar drove them around the Old City in his Volkswagen Golf and they took photos. Bashar was young. He knew how to use computers. He had been a doctor. He had studied in London. His wife Asma, Razan liked to say, was a babe. *Vogue* put her on the cover ("A Rose in the Desert").

But inside the regime, money and power flowed to a narrow group of individuals around the new President. Cousins, trusted friends, influential families—the insiders won fortunes in oil, telecommunications, and car dealerships.

Razan, already impetuous and rebellious and flirting with Marxism, explained to Mariam how the system worked. She lay on their dorm room floor in a white tank top and jeans taking slugs of vodka off the bottle, a cigarette-clotted ashtray next to her head. "The money and licenses and positions are controlled by Bashar and a few people around him," she said. "Then they carve it up and give it to a second tier, who does the same for the third, and so on." She put down the vodka bottle and dragged on her cigarette and stretched her arms along the carpet until her shirt pulled upward and her dusky midriff was bare. She'd had her belly button pierced. Complete scandal. "It cements Assad's control over Syria. *Suriya al-Assad.* Assad's Syria." She gave a wicked grin and handed the bottle to Mariam.

Mariam set down her drawing pad and took a swig, arching an eyebrow at her cousin. Mariam scanned the room, imagining where the *mukhabarat* may have installed microphones. Razan did not care. She smiled and asked Mariam: "Do you know where it all goes?"

"Downstream," Mariam said as she drank the cheap vodka.

Razan opened the door to their shared closet and dangled a pair of Louboutins, instantly recognizable from their red soles. Not that Mariam had any difficulty identifying the five-inch heels. They were hers. One of several pairs that she owned. "From Assad to our closet,"

Razan slurred, the vodka's bite now settling in. "A few detours along the way, of course. Through the military and the SSRC to our fathers, then to us." She rifled through the jewelry drawer, holding up gold pieces as she continued her monologue. Then she cupped her breasts and feathered fingers over her forehead—recently augmented and injected, respectively—and said: "Courtesy of His Excellency Bashar al-Assad" and curtseyed and laughed with a snort like Mariam's. She lolled into the wall from the booze.

"*Habibti*, we've got to be there in fifteen minutes," Mariam said, looking at her watch. Politics dropped, Mariam and Razan set out to party. They put on the shoes—"Assad's Louboutins" said an increasingly tipsy Razan—and tight little dresses and caked-on makeup, and took a cab to the Art House Restaurant, which had been rented to celebrate a friend's birthday. As the cab flew down the streets of Damascus, Razan leaned her head onto Mariam's shoulder.

"What happens to us when life catches up?" Mariam asked.

"They're going to breed us," Razan said.

"I think you're right."

"The only way to avoid the breeding program is to get a good job," Razan said. "That way we have options." She sat up and looked out the window. Mariam did the same, the city full and lustrous through the window. Damascus, oh, Damascus. Mariam loved then how it glowed in its center, like a pulsing neon heart feeding the country's gangrenous body.

She could almost forget the heaviness on her chest. Almost.

Mariam remembered more vodka and dancing and kissing one of the boys from history class, but then Razan, that evil glint in her eyes, said, "Let's take a field trip, *habibti*." And her cousin—God help me, Mariam thought—somehow snatched a friend's car and she was driving them east on the M5 out of the city toward the suburbs. Mariam thought maybe she'd blacked out, couldn't remember much about leaving Art House. Then Razan was smoking and the windows were down. Enrique Iglesias blared from the radio while Razan drummed the wheel with her palms and danced in her seat. The freeway lights spun as Mariam fought the slide.

After what seemed like thirty minutes—but may have been longer,

Mariam was not sure—she asked Razan where in the hell they were going. "Out, *habibti*," she said. "To see the sights." Razan had sobered up a bit. The car mostly moved in a straight line, anyway. But around a place called Harasta, Mariam saw a strip of metal in the road and Razan plowed into it and they heard a dull pop. Razan started cursing, reviewing the glowing dials, putting her fingers on them like they were talismans. Razan turned off the M5. The streets were dark and Mariam could feel eyes behind shuttered windows examining the tinted BMW. They passed several mosques, an electronics store, a restaurant abandoned to stray cats. Mariam saw a woman in a niqab—unseen in central Damascus—walking behind a man and a flock of young children. Refuse piles dotted the streets. Razan dodged a garbage bag as she passed another mosque, cursing, the tire now flapping as the road shredded it to ropes. "Don't think they're used to seeing Christian women driving BMWs," Razan screamed over the noise. The stress ushered Mariam from the vodka fog.

Then the tire gave out and the rim hit the pavement. Sparks flew. Razan cursed and sputtered the car to a stop in a nameless darkened street. They found the spare beneath the trunk but neither knew how to change a tire.

Together they reviewed the darkness—Where are the streetlights?—and the bone-deep quiet and the sewer smell wafting into the air. Mariam said: "We're fifteen minutes from home and I've never felt farther."

"Which suburb is this?" Razan asked.

"You drove, idiot."

"So?"

"We passed Harasta, right?"

"Yes."

"Douma, then. It is Douma."

They strolled looking for help. Two half-drunk, uncovered Christian girls dressed to party. Miraculously they found an auto body shop a few blocks north. It was now past midnight. The shop was dark, but Razan knocked anyway.

"Razan, what are you doing? It's the middle of the night."

"How much money do you have?"

"Not much."

"We'll give them what we have."

On the third knock a man with a thick black beard and a jagged face opened the door. Seeing two strange women on his doorstep, he immediately shut it. Razan raised her fist to knock again, but Mariam caught it midair. "No," she said. "Enough."

Bickering, they'd turned to leave when the door opened again. An old woman stood in the entryway. She wore the niqab. "What do you want?" she asked.

"We broke down a few blocks that way," Mariam said. "Flat tire."

The woman waited in silence as if this were a bad answer.

"We were hoping you could call a taxi for us or have someone look at the car," Mariam continued.

"You know the time?"

"Yes. We're sorry. We just broke down."

"Where were you going?"

"For a ride," Razan said.

The woman stared at Razan like this answer was ridiculous. Mariam found herself agreeing. She watched this woman, nearly completely covered, and Mariam registered cosmic embarrassment for existing in this awful moment. She wanted to throw her Louboutins—Assad's Louboutins—in one of Douma's trash piles. The woman may have had the same thought, because she stared at Mariam's shoes for a beat, then looked up at her face.

"Come inside," she said.

She led them through a cramped hallway into a kitchen and gestured to a grimy plastic table. She left to speak with her husband. The door to a back room was ajar. Mariam could see at least eight, maybe nine children sleeping on ratty blankets spread on the floor. When the woman returned, she saw Mariam looking at the children and said: "Six are mine, the rest are my husband's family from the east. The drought destroyed their farms and herds. They had nowhere else to go. My husband will go look at the car. Where is it?"

"A few blocks that way," Razan said, pointing. The old woman nodded.

"It's a BMW," Mariam said, hoping the old woman would let that go.

Again the woman nodded. Mariam thought she could see her face crease with a smile beneath the niqab, which she now removed in the presence of the two women. She had a craggy face, gray hair, and corn-kernel teeth. It was impossible to tell how old she was, but Mariam could tell from the symmetry of her face that she'd been attractive before life intervened.

"I'm Mariam," Mariam said. "And this is my cousin Razan."

"Umm Abiha," the old woman said.

Her husband walked through the kitchen carrying a toolbox and avoiding eye contact with them. Umm Abiha told him about the car. Razan slid the keys toward him and he picked them up from the table. As he extended his hand, Mariam saw the knife scars and burn marks covering his left arm, recounting a history with blades and fire. Many of the burns were small and circular. Razan gave a lingering stare that did not go unnoticed by Umm Abiha. After her husband left, she stood to heat a rusted teapot. As she opened a cabinet searching for the tea, Mariam's shame flowed again as she reviewed the sparse shelves and the skittering roaches. She thought of her own mother's pantry, always stocked with fresh bread, vegetables, and spices.

"Saydnaya," Umm Abiha said.

"What?" Razan said harshly. She was not reading the cues right. Probably the fatigue and the vodka.

"The burn marks you noticed on my husband's arms. He received those in prison. Saydnaya. He was there for three years."

"I'm sorry," Mariam said. "We didn't mean to stare."

Umm Abiha set the teapot on the burner and lit the flame. She sat back at the table. "They said he smuggled weapons," Umm Abiha said, again as if reading Mariam's thoughts. Then she shrugged as if to say, *Who knows if it's true?* The teapot whistled and Umm Abiha poured three cups of bitter tea. Razan asked for sugar; Mariam kicked her under the table.

Umm Abiha's face flushed and she shook her head. "We don't have any," she said. The old woman sat down and stared at Mariam. The rest of her looked tired, Mariam thought, but the eyes were lively.

Embarrassed by these Christian *sharameet* Mariam figured, Umm Abiha sat and sipped her tea like an instructor considering a punishing lesson. For a while no one spoke. A frail girl emerged from the back room and sat in Umm Abiha's lap staring at Mariam and Razan.

"Before prison my husband used to farm here in Douma," she said. "Apricots, mostly. It was beautiful. Now there are more wells and less water and the *mukhabarat* check on him frequently. He works in the auto body shop with his brother." Umm Abiha looked at Razan's necklace, her earrings, and the dress hemline. Razan's eyelids sagged, then rocketed upward, then fell. She had not touched her tea.

"You live in the Old City?" Umm Abiha asked Mariam.

"Yes," Mariam said. "We're at Damascus University now."

Umm Abiha nodded. "You are married?"

"Not yet."

"A shame. You are beautiful." Umm Abiha excused herself to put the child back to bed. Razan had fallen asleep seated at the table.

Umm Abiha's husband returned, walking briskly through the kitchen. He murmured a few words to Umm Abiha and handed her the keys. "He changed the tire," Umm Abiha said.

Mariam opened her purse, but Umm Abiha raised her hand. "No." The final word. Mariam nodded and removed her hand from the purse.

"Thank you."

She was about to wake Razan when Umm Abiha slid her chair toward her. She took Mariam's hands in her own and stared at Mariam's teeth, smiling with her own knobby set.

Umm Abiha picked up Mariam's hand and placed it on her own furrowed cheek, ran it down past the rotting teeth and the bony neck onto flattened breasts that had nurtured six lives. She held Mariam's hand on her heart and Mariam could feel it beat and pulse.

"Time to go, Mariam," she said. "But you remember this. You remember me. A slave outside your gates."

INSTEAD, SHE HAD TRIED TO forget. But now Mariam looked back to catch another glimpse of the woman on the protest poster. "Donkeys," the driver muttered as he managed to clear the crowd and accelerate the car. Mariam lost sight of the poster as the gates swung shut, still uncertain if it was Umm Abiha in the photo. She closed her eyes and sucked in a deep breath, then pushed it out as if expelling the memory.

INSIDE THE EMBASSY, MARIAM KNOCKED on the door leading to the *mukhabarat* station. A sweaty Mohannad answered. She thought of the silly report she'd filed on her brief conversation with Sam from the reception earlier in the week. She wondered what he'd done with it.

"I need the files I sent from Damascus," Mariam said. Mohannad nodded and told her to wait there. He returned with a large stack. Mariam sorted them, then took the single sheet containing the list of Fatimah's relatives. She folded it into an envelope and placed that in her purse.

She returned to the embassy car in the motor pool, Mohannad in tow, trying to ignore the threatening chants of the crowd outside rising over the gates. As she stooped into the open door, it registered that she'd never even considered reporting to Mohannad her second, clandestine meeting with Sam. They drove through the gates. The driver honked, screamed, and flung obscene gestures to the mob as he forced the car back through the crowd.

SHE WOULD MEET FATIMAH AT a small apartment owned by the Syrian Embassy. The Paris real estate was expensive, but the apartment, like most Syrian government property, was dingy. The heavy wooden furniture, musty rugs and drapes, and portraits of Hafez al-Assad gave it a dated look. Mohannad entered, swept the apartment for listening devices, then went to the hallway door, outside of which he would stand watch. Mariam sat in the apartment's cramped drawing room on a weathered burgundy sofa with grease splatters on one of the pillows. She waited.

After a few minutes Fatimah entered, Mohannad behind. She had short, curly, reddish hair, her face plump like a cherub's. Fatimah's fighting eyes were still there, gazing into Mariam as they shook hands. Fatimah wore a black pantsuit and a frilly blouse with white polka dots. Around her neck she wore a scarf emblazoned with the tristar flag of the rebellion. She sat across from Mariam. Mohannad decamped for the hallway. An embassy attendant entered with cardamom tea.

"Thank you for meeting me," Mariam said.

"Where is Bouthaina?" Fatimah said.

"On pressing business. I am empowered to speak on her behalf."

Fatimah nodded as she stirred sugar into her tea. She pulled aside her scarf and unfurled it on the couch so Mariam could see the triplet stars. "You are General Georges Haddad's daughter?"

"Yes."

Fatimah sighed as the stirring spoon clinked onto the plate. "Do you know how many of these discussions I have had? They all follow the same script: tea, pleasantries, then a reminder of the futility of my position, a lecture on the jihadi underpinnings of the rebellion. Then, finally, the offer, its price, the accompanying threats." She took a sip of tea. "I cannot, though, remember a messenger as elegant as you, Mariam. I do give them points for that. You are a credit to the regime's creativity and the image-conscious nature of our venal President. But unless you are not following the script I described, I would suggest you move straight to the offer, what it will cost me, and what you will do if I do not comply." She put her teacup down and regarded Mariam.

"The offer: you come home. The price: descriptions of the rebellion in several European newspapers as a jihadi front, and silence upon your return. You live out your days in your childhood home." Mariam sipped tea, the hot liquid flowing past the ache in her gut. She removed the envelope from her purse and put it on the table.

Fatimah blinked at Mariam. "The threat?"

"Yes."

The oppositionist opened the envelope and scanned the list of twenty-two names. At the top: An elderly mother. Eighty years old. She looked up at Mariam.

"When I was young, I could not comprehend how anyone could support the government. I hated those who did. I would not speak to them. But as I've aged I realize that we are born into a world, a family, and there are constraints. There is a system. Some people—the French, the Americans—are born into worlds that offer immense freedom. But we were not. We are Syrians. We are caged from birth, for reasons deep in history. I do not hate you, though you've just threatened my mother. You are doing what you should to keep your family safe, to afford nice things, to eat well. But do not be deceived, you still have a choice. It is just a difficult one."

Mariam finished her tea and set down the cup with a clatter. Her chest felt heavy again.

Fatimah folded the paper and slid it back to Mariam. "The answer is no. I am a free woman. I intend to stay free."

THAT AFTERNOON IT RAINED, AND the clouds hung thick over the city. Mariam returned to the embassy to draft the readout of the meeting. Bouthaina had departed for Syria. The official talks were in disarray and the President was preparing to give a speech announcing their end in front of the rubber-stamp parliament in Damascus.

After she finished the report and sent it to Bouthaina's secure Palace email, Mariam went to a café around the corner from her hotel. She opened a notebook to journal but could not put a single line on the page. She closed it, pulled out her phone, and, after hesitating for a moment, called Bouthaina.

"Have you read my email?" she asked.

"Yes. To be expected. She needs to think on it. You need to take another pass at her. She'll spend the rest of the day debating the decision.

Excuse me one second." There were muffled noises in the background as her boss spoke to someone else. Mariam put her pen on the paper but it did not move.

"Are you still there?" Bouthaina said.

"Still here." Mariam was looking down at the blank page in her notebook, which seemed to be taunting her.

"I'll call Ali Hassan now, but I think we tell Fatimah that her mama will be brought in by the end of the week if she does not comply."

"Agreed." Mariam clenched her jaw.

"Good. You stay for the follow-up. 'Bye."

Mariam ended the call, then looked around the café. The woman at the counter was flirting with a college student ordering a coffee. Mariam opened her wallet, removed the napkin, and spread it on the table. She looked at the phone number and remembered the feel of his hand.

She dialed the number.

10

CIA PREFERRED TO PICK THE MEETING SPOTS, BUT SAM had stressed in his cables to Langley and Damascus that proposing an alternative would spook Mariam. So a rapid investigation took shape. CIA ran the address through dozens of databases to check for any mentions in intercepted terrorist communications. EUR Division, using a cover company to make the inquiry, confirmed the validity of the address and business with the French tax authorities. The BANDITOs staked out the entrance and did not spot any hostile surveillance. Rami even toured the studio, noting a single security camera outside. The place checked out.

Now Rami and Elias waited outside Mariam's hotel. Sam and Yusuf were in an alley two blocks from the address Mariam had provided. There had been more rain and the city streets were now cool.

"She just left the hotel," Rami said over the encrypted radio.

Mariam had instructed him to wear athletic clothes and arrive at six. She'd told him to expect a private lesson from one of her old friends. "She's going to kick your ass," Yusuf whispered to Sam with a wide grin. Probably true. *CIA officer incapacitated by Syrian developmental during Israeli martial arts exercise.* Now, that would be an embarrassing cable.

"She's doing something interesting," Elias said on the radio. "She's on foot headed toward Saint-Germain but she's traveling in a zigzag route. Plus a few turns and reversals that we didn't expect. Pretty simple but threw us off."

"Sad if you get spotted by an amateur," Yusuf said.

"We're better than the *mukhabarat,*" Rami said. "We'll be fine."

"What nationality was the instructor who gave you the tour of the studio?" Sam asked into the radio.

"Israeli."

Sam smiled and thought of a young Mariam, seventeen years old, sneaking out of her parents' apartment with a bag of workout gear slung over her shoulder to train under an Israeli.

"She doesn't want the *mukhabarat* to see her," Sam said. "She's running a surveillance detection route."

APPROACHING THE BUILDING, SAM SAW the worn, handwritten label, "Krav Maga-Paris," and buzzed the adjoining button.

"*Oui?*" came a scratchy, metallic voice out of the tiny speaker.

"I'm sorry, I don't speak French," Sam said in butchered French. Sam's only experience with the language had been when he spent two weeks running an operation in Morocco during his Cairo tour. He served in the Sandbox where Arabic, not French, was the language of the asset recruiters.

A laugh. "You are right. Sam Joseph?"

"Yes."

The door clicked and Sam jogged up the winding cement staircase to the third floor.

He found Mariam inside, stretching on the padded floor. She smiled at Sam. She wore stretchy tight black pants, scuffed tennis shoes, and a black racerback top. The instructor shook Sam's hand and introduced himself as Beni. "I'm always honored to have one of my old students come back," he said. "And it's even better when they bring a sparring partner." Beni had the physique of a man in his mid-thirties but his weathered face and shaggy gray eyebrows put him closer to sixty. He spoke English with a mutt accent blending French and Hebrew.

"Have you sparred before, Sam?" Beni asked.

"Yes. Karate lessons when I was a kid." He omitted the hand-to-hand combat at the Farm and the refresher lessons before Baghdad.

Beni laughed—a big, guttural laugh that was impossible not to like. "We'll make sure you are well protected from Mariam. She was one of my more, how do you say, enthusiastic students."

At that, Mariam grinned and then tossed Sam a helmet, vest, and a pair of gloves. "I thought we could start with some light sparring," she said. "You can help me dust off the cobwebs from Damascus."

Beni coughed and looked at Sam. "I assume you did not bring protection for the, uh, how do you say politely?" He pointed at Sam's groin. Mariam snorted.

Sam smiled. "I did not."

"I have a rental. Lightly used."

SAM RETURNED FROM THE BATHROOM, fiddling with the plastic that would protect him from this wildling Syrian woman.

Beni gave him an imploring look of unspoken yet clear concern for the well-being of Sam's groin, so Sam nodded once to signal it would be fine. Beni nodded back and then turned to Mariam. "Let's start with some light contact."

Sam and Mariam tapped gloves. She circled. Beni watched from the sidelines. "Krav Maga is not about forms or beauty," he explained to Sam. "It is about destroying an opponent using any means necessary. You do not just defend yourself, you become the attacker to destroy the threat."

Mariam came at him first with a few straight punches that he dodged. When she was in close she threw a knee into his vest, scoring a direct hit. She thrust it in again, then backed off, circling once more. The strikes were sharp and quick. She stared him down, eyes narrowing from inside the helmet. He could feel her energy and tried to sense her next move.

She came in with more straight punches and fast footwork. He stepped back and blocked two strikes with his forearms.

She circled. The case danced through his mind.

She agreed to have drinks.

She shared secrets.

She is sympathetic to the protesters, even if she denies it.

She called back after saying no the first time.

She brought him to an intimate place, one she knew would be devoid of hostile surveillance.

She is trying to physically harm me.

She wants to fight.

He jumped back as she came in with a kick at the groin. "Turn the attack around, Sam," she said. "Come at me." He'd wanted to avoid an actual fight to keep his cover intact. The State Department guys didn't get this kind of training.

Screw it. He landed three quick jabs into her vest and helmet, she kicked him in the stomach, then stepped in and struck his head with the tip of her elbow as her knee connected with his groin. He grunted. He hit her vest with a fist, then kicked at her legs to get some distance. "Come on, come at me," she said, clapping the gloves together.

He did.

But now they were reading each other. She blocked each jab, he blocked the kick, ducked an elbow, then she tried to drive him into the wall with a choke. Beni whistled. Sam smacked her arms down like they'd taught him at the Farm, she threw a fist at his helmet, and he dodged it. She cursed in Arabic and came at him again. He ducked and went for a jab into the area above those lovely hips. She stepped back, smiled like the devil, and returned with a groin kick that he caught. He twisted her leg and she collapsed faceup but scuttled backward, right knee folded up like a scorpion tail. When he stepped forward she thrust it into his shin. He tried to get closer, but she kept scuttling away as she kicked from her back. He stopped, she jumped up, knocked her gloves together, cursed, and came right back for more.

But instead of kicks or punches, she lowered her shoulder and bowled into him, knocking him off balance, her body weight taking them both to the floor. Then she was on top, her legs pinning his arms and raining blows down. He was cursing, wincing. Beni whistled, said, *Arret, arret.*

Sam smiled as her eyes flickered inside her helmet, like she wanted to bed him or kill him, maybe both, he couldn't tell.

She dismounted and strutted to the corner for water. He watched her bob away and heard the sound of Beni's voice asking if he was all right. The instructor offered a hand to help him up.

HE FIGHTS WELL, MARIAM THOUGHT. He has been trained. Karate when he was young? Please. He moves like someone who has been taught. She wanted more of this, of him. It took her back, away from Fatimah and the war, toward the Paris of her youth and the lightness of breath, which she felt now, though her lungs burned hard and her muscles were sore.

"The weapons, Beni?" Mariam said.

The Israeli nodded and turned to Sam, who had barely gotten off the floor.

"Sparring is helpful, but Krav is really about training for practical, real-life situations," he said. He arched a bushy eyebrow. "You said only karate when you were younger? Nothing more?"

"That's right. And a few street fights, I guess. Poker games gone bad, that kind of thing."

"I see," Beni said, intonation hinting that he in fact did not. Mariam did not, either.

"Maybe he pulls a gun on me?" Mariam said. She took another drink of water and spat the saliva congealed around her mouth guard into a sink.

Beni nodded, retrieved a fake handgun from the wall rack, and gave it to Sam. "You come up behind her, point the gun at her head, demand money? You pause enough to give her a chance to respond, but after that, pull the trigger if you get the chance. I judge who wins, *d'accord*?"

Sam nodded, weighing the gun in his hand as if to ensure it was, in fact, fake. Mariam sat in a chair. He approached from behind and pressed it into the back of her head.

"Give me your purse," he said.

She snatched the weapon with her right hand and brought it into both hands as if it were her own, then stood, straightening his arm and spinning clockwise with her shoulder pressed up, under his elbow, keeping him taut. She tightened her grip with her left hand, released her right, and reached around his front to hit him in the face mask. He gasped, and his body went a little limp. She spun around, pulled his arm, and folded it around his back as if preparing him for a royal bow. She gave a quick jab to the back of his skull—another gasp, his body flopped—then took his shirt collar in her left hand, yanked it down, and jumped into the air. She drove the plastic gun into the top of his vest, just below the neck.

He collapsed and rolled onto his stomach. The whole thing had taken four seconds.

He got up, eventually. Beni asked if he was all right. "My ears are ringing," Sam said as he went over to the sink, pulled off his face mask, and spit. He caught his breath as he watched the blood run down the drain, and turned back to Mariam with a wry smile visible through his face mask. "When is it my turn?" he said.

Beni laughed, smacked Sam on the shoulder, and went to the wall rack for a club. "Mariam comes at you with this, *d'accord*?"

Sam nodded and went to the other side of the mats.

The club attack was one where the normal human instincts would get your arm broken. An attacker comes at you with an overhand strike, you put up your arm, the blow shatters your radius or ulna. You collapse, they beat you to death. The key was to run toward the strike, arms extended in front, protecting the head while making it nearly impossible to break the bones. Then you fight—elbows, teeth, fists, head butts, whatever. The club's advantage has been neutralized by the close quarters.

She looked at the club and thought of the *mukhabarat* man driving the truncheon into Razan's eye, her cousin's helpless blocks, the screams. You did nothing, girl. You watched.

She ran at Sam, club in the air. He did not raise his arm but instead came at her, closing the distance. She went for the head, but he dodged and her strike harmlessly glanced off his left shoulder and they were in close. She felt her grip on the club quiver as he got hold of her club hand and compressed the bunch of nerves between her thumb and forefinger. The club dropped onto the mat. He gripped her wrists, firm but not painful, and she locked on his eyes, waiting for the jab, the knee, the finisher. Her muscles, bones, they were all sore. She wanted water.

He held her wrists, hesitating to deliver the blow. Looking into her eyes.

She head-butted him directly in the face mask. He grunted and fell back.

Beni laughed and whistled to call the fight.

SAINT-GERMAIN AT NIGHT: THE RAIN gone, the leafy avenue was now clotted with Sorbonne students ambling through clouds of cigarette smoke and café-goers sporting evening wear, wet bottles of Sancerre sweating in their tableside buckets. They walked together down the boulevard, maybe unwise, but the BANDITOs said she was black and Sam knew he was. They'd changed from their athletic clothes, but Sam still sported a bruise on his forehead from the head butt, which, she admitted, had struck a little high.

They found a sleepy brasserie and ordered too much food. Foie gras, duck confit, a white bean cassoulet, a plate of fries, at which Mariam sniffed. She ordered the wine. He paired a beer with the fries. "Just one," he'd said. She laughed. "If anyone back home saw me drinking wine with fries, they'd kill me."

"And where is home for you now, anyway?" she asked.

"Right now, it's D.C. I'm covering the Syria Desk at State before my next posting, so I have an apartment in the District."

"Ah," she said as the waiter brought out the duck. She placed her napkin on her lap. "Dogs?" she said, wrinkling her nose.

He shook his head.

"Cats?"

He smiled. "No, no pets."

"Girl?"

"Not anymore."

"I can picture this place. There is horrible beer in the fridge and nothing on the walls."

She was pretty damn close, though she'd missed the fact that there was not much furniture on the floor, either. The fridge was also empty. He laughed and ate another fry. "You're not wrong, but it's an interim apartment until my next post. So I won't be there long."

"Where will you go next?"

He debated telling her about Damascus but decided to hold back for now. "It is still undecided, but probably somewhere in the Middle East."

She nodded and took a bite of bread.

"Where is home for you?" he asked.

"I have an apartment in the Old City."

"I take it from that look that you don't have a dog?"

"No. Filthy creatures."

He laughed, remembering his tour in Cairo and the aversion to dogs common in the Arab world. "A cat, then?"

"No."

"Boy?"

"Girl. Very scandalous." She winked and he laughed.

"Razan?" he asked.

"Yes. She's staying with me. Our apartment, unlike your sad bachelor pad, is nicely furnished and stocked with food."

The waiter returned to clear some of the smaller plates. Sam decided to use the gap in conversation to elicit something. He needed to show progress to Langley. "How are the meetings going?" he asked after the waiter had disappeared.

She picked at some of the duck, working a cord of meat from the bone. "Not well. The talks collapsed today. My boss has gone home. My meeting with Fatimah Wael, one of the oppositionists, went poorly."

Sam dunked a fry in ketchup as Mariam eyed him. She'd shared her first secret. He bit the fry and took a sip of beer.

"I'm sorry to hear that," he said, debating how hard to push. "Are you leaving early, too?"

She shook her head. "My boss asked me to stay a few more days to follow up with Fatimah."

He nodded, understanding he should not press too hard. Mariam's phone rang and she looked at the number.

She grimaced. "I need to take this." She walked out of the restaurant. Sam finished his beer and refilled their wine. He'd grown more assured that CIA had an ideological angle to play with Mariam. But the intimate conversation and the charged sparring: it worried him, on two counts.

First count: That he wanted her. He couldn't deny it. It was also a major problem. A case officer romantically linked to an asset was cause for separation from CIA. A violation of his oath of service and probably a dozen Agency regs. And yet, he doubted his self-control if the issue were pressed. Second count: His recruiter instincts judged the best path to putting this asset in harness was kindling the spark of romantic energy. He was less certain the usual approaches to shuffling a developmental through to recruitment would work: the amenities provided to drive reciprocity, the unstated authority, the excitement of espionage. Sam thought she wanted him. That the romance would propel the recruitment. What would Bradley say? He'd say that you're delusional, Sam.

Mariam returned and sat down. "Fatimah is traveling tomorrow. Her family has a home near Villefranche-sur-Mer, on the coast. She has agreed to meet me there. I will go tomorrow morning."

"She must have been intrigued by your meeting, to agree to another," Sam said.

Mariam spread foie gras on a toast corner. "Yes, but I cannot imagine why."

"Why not?"

"Because I threatened her family if she did not denounce the opposition. We are doing this with all foreign-based oppositionists. I run the program inside Bouthaina's office." Mariam now looked off, out the window, and took another bite of the toast. She looked back at him. "This is widely assumed, no?"

"Of course." But it had not been confirmed by an unvetted contact with firsthand access, he thought. Until now.

"You said you are staying for a few more days in Paris?" she said.

He nodded and decided to put it on the line. "I had planned to. But what if I came to Villefranche while you were there?" he said. "For a few days."

She dipped one of the remaining toast points in the foie gras and washed it down with a gulp of water. She gave him that look he'd see at the poker tables when an opponent would lay down with shaky fingers what they thought could be a winning hand. "I think I would like that," she said.

THEY WORKED THE LOGISTICS OVER crème brûlée: she would take the train down to the coast tomorrow morning, he would follow in the afternoon, find lodging—a safe house, he thought, hoping Shipley had one nearby—and wait for her to propose a time and place to meet. As they spoke, his mind meandered through the half dozen cables he knew Langley would need that evening.

He checked his phone. Nothing from the BANDITOs. They hugged and held a long embrace, eyes locked, both sensing the boundaries, the intentions, the expectations. She pressed her forehead into his, avoiding the bruise, and leaned back.

"Softer than the head butt," he said.

She snorted and smiled. "You hesitated."

He looked around. They had closed the restaurant down.

"Tomorrow in Villefranche?" Sam said.

"Tomorrow in Villefranche."

She kissed him on the cheek and left, door jangling behind.

Sam wiped off the red lipstick in the bathroom before the outbound SDR. Sam's reflection reminded him that he'd just violated Agency Regulation 22-345—"Restrictions on Contacts with Foreign Nationals." His reflection shook its head in reproach, then disappeared.

11

ARTEMIS APHRODITE PROCTER WORE A LIME-GREEN velour tracksuit for the secure video teleconference. Sam and Shipley sat in Paris Station, Bradley at Langley, Procter in Damascus. Sam's late-night cable on the Mariam case had tickled a list of interested parties so numerous—Syria Reports, Weapons Intelligence and Counterproliferation, the Medical and Psychological Assessment Center—that Bradley had organized a quick huddle to talk ops with only those that mattered.

"What is that neon animal you're wearing?" a very pixelated Ed Bradley asked.

"It's a velour tracksuit, you ignoramus. Casual Friday here in Damascus Station. You like it, by the way?"

"It's a good look. Reminds me of a Ukrainian mobster I was developing a few years back," Sam said with a smirk.

Procter told him to shut up, tied up her curly black hair, and then picked up something yellow. How close do you think we are?" she asked.

"Close."

"How close?" Procter shot back, though she wasn't looking at Sam. She was struggling with what looked to be a small package of Starburst.

"She's disillusioned with the government and her job. She's offering more and more each time we meet."

Procter, apparently having succeeded in opening the wrapper, popped a candy into her mouth and began to chew loudly. "We can work out the details here in Damascus," she said. "But from my standpoint the critical hurdle to clear with Mademoiselle Mariam in France, before she returns to Damascus, is to get her comfortable with the idea of meeting with an American out of the public eye."

Procter picked up a whiteboard marker and twirled it in her fingers. "Let me get you up to speed on what's happening in D-town, Damascus, the oldest continually inhabited city on the goddamn planet," she said. "Things have gone downhill since your last visit."

Sam opened his mouth to speak, but Procter steamrolled on. "There is literally no reason for an American to meet a Syrian in Damascus right now. They don't invite us to the cocktail parties. Reasonable, I guess, given we told Assad to step aside, but still rude, a tad uncouth if you ask me." Her hands left the frame, and when they returned the marker had been replaced by another candy. She tossed it into her mouth. Her eyes held the screen as she talked. "Best-case from Damascus Station perspective is Mariam leaves France with a safe house address and a basic commo plan. Signal site, dead drop combo probably. We've got no short-range comms available, and before we get her on a fancy device, I'd suggest we get something we can corroborate."

Sam nodded in agreement. "The Iranians run dangles at us all time, and they're coaching the Syrians. We need to be sure. I'll work to get something good from her." Sam had zero doubt about Mariam's credibility, but there was still a process to run. And it was true that while she had provided sensitive information, none of it would do any damage to the Syrian regime. CIA needed more to vet her properly.

"Chief, how is the security situation impacting asset—" Sam said before Procter cut him off.

"Yeah, yeah, yeah," she said, bobbing her head. "The asset meetings? It's been an issue. A manageable issue, though, okay? We don't need the security guys yet—thank God, that sure as shit kills the mood in meetings. Central Damascus tends to be fine, like it was when you drove in to get KOMODO and Val. Government controls it. Occasional suicide bombings but rebels don't run the turf. We've also noticed that the Syrians have redirected surveillance resources against the rebels, so some days they don't really tag us. Though if these guys decide to bumper-lock you, they can swamp us with bodies—not top-notch tradecraft, but it's their turf and they know the streets. They can slog up a good route with lots of fixed surveillance positions.

"Point being," Procter continued, "developing Mariam in Damascus will be a real treat. Obviously, the Syrians are going to watch you twenty-four/seven for at least the first few weeks. They'll harass you. Maybe break into your apartment, maybe knock on your car window when you're sitting in traffic, smile at you with a big toothy Syrian *mukhabarat* grin. Maybe someone takes a dump on your bed. All of these realities will shade development," Procter concluded. "The more work you do in France, the better.

This time she let Sam get it out: "I'm going to try to recruit her this week. At least take a shot."

"Atta boy," Procter said.

"Shipley," Bradley said. "Can we get a safe house near Villefranche?"

"I've got one down there," he said. "But it will beg questions as to how a diplomat could afford the rental fees," Shipley said.

"You said in one of your cables that you told her about Vegas?" Bradley asked.

"That's right. I could tell her I paid for it with my winnings," Sam said.

"Hope you were good," Shipley said. "This place is wild."

SAM TOOK THE TGV FROM Paris to Nice and as the graffiti-painted concrete of Paris's slums receded to the bright greens of rolling farmland, he wrestled with a thought that had nagged him all week: Who were the three Syrians that had followed Mariam in Paris? He'd originally dismissed them as embassy *mukhabarat,* but for some reason his mind could not put the issue to rest. The three Syrian men were not trained in surveillance. It felt like a plot, a setup.

He ordered coffee from the dining car. Spotting the BANDITOs at a table on the far side, he returned to his seat without a word. Sam watched pastures and vineyards and small villages fly by. He thought of how he would try to recruit her, sharpened his assessment of her personality and motivation. He began drafting the recruitment cable in his head: the comprehensive agent assessment, commo plan, financial arrangements, the ops program to produce intelligence. If he succeeded it would all generate a cryptonym to signify Langley's blessing that the recruitment was made or at least far enough down the path. One plank of the strategy remained vulnerable. He had no plan for how to manage his feelings for her.

The train sped toward the coast, stopping in Avignon for mechanical problems. He left his seat to stretch on an open-air platform that was flanked by cypress and caught the clean spring breeze of the Provençal countryside. It reminded him of Mariam's hair.

MARIAM WALKED FROM FATIMAH'S WATERCOLOR home onto the Saint-Jean-Cap-Ferrat peninsula, taking the narrow trails hugging the coastline. Mohannad had tried to follow her to Villefranche, but Mariam had asked Bouthaina to intervene and her boss had won the battle, arguing that Mariam would be more persuasive without a mouth-breather over her shoulder. She had four days alone on the French Riviera. She could hardly believe it. In fact, she'd wondered—still did—whether it was some kind of trap set by Bouthaina or the *mukhabarat*.

Now Mariam watched a small white sailboat plying the waves into the horizon as Fatimah walked beside her in silence. They turned a corner and the view widened to an expanse of wave-smacked coastline bearded with scrub and pines. Across the bay she could see Villefranche's red-roofed homes, the village a seaside smattering of yellow and ocher resting on the hillside like so many shoe boxes.

"Thank you for meeting again," Mariam said.

"I felt we had more to say to one another," Fatimah said.

"What do you mean?" Mariam asked.

"I think you know."

Mariam stopped and put her hand on the oppositionist's shoulder. She held Fatimah's eyes for several significant seconds. "I'm afraid I do not." She started moving again, Fatimah a pace behind.

"I can tell that you are not an Assadist," she said, catching up. "Why not help us instead?"

Paranoia, birthright of all Syrians, now took hold. She considered the angles, the possibility of deception and subterfuge. Fatimah could be a *mukhabarat* plant inside the opposition, trying to recruit government officials to test loyalties; she could be an informant for Bouthaina; she could be what she appeared: a well-meaning, hopeless idealist.

Mariam wanted to say: *I cannot understand where this rebellion ends, Fatimah. There is no government-in-waiting if Assad leaves. There is only fragmentation and incoherence. That is why I will not join you.*

Instead, she narrowed her eyes and said: "I see, a pitch of your own."

They rounded above a small pebbly beach. Topless sunbathers sprawled on the rocks like seals. Fatimah smiled. "I'm always amazed at how peaceful it is here. A war ravages our country, and just across the Mediterranean they sun themselves like little gods. I want Syria to be like this. I suspect you do, too."

She wanted to say: *I do,* okhti, *sister. I want this more than anything.*

Mariam said: "Have you reconsidered my offer?"

Fatimah ignored her. "Why not defect? Join us here in Europe."

She wanted to say: *Because I am not a coward.*

Mariam said: "Fatimah, you are trying my patience."

Fatimah stopped and turned to Mariam. "Arrest my mother if you must, Mariam. But beware: You are midwifing the slaughter. I hope that your soul is prepared."

She wanted to say: *And you are right. I am not prepared.*

Mariam said: "And you are midwifing jihad, Fatimah."

Fatimah stopped at the end of the trail and looked out toward the ocean. "You've made your choice, then?"

Mariam did not answer the question and could not look at Fatimah anymore. She focused on the line where sea met sky. "You have two days to decide. Come home and we will not arrest your mother. If you stay here, I cannot help you."

Mariam turned and left in silence. Levantine paranoia in full bloom, she called Bouthaina to provide a full report and to recommend the immediate arrest of Fatimah's geriatric mother given her ongoing support to enemies of the Syrian Arab Republic, both foreign and domestic. "She is stubborn, I told you," Bouthaina said. "Hold out for a few more days, see if she comes around."

Mariam felt bone-tired as she arrived at her hotel. In her room she lay on the bed, mind racing with Fatimah's questions and a phone number she should not dial. She got up, stripped to her underwear, and ran through the kicks, punches, and elbow and knee movements Beni had shown her in Paris long ago.

Mariam then considered the loose threads that she had knit together on the train ride down to Villefranche: his fighting skills, the confidence, the suggestion of following her to the Riviera, the coy questions. She had met dozens of American diplomats. Sam was not one of them.

Now Mariam realized that she hoped she was right.

SAM'S FIRST THOUGHT UPON REACHING the safe house was that he'd signed up for the wrong CIA Division. The properties he'd used during his tours in Egypt and Iraq had been dusty, smelly, and typically lacked working plumbing and air-conditioning. At a safe house in Anbar a camel spider had once jumped from a shelf and bit one of his assets on the neck. In Cairo, he'd had to replace an inoperable toilet with an old twelve-gallon paint bucket.

In this case *safe house* was a misnomer for a stone chateau in the medieval hilltop village of Èze, twenty minutes east of Villefranche. The town was perched more than one thousand feet above the Riviera's beaches on an old Roman road. Now it was home to several dozen elderly natives and an equal number of fabulously wealthy Europeans and Americans, keen to sun themselves on the Riviera in privacy.

Sam found the key, hidden in the flower beds by a Station support asset, and entered the chateau. He turned on the foyer lights. The walls were exposed stone, the furnishings French antiques. He made a mental note to avoid opening bottles on the tables here. There was a terrace with sweeping views of the Côte d'Azur, seven stately bedrooms, and two stocked kitchens, one of which had been for the servants. There were even beers in the fridge. He took an inventory of the food against the list he'd requested in Paris. He opened a beer and walked out onto the terrace, where he texted Elias to confirm the BANDITOs had assumed their watch outside Mariam's hotel in Villefranche.

MARIAM LAY ON THE BED watching the fan rotate lazily overhead like a clock counting down to a decision. What are you doing? You can still walk away from this. Get on a train for Paris and fly home. But now, if you call him, well . . .

She donned a pair of tan espadrilles that laced up the ankles and a knee-length blue-and-white-striped poplin sundress she'd picked up in Paris.

Then, after ten more minutes of staring at the ceiling, her mouth chalky, she used her room phone to dial the number Sam had provided.

THE BANDITOS, EATING PIZZA AND holding watch outside the hotel, said she was black, so he picked her up in the rental car. A restaurant in Villefranche would be natural, but he wanted to get her comfortable meeting in discreet locations. The safe house was perfect. He wondered if she would parry, maybe suggest a cozy place in town.

"I thought we could cook dinner," Sam said as she hopped into the car and smoothed her dress over her tan legs. As he kissed her cheek, he noticed little sun freckles below her eyes. "What do you think about going back to my villa? Twenty minutes east, in Èze, beautiful place. Little medieval village."

"That sounds wonderful," she said.

They took the Moyenne Corniche, the Roman road that carved the ridgeline of the cliffs along the sea. The lights of Nice and Villefranche filled the western horizon, and Monaco twinkled to the east.

"I got word today on my next tour," he said. "Damascus."

She rolled down her window and put her face into the evening breeze until it whipped back her hair. "That is wonderful news, Sam," she said, still looking out the window. "Maybe we will get to see each other again."

"I would like that," Sam said. He now lowered his window and took in the sea air. "I'll never get used to this."

She smiled and said nothing.

Inside the chateau, she asked the inevitable question, albeit tactfully, in intentional Arabic so she could be sure of his answer: "How did you find this place?"

"I had a good weekend in Vegas a few weeks back," he said. "And found the right local agent." She ignored the answer, instead stepping into one of the bedrooms to take in the ocean view, now a black wall on the horizon. Sam followed slowly. She knew it was a lie and was tolerating it for now, he thought.

"What are we going to cook?" she asked, nodding toward the kitchen.

He smiled. "I thought we could cook spaghetti."

She arched an eyebrow. "Spaghetti? You?"

"I've got a couple good dishes. This is one."

He guided her into the kitchen and laid the ingredients on the counter. He asked her to chop the onions and carrots and celery.

"You trust me with the knife after . . ." She put a hand on her hip and pointed at the bruise on his forehead with the blade. "Your accident." She laughed.

He touched his forehead and smiled. "That's why I'm across the kitchen, keeping my distance."

Sam put a baguette on the counter and sliced it, then pooled olive oil and balsamic on a plate and sprinkled coarse salt on top. He presented a bottle of wine—Shipley had recommended it—and she laughed and nodded, but he decanted a glass for her to taste anyway. She couldn't hide her surprise. "Maybe, like fighting, you know more about wine than you let on?"

"I wish. Good recommendation at a shop in Villefranche, though the guy selling it clearly did not care for my French."

He mounded flour and egg to make the dough for noodles.

"How difficult are the politics at the Department of State?" she asked as she chopped.

He laughed. "What do you mean?"

She wiped her eyes from the onion, then her face flushed. "Well, I'll give you an example." She stared at him with a look that said, *Listen to me, right now.* "My team at the Palace controls the file on the foreign-based opposition and the government's media profile," she continued. "Ali Hassan's Security Office is the central hub for Syria's security services and *mukhabarat*. He spies on the spies, so to speak. If the President wants a traitor found, he uses Ali."

Sam, hands crusted in dough as he worked the flour and eggs together, took a sip of wine and looked at Mariam as if this were a perfectly normal conversation, though his mind was already writing the cable to Langley. He didn't notice the bits of dough and flour he left on the wineglass.

"The other large group in the Palace is commanded by Jamil Atiyah. He and my boss, Bouthaina, detest each other. He is also a pedophile."

Sam stopped working the dough and looked up with a grimace. "A pedophile?"

"Yes. It is well known."

"Well, I can't say I have to deal with any pedophiles in my office, so I may not be able to help you there. But there are plenty of assholes where I work."

"I'm done chopping," she said.

He poured a generous amount of olive oil into a pot and scraped in the onions. Once they were translucent, he dropped in the carrots and celery.

"Now we have to squeeze these tomatoes," he said.

"We are not going to do anything. *You* are going to do it," she said, sipping more wine. "I don't want sauce all over my dress." He smiled, and for a moment forgot he was trying to recruit her to work for CIA.

He dumped the tomatoes into a bowl and squeezed them between his palms until they were liquid. Dumping them into the pot, he added water, red pepper flakes, and salt.

"Where did you learn this recipe?" she asked. She sat on the counter drinking the wine, watching him work.

"My grandma. She was Italian and grew up in New York."

"But you only learned one dish?"

"Just two, actually. She was a really mean old lady."

Mariam snorted and tossed a rag at him.

As the sauce simmered, they worked the dough through the hand-rolling machine Sam had found in a cupboard, laughing as they tried to manage the ever-thinning sheets. His hands stuck to the dough and she threw flour on him. He tossed some back and she dodged it. "I forgot how quick you are," he said. "And I should be careful, because this time I don't have any protection." He pointed to his groin.

She laughed. They rolled out the noodles and placed them on sheets of wax paper, waiting for the sauce to thicken. He poured more wine for both of them, against his better judgment.

"You were saying?" he said.

"Oh yes. Bouthaina and Atiyah despise each other. Bouthaina, as everyone knows, is the Republican Guard commander's girlfriend." She stared again, eyes saying, *Listen carefully, American. I am explaining how things work.*

Sam knew this would be news to CIA. During their late-night run to the Langley hot dog machine, Zelda, the analyst, had indulged Sam with salacious gossip on Assad's mistresses and which senior officials were faithful to their wives and husbands. But this had not come up. Sam believed that so far he'd elicited sufficient information for maybe three intelligence reports, all of which would make the analysts salivate.

Mariam continued: "Bouthaina and Rustum want to destroy Atiyah by assembling evidence of his corruption. And he of course is fighting back, creating problems for our office. Do you have politics like this?"

He found a large pot in one of the cabinets and began filling it with water. "Depends on what you mean by politics. We have officials—"

"At the State Department." Said with intention, to see how he confirmed it, to sense if he was lying.

"Yes, at the State Department."

She held his eyes for a beat, but he kept talking as though he did not notice.

"We have competitions for influence all the time," Sam continued. "One official gets in the secretary's good graces, another is on the outs."

"Yes, of course, but our politics are more. What is the word in English? *Savage*. More savage." She had switched to English. "For example, Bouthaina presented the President with more evidence of Atiyah's predilection for underage girls. When Atiyah discovered this, he sent people to assault a young man in our office. Nearly killed him, to send a message to Bouthaina: *Don't fuck with me*." She jumped down from the counter to stir the sauce.

"How is Bouthaina fighting back?" Sam asked in Arabic.

"Bouthaina has already found accounts previously unknown to the President. For baksheesh. Corruption money. Everyone in the regime has them, but she found his. She's also assembled the lists of underage girl he has bedded. It is extensive."

"Pedophilia isn't enough to take him down?"

"I don't think so. It sullies him, but Bouthaina will need more. The relationships with girls were already well known inside the Palace. The President trusts Bouthaina, he trusts Rustum. But he also trusts Atiyah, as his father did. He has hesitated to make a decision. And so the combat continues." She shrugged.

They boiled the pasta, then strained it and placed it in bowls. He poured sauce on top, then a dollop of ricotta. Mariam plucked basil leaves from a plant in the kitchen and sprinkled them on top. They brought the bowls, another bottle of wine, and the bread to the terrace. A gentle breeze curled their hair and clothes as they ate. He brought his chair around to her side of the table, and when they'd finished eating she asked what would happen in Damascus.

"I'd like to continue seeing you," he said.

"Me, too."

"It will be different there," he said. "More restrictions."

She ignored this. He poured more wine. They were sitting very close.

Then their heads drew closer and they kissed, long and wet and slow. He ran his hands through her hair. Soon they stood together, still locked, and began sliding toward one of the couches. Hands moved to unbuckle, slide, unzip. Somehow, at just the moment he'd begun slipping his hands beneath Mariam's sundress, he summoned the self-control to realize that if this happened at all, it would be cause for his dismissal and, also, that if it happened *before* the recruitment he would never be able to separate the romantic pull from the motivation to spy for CIA.

He pulled his lips back from hers. "Maybe we should call it a night," he said.

Her hair was tousled, lipstick smeared, dress pulled sideways or up or down depending on what it covered. His belt was unbuckled, pants unbuttoned, shirt in process. She leaned back, darkened face reflecting a brew of disbelief and queenly wrath. She stomped to the bathroom to repair herself and reappeared in the kitchen, bathed in dark energy, as he set the dishes into the sink.

"I need a ride back," she said.

"Mariam, I —"

She held up a hand. "I need a ride back," she repeated.

They drove to Villefranche in silence and Sam realized he may have just shit the bed, as Bradley liked to say. He took some comfort in knowing that if she'd required his love to work for CIA, the recruitment would have been doomed from the start. But as he looked at Mariam, pressed into the passenger door as if trying to maintain maximum distance from him, he realized turning her out had been a mistake.

When they arrived at the hotel, he asked if he could walk her upstairs.

"You are not getting a second chance tonight, you understand?" she said, staring out the windshield.

"Yes."

He followed behind her through the lobby and up a winding staircase to her third-floor room, hoping for an opening to set up another meeting.

"This is my room," she said, turning around and planting her back against the door to signal end of the line.

"Can I see you tomorrow?"

"Maybe. I will text you."

"Can I come in, just for a few minutes?" he asked. "To explain."

She nodded and put the key in the lock and turned the doorknob. He took a step farther, toward the open door. She walked inside. That's when he noticed the scratch marks on the doorknob and the flakes of chipped blue paint on the wood. The room was dark. Mariam fumbled for the light switch, saying again that she was tired and that he had exactly one minute to explain things.

She flicked on the lights.

And there they were, the three Syrian watchers from Paris.

The thick one wearing jeans and a Pink Floyd T-shirt holding a baton and handcuffs, the other two with pistols fitted with suppressors, flanking him in hoodies and slacks. One entirely in gray, the other in black. Everyone was surprised to see each other. Sam did a double-take at Pink Floyd, who yelled at him in Arabic, demanding identification. Sam looked around for a weapon, saw a lamp on the desk, and quickly ran the scenario: A kidnapping, not an assassination, because we'd already be dead. If they take her who knows what happens?

Sam put his hands up. Mariam did the same. She was telling them that she'd met Sam in town when he stepped forward and said in Arabic that this was a big mistake, he would cooperate. Pink Floyd approached Sam and said turn around. He gestured with shaky hands. Sam took a step forward with his hands up and Pink Floyd came toward him. Sam head-butted, driving his forehead into the man's nose. He heard the crunch and then he tore the baton from Pink Floyd's hand as he drove a knee into his groin. He swung the baton down on the man's skull, ripped the marble desk lamp from the socket, and threw it at the guy in the black hoodie, who had not yet managed to raise his gun. The lamp struck him in the chest, sending him back on the bed.

Now Mariam was moving, sundress flapping behind, as Gray Hoodie watched his comrade collapse onto the bed. Her quick front kick sent the man's pistol skittering across the floor, but he blocked her first hammer-fist and pushed her back, creating vulnerable distance. He dove to the floor for the gun, but Sam was already grasping for the weapon from Black Hoodie, who was sprawled on the bed.

Finally feeling his fingers tighten around sweaty gunmetal, Sam fired twice, and Gray Hoodie fell back into the desk. Black Hoodie was on the bed, holding his stomach where the lamp had struck him. He tried to sit up while drawing a knife from its sheath. He lunged at Mariam. Sam fired three times, striking the man's neck, head, and shoulder, until he collapsed back onto the bed and lay buns-down on the sheets, lifeless eyes watching the rotating fan. Sam walked over to Pink Floyd to see if he was alive. He wanted to ask questions. But Sam's blow had shattered his skull and his body was slumped on the floor. He had no pulse.

Mariam stood up. Her chest was heaving, her eyes gigantic.

Sam quickly checked the pulses of the other two and felt nothing. "Shit," he muttered. "Shit."

When it hits the fan, get off the X. "We need to go," Sam said as his training kicked in to manage the surging adrenaline.

She was right there with him, had already started throwing everything in her suitcase. "Now you tell me the truth, you understand?

"Understand?" she yelled.

12

IF THE HOTEL LE PANORAMIC HAD BOTHERED TO invest in even the most basic of security systems, the camera on the third floor would have shown a tall American man and an Arab woman hanging the DO NOT DISTURB sign on the door of Room 302 at 12:38 a.m. Another camera would have shown the same couple walking quickly through the lobby. The woman was making irate gestures toward the man with her right hand while gripping the suitcase with her left. The man, who had no luggage, grasped her hand as they marched toward the door. The camera would have also caught part of a blouse peeking through the woman's suitcase zipper as if it had been jammed inside at great haste. There was also a speck of blood on the woman's forehead, which she had missed in what the viewers might have assumed was a hasty face-washing attempt. Her shoulders and the hair at the top of her forehead looked very wet.

But, as Sam guided Mariam out of the lobby, he noted with relief that the hotel did not have any visible security cameras and that the receptionist at the front desk was sound asleep.

Three problems instantly became clear as they passed through the lobby and jumped into Sam's parked car. One, quite pressing, was to calm Mariam, who was nursing a bruised hip and asking a steady hum of uncomfortable questions.

The second was where to go. The Èze safe house seemed like the lucky winner, so they tossed Mariam's suitcase into the rental car and drove back onto the Corniche toward the village, the silence punctured regularly by Mariam's string of Arabic profanities. He held tight on the wheel and double-checked his speed to keep it below the fifty-kilometer-per-hour limit.

The third, and most problematic, was what to do with the bodies. Sam had no idea if someone had heard the shots or the fight. If they had, the French police would be there in minutes. If not, they had time. The triple homicide ensured that no one in Syria could link Mariam to the CIA. He hoped to unsnap the connection between Mariam and the bodies.

Holding the wheel with his left hand, he picked up the phone to dial Shipley. Mariam asked who he was calling.

"My boss in France," he said.

"Wait. Before you do. I know at least one of those men. The big one. He works for Atiyah. He's *mukhabarat*."

"Based in France?"

"I don't think so. Kidnapping?"

"A poorly managed one."

She smacked the dashboard. "Fuck," she yelled in English.

Sam dialed Shipley just outside Beaulieu and told him what had happened. The Chief sat in silence for several seconds. Sam saw the sign for Èze and began to slow the car. Mariam rubbed her face with both hands.

"Go to the safe house now," Shipley said. "Take the Syrian with you. I'll send a team to dispose of the bodies unless the police get there first. I have a crew of support assets who can do this sort of thing."

"How do you want to, uh, write this up?"

"You're sure the kidnappers were Syrian? Not French? Not French North Africans?"

"I am sure at least one was sent from Syria. Mariam recognized him from Damascus."

"The others?"

"We think they are Syrians."

"As far as I'm concerned, there is little upside to an official reporting stream on this. Our team is okay, the Syrian is fine, three kidnappers are dead. Though if any of this turns up on French police blotters, you'll never be able to come back to France."

"I'll take those odds."

"Have your surveillance team watch the hotel for police. My team can be there in a few hours. If the police arrive, the Syrian will either have to run or turn herself in." Sam heard the Chief breathing into the mouthpiece. "Keep me updated." He hung up.

MARIAM TOOK A SHOWER WHILE Sam positioned the BANDITOs. Elias drove to Èze to retrieve Mariam's room key for onward passage to Shipley's cleanup crew. Thirty minutes later Rami called and said the police had still not arrived and the hotel was quiet.

Sam called Shipley, who told him the team would be in Villefranche in two hours. They would beat the maids to the room. Shipley said they would come to collect the clothing worn and weapons used during the assault. "Put everything in a garbage bag," Shipley said. "Leave it outside."

"What are they going to do with the bodies, Chief?"

Shipley grunted. "They'll bring saws and acid and a few suitcases and shit. More questions?"

After he hung up, Sam placed each article of clothing he'd worn into a garbage bag and took a hot shower. Then he sat on the terrace with a beer. The evening was cool and pleasant, the moon fat and bright as clouds thinned in the night sky. He knew she knew. He took a long swig of beer. It was time.

She brought a bottle of wine onto the terrace and sat across from him, drinking half a glass in silence. She wore a robe and her hair was wet from the shower.

"Where are your clothes?" he asked.

"The bathroom."

Sam stuffed them into the same garbage bag along with the confiscated pistols and baton and placed it outside as Shipley had instructed.

He returned to the terrace to find Mariam pouring herself another glass of wine.

"I have questions," she said. "I will go first. Then you can ask me yours."

"Sounds good."

"You are CIA?" she said.

"Yes."

"Your real name is Sam?"

"Yes."

"You are really from Minnesota? You spent time in Las Vegas? Your background, is it all true?"

"Yes."

"We are in a CIA property now? None of this nonsense about you renting it with gambling money."

"Yes. A safe house."

"You are really going to Damascus next?"

"Yes."

"You fight well because you have been trained?"

"Yes."

"Why were you in Paris?"

"To talk to you."

"To try to recruit me."

He finished his beer. It was not a question. Still, he would answer. "Yes. To recruit you."

"You did not stage these men in the hotel?"

"You Syrians really are paranoid—"

"Answer the question."

"No. We did not stage it. I was as surprised as you."

She gulped more wine. He noticed that she was not shaky. She was composed. She'd seen death before.

"Do I need to flee France?"

"I don't think so. Police have not been called. Cleanup crew is on the way. We'll know more in a few hours."

"The chemistry between us. It is real, or you faked it to recruit me?"

"Real. Very real."

"I'm done now." She closed her robe tighter against the gusts of hilltop wind and looked out toward the ocean.

He set down the empty beer bottle and dragged his chair closer to take her in: the eyes, hand movements, the position of her head. It would all matter for what was coming.

"You've seen murders or killed someone before?"

"Yes. There is a war in Syria, Sam."

"But more than that. You've done it yourself, haven't you?"

She ran a hand through her wet hair, untangling a knot. "Yes. Once. In Damascus when I was twenty. Someone tried to rape me. He did not succeed. I killed him. It does not bother me, in case that was your next question."

"It wasn't. I already knew that. Why did you tell me about the Palace tonight?"

"I wanted you to know."

"Why?"

"Because I must do something."

"Would you like to work together?"

"Do I get to work with you?"

"Yes. We would work together in Damascus."

"Tell me what this would look like."

SHE PUT THE LEVANTINE NEGOTIATING sensibility on full display and kept the conversation going without actually saying yes. He marched through the flow on the terrace: we give you a crash course in France; a communications plan so we can talk inside Syria; an address where we can meet in Damascus; a list of topics we want to know more about; we make financial arrangements.

She held up a hand. "I do not want money. I am not a mercenary."

"I understand, Mariam, but we'll hold it in escrow. For later."

"I would never leave Syria. It is unnecessary."

He dropped the subject. Money would flow into an account. Finance would keep records. If she defected or retired, it would be hers. CIA kept its promises to its assets. Sam had once delivered ten years of back payments that an asset had missed because the guy had been in prison for spying. He'd sat across from the man on a train and slid a duffel bag filled with cash toward his feet. "From your American friends," was all Sam said as he walked away.

"You will show me how to move to get to the safe house without the *mukhabarat*?"

"Yes. We will—" His phone vibrated in his pocket. Rami. It was almost five in the morning. He was wide awake.

"What's up?"

"Cleaners just left. Guy at the front desk is literally snoring. No police."

Thanks. He dialed Shipley next. "Does she need to get out?" Sam asked.

"No. My team says the room is clean."

He looked up at Mariam, who was leaning against the terrace's wrought-iron railing, scrutinizing him. "Maybe she checks out tomorrow morning and relocates here, to Èze?"

"She's okay with that?"

"Yes."

"Fine. Call me tomorrow." The line went dead.

"We are okay, yes?" Mariam said, and Sam wondered how much of the conversation she had heard.

"Yes. You should check out tomorrow morning. Relocate here if you're okay with that."

"How do I handle this when I go back to Syria?"

"The kidnapping attempt?" She nodded. "I'm not sure you need to do anything right now. Atiyah is going to assume they failed, say nothing, maybe regroup for another try. None of this was official."

"That's the problem with Syria, Sam. You never know."

13

SAM DRAFTED THE CABLE AFTER MARIAM FELL ASLEEP in one of the bedrooms and sent it encrypted to a BIGOT list sufficient to wake the CIA's slumbering bureaucracy. The bipolar nature of the Agency never ceased to amaze: CIA had the ability to find and kill a person in the remote Hindu Kush, and on the other hand he couldn't find a working stapler at Langley. And so it was with Mariam's recruitment.

Procter set to ensuring the prized asset would have what she needed in three days when she returned to Damascus. The Chief sent a map of potential dead drop locations, signal and brush pass sites, and two safe houses in the Old City. There were reams of satellite imagery. It all had to fit with Mariam's pattern of life. Sam would have to build it with her here in Èze. Luckily, a few days was a lifetime to spend with an asset.

He could not sleep, so he made coffee. It was seven a.m. The sun had begun peeking over the horizon. Mariam was still asleep. As he waited for the grounds to finish steeping, he could smell the salt from the sea and hear the waves crashing into the rocks below. He pressed the plunger, poured a cup, and stepped out onto the terrace to watch the sunrise. Only the sound of the waves and a solo car horn disturbed the dawn-quiet streets. He sipped the coffee for a few minutes before returning inside, where he pulled up Procter's maps on a secure tablet.

Then there was Langley's torpid bureaucracy. He'd asked for a trainer to coach Mariam on SDRs. No one available. Procter had gone berserk and used the word *dogshit* in official cable traffic. Said we have a plum asset here, a Tier 1 country, and a Palace adviser at that and you can't get us someone? Fuck's that about? It had not worked. Sam and the BANDITOs would have to handle it.

Mariam emerged from her bedroom and started rummaging through the cabinets before closing them very loudly. "Everything in the world, except for tea," she said, then poured herself a cup of coffee and sat on the couch next to Sam.

"Before we start," he said. "A promise. We tell each other the truth about everything. No walls. No half-truths. No lies." He'd given the same pep talk to other assets, but they usually were not in bathrobes. Now he evaluated Mariam's eyes, looking for deception, for courage. He saw honesty. He saw fear. It meant she understood the weight of her decision.

She held his gaze. "I promise, Sam."

"So do I, Mariam."

"Now, where do we start?"

They spent four hours reviewing her life: family, work routines, friends, frequented restaurants, enemies, blackmail risk. They consulted the maps. She pointed to her apartment, the Palace, her parents' home.

In the early afternoon Mariam went into the village to buy sandwiches and call Bouthaina to report on the lack of progress with Fatimah. Sam fired up the encrypted cable database on his tablet and saw the good news:

1. NE DIVISION CONCURS WITH C / O GOLDJAGGER ASSESSMENT OF REF DEVELOPMENTAL'S MOTIVATION AND PROGRESSION TOWARD RECRUITMENT.

2. RECOMMEND GENERATION OF CRYPTONYM PENDING COUNTERINTELLIGENCE CONCURRENCE.

3. WE LOOK FORWARD TO REVIEW OF GOLDJAGGER'S COMMS AND OPS PLAN.

Burt O. GOLDJAGGER was Sam's "funnyname," his alias used in written cable traffic to avoid printing his true name on documents. Such names were frequently ridiculous. Sam had heard that a computer program generated them using a British phone book from the 1950s. Procter found the name amusing and had taken to calling him Jaggers. Sam saw another cable, this from Counterintelligence, CI.

1. CI DIVISION CONCURS WITH RECRUITMENT AND SIMILARLY LOOKS FORWARD TO COMMS AND OPS PLAN.

2. REF DEVELOPMENTAL NOW ENCRYPTED BL/ATHENA.

ATHENA was perfect. A huge improvement on his last recruit, who'd been encrypted SLIMER.

He called Elias and asked the BANDITOs to meet in Nice the next morning for Mariam's crash course in surveillance detection. The town's cramped old city was the closest terrain to Damascus here in southern France.

Sam banged out a cable for Procter with a proposed comms plan and follow-up questions for the Chief based on his discussions with Mariam that morning. He attached a picture of a map he'd drawn with Mariam that traced her jogging route through Damascus and up Mount Qasioun overlooking the city. He wanted to know if Procter could find a suitable drop site on the mountain. He sent the cable, closed the database, and refilled his coffee.

Mariam returned with lunch: a tray of salami-and-butter sandwiches, bottled water, salad, and quiche. She explained that Bouthaina had instructed her to try for one last meeting with Fatimah. It was a gift. It bought them more time. As they ate, he explained that he'd asked Damascus for a drop site. "We can go to a trail nearby, maybe this afternoon, and I'll show you how to manage the drops," he said. She took a sip of mineral water, thinking something.

"What's up?" he said.

"Can we talk a little more about the Palace? For me to understand the information that is helpful to you."

"Sure."

"For example, what if Bouthaina was facilitating strange financial transactions for the Republican Guard?" Mariam said. "Would that be interesting?"

"That would be very interesting."

Mariam took a sip of water. "Rustum appeared in Bouthaina's office a few months back for a meeting. It hasn't happened before or since. Bouthaina includes me in almost everything, but this one she handled alone. After the meeting she told me why. She shouldn't have, but she did: the Guard needs to procure equipment clandestinely. The sanctions are biting, and they don't trust the SSRC shell companies to manage sensitive transactions."

"She said 'SSRC'?" Sam asked.

"Yes."

"Interesting."

Mariam continued. "Bouthaina creates the shell companies using a network of friendly Syrian businessmen. Most are in Beirut. Some are in Amman, a few in Cyprus, in the Gulf. I helped with six transactions. I don't have the full picture."

"All unique to the Palace?" he asked.

"I think so. The funds come from bank accounts associated with the Republican Guard and are put into several held by Bouthaina at the Palace. Then we wire the money to the shell companies, who are presumably purchasing something for the Guard. It makes Bouthaina nervous. But here is the most interesting part. I did some research on one of the shell companies. The internet searches turned up nothing. They don't have a website. But I checked a Palace database and found that an identical shell was established in 2002 to conduct business for the SSRC."

"I know where you're going with this," Sam said. "Chemical weapons. But they could be using the same shell now to buy something else. Pipes, bolts, scissors."

Mariam nodded. "True, but I called the company because I was curious. I told them I was in Finance—asked if they could read back the items on the bill of materials. I told them the scanner had done a poor job. It was one item: isopropyl alcohol. It is required for sarin production. I know because Bouthaina's office had to respond to questions about the Europeans banning chemical exports to Syria."

"Do you know how much money was transferred into that shell company?" Sam asked.

"Ten million U.S. dollars."

"Any ideas for how we could get access to the full list of shell entities and the transactions between those firms and the Palace?"

"I expect it is on Bouthaina's computer."

"She ever leave you alone with it?" he asked. Worth the risk, he knew, but it was just a little hard to be objective with her folded up on the couch reviewing the maps with that white underwear peeking out.

THEY DROVE THROUGH BEAULIEU-SUR-MER AND parked on the northern tip of Saint-Jean-Cap-Ferrat. They dressed casually as if going for an afternoon stroll. Mariam wore jeans, a Breton-striped top, and white tennis shoes. He wore jeans and a gray T-shirt. The dusty paths circumnavigating the peninsula would be a reasonable proxy for a running-trail drop site in Damascus. It was late afternoon, the sky cloudless, the trails peopled but not full. A young couple, hands in each other's back pockets, strolled past. Sam and Mariam spoke in Arabic.

"You are not allowed to love your agents because it makes you less objective, no?" she asked.

"That's right."

"And what happens if CIA discovers our kiss?"

"I would be okay. They would ask a lot of questions. Maybe give me a poly—"

Sam stopped talking. A couple pushing a stroller turned a corner in front of them and walked past.

He continued: "They might give me a polygraph. But I'd be fine. A kiss is different from—"

She completed the sentence in English: "Sex."

The switch from Arabic threw him off. "Yes. For that they might fire me. Full-scale review, that kind of thing. I know a guy who slept with an agent. They benched him for two years."

"What is benching?"

"It means he sat at a desk doing nothing."

"I see."

They continued walking and he shifted to a less arousing subject: dead drops.

"A good site," he explained, "harmoniously balances physical cover and flow. The former because it has to be hidden, the latter because the agent and the handling officer need to travel past, ideally at an unbroken speed, to retrieve the object. The two are always in tension. The more flow, the less hidden it will be. The more covered an object, the crummier the flow. I once used a taxidermied cat tossed near a construction site. The agent would stuff papers and messages in a compartment that had once held intestines. No one touched it. But it was too hidden: the area contained other roadkill and the agent could not locate the right animal, which broke his flow and eventually forced him to abandon the pickup."

She snorted. "You can't be serious."

"I am."

"No cats for me, please."

He shook his head. "No cats, I promise. I think we'll use trash, maybe a can lined with adhesive to hold paper on the inside, with a top you can pull off."

He found a promising site on the western side of the peninsula: a trash can next to a short rock wall, garbage strewn about. He found a can and worked the top off with a pocketknife he'd brought along.

"This is as good as any we'll find," he said as he rifled through the trash until he found a napkin. He shoved it inside the can and tossed the can into the pile. She wore a sour frown as she surveyed the trash.

"This whole thing is less glamorous than people think," he said. "It's trash and dead cats more than anything else."

THEY PRACTICED FOR TWO HOURS, stopping whenever pedestrians approached. Sam took video on his phone as she repeated filling and retrieving contents from the can. She was a quick learner, and the Krav helped. She could move fluidly. She could move solidly. She could move with intention. He filmed on his phone from all angles and by the end of the afternoon her movements completed the cover: a jogger tying her shoe in about three seconds.

At sunset she said she'd had enough, but he insisted on one more retrieval. He filmed from behind as if he were a *mukhabarat* tail. She jogged to the trash pile, slowing on her approach. When she reached it she bent at her waist, legs soldier-straight, body folding into a ninety-degree angle as her chest plunged toward the ground and her buns jutted out.

The jeans were tight and majorly distracting from the dead drop evaluation. She looked back at him with a wicked smile. Then she straightened her back, stood erect, and pretended to take a sip from the can. She winked.

"I think we'll call it there," he said.

14

THEY MADE THE SECOND RECIPE FROM HIS GRANDmother, a cacio e pepe—bucatini lathered in twenty euros of melted pecorino dusted with ground black pepper. They lit some candle lanterns and scattered them across the terrace. Mariam wore a red floral-print sundress, sandals, and gold hoop earrings with her hair flopped halfway down her back, whorls untamed.

She had discovered the wine cellar after they reviewed the videos of her dead-drop training and took a Tuscan red. Sam asked if it was expensive. She rolled her eyes. "That's not the point," she said. "We want to find something that will pair well with the pasta. This Sangiovese will be good."

"So is it expensive?"

"Yes."

"Good."

Another eye roll.

"Thank you for coming to the hotel room," she said after they sat down and clinked glasses. "For saving me. I realized this afternoon I had not said that."

"You would have done the same for me."

"I know. But still."

They ate for a few moments in silence, then she set down her silverware. "I am scared. Scared to go back. To take the first real step."

"We'll do this together," he said. "I will protect you."

MARIAM STARED INTO THOSE EYES and realized at that moment why she wanted him. In some strange world this was now one of her most intimate relationships. He knew everything about her, they'd shed blood together, and he knew her darkest secret. In Paris she'd felt the chemistry, but now it was more: a raw and unconsummated emotional intimacy. She wanted more. She wanted it all.

"I know you will protect me," she said. "This is your job, no? Recruiting spies, obtaining their secrets. But what happens if I am caught?"

"Mariam, don't—"

"Let me finish. If I am caught they will torture, then murder me. You get to go home. I am putting it all on the line. You are not. This is a fact."

"It bothers you."

"Of course. Our relationship—our partnership—is special. I don't really know how to describe it. It just is." She leaned forward, pointing at her heart. "So I want more than the typical agent gets."

He shifted in his chair and looked down the cliff toward the moonlit sea. He absentmindedly swirled the last of the wine around in his glass and she noticed as he gazed, hypnotized, into the ink that for a moment he'd traveled elsewhere. He ran both hands through his hair, then put them back on the table. Mariam could see the sweat dappled on the cloth. He looked into her eyes to check for the trust before he began speaking.

"I will tell you something no one else knows. Would that help?" She said she wanted to hear.

"I have three brothers. But once there was a fourth, Charlie. He was the baby. Four years younger. Crazy funny kiddo, my parents say so now, I knew it even then. Blond hair, big blue eyes, easy smile. He would make crazy faces and dance around to music. Life of the party. Charlie and I always got along. We had fun together. I was old enough to take care of him, he was old enough we could have fun."

She saw his jaw cement in place, just like she did when she wanted to cry but forced herself to soldier on. She said nothing.

"I remember this one time. Charlie's four, four and a half. I'm eight or so. Our oldest brother Danny is studying for a math test and not getting it. He's crying as my dad tries to help him work through the problems. My dad suggests he cool off a little, take a break, and he leaves the kitchen. Anyways, Danny is sitting there at the table crying. Charlie sidles up next to him, scans over the textbook like he can make sense of it. He closes the book and puts his arm around Danny and tells him it will be okay, you'll get it eventually. This four-year-old kid comforting him. Danny puts his head on Charlie's shoulder."

Sam laughed, wiped the right corner of an eye, and took a sip of wine. "Charlie puts his right finger in his mouth and licks it, nice and juicy, then shoves it in Danny's ear, telling him the math problems are easy, he'll figure it out."

Mariam laughed and almost coughed up wine. "What did Danny do?"

"He yelled and ran after Charlie. Failed the math test, if I recall."

She saw his jaw clench again. They passed several seconds in silence. Insects were humming on the hillside and murmurs of a crowd floated upward from the narrow medieval streets.

"It was a few months after that," Sam said, "me and Charlie are the only ones at home. Mom needs eggs from the store. Ten-minute walk, we did it all the time. She says you go with Charlie. We take a baseball with us. We're tossing it around, Charlie demanding I throw a couple fly balls, wanting me to run ahead, then throw it high. This road is never busy. Still, I know it's a bad idea. But there's Charlie, making the pouty face, yelling. Finally I give in, run about twenty feet ahead. We've come up a hill at this point, beyond Charlie it crests down. We're on the shoulder and it's flanked by these big pines. I toss it very high, kind of angry because Charlie's been a brat. It glances off a tree branch and toward the road. I never saw the car coming. Black pickup, running at a nice clip up the hill. It was clean, docs said he didn't suffer. I lay there with him on the road, for how long I have no idea. His eyes were open, like he was still locked on the ball. The idiot driver holding his head in his hands, pacing, muttering. No one ever found the baseball. I left it there, never told anyone about it."

She now clenched her own jaw. "It is not your fault, you know. You did not run him over."

He took a deep breath and refilled his wineglass. The pasta was cold. "We should probably put this back on the stove," he said.

Standing in the kitchen, she kissed him. "Thank you for telling me," she said.

They were ravenous and ate from the pot, joking about their fight in Paris and her suggestive dead drop and something she had spotted as she'd tried to remove his shirt the other night.

"Let me see," she said, pointing at Sam's left shoulder blade. "I could not get a good look the other night. This is still a secret."

Sam lifted the shirt up his back, exposing the word *Clarity* tattooed on the left blade.

"What does it mean?" she asked. "And why is everything behind the *i* all discolored and shitty?" she said in English.

"You mean shoddy?"

"No," she said with a half smile.

His shifty body language said he had given this speech before and hated it. She ran a hand along his back. It was nice and strong. Except for this tattoo, which she did not like.

"Clare was my high school girlfriend," he said. "One night we got drunk. We went to a tattoo parlor and got each other's names on our backs. When we broke up, I couldn't afford to get the whole thing removed, so I had a guy try to remove the *e* in her name, then finish the word into *Clarity*. At the time, it seemed profound."

She cackled, then snorted. A whip of bucatini almost escaped from her mouth, splattering a few flecks of cheese on her dress. She wiped them off, laughing. "I paid to have my Assad tattoo removed from my bottom. Worth every Syrian pound." She winked. He laughed and kissed her, his confidence and looseness returning, she could tell, as his mind distanced itself from his brother.

Laughing, they went into the cellar to find more wine.

WHEN THEY'D ALMOST FINISHED THE next bottle, Mariam asked how frequently they would see each other in Damascus. "It really depends," he said. "But ideally only when necessary. It is obviously dangerous to meet face-to-face there. For your safety we should communicate as much as possible through the drop site. Eventually, we'll get you a device."

"And the training you are giving me tomorrow?" she asked.

"Surveillance detection routes. SDRs. How to ensure the *mukhabarat* is not watching you before we meet. We'll also do brush passes. There is a lot to cover." Sam did not describe the nausea he felt at her going back inside.

"So we have two days, then who knows," she said, not asking a question.

They sat on the terrace couch and melted into a sweet silence, facing the coastline as they emptied their glasses and nestled into each other. It felt for a moment like they were a normal couple. They stayed there for a while, soaking in the vast black night, until he kissed her and she kissed back, and soon the very natural feeling of leading Mariam toward the master bedroom of a CIA safe house took hold, their mouths locked, lips moving to laugh or kiss or gently bite, and they were standing by the bed when she slipped from her sundress and her underwear and he was catching up, almost tripping like an idiot over his jeans, and he heard that snort and felt soft hands grip him as he drew her body close and they fell onto the bed, laughing like friends who'd just discovered they could somehow be closer to each other, had just found the secret, couldn't believe it had escaped them this long.

Oh fuck, she said in English, fuck *habibi*, her head back on the pillow, once he was inside. He pressed his forehead on hers and kissed her. Her skin glistened and her thick hair, wet at the forehead, stuck onto her face and the pillow, her body seesawing underneath, everything in rhythm, that lipstick everywhere, a crime scene. He felt warm and could smell nothing but the lavender, hear the clink of her earrings as they found a rhythm. He escaped from the moment just once, to realize it seemed right and normal to now be with Syrian Palace official and recruited CIA asset Mariam Haddad, cryptonym ATHENA, in violation of the CIA's code of conduct and probably a half dozen federal laws. But Mariam was straddling him, her head tossed back, their hands white and clasped together, and the thought evaporated.

She fell asleep first, as the dawn light reached through the windows. Instead of sleeping, Sam worried. He thought of his agent servicing a dead drop. Eliciting information. Running an SDR. In Damascus. Sam's eyes caught Mariam's discarded bra, now twisted on the floor. What in the hell have I done?

Mariam rolled closer to him, still asleep, breathing deep and peacefully.

15

THEY SHUFFLED AROUND THE SAFE HOUSE COLLECTING clothes, tidying the bedroom, scraping congealed pasta from pots. Of the lovemaking they said nothing. It had been natural, fun, normal, in a bizarre way. He made eggs and toast and they drank coffee on the terrace, watching waves crash into the rocks as the heat climbed up the hilltop.

Sam reviewed Procter's maps of Damascus on his tablet while Mariam showered. She emerged in the living room toweling off her wet hair and asked what time they were going into Nice. She smiled at him as she wrapped the towel around her wet hair. He said, "We've got about ten days of work to do in two, time to get dressed, *habibti*." He didn't realize he'd called her *habibti*—dear, baby, my love—it just slipped out but did not go unnoticed. She smiled at him for a moment, then walked off to change.

They spent the morning drinking coffee as they tore through the classroom segment of surveillance detection. She was a star pupil—attentive, curious, eager to learn. The coffee, however, was treated with disdain. "It is black tar, Sam," she said, wrinkling her face as she took small sips. "This is a drink for savages."

He taught her everything: the basic setup, the moves, spotting repeats, how to build the SDR into your pattern of life. The classroom lecture, he knew from the Farm, could only do so much. You had to get on the street.

She was close enough that he could smell her hair and see the outline of her breasts under the clingy shirt and— Stop it, idiot, this is her preparation for Damascus. Time to focus. You get one chance at this.

"Some of these ideas we'll just have to practice out there, just so you know," he said, pointing down the coastline toward Nice. She nodded and scanned the maps, knees bouncing, ready for action. "Time to go," he said.

His phone rang as she packed her purse and changed into tennis shoes in her bedroom. He did not recognize the number.

"Hello?" he said.

"It's Procter."

"Chief, what's up?"

"I just landed in Nice. Spur-of-the-moment thing, so don't think I don't trust you, I just want to meet our girl myself before she disappears into Damascus. Your cable said SDR training today. Put me in, Coach."

SAM HAD DESIGNED SEVERAL RUNS crisscrossing Nice's Vielle Ville, a warren of medieval streets that resembled the terrain in the Syrian capital, the gelato boutiques, fedora-clad tourists, and watercolor buildings standing in for Damascus's bombings, militias, and general mayhem. The BANDITOs and Procter would play the opposition. Damascus would be hellacious; they would be demons here. They brought out the heavy weapons: encrypted earpieces designed to look like Apple AirPods, several rented Vespas, disguises—mustaches, fake guts, new clothes and shoes, makeup—a nearly silent microdrone—unpermitted for aerial operation in France, but screw it—decked out with high-def and thermal imaging feeds, subminiature cameras embedded in sunglasses, messenger bags, and fedoras connected to an encrypted satellite link that beamed everything to the mother ship: a delivery van manned by Procter. Sam and Mariam sat at a brasserie on the city's far western edge reviewing a tourist map of the city, debating the route.

They drew one up. Long, exhausting, just like Damascus would be. He decided not to tell her about the drone. Evil, indecent, really.

MARIAM NOTICED AS THEY PLANNED the routes that she loved this, wanted more of it even though she feared returning home. Twenty minutes in, she spotted one of the watchers dressed like a bum—shoes were clean and new, not a bum, she said later in the debrief—in a fixed position outside a Best Western, then successfully forced a couple tails into a wagon train on the way up the hill to the castle. She had the instinct for this, she knew. She could feel the opposition at work. Maybe the fruits of Syrian paranoia, of living in a place where you could always be under surveillance. The tingle again, a jolt down her spine. Her scans for surveillance turned up nothing. Three stops, a half dozen turns, she wound through the cramped little streets and decided she needed to quiet things down. Off the Cours Saleya she passed a sunny yellow baroque church covered in ornate sculptures. She was certain the tails had disappeared, but the tingle remained. She stepped into an Italian restaurant at the foot of the church and went into the back courtyard.

An old woman opened a window and began hanging laundry. Mariam looked up and saw a metallic glint in the blue sky. And then the tingle again, her heart rattling against her ribs. If this thing was what she thought, it was being used to deploy the teams. She could evade or spot foot operators and they'd just regroup later.

For a beat her throat went raw, the sweat picked up, then she left through the service entrance. On the hot street she sensed immediately the watchers returning. She executed a set of quick turns near a cathedral and calculated she probably had thirty seconds, how had Sam described it, *in the gap*. Free of surveillance. She ducked into a kitschy tourist stand and paid cash for a large T-shirt intended for an English-speaking audience (NICE IS NICE), a baseball cap (I ♥ NICE), and a cheap yellow scarf. She stuffed them in her purse as her count reached twenty-five and reappeared on the street.

She melded into a thick crowd near a library and then broke free into a quarter of quiet side streets filled with empty kebab, Indian, and Italian restaurants. She was moving well now, she sensed, knowing when to accelerate, when to stop and dawdle, and she was very close to where she planned to lose the thing buzzing above her, which she now knew was an incredibly small surveillance drone.

She went into a den of streets as narrow as anything in Damascus, with bright restaurant awnings meeting in the middle to blot out the sky. As she marched onward, she put on the hat, the horrendous T-shirt, and tied the scarf up around her neck. When she emerged from the awninged alleyway the tingle disappeared. She pressed on toward the "safe house," a sidewalk café called René Socca. She started using the terrain to her advantage: turning, stopping, executing what she thought was a very nice corner hang—no one followed—and finally overshooting Socca to sit at another café three blocks north. She was black. The drone was gone, searching for a woman in a navy T-shirt and capris instead of the tackiest Arab tourist in southern France. When she started out again she did the final checks, scanning every passerby against suspects she'd seen earlier in the day, looking in parked cars without turning her head.

Black. I am black, she said to herself.

She found a table and ordered a glass of wine.

Sam and Procter found her on the second glass, still wearing the hat, the impossibly tacky T-shirt, and a victor's grin.

"It's been fifty-one minutes," she said, smiling, as Sam and Procter approached. "You two hold the table, I'm going into the bathroom to change. I can't spend another minute in this thing." As she brushed past, she thought that Sam looked like he wanted to kiss her.

THE GROUP DECAMPED TO THE safe house to debrief. Procter wheeled in her suitcase saying she needed a place to stay and would use an available bedroom or a shitty blow-up couch, I'm not picky. Sam wondered what Mariam would think of her.

The BANDITOs brought the food. "Pizza Hut delivery," Elias yelled as the brothers opened the door carrying several pizza boxes. Luckily, they were only messing with him. They had actually found a respectable Sicilian place in Villefranche. The BANDITOs watched the video and coached Mariam. "Tremendous first day, Mariam," Procter said. "We do it again tomorrow until your feet bleed." Mariam raised an eyebrow, then laughed.

Procter motioned Sam into the kitchen as the BANDITOs explained how Mariam could make her visual checks less obvious as she executed a turn. He followed the Chief.

"I think we've got the comms plan settled," Procter said. She opened her tablet and explained they'd taken an extensive library of photos along Mariam's running trail. Procter paused on an image that caught Sam's eye. There was a fork in the running path, with a crumbling retaining wall separating both sides and trash heaped alongside. It was remote and consistent with her pattern of life.

"This is the spot. We'll use a can, like you did in practice. We'll use the signals we talked about. She puts the blinds halfway up in her apartment if she's loaded the drop. We use graffiti outside her apartment. We do this for a bit, get everyone comfortable, then we'll try to get her a device."

Sam nodded. "Good, I'll walk her through it." Procter put the tablet aside and asked for his assessment of the case as she pushed buttons on the coffee maker. Sam had used the French press, Procter insisted on the machine. It beeped twice, then powered down. "Dammit," said the Chief, smacking the water compartment.

"She's doing excellent so far." Sam remembered Mariam smiling as she bent over to sip the can. "Great movement, great instincts. She's a natural."

"Let's hope she can transfer those skills to D-town," Procter said.

Sam wanted to change the subject. "Any follow-up on the call to Ali?"

"Nothing. Syrians continue to deny any knowledge of Val's whereabouts and offer to help us locate the criminals or terrorists that kidnapped her. Fuckers." Procter smacked the coffee maker again. The machine finally hissed, and soon a trickle of coffee began filling the pot. Procter peered out toward Mariam and the BANDITOs to ensure she and Sam were alone. "Bradley says that POTUS got pretty worked up about it at the last Syria Working Group meeting. Everyone is sick of their games."

Now Sam turned to make sure all four Syrians remained in the living room, out of earshot. "The longer they hold Val, the more likely it is that they're wringing her for information. We've got to do something."

"I know, I know. And I meant what I said. If Ali hurts Val, we'll take his balls."

A FEW DAYS WITH A highly placed, valuable agent was rare, a gift from the intelligence gods.

So Procter and Sam peppered Mariam with questions dispatched in a requirements cable from Langley. The pressing issues the White House, NE Division, and the analysts wanted to know about: how her office worked, the President's views on the war, the plans and intentions of senior military and security officials. The banter was relaxed. Mariam and Procter seemed to enjoy each other's company. The Chief somehow stuck the landing on an obscene joke about the President's virility, complete with hand gestures, many of which were biologically and anatomically impossible. Mariam snorted in delight.

They all went to bed early, exhausted from the training. "Another circus tomorrow," Procter said. "Much to do."

Mariam kissed Sam's forehead in the hallway after Procter closed her door. "I like her, Sam," she said. "This team. It feels right to me."

THE NEXT DAY WAS BRUTAL, hot, and exhausting. "But the girl can feel the street," Sam told Procter inside the surveillance van as she threw the drone again and the BANDITOs lost her somewhere east of the castle six hours into the second run. Procter watched video of her dead drop and pronounced it *parfait* ("PAR-FAT"). Sam noticed Yusuf shudder as the Chief butchered his second language. The Chief gave Mariam a big hug at the end of the day. "We will do great work together, Mariam," Procter said before departing to return to Syria.

Mariam tried, for the last time, to contact Fatimah. She could not get through, and called Bouthaina to provide a report. "Time to come home, Mariam," Bouthaina said. "The *bint mbarih* has made her decision."

Now knowing it was their last night, Sam and Mariam drove the Moyenne Corniche, ostensibly so he could explain some of the mechanics of vehicular SDRs but in truth because he wanted to be alone with her and had become paranoid that Procter had bugged the safe house. They also had to talk about Uncle Daoud.

They drove toward Monaco. A few stars peeked admirably between the haze. He pulled into an overlook. The cliffs below collapsed into a forest of palm and citrus overlooking a white beach. A few other cars were parked at the far end of the overlook, the occupants necking inside.

For a while Sam and Mariam looked out in silence.

"Daoud?" she said finally, scanning to the left to ensure they were out of earshot.

"What do you think?" Sam said.

"He will not work for CIA," she said. "But I think he would tell me things he should not. He may assume his information would go somewhere else, but he would not ask where, I think."

"You said he has grievances?"

"Yes. Razan. He is enraged at her treatment. And he, like many people, does not support the indiscriminate killing. He also does not want to see the gas used. He is a patriot. He understood why it was necessary to deter Israel. He does not think it should be used on Syrians."

"You've talked about this?"

She put her hand on his leg with a look that said, *Let me explain Syria, silly American.* "The conversations are more guarded, more vague," she said. "In Syria we do not have such frank discussions because one can never know who is listening.

"If I ask him questions, I will say the Palace is asking. It will allow him to speak candidly."

"Just be careful."

She rolled her eyes and turned away.

Sam moved on: "What do you think he could provide?"

"He is responsible for the stockpile in the capital, so he would know if the regime is planning to use the sarin in Damascus. He would also know about the security situation at the sites."

Sam nodded. "Whatever you can elicit would be extremely helpful. It would be a priority for us."

MARIAM INVITED HIM TO SHUT up by kissing him hard on the mouth. Then they awkwardly slid into the back of the car. He went first, she followed. Soon she was being rocked back and forth and squeezing her muscles and it was starting to feel good, that swelling expanding to fill her body. And his hands were knotted in her hair and his eyes were stuck on hers and he'd put his back up a bit to get the angle right, sensing where she wanted the pressure. When it was done, they lay winded in the backseat. This is how the weighty decisions get made, she thought as they breathed together.

I did nothing.

Not anymore.

PART III

Bombs

16

THE NEWS ARRIVED ON LANGLEY'S SEVENTH FLOOR courtesy of a Syrian document thief who photographed sensitive files for a generous monthly stipend. Bradley, briefing the Director, said his reporting was firsthand and reliable. The document and accompanying photo were almost certainly authentic. The Director summoned Procter back to Langley for consultations.

For the next twenty-four hours, a small team from Security scrubbed Val Owens's medical files and prescription records. They interviewed CIA psychologists. A team of doctors, pathologists, and coroners pored over the single photo. In the end, the lies in the document and the truth in the photo set in motion a late afternoon meeting with the Director. The whitewashed meeting record was placed into a Restricted-Handling compartment ineligible for declassification or Freedom of Information Act release. If read, the document would have revealed that between minutes fifteen and seventeen of the discussion, Chief of Station Damascus Artemis A. Procter "interrupted Dr. Pan to clarify the level of certainty in her medical judgment before speaking at length in an uninterrupted and vulgar monologue about the appropriate methods for revenge."

SAM WAS AT THE OFFICE of Medical Services—the Agency doctors—completing bloodwork in advance of the Damascus tour when he saw a patch of black hair appear outside the lab. Procter opened the door, pushing past the doctor, who wisely remained silent after sizing up the Chief. Sam had no idea Procter was in town.

"Let's get some air," she said. "Take those needles out and let's walk."

They left the Original Headquarters Building and made for the forested running paths off Chain Bridge. The afternoon was muggy, and he could feel the sweat collecting on his back and legs as they walked. Procter did not have a drop of perspiration on her face, a miracle given that she was clothed in a tweed skirt and maroon blouse. When they reached the paths, Sam's white shirt was soaked in sweat.

Procter accelerated, still holding the silence. Sam found himself struggling to keep pace, though Procter's legs were almost a foot shorter than his own. A runner huffed past. They walked in silence until the man turned the corner and was out of sight. Sam zigzagged across the sidewalk searching for shade. Procter, face bone-dry and chalky white, tore a straight line through the sunshine until they reached a remote part of the path.

She stopped.

"Val is dead," Procter said suddenly. "News arrived early yesterday. Ali Hassan killed her during an interrogation." She spat.

Sam walked off toward a bench and sat down. He watched leaves rippling in the late afternoon wind. He rubbed his hot forehead with a sweaty hand. For some reason he anchored on the small things, the details. Strangely, he thought of Mariam and wanted her here with him. He wanted her skin on his. He watched another runner go by. He rolled up his sleeves and stupidly smoothed his tie.

Procter looked around. They were alone. She stared at Sam, his face dripping with sweat, and removed a rubber band from her pocket. She tied her curly black hair up into a lopsided ponytail. Then she removed from her tweed pocket two pieces of folded paper and handed them to Sam. Drops of sweat plopped onto the paper as he unfolded a picture. Sam had seen death before. As a boy, in the shadows of a north woods pine forest. As a man, in the muck and sand of Baghdad and Anbar. He looked at the paper into Val's lifeless eyes.

"They took her fucking scalp," Procter said. "Agency docs and photography experts could see a thin incision in the photo, despite the makeup. They scalped her, then sewed it back on for the picture."

Fighting a surge of nausea, he folded up the picture and handed it to Procter. They watched another runner pass by. She joined him on the bench.

"Read the other one," she said. He unfolded the second piece of paper and read the English translation:

15 APRIL

FROM: BRIGADIER GENERAL ALI HASSAN, DIRECTOR, SECURITY OFFICE OF THE PRESIDENTIAL PALACE

TO: HIS EXCELLENCY, PRESIDENT OF THE SYRIAN ARAB REPUBLIC BASHAR AL-ASSAD; LIEUTENANT GENERAL RUSTUM HASSAN, COMMANDER OF THE REPUBLICAN GUARD

SUBJECT: CIA OFFICER IN CUSTODY

CIA OFFICER VALERIE OWENS, UNDER COVER AT THE AMERICAN EMBASSY AS A SECOND SECRETARY, PASSED AWAY FROM HEART FAILURE DURING A ROUTINE INTERVIEW. PHARMACEUTICALS AND ANTI-DEPRESSANTS OBTAINED FROM HER RESIDENCE INDICATE OWENS SUFFERED FROM HIGH CHOLESTEROL, STRESS, AND PANIC ATTACKS. THE SECURITY OFFICE REGRETS MS. OWENS' UNTIMELY DEATH.

He folded the paper and handed it back to Procter. "Agency docs reviewed Val's records, so we know the stuff about the drugs is bullshit, by the way," Procter said as she placed it in her pocket. "Ali made that up to cover his ass. The Director is going to push the White House for a lethal finding. But I have no confidence we'll get it. These things are hard. They take time. However, I have a particular goddamn problem with CIA officers getting murdered."

A covert action finding with lethal authorities, Sam knew, would be required for the CIA to retaliate for the killing. Findings required a robust intelligence justification and had to clear Office of Legal Counsel review at the Justice Department, not to mention the CIA's in-house Office of General Counsel. Tricky, because an executive order from the Reagan years applied a blanket ban on assassinations.

"I want a plan so we're ready when called," she said. "Off the books. You come to Syria. You bring the BANDITOs back to Damascus with you. I want you to run them to build a plan to take Ali out, in case we need it." She continued staring ahead, unflinching.

Another runner went by. Sam stood. "I'm going to get out of here for a bit, clear my head before Damascus."

"Good idea."

He knew that visible emotion would dampen Procter's enthusiasm for his involvement in the case, so he kept his words simple and direct. "It will be an honor to join the hunt in Damascus," he said. "Thanks for giving me the opportunity to be involved."

Procter nodded. "Welcome to the show."

SAM HAD A WEEK BEFORE departing for Damascus, so he flew to another desert to forget. Las Vegas was at full fever pitch: the glitter of the Strip, the bending palms, the booze and grime underfoot everywhere, on everything.

He was a little drunk and on a heater.

If he'd been a different man with a different past, he'd have already considered how to spend the $22,750 in winnings now stacked in towers on the green felt of his old table in the Bellagio's poker room.

But he'd made choices, and of the haul he would keep only a single hundred-dollar bill to cover the post-game buffet for two. The Vegas trips had become a kind of cathartic ritual after tours or nasty operations. He'd had the professional misfortune of serving in cities that frowned on gambling: Cairo, Riyadh, Baghdad. Sam could—and did—ravage the embassy and Station house games, but the struggle was less fiery, more like a slow-motion surrender of the opposition than the gladiatorial showdown he relished. The cards were peacetime's combat. It was substitute spycraft where money, not an asset's life, was the only thing on the line.

Sam wore an old gray hoodie that felt lucky. He now stared across the table at the chubby suited Brit, the single caller to his raise. A bluff, really. Sam had nothing but 10-8, but he sensed an opportunity.

The Brit coughed, showing his nerves.

The flop came: two of spades, four of hearts, queen of spades.

Sam checked. The Brit bet $500. Sam recalled his opponent's betting patterns. His previous maximum had been $200 and his stack was about the same size then. It's not betting inflation. If he landed a queen, he'd bet lower to lure me in. Make me comfortable. He wants me out of the pot. Maybe ace-king? Pocket jacks? Tens? Flush draw?

Sam re-raised another $500. The Brit called.

The turn: nine of diamonds.

The Brit smiled, just a little, as he played with his chips. Sam had seen this hundreds of times on hundreds of people: the watery smile of a man convincing himself of something. The cough had vanished.

The Brit bet $750. Sam stared at the man. Dress shirt clinging to the gut is heaving a bit. He's trying to control his breath. If I go at him again and he sticks with me, he's paying for the flush draw.

Sam re-raised another $1,000.

The smile vanished. The Brit looked again at his cards. The final release of a hand with unmet potential.

The Brit tossed the cards to the dealer, who raked the pot toward Sam.

"What'd you have, you don't mind me asking?" said the Brit.

"Queens," Sam lied.

The Brit nodded and took a sip of his whiskey. "Damn. Well played."

Sam felt a hand on his shoulder. "Time for the buffet? Dinner ends at ten."

Sam ran his hand along the felt, fluttered his fingers along the clay chips, took their weight in his hands. He closed his eyes and inhaled the reassuring, musty smell of a table in action.

SAM STROLLED TO THE CASHIER with Bellagio resident, late-night buffet partner, and occasional CIA talent spotter Max Huston. Huston had introduced Sam to the CIA. Huston's relationship with the Agency was unofficial, ad hoc, shadowy. Huston found talent in Vegas and directed them to Langley recruiters. He was not paid. He'd told Sam once, after a half dozen vodka sodas, that he was merely doing his civic duty, sticking it to the commies and the Russkies and the Qaeda camel-humpers. "CIA has to have the best, not just the Ivy pricks," he said with one eye open, the other flickering off and on. "CIA needs the girls and guys who know how people work, Sam." Six months after meeting Max Huston, Sam had been in the Field Tradecraft Course at the Farm, the first test given to new case officers to determine if they had the mettle required for the Mission.

"Good hunting tonight?" Huston asked, sipping at his vodka as Sam slid the chip tray through the slot to the leathery cashier behind the glass.

"Yes. Like old times."

"Good man."

"Can you break it into two checks and one single bill?" Sam asked the cashier.

Huston laughed.

"Of course." The cashier's brow crinkled. He eyed Huston, then the dwindling vodka. He tried to smile.

"One check for ten thousand to Sam Joseph. Me." He slid his driver's license through the slot. "A single hundred-dollar bill. Then one more check for the remainder made out to Clara Grace Joseph." Sam spelled the name.

Huston chuckled and finished the vodka. "What does she do with the cash?"

"Before Cairo she bought a car."

"Baghdad?"

"There was no check before Baghdad."

Huston grinned. "I know."

Sam pulled a pre-addressed envelope from his jeans pocket:

CLARA GRACE JOSEPH
15 BIG RICE ROAD
SHERMANS CORNER, MN 55395

He slipped a check for $24,480 into the envelope and asked the cashier for a pen and a slip of paper. On the paper he wrote: *For anything. I love you, Mom.* He put the note into the envelope and sealed it.

"She's a lucky mother," Huston said. "Even though you broke her heart. Now, the buffet. I will also note that, as usual, you have not withdrawn funds sufficient to cover my drinking habit."

SAM STACKED HIS PLATE WITH a pile of seafood and slid into the booth across from Huston, who was already downing another vodka. He'd ordered one for Sam.

"I always appreciate my former students letting me know when they're in town." He raised his glass. Sam did the same. The vibe was energetic amid the din: plates clattered in the kitchen, a group of drunken Chinese businessmen hooted from across the room, Huston raised his glass to three attractive women strolling by, their skirts impossibly short, painted on, their hair bleached into downy oblivion. He looked back to Sam, who had started in on the snow crab. Huston's brow furrowed. "Something wrong?" he said.

"Yes. We lost someone."

Huston grunted and raised his glass. "Can't say more, I imagine?"

"No, unfortunately."

Huston cut a chunk of prime rib. "Bradley get you involved?"

"Yeah."

"You're his fixer, you know that, Sam. That's why he puts you in the action."

He raised his glass so Huston could not see his lips purse. He hated hearing himself described as a fixer for Bradley—because it was true.

The Chinese businessmen erupted into raucous laughter as one fell out of the booth. The waiter stepped over him. "You miss this place?" Huston said, changing the subject.

Sam looked at the businessman, now clinging to the edge of the table, trying to stand amid the whoops of his inebriated colleagues. "Just your smiling face, Max."

Sam was about to pull the rip cord after two more rounds of vodka, one more trip through the buffet, and a thick finger of a peaty scotch that Huston habitually insisted was the only appropriate nightcap. It had a name Sam could never remember. Then Huston pointed his empty glass toward one of the televisions mounted above the prime rib carving station.

Sam turned around and read the CNN chyron: *U.S. official killed in Damascus.* Then the caption: *Senior national security officials have told CNN that Valerie Owens, a U.S. diplomat, has died in Damascus. The Syrian government has not released an official statement.*

SAM HAD POLISHED OFF FOUR bottles of mini-fridge whiskey and now stood facing the Strip below with its illuminated fountains, the Eiffel Tower replica, mountains shadowed in the distance.

The Bellagio fountains, white sunbeams in the night, licked skyward.

This is why you left. This city dances, oblivious, and the war happens elsewhere. He wondered what Mariam would think of this place and felt a pang of nostalgia for France. Before Mariam had disappeared back into Damascus. Before he'd seen that picture of Val.

He opened a fifth bottle of whiskey and downed it quickly. Fucking media leaks. Val had served in secret and was entitled to be buried that way. Instead, some goddamn college yearbook photo was splashed all over the news. It made him furious. He lay on the bed and waited for sleep, but in its place was a mental slideshow of a dead friend and her crazy laugh from Baghdad. When daybreak finally arrived, he brewed coffee on the room machine and drank it in silence watching the fountain, now naked and unilluminated in the comedown of the Vegas dawn. He set down the coffee cup and turned one of the empty Jack Daniel's bottles over in his hands.

Drinks back home in a few weeks, Val had said.

VAL OWENS DIED BEFORE THE annual Memorial Ceremony, so the stone carvers had time to chisel the 134th star into the marble wall exactly six inches to the right of the 133rd. The calligrapher inking the mortal harvest into the goatskin-bound *Book of Honor*, held in a case jutting from the wall, added a similar black star but no name. Valerie Owens was under diplomatic cover at the time of her death and her role at the Agency remained classified.

The lobby was crammed with Agency brass, approved reporters, families of the dead, and anyone else able to squeeze into the Original Headquarters Building lobby. The Director did not utter her name during the ceremony. Unwashed masses, lacking blue badges and Top Secret/Sensitive Compartmented Information security clearances, filled the audience.

Sam stood in the back. Scanning over the seated crowd, he saw a middle-aged woman with tousled gray hair in the front, sobbing as the Director described the recent loss of a case officer in a Middle Eastern country. It was Val's mother, Joanna. Val's dad was dead.

Sam had never thought much about CIA officers killed in the line of duty. Most were Special Activities Division paramilitary guys—Ground Branch, typically—who died in a war zone engaged in something that more closely resembled combat than it did intelligence collection. But this was different. Looking at the star, it was as if Val had been annihilated save for an etching in the wall.

The Director thanked everyone for coming, praised the fallen with vague honorifics, and the crowd began to shuffle away. Sam cut through the crowd for Joanna Owens. Her cheeks were red, eyes wild with the despair of a mother who'd outlived her only child. Sam shoved past a faceless well-wisher and gave Joanna a bear hug. "I knew her in Baghdad, she was like a sister to me then," he said. "I'm so sorry." Joanna cried. He stood back, wanting to say that CIA would do its best to find her daughter's killer. But he had no idea if Joanna knew her daughter had been murdered, or if Langley would ultimately try to avenge Val. He held her eyes. "I'm so sorry," he said again. She sniffled and nodded. Guilt rising, he turned away and pushed through the throng to leave the lobby.

SAM TRAVELED TO DAMASCUS ON an economy-class ticket purchased by the Global Deployment Center under Agency Regulation 41-2, stipulating that any journey must "meet or exceed thirteen hours in duration, including layovers, to merit the purchase of an airfare above Basic Economy Class—or its nearest equivalent—on a U.S. carrier (Delta, American, United, etc.)." He'd argued with the old lady in Deployment that a good night's sleep in a lie-flat seat would really help the jet lag, but she didn't budge. The lowest available fare had a total one-way trip of twelve hours forty-seven minutes.

Sam connected through Vienna because Austrian Air was one of the few Western carriers still flying into Damascus. He was just nodding off when the pilot announced they'd begun the steep descent into Damascus International Airport and everybody just hold on tight. He did not explain why, but Sam knew: a rapid drop lowered the aircraft's profile in case rebels wanted to sling a shoulder-fired missile into the plane. His stomach swung past his head as the pilot dropped through the chop.

Out the window he saw the smoke wafting in columns from a few of the embattled suburbs and the sprawl of stone apartments coating the desert floor. From the air the suburban ring around the city appeared like an endless string of cinder blocks. The city center, the ancient Old City, was dotted by minarets and the green of parks. It was beautiful from the air and for a moment allowed him to forget the danger Mariam faced, to push from his mind Val's scream as he'd careened out of Damascus during his only previous visit to this city.

The wheels slammed into the runway and the pilot offered a half-hearted welcome. Sam looked around. No one appeared thrilled to have arrived.

SAM DEPLANED AND FOUND THE embassy expediter waiting at the gate, as specified in the cable confirming his PCS (permanent change of station) to Damascus. The man shook his hand, welcomed Sam to Syria, and he hustled them off at a near-run. Clearing passport control, they arrived at baggage claim, where Procter waited. The Chief, unsmiling, sported aviator sunglasses and an olive drab blazer meant for a polar climate. In the presence of the expediter—a Foreign Service National, or FSN—they said nothing. Sam collected his single suitcase from Damascus International's baggage claim area: conveyor belts inoperable, the bags collecting in sloppy piles, passengers thronged about like the refugees he'd seen jostling for sacks of flour in Baghdad. Whisked through customs, he wheeled his bag through the dusty terminal and into the blazing light of the afternoon.

Like all competent expediters throughout the Arab world, the man had parked illegally: a white embassy Land Cruiser sat smack in front of the terminal with its flashers blinking. Procter waved the expediter off, sending him to another car—no doubt parked legally, some distance away—and took the wheel. Sam opened the back to toss in his suitcase, noting the odd presence of a shovel before hearing the Chief's comforting first words: "Rebels kidnapped some Republican Guard guys on the airport road this morning, so I'm here to keep you safe, make sure you don't end up dead on day one."

Five minutes into the drive, they hit the first checkpoint. They showed their black diplomatic passports and were waved through without even a quick examination of the bags in the back. The airport was thirty minutes southeast of the city. "We'll go from war to peace in about twenty minutes," Procter said. Sam took in the palm trees, the ubiquitous billboards littered with regime propaganda, and the cinder-block suburbs. The situation had worsened since the operation to rescue Val and KOMODO. As they neared the city, they passed shuttered strip malls, restaurants, and auto-body shops that appeared abandoned to some long-ago apocalypse.

Procter played tour guide as they drove. "Rebels have started to hit regime soldiers and militia on this road," she said, gesturing to the scrubby plains flanking the airport highway. "Sometimes it's kidnappings, sometimes they fling a goddamn rocket-propelled grenade into the car like *whoosh*." The Chief made an unsettling gesture toward the Land Cruiser's windshield. "Before you move around in this city you make peace with your god."

When they reached Jaramana, another restive suburb, they hit five more checkpoints. Each uneventful, yet pulse-quickening with uncertainty. Procter, rolling up her window after checkpoint number five, captured the feeling well: "Never know when one of these teenagers is going to decide to have some fun with us." Three attack helicopters hovered above the suburb, machine guns rattling into the rubble. The Guard had blocked off the entrances, but Sam could see that most of the buildings inside had been shattered: whole sides cleaved off, concrete pockmarked by shell fire, surfaces soot-blackened from explosions. "It's like Afghanistan in there," Procter said. "Without the joyful atmosphere."

The world brightened inside central Damascus. Shops were still open, sidewalk cafés peopled, buildings whole, traffic bustling. Procter parked her car on the sidewalk of the circle outside the embassy. "I'll show you around," she said, unbuckling and jumping out of the vehicle. They left Sam's bag in the trunk and walked west outside the embassy's white stone walls. The stone was about ten feet high, topped by another fifteen feet of fencing designed to prevent climbers from gaining a foothold. "No real setback from the road here, huh?" Sam said.

"Yep, big-ass problem," Procter said. "Back in '06 some terrorists tried to drive a truck bomb through the front door. Not much stopping anyone, except the midget pylons on the sidewalk." They entered on the western side and went through the metal detectors under the watchful eyes of three Marine guards. Sam already had his badge, so they walked into the embassy's chancery building and Procter gave him the codes to open the doors. "Floor two," she said, "the State bigwigs. Ambassador, Deputy Chief of Mission, the Political and Economic Sections. Ambo has a SCIF in there we sometimes use for briefings. Third floor is Marines and the commo freaks, all their antennas and shit. That, by the way, is where we rally if things go all Tehran '79 on us," she said.

"Now the basement," she said, pointing down a plaster-flaked hallway with a spasmodic bank of fluorescent lights and a bathroom—door ajar—at the end. "This is us. Welcome to Damascus Station." She approached the metallic vault door, punched a code, and heard the buzz. She swung open the slab.

Sam had become accustomed to the rustic nature of the CIA's Middle Eastern real estate during his first tour in Cairo. Damascus Station was no different. It was bathed in artificial light and held fewer than ten desks, all eerily empty as though there had been layoffs, or a plague—not impossible, given the recycled air. The austerity sprang from the fear of ransacking. Hard drives were removed from the computers each evening, papers shuffled into the acid-boosted shredders or safes, and personal effects were discouraged. Television monitors beamed security footage of the area outside the Station's heavy vault door.

Procter walked him to his desk. The rebel flag and a portrait of Bashar al-Assad fluttered in front of a vent.

The first thing he noticed in Procter's office was the shotgun.

One of her Moscow case officers had mentioned it. Procter kept a Mossberg combat shotgun propped in the corner of her office next to the trash can, a gross violation of several Agency regulations. A sign taped above it read PULL IN CASE OF HOSTAGE CRISIS.

When he entered the prison-cell office—windowless, ten-by-five, furnished with only a small desk and a table—Sam saw that her desk was covered in greasy wrappers and pita crumbs. Procter removed her blazer and tossed it on the floor. She wore a black tank top, and with her back turned he could see imprinted on her lats a tattoo of seven simple stars in a line, the words *IN HONOR* marked above. A personal memorial wall inked on her back. Procter then explained she wanted to dive into the ATHENA ops plan, which Sam thought was pretty aggressive given he'd been in Syria for about an hour and a half and had not slept in a day. He recalled the verdict on Procter: Energizer bunny. She stood at her empty whiteboard and picked up a red marker as if she had an idea. But she wrote nothing. Then she set the marker down. She looked at her clock, then pointed at the door.

"Time to get out so I can meditate."

17

THE PACKET OF SVR INFORMATION ARRIVED IN ALI'S office on Wednesday, as it did every week, one of the fruits of an agreement struck between Assad and Putin for Russian support against the rebels. The new intel from Russia's Foreign Intelligence Service was an improvement from the drivel the SVR provided prior to the unrest, in the salad days when Syria had not been at the heart of the proxy war between Washington and Moscow.

Ali, flipping through the papers, learned that the Americans, even after the recent arrests, had recruited a new source. He read an intriguing report titled: "SYRIAN PRESIDENTIAL PALACE PERSONALITIES AND POWER DYNAMICS." It was very accurate.

It concluded with a short commentary paragraph drafted by the SVR's Middle East Department in clunky Arabic:

SVR SOURCE ALSO REPORTS RUMORS OF NEW, HIGHLY-PLACED CIA ASSET IN SYRIA. SOURCE ELICITED INFORMATION DURING INFORMAL EXCHANGES. SVR FOLLOWING UP TO PROVIDE MORE DETAILS.

The SVR did not describe their source, but Ali assumed the Russians had an asset inside the CIA or the Israeli Mossad, because the digital scan of the actual CIA report in the packet had a banner that read: "TS//HCS//OC REL ISR." The "REL ISR" meant it had been cleared for release to the Israelis.

Ali called Kanaan and asked for the reports from the U.S. Embassy. The *mukhabarat* officers monitoring the building submitted daily reports logging the arrivals and departures of every American.

Waiting, he finished a cigarette and called Layla for no reason.

Layla was explaining that the electricity was out, an increasingly common frustration even in Ali's neighborhood, when Kanaan entered with the papers. He left them on the desk. Ali told Layla he would call her back.

He started reading. There were pictures and commentary on each American official. Some were listed as "Suspected CIA" or "Confirmed CIA." These categories represented more than twenty names. Then he saw a name he did not recognize: Second Secretary Samuel Joseph. Nor did he recognize his face, which he now saw in the grainy pictures of Mr. Joseph entering the embassy at 7:56 a.m. and departing again at 11:45 a.m., probably for lunch, then heading back for the afternoon before clocking out for the day at 6:48 p.m. The report labeled him "Suspected CIA" and noted that he'd been in Damascus for two days.

He called Kanaan and asked him to scour the records departments at the various *mukhabarat* agencies to determine if they knew anything about this Samuel. Ali closed the reports and shifted to the other pile of paper on his desk. Ali wore the unofficial uniform of the Syrian *mukhabarat:* plain white collared shirt, loose-fitting black slacks, and scuffed black leather shoes. Nondescript, functional, and cheap—an international detective uniform. The top two buttons of his shirt were undone because of the heat. Another summer of war on the way, he thought. Certainly not the last.

He turned his chair to the window and scanned the eastern sky, the sun's hazy rays illuminating the city's rebellious suburbs. He thumbed through a report on Republican Guard operations in Douma. Rustum's men had finally sealed off the district last night, closing down what they thought was the last of the tunnels. The strategy was collective punishment: seal off a restive area and contain the population until they hated the rebels for inciting the regime's terror. Until they turned on them.

Then he came to the pictures. Victims with names, some biographical information, causes of death. Some pictures only included pieces of the dead, the remainder presumably lost or misplaced amid the skittering bullets, mortar fire, or jerry-rigged bombs dropped, inaccurately of course, from the government's ancient fleet of Soviet fighter planes. All the victims were emaciated, many were children. He put the report down. His mind drifted to his own boys, and then to the conversation with Layla when it all began.

APRIL 2011. IT HAD BEEN the first spring in the new and crumbling Syria, just four weeks after the protests started. They'd left the twins with Layla's mother for the afternoon and taken a basket stuffed with mezze and Syrian wine to a secluded ridge on Mount Qasioun overlooking the city. He felt the anger in the air and knew then that everything was falling apart. He told Layla so. The *mukhabarat* shooting innocents, the demonstrations growing, the criminals and jihadis lurking in the shadows, the kidnappings and torture, the rebels painting red X's on Alawi doors to mark them for death. The chaos was embryonic, sure, but it was there. He was looking closely, tracing its patterns to understand if he would survive. He and Layla talked through the choices, as everyone did: leave, stay and support the President, join the demonstrators, keep your head down.

They were all bad options.

But the choice had been simple. They did not have the resources to take their extended family along if Ali fled. And, given his role in the regime, he could have been arrested for war crimes depending on the destination. Leaving Syria would be a death sentence for many relatives, and potentially for him. Defection to the opposition would be even worse for his family. The government would arrest them, confiscate their property, torture and kill a few to make the point.

"What do you think of Assad?" Layla asked after her third glass of wine. "Do you support the government?" She'd never asked before, and he'd never volunteered an opinion.

Ali decided to tell Layla the truth, knowing he never would again. "Assad is going to kill his way out with all of us lashed to his throne. He will take our souls."

That sufficed for an answer because it left just one option. Stay put, keep your head down.

He had felt like a coward. He still did.

KANAAN VICTORIOUSLY WAVED A FOLDER in the air as he entered Ali's office. He slid a copy across the desk. "Something interesting from one of the officers in Paris. Mohannad al-Bakry. One of the clerks in records knows him. Notorious for over-filing. He drafts regular surveillance reports on the embassy staff. They of course despise him."

"Naturally."

"But in this case al-Bakry's fastidiousness has served us well, because he filed a report just a few weeks ago mentioning Samuel Joseph."

Ali's pulse jolted. He again felt like a detective beginning to unravel a long thread. In this moment he was an investigator, not an accomplice to mass murder.

"It describes an interaction between Samuel Joseph and a Palace official named Mariam Haddad," Kanaan continued.

"Haddad?" Ali's brow furrowed. He lit a cigarette.

"Yes, old Damascene Christian family."

"Everyone knows them. What does the report say?" Ali asked.

"Well, al-Bakry writes here that Mariam and this Samuel struck up a conversation at a diplomatic event in Paris. Apparently he tried to warn her against speaking with Americans, but she told him off. He describes the interaction as 'warm and friendly with amorous overtones.'"

Ali laughed. "She might have just thought he was an attractive American diplomat and struck up a conversation to pass the time. And why not tell al-Bakry off? She comes from a good family, she can tangle with a low-level *mukhabarat* officer."

Kanaan reached into his briefcase, pulled out a photo, and slid it to Ali. "As you can see, she is quite—er—striking. It is easy to see why al-Bakry may have been jealous."

Ali looked at the picture of her state identification card. Long dark hair, lightly spun and whorled like Layla's.

"Let's talk to Mariam."

"Of course, General, I'll arrange it."

The desk phone rang as Kanaan stood to leave. Unfortunately, Ali recognized the number. "Hello, big brother," he said.

"Little brother," said Rustum. "I am running an errand tomorrow and had a question about a detail from Marwan Ghazali's testimony." At the mention of the dead spy, Ali again felt Rustum's weight pinning him down in the interrogation room. He coughed.

"What detail?" Ali said.

"In one of your reports you wrote that Ghazali said he provided a list of SSRC employees to the CIA. Potential sub-sources, I believe. He claimed they were unwitting."

"That's right," said Ali. "We've been monitoring many of them, just to be sure."

"Was Colonel Daoud Haddad on the list?"

"He was not on the list," Ali said. Rustum hung up without a word.

Ali set down the desk phone. A lack of caffeine had turned into a throbbing headache and he wanted to think about an investigation. Anything other than Rustum, Basil, Marwan Ghazali, Valerie Owens. He dismissed Kanaan and asked his assistant for tea. Then he creaked back in his chair, pressing his thumbs into his temple to dull the pain. He wondered if Samuel Joseph's arrival was connected to the CIA's new source. The CIA Station transitioned officers frequently, he knew. It could be just another rotation. But what if the two were linked?

He did not yet know how Mariam fit into the picture, but something spoke to him from beyond the reports, something buried deep in the maze of his investigator's brain. There is something here. Unravel it.

18

RUSTUM'S ARMORED LEXUS SUV ZIGZAGGED THROUGH the concrete barriers outside the airfield and pulled onto the tarmac. Several staff cars, including Basil's, were parked in a triangle next to a Russian-made MiG-29 bomber that was fueling on the runway, their headlamps illuminated in the early morning darkness. A tractor-trailer pulled between the cars and the plane. Rustum signaled to his driver to stop. Armored personnel carriers maneuvered into positions covering the airfield's perimeter as a helicopter whirred overhead. Jumping down from the car, Rustum nodded to Basil and approached Colonel Daoud Haddad and one of his technicians. The men stood over a computer resting on the hood of a battered white Toyota pickup. Flaking paint on the door marked it as SSRC.

They shook hands as a bomb lift truck drove toward the plane. "Colonel," Rustum said as they shook hands. "Thank you for arranging a team so quickly. This is a highly sensitive matter. I am glad you could personally oversee it."

"Of course, Commander," Daoud said.

As the lift truck passed by, Rustum noticed Daoud eyeing the green paint on the bomb's midsection, the Soviet indicator for chemical munitions. Basil sidled up next to Daoud, who took a step away, smiling politely as he did so.

"We'll need your men to load the components into these bombs and one of your technicians to interpret the results of the test," Rustum said. "We've installed sensors at the site."

Daoud nodded. "We are not going to the proving grounds for the test?"

Rustum shook his head. "No. Somewhere else today. A new site." Daoud huddled up his team and explained the requirements. Their forklift carried the drums alongside the bomb lift truck. The operator had opened the munition's compartments and Daoud's team filled them with care, measuring the output of each component using sensors on their rubber vacuum hoses. Daoud gave Rustum a thumbs-up fifteen minutes later as the bomb lift operator drove the vehicle away from the plane. The pilot was now in the cockpit performing preflight checks.

"A very light wind at the site, Commander," an aide said to Rustum.

He nodded. "Get Daoud and his team loaded up, let's go."

THIRTY MINUTES OUTSIDE DAMASCUS, THE convoy of Rustum's staff car, three Republican Guard jeeps, and two armored personnel carriers stopped on a hilltop stretch of road overlooking the village of Efreh. The town, perched on an opposing hill, was a ramble of stone huts cut by a single road, a mosque on the southern end. Rustum saw the lights of the bomber appear to the north, beyond the village. It was still dark. The only light in Efreh came from a small hut, a fire still burning on its roof. Rustum had not wanted to bring another SSRC official into his confidences, but he required Branch 450's expertise today in Efreh, and Colonel Daoud Haddad was considered loyal.

Rustum kicked his boot into the gravel and got out of his car to stretch. "Bring Haddad over," he told his aide. Haddad hustled over. "Commander?"

The captain spread a map on the hood of the Lexus. It was spotted with red dots. "We've placed sensors in a grid pattern throughout the village," Rustum told Daoud. "We've also put some of them in an old tunnel complex the terrorists used. We want to see how effectively they spread underground. Now tell me, where should we drop the bombs?"

Daoud now picked at the back of his neck as he looked from the map to the village, asking one of his technicians for the wind speed and direction. Presently, Daoud pointed to a spot on the map a few hundred yards south of the village. "Given the light southern wind, I would drop the munitions here. The wind will then carry them over the village."

Rustum nodded and gestured toward his aide for the walkie-talkie. The jet now circled overhead. He clicked the walkie-talkie and read the coordinates from the map.

The explosions tore into an olive grove on the hill's southern tip. Four plumes shot skyward, then clumped together and eventually engulfed Efreh. The town was empty and silent. Rustum watched through binoculars, his gaze settling on a single home resting in the shade of the mosque. Some of the men played cards on the armored vehicles. Daoud stared at the computer screen with his technician.

One of the officers wandered between vehicles offering cigarettes. A few sat asleep and upright in the armored personnel carrier's ragged leather seats. Basil whittled on a stick with his knife, staring at the same house in the village. He had overseen the operation to clear the village, and it had been bloody.

"We should take Haddad in with us," Rustum said. Basil nodded, keeping his eyes locked on the house.

The smoke dissipated as the sun rose.

After twenty minutes Rustum approached Daoud and the technician and asked for a preliminary report. Sarin, he knew, is deadliest when inhaled as an aerosol. The sensors he had ordered his men to place throughout Efreh would monitor the sarin's airborne persistence and the radius of contamination. In some parts of the test site the toxicity would be sufficient to kill everyone. In others, people would merely become sick.

"The coverage is good, Commander," Daoud said. "I'm seeing lethal persistence in most sectors. The exception is the row of sensors at the northern end. There I'm seeing concentrations that would lead to severe, not lethal, effects. The winds were calm, which also helped focus the dispersion." Daoud's voice was pinched. The man could tell something was wrong.

Rustum placed a hand on Daoud's shoulder. It was time. "Shall we examine the town, Colonel? A few of my men have not seen it since the clearing operation. They are anxious to return." He smiled at Daoud.

Daoud looked down at the village. "To gather up the sensors, Commander?"

Basil laughed.

ALL OF THE SARIN HAD evaporated—Daoud, to Rustum's irritation, had explained it to them twice—but Rustum had a healthy respect for the gas and ordered the small search party to don protective suits. They entered the first home. Plastic chairs were overturned near a woodstove. Spent rounds littered the floor by the window. A selection of clothes—a white shirt, a baby's left shoe, a kaffiyeh, camouflage vests—lay crumpled about, mapping the transition from home to rebel outpost. Rustum saw the hatch built into the flooring. It was nailed down from the outside, and he motioned for two men to pry it open.

It creaked as they worked it loose with crowbars and knives until the men succeeded in tearing it loose. One of the officers threw it aside and disappeared into the darkness down the plywood ladder. Basil followed him. Rustum smiled through his fogging mask and slapped Daoud, now ashy white, on the back. "Your turn, Colonel," he said. Daoud looked toward the door, then at the baby shoe. He nodded and slowly descended the ladder. Rustum followed, his eyes adjusting to the tunnel's blackness as he reached the bottom, nearly twenty feet beneath the hut.

Daoud faced one of the walls, his mask on the floor. He was hunched over and dry-heaving. Rustum slapped Daoud on the back. "You are like a blind painter, my friend, finally seeing your handiwork for the first time." He laughed. "What do you think?"

Basil swept his flashlight over the bodies before focusing on a man who looked about seventy. Rustum saw the spittle around the mouth and the throbbing red haloing the eyes. He patted the dead man's cheeks. Basil walked farther into the tunnel to inspect the line. He stopped and knelt over a teenage boy. "This one almost bit his hands off trying to escape, Commander."

"Are they all dead?" Rustum asked.

"It appears so."

Rustum took Daoud's shoulder and pointed him down the line of fifty-seven bodies. They'd counted the prisoners after the operation to clear the village. "They'd have done the same to us if they could," Rustum said as he kicked at a woman's bare foot. "Even the women. Do not forget that, Colonel."

Daoud stared down the corridor.

"I count on your discretion," Rustum said. "You are a good soldier." He led Daoud farther into the tunnel, stopping when they came to a young girl with closed eyes and an open mouth. "Even if your daughter does not know when to keep her mouth shut."

19

ON HIS FIRST WEEKEND IN DAMASCUS, SAM WALKED the Old City to see the typical tourist sites: the Umayyad Mosque, Souq Al-Hamadiya the Street Called Straight, the Ananias Chapel, a half dozen more. He took pictures, he purchased trinkets and swag with Assad's face on it for his brothers. He smiled stupidly at checkpoints, handing over his black diplomatic passport and explaining how grateful he was to be in Damascus. He stayed in the pocket of the city center. The route appeared normal for any new American diplomat. And it was.

The stops were preparation for a set of SDRs he'd designed since leaving France. He scanned for fixed surveillance, for cameras, he took in the city's terrain and its feel. He felt watched everywhere.

He drank bitter coffee at a tumbledown café in Kafr Sousa as the afternoon *salat*, the call to prayer, rang out from the muezzin loudspeakers. When it concluded, he left and walked toward a jewelry store, where he planned to purchase something for his mother. On the way he strolled past a building marked SYRIAN ARAB REPUBLIC MINISTRY OF AGRICULTURE AND AGRARIAN REFORM.

He passed another building up the street and saw a bank of windows facing the road. He noted the address, the phone number for the leasing company, and then the *mukhabarat* tail bumper-locking him. He continued to the jewelry store, where he examined the inventory for an hour: silver, ornate gold, mother-of-pearl. He settled on a big silver ring. Crafted in Aleppo, it resembled a flower.

The poor *mukhabarat* guy looked very bored as he watched the shopping trip from outside the store.

THE BANDITOS HAD ALSO ARRIVED in Damascus.

Sam—in his role as State communications officer (second secretary)—had called Rami from his office and asked if he and his brothers would consider discussing the business environment in Syria with the ambassador. "We would value your perspective on the economy, given your vast commercial interests," Sam had said.

The brothers had made the requisite calls to clear a meeting at the U.S. Embassy: the Interior Ministry, Military Intelligence, General Intelligence, Political Security, Air Force Intelligence, the Palace. All consented. Military Intelligence faxed talking points to use with the Americans. Rami threw them away.

Sam greeted the brothers at the embassy, ushered them into the chancery, past the ambassador's office, and into the metallic SCIF used by the State Department team upstairs.

Instead of the ambassador they met with Sam and Procter for two hours. They covered the waterfront: safe house provision, the logistics of reopening the family's Damascus villa, the creation of a business rationale for their return.

"Guys, no one is going to ask questions as long as we make the right payments," Yusuf said as he picked at a hamburger from the embassy commissary. "There is a long list of bribes, but once that's done they won't care why we're back. Lots of sons of the regime sunning themselves in Beirut, like we were."

The CIA would put $500,000 into the BANDITOs' escrow account to cover start-up expenses. Sam slid the address for the building he had scouted across the table. Yusuf picked up the paper, read it, and handed it back.

"We'll take care of it," Yusuf said.

"We still need the high-level accounting, like before," Sam said. Always an embarrassing topic. Sometimes DO Finance audited operational accounts and asked nosy questions.

Elias laughed. "We should work for the DGSE, no way the French are asking for paperwork."

"Just don't write down the bribes," Sam said.

A CHUNK OF THE BANDITOS' cash went toward the provision of a new safe house (Directorate of Operations Finance category: Housing).

Rami, under the auspices of a shell company, had paid six months' rent on a cramped ninth-floor office. Sam had specified the location, including the required view, but not the target. Not yet.

The SDR to the new office required ten hours. Rami greeted Sam at the door and apologized with a grin that they'd already eaten dinner. "We started doubting you'd make it. We left you some cold shawarma, though."

The office was a testament to whitewashed corporatist style: particleboard desks, faux-black-leather chairs, disconnected Avaya desk phones, cheap gray carpet. It could have been anywhere. But it was in Kafr Sousa, one block from the Security Office.

Yusuf showed Sam the two cramped cubicles and led him into the conference room. The air smelled of chemical wash and paint. A fluorescent light hummed above. The room hurt Sam's eyes.

"Internet and phones will be connected on Tuesday," Rami said.

"Good. I'll send someone to sweep the place on Wednesday," Sam said. A tech from the Station had visited yesterday for the initial scrub.

Sam poured a glass of lukewarm white wine and picked up the shawarma, its once-white wrapper now translucent from grease. They sat at the table. Elias refilled his glass and smacked Sam on the shoulder as he walked behind him.

"Good to be back in Damascus," he said without conviction.

Sam lifted his glass. "To our work together."

"And that we all make it through the war to grow old," Yusuf said. They clinked glasses and drank.

"Let's talk about the view," Sam said, knowing he had about fifteen minutes.

Elias stood and motioned toward the cubicles. Sam and his brothers followed. Elias and Sam squeezed into the cubicle closest to the conference room. The square window, cut into the middle of the wall, provided a direct line of sight to the Security Office's main entrance. Elias oriented Sam.

"Two entrances, far as we can tell. This one and a smaller one on the western side. Used to be the Agriculture Ministry. Obviously, it's not anymore."

The entrance was about two hundred yards down the street. Sam could see the concrete berms, a small guard hut, and a manually operated gate. Three guards holding AK-47s loitered outside. Behind them, a cinder-block wall surrounded the building.

Sam looked at the street below. Cars were parked on the sidewalks. He saw *mukhabarat* officers weave between them as they approached the gatehouse, where they would flash a badge before walking into the entrance courtyard. He looked down the road at the parked cars and the *mukhabarat* officers snaking around them. He watched a man bump into the trunk of a car as he walked past.

They returned to the conference room and sat down. Sam pulled a photograph of Ali from the compartment in his bag and put it on the table. He registered the thought that he was usually planning to recruit foreign officials, not kill them. The prospects of a lethal covert action finding against Ali Hassan had changed all of that.

"This stays in this room, no outsourcing. It's a lot to ask, but I need some combination of the three of you to hold watch here for a week. I want to know when this man, General Ali Hassan, enters and exits the building. The usual. Time-stamped logs, photographs, and the street he takes when he arrives and exits."

Rami looked at the photo and asked: "Who is he?"

"Runs the Palace's Security Office. Bad dude."

"Want us to follow him on the street?"

"Not yet. Just the building for now. And all watching from this office."

Elias smiled, watching Sam's brain work through the angles. "I wish I knew what you were thinking right now, man," he said.

"Trust me, you don't."

20

THE USB STICK JAMMED INTO SAM'S RIGHT RUNNING shoe had arrived in an orange diplomatic pouch. It had been designed by the CIA's Directorate of Science and Technology at exceptional cost to the American taxpayer, contained fifty terabytes of storage, and housed a malicious software program that could pirate the contents of a computer in ten seconds. That did not sound like long, but it would feel like an eternity for Mariam. She'd agreed to the idea in France. It was part of the deal, they both knew. She had signed up to work for CIA. But he still felt sick. His feelings for her nagged. They made him feel less like a CIA case officer and more like a manipulative boyfriend.

The stick pinched his heel as he jogged past a restaurant onto one of Qasioun's overlooks. He stopped and stretched, using the opportunity to again check for surveillance as he took in the view. The evening was cool for summer, and a light wind bristled the pines. The lights of central Damascus illuminated as homes and shops and restaurants prepared for the evening. The suburbs were dark.

At the start of his run, near his apartment, a *mukhabarat* gorilla had aggressively bumper-locked him. He'd been a hair tweaked because this was just no fun, having a constant shadow on you.

Now, near the drop site, he felt black.

"HOW FREQUENTLY DOES SAMUEL JOSEPH exercise?" Ali asked Kanaan after waving off the surveillance team. They'd needed the resources for another operation against a man suspected of smuggling weapons for the rebels.

"Probably twice, maybe three times each week," Kanaan said. "Very normal for him."

Ali stared at the map. The single team had tracked him for an hour on a winding run around central Damascus. It had been a waste. He lit a cigarette, wondering if Samuel was a dead end. Then he heard again the little whisper in his head, the one that helped him track down a serial killer on the coast all those years ago, and now it said, *No, you keep at this American*. Ali took a long drag on the cigarette, snuffed out the butt in his ashtray, and called Layla to hear her voice.

FEELING ALONE, SAM CHECKED HIS periphery and the hills above without moving his head. Nothing. The path ahead cut steeply upward until it turned to the right. He began sprinting up the hill. His legs and lungs burned. Cold sweat ran down his forehead. The path evened out and he emerged from the pines. He saw the retaining wall drop site twenty yards ahead. It looked identical to the image from Procter's tablet in France.

He sprinted closer, now risking an obvious look back to see if anyone trailed him. He was still alone. Ten feet from the trash pile, he eyed the unlabeled can. Kneeling down, he lifted the lid from the can, pulled the USB stick from his shoe, and placed it inside.

He finished tying his shoe and set off down the path.

TERROR HAD ACCOMPANIED MARIAM SINCE France. She lay with it in bed, recognized it in Razan's eyes. It pricked her neck when she strolled the Old City. She waited for the *mukhabarat*. She waited for

Jamil Atiyah's assassins to return. She used the moves Sam taught her in Nice to watch for the watchers. She carried a hunting knife in her purse and in her room practiced unsheathing it, gutting an assailant, slashing the neck and chest and face.

She also felt the lightness return to her chest, because she'd chosen a side and taken back control. The fear, oddly, confirmed the righteousness of her decision to spy. The espionage set her against a murderous government, but the fright lingered because the opponent still stood. She had not yet won. Maybe she never would.

Now, in her office, Mariam rubbed her clammy palms into the couch's upholstery and checked her face to confirm she was not sweating as she slipped the USB stick into the pocket of her own binder, closed it, and spread Bouthaina's folder on top. She checked the time. Two minutes until her meeting. She started walking down the hall toward Bouthaina's office, careful not to move too quickly. She noticed her hands did not shake but her heart was racing.

Mariam had asked for an evening meeting at the time when Bouthaina usually took a call from Rustum. Sometimes business-related, sometimes amorous, but always a distraction for several minutes. Sometimes she would shoo Mariam from her office, others Bouthaina would decamp into her palatial washroom. Occasionally, but rarely, she would take the call in front of Mariam. She hoped that would not be the case tonight.

Bouthaina waved in Mariam, who took a seat. Bouthaina donned her Chanel tortoiseshell reading glasses and joined her at the table. Mariam slid the top binder to Bouthaina and began an update on the latest divisions inside the National Council. All of it unsurprising, salacious, delightful to Bouthaina's destructive sensibilities. "We don't even need to do anything, do we, Mariam? They destroy themselves."

Mariam had just finished when Bouthaina's mobile phone rang. Mariam heard her voice shift, almost imperceptible, but she understood the softening tone indicated Rustum was on the other end. Bouthaina excused herself and went into the washroom, closing the door behind.

Mariam stood by the table. Her whole world the toxic USB stick and the stream of sweat on her back. She remembered something Sam had told her in Èze: the operation itself is usually short. The setup, the planning—now, that's arduous. He'd said the Science and Technology folks work on this for years. Probably millions in R&D. Lots of people behind the scenes making it all happen. Analysts, techies, the operators, logistics in Damascus. But it all depends on someone like you having the courage to go into an office and put this into a forbidden computer. Ten seconds, he said, but everything is on the line.

She slipped the USB stick from her own binder and picked up Bouthaina's documents. At the desk she set down the documents—the alibi for her relocation here—and flicked open the cap of the USB stick. She stared at it for what seemed like hours, her conscience struggling to keep pace with the facts unraveling before her. She'd already committed treason, she figured. But had she? Maybe now is the time to walk away. Smash this with a hammer and dump it in the trash.

Her mind never raised the counterpoints because she just stuck the damn thing into the computer and sat down at the desk and began shuffling the papers around as if preparing to leave the binder for Bouthaina to read later.

Then Jamil Atiyah swung open the door.

21

MARIAM'S SKIN WARMED AS IF SHE'D BEEN ROTATED over a fire but she said nothing, looked at him, and smiled big and white.

Atiyah's eyes locked on Mariam, then the desk, then scanned the room, searching for Bouthaina. From her fogged periphery Mariam registered the USB stick blinking green but she could not remove it with Atiyah watching. Atiyah gave a menacing smile and clicked his tongue. He entered the office and closed the door.

"Getting accustomed to the boss's chair, Mariam?" he said.

"Just laying out documents," Mariam said, trying not to stare at the USB stick.

Atiyah had cast an eerie shadow over her life since Villefranche. She assumed he'd intended her as a sacrifice in the race with Bouthaina for Palace prestige, but she still did not really understand why he had targeted her. Now, in Syria, she watched, looking around corners and waiting for the tingle that would announce the presence of his thugs. There had been nothing, and, as Sam told her, that was the maddening part. She could never be sure. The stillness might be a trap.

Atiyah was bald and muscular, but his face and mustache drooped like melted wax. "He looks like that from all the sex," Bouthaina had explained once. "You can't bed thirteen-year-olds and look presentable." Now he looked toward the washroom as a hushed and sexual phone call unfolded inside. Murmurs escaped from beneath the door and a smile spread across Atiyah's face.

"Can you retrieve her? I need her in my office now."

Mariam considered her options. She could not pluck the USB stick from the computer while he watched, and she could not disobey Atiyah. If Bouthaina actually went to his office, Mariam might have a chance to retrieve the thing and leave. Her spine was now a rolling stream—thank God she'd worn a black dress—and her vision was clouded. She realized, though, that she was smiling pleasantly and walking smoothly.

Mariam knocked on the washroom door. "Bouthaina, Jamil Atiyah is here for you. He says it is urgent." She knocked again, this time a bit harder. The murmurs stopped. She heard a harried voice that ended the phone call. Bouthaina opened the door, her cheeks flushed, eyes feral. "Jamil, to what do I owe this honor?" she gritted out.

Atiyah wore an amused smile as he stared past Bouthaina into the washroom.

"My office. Now," he said. He smirked at Mariam, then spun around and left. Bouthaina hustled to her desk in manic silence and began searching for something. Her right hand grazed the USB stick. "Can I do anything, Bouthaina?" Mariam heard herself say. She did not know if she was still standing, but she realized she was smiling like a good subordinate.

Bouthaina looked down at the computer, toward the USB stick. "Nothing now. I'll handle this." She found the folder she sought and stormed from the room.

Mariam would not remember the full chronology of her return home that evening. In its place: fragments. Standing over Bouthaina's desk, yanking the USB stick. Her own office, stuffing a binder in her purse. Dark open skies above the city as she strolled home. The *whump-whump* of mortar fire as if heralding her treason. Falling into bed in her sweat-soaked dress.

And through the adrenaline one sensation above all: her chest airy and unburdened. The absence of the hand that had pressed her down since youth. But my god, the terror.

DAYS LATER THE LITTLE USB stick still felt radioactive. Mariam wanted it gone. So she'd stashed it in the bottom of a vase in her bedroom and loaded the dead drop asking for a brush pass at the site she'd reviewed with Sam back in Èze. She had debated dead-dropping the stick in the can, but it seemed risky. No, it had to be in her possession until she gave it to Sam.

Now Mariam wove through the bustle of the spice market, the Souq Al-Bzouriye, examining the powdery goods as she had as a little girl. She stopped at her favorite stall and took in the scents of star anise, coriander, cinnamon, cardamom, thyme, and a hundred others she couldn't even name. When she was young, she'd enjoyed walking this market with Razan. Now, her purse stuffed with a brown plastic bag filled with cinnamon and a USB stick containing stolen material, she felt her heart crawling around inside her chest amid the usually comforting hubbub of the market. She haggled and purchased a bag of cinnamon identical to the one in her purse. She glanced at the clock on her phone. Just a few minutes. Two more cross streets, then a sharp left.

The covered market defended shoppers from the sun, but Mariam registered slickening sweat on her lower back. The heat and stress were making her feel delirious and she started thinking of the mountain of pain she would climb if the *mukhabarat* saw the brush pass. They'd ask her to start writing and, eventually, would find a lie. This was the torturer's base camp. Then they would move to a light beating, then more questions at a table, then onward to an "examination" administered by some handsy erotomaniacal lesbian, before reaching the sadistic hilltop: the voltage. However one reached the summit, they always found the same thing waiting: the hangman. For all the barbarism, it was paperwork that made the final push toward the noose: drafted by the *mukhabarat,* approved by a Supreme State Security Court magistrate, and embossed with Assad's signature and the *quraysh* hawk of the Syrian coat of arms. Then, a great mercy, the whoosh of the floor disappearing and the final crack of her own neck. Peace.

She reached under her black T-shirt and squeegeed her lower back with her fingers. She pulled her phone from her jeans pocket and checked the time. Mariam took the bag of cinnamon from her purse, the one with the USB stick in it, and brought it to her face. She closed her eyes and inhaled the spicy sweetness and then resealed the bag. She put the bag in her right hand and turned left, back into the spice market, hugging the corner as she walked. The aisles were packed, and Mariam bumped into a woman in a silky pink hijab, apologizing as she double-checked her grip on the bag.

Don't drop it. Don't stop walking. And don't look at him.

Mariam saw Sam appear on her right as she turned the corner. Then she felt him press an identical bag into her chest. She secured it with her left hand while he took the one containing the USB stick from her right. Maintaining her strolling pace, Mariam slid the new bag down to her right hand, where the old had been.

It took less than a second.

Mariam walked to another spice stall and purchased cardamom, relishing the fact that her hands did not shake as she paid. As she left the stall, she paused again to look at the array of spices. The colors had never seemed so vibrant, so alive.

22

"WE ALL KNEW ATHENA'S INTEL WOULD MAKE WAVES," Procter said. "I just didn't expect it to drown us. How's the lady analyst, by the way? Esmerelda? Isn't that the chick from *The Hunchback*? She's a Syrian-Mexican-American, you know." Sam stared blankly, wondering where she was going with all this. "Her dad's one hundred percent Syrian, born in the States, and her mother's a Mexican," Procter said. "Born in Mexico. Now, is Esmerelda a Mexican name?"

Sam shrugged. "I have no idea, Chief. She goes by Zelda. I don't know about the Spanish, but she speaks passable Levantine Arabic."

Zelda Zaydan was the topic of conversation because she had arrived in Damascus on TDY, temporary duty, to exploit the intelligence from Bouthaina's computer. The part about the name agitated Procter, for some reason. "That's like me saying you can just call me Temis. I go by Temis from now on. Whatever." She gave two thumbs down. Sam pressed on.

"Zelda's getting her TDY pack set up now," Sam said, not taking the bait. "Techs say the exploitation computer arrived from Fort Meade this morning." The machine, unconnected to any Agency network, would test if the Syrians had infected the USB stick with malware. The Diplomatic Security team had also scanned it for explosives and poisons. The odds were slim, but Hizballah had placed explosives in cell phones they knew would be captured, hoping to blow an officer to smithereens as the CIA tried to crack into it.

"Perfect, just in time," Procter said. "Girl's got a ton of work to do."

ON THE FIRST AFTERNOON SAM noticed a thick stack of printed reports on Zelda's desk. The top one, a DI assessment, was titled "Intelligence Assessment—Chemical Weapons Programs: Case Studies from the Soviet Union, Egypt, Iraq, and Syria." She also had a book under the stack, *Nerve Agent Precursors and Production Methods.* Zelda saw him looking at the title. "That's a good one," she said. "Commissioned during the Reagan administration. It's got the recipe for industrial sarin used in the U.S. and the Soviet Union. Syrians use a very similar cookbook."

Zelda stood to stretch. Sam flipped open the book. "So, how are you going to do this?"

"I start searching for every possible sarin precursor chemical, scouring every bill of materials on this computer," she said. "Then we'll have a list of suspected shell companies. From there, we can burrow back and follow the money into the Palace. Assuming most of the accounting is complete, we should be able to see the quantities."

She put her hands on her hips and blew a giant gum bubble. She spat out the gum and put on her headphones.

IT WOULD TAKE TWO DAYS to get an answer, during which Zelda drank, Sam estimated, five gallons of bitter Station coffee and slept for a total of four hours. The lack of sleep was Procter's fault. The Chief, anxious to peel the onion on the op, gave Zelda an absurd deadline to speed things along. "We make her earn her TDY per diem," Procter had said. "All hundred and thirty-eight dollars of it." So when Zelda beckoned Sam and Procter to her desk thirty-six hours later, the analyst looked run-down. This, he thought, seemed to please Procter's managerial sensibilities. Zelda's clothes were rumpled and there was a streak of labneh on her pants. But the analyst was smiling. Procter nodded at the wall. "Analyst brain aneurysm?" she said.

The flaking plaster wall had transformed into a shotgun blast of dozens of Post-its. They were organized into a pyramid, the top of which read "Sarin." Below that were two cards listing the binary components: methylphosphonic difluoride, or DF, and isopropyl alcohol, which Zelda abbreviated as IA. Cascading down were the building blocks of each, like a detonated periodic table: methylphosphonic dichloride, methyldichlorophosphine, hydrogen fluoride, among many more Sam could not read.

Procter wheeled over a chair and sat. "Hit me."

Zelda nodded and positioned herself in front of the littered wall. "Bottom line is they've set up a network to boost their sarin stockpile, facilitated by the Palace, probably for the use of the Republican Guard. I've found evidence that Bouthaina has helped purchase most of the precursor chemicals. At least the ones they can't fabricate in their own factories. Most of it is being shipped to fronts in Lebanon, some in Turkey. From there it's likely smuggled into Syria."

"How much have they procured?" Sam asked.

Zelda opened Excel on her Agency computer and looked at a table. "We're probably missing pieces, but if you add up all the precursors you get something like two thousand metric tons."

"That sounds like a lot," Sam said.

"It is," Zelda said. "Rough rule of thumb for industrial sarin production is inputs weigh eight times the output. So, assuming they cook it right, you get two hundred and fifty metric tons of sarin. Enough for a massive attack. Based on some of these purchase dates, I'd expect they're well into production at this point."

"They could just be sending it to the SSRC for production and storage, right, Jaggers? Procter said, pointing at Sam.

"Jaggers?" Zelda asked.

"GOLDJAGGER." Procter rolled her eyes at Zelda. Sam had never communicated via email with the analyst, so she'd never seen his funnyname. "Joseph's pseudo."

"Ah. Got it. That's a terrible pseudo. Debman's is Willy T. PECKER. He applied for a change. Anyways, on your question, they could be sending it to the SSRC, it's true, but the SSRC production facilities and stockpile have been quiet for almost a year, according to the Israeli SIGINT and imagery. And the Syrians know they have a stockpile sufficient to deter the Israelis from taking out the regime."

Zelda had picked up a pencil and now tapped it on the wall like a metronome, metering her thoughts. "If the Syrians believe their deterrent is secure, why would they buy two thousand tons of precursor material, presumably adding to an already sufficient stockpile?"

"Because they want to use it on the rebels," Sam said softly.

Zelda leaned against the wall, staring into the spackled ceiling tiles. "A lot of it."

"And they don't think they can use the current stockpile because we and the Israelis would detect transport, mixing, and preparation," Sam said.

Procter had started nodding her head vigorously.

"They're right," Zelda said. "Rustum Hassan is no dummy. He knows we've got the SSRC sites scoped for perpetual satellite coverage. We would see the stockpile moving or being prepared. If you want to use the stuff, in combat, right now, you separate it from the SSRC. Set up a compartmented program."

"Where the hell is all of it?" Procter said. "Two thousand tons of material means they have an industrial facility somewhere in-country that's just churning sarin out."

Zelda smiled. "Bouthaina made a mistake in an email, told one of the brokers to send something to Jableh, then changed the location to another Republican Guard facility. I checked it out. NGA did a report on an 'Enigmatic Facility' "—she wiggled her fingers in air quotes around the phrase—"that was located near Jableh. This is nine months ago. Said something was under construction. No flybys since. We should check it out again."

Sam pointed a finger gun at the Assad wall poster and pulled the trigger.

ARTEMIS APHRODITE PROCTER HAD A complicated reputation inside the National Reconnaissance Office and the National Geospatial-Intelligence Agency. There had been some unpleasantness back in Kabul when an argument had concluded with the shoving of two satellite imagery analysts down a flight of stairs in the middle of a Predator op against the Pakistani Taliban. "Accidental," Procter always said. "Unfortunate."

The drama had made it challenging for Procter to conduct resource negotiations with representatives of either agency.

So she called Ed Bradley to grease the skids. "Ed, can you get those nerds to give me a bird?"

BRADLEY CALLED THE CIA'S NATIONAL Reconnaissance Office liaison with the coordinates for the Jableh facility. The liaison scanned a real-time feed depicting the NRO's available orbits, a view so highly classified that his grandchildren would not live to see its public release. The liaison thought the Misty-3 satellite platform might work and called the Mission Manager to provide Jableh's coordinates.

"Well, shit," the NRO Mission Manager said at the morning meeting, sniffing at his coffee cup, itself probably classified, shaped as it was like Misty's balloon and inscribed with the words *Smile, you're on camera.* "We don't have an unlimited supply of these damn birds." By evening the Mission Manager, cranking through his sixth cup of Misty balloon coffee, stood twitching over a greaseball technician who fired Misty's ion thrusters at the satellite's orbital apogee, settling her into a path that would cross Jableh the next morning, local time.

Misty crossed over at precisely 6:43 a.m. local time and snapped seven pictures of the complex with its nine-foot panoramic camera. The images, sent to Washington via an encrypted link, revealed three large warehouses, a collection of tractor-trailers, parked cars—including several marked with the insignia of the Republican Guard—and a small barracks nestled into a mountain valley. The kicker, though, was a cargo truck with a visible license plate. The imagery was distributed to NGA's Middle East and North Africa Analysis Division, where an analyst listening to Tchaikovsky's Piano Trio in A minor on noise-canceling headphones drafted a report eventually disseminated under the title: "15 JUNE: JABLEH COMPLEX ACTIVITY INDICATES REPUBLICAN GUARD AND SSRC AFFILIATION." The analyst's commentary boxes were verbose, but he was a stickler and had run the traps, including typing the truck's license plate number into numerous NGA databases.

The truck, it turned out, was owned by the SSRC's Branch 450: chemical weapons security and transport.

23

AS THE SHELLING PICKED UP AND THE REGIME'S CONTROL of the capital weakened, Damascenes increasingly stayed indoors: the glances furtive, the café sidewalks empty, the neighborhoods insular and vigilant, the restaurants shuttered at random. The electricity was erratic, the darkness like a plague that had even spread to the rich quarters.

So when Uncle Daoud asked to see Mariam and Razan, instead of going to a restaurant the cousins strolled four blocks to Daoud's apartment for a home-cooked meal of dawood basha. They had gathered in the dining room when Aunt Mona had been alive, but no one enjoyed staring at the seat she'd occupied since the family had moved into the apartment in the eighties. Daoud had removed her chair, but that almost made it worse. So, without acknowledging why, they ate huddled around a small table in the kitchen.

Daoud asked questions about the doctor's assessment of Razan's eye, about what she had been reading, about her friends. He was trying to be a good father. Razan was not interested. She sat in her chair picking at the meatballs, wine untouched, eyes—patch still there—focused on the refrigerator behind her father. Mariam wanted to slap Razan for being such an ungrateful *sharmoota,* a petulant child. Give your father a break, we all serve a government you despise—and he's done what he's done so you can eat. Worried that the inner monologue might escape, Mariam took a large sip of the Lebanese wine.

"When do you think you will go back to work?" Daoud asked Razan, who was presently staring down at her plate with her one good eye.

"I don't know." She set down her fork and excused herself for a few minutes.

Daoud smiled at Mariam with exhausted eyes. She scanned his face, suspecting this might be the night. You're not asking him to spy for CIA, Sam had coached, you're asking him to cross a line with you and you only. To share something he knows he should not. He can suspect you work for an intelligence service, but you never mention that. Sometimes CIA may fully recruit a subsource, but often the relationship remains between source and subsource. Am I recruited? Mariam had asked. He'd not wanted to answer that question. It made him uncomfortable, she could tell, and she had felt the same way.

Daoud's back was hunched and his sagging belly made him appear fifteen pounds heavier than he'd been at her cousin's engagement party. His chestnut hair was wispier and thinner than she remembered. He looked like a rumpled scientist who'd just learned an experiment had failed. To her, he mostly just looked sad.

Razan returned to the table with mottled cheeks and wild eyes, ready to spar. She'd made decisions in the bathroom and looked like she wanted to have it out with her father. Mariam was now a bystander.

"I need to speak with you as my father," Razan said. "Not as an employee of the SSRC." He nodded, but his face said he did not want to hear it. "I want to work again with the Coordination Committees," she said as if she was taking a job at a bank. As if middle-fingering the all-powerful Assad were a normal profession.

Daoud was angry now, jaw set, back upright. "Razan, oh, God, no—"

"Stop, Papa, let me finish. I cannot sit by and let our country be destroyed. The protesters are weak, but they are right. I want to be on the right side. The moral side. God's side."

Daoud rubbed his hands through his thinning hair and pushed his chair back from the table. He stared angrily at Razan. "God is not in Syria now, Razan, in case you have not noticed. We've been abandoned to the chaos. There is nothing to do but keep our heads down and ride it out. And if you must bring God into this, what good will come of joining the opposition, eh? You want to help them bring their bloodthirsty jihadi Allah to our country, to kill all of us?"

Now he pointed at the eye and he was crying, and Mariam felt shame at being here in this kitchen, as her uncle came to pieces. "I've already lost your mother," he said. "Don't leave me alone here, in this hell. I can't lose you, too, Razan," he whispered.

There was more to say, but it would have to wait, because someone knocked at the door.

Mariam had the dizzying sensation of watching her body from outside herself. The knock. Syrians knew the knock. Daoud and Razan's eyes confirmed it. Mariam thought of Bouthaina's computer. I didn't make it very far. Short run, even for a spy. She stupidly remembered asking Sam how long most spies served. It depends, he'd said. On what?

Daoud got up to answer the door. There were two *mukhabarat,* and they flashed badges from Political Security. One was barrel-gutted and jowly, carrying fifty pounds more than Daoud. He had a cauliflower nose and a droopy mustache. The other, his subordinate, was short and mousy with a turned-up nose and timorous eyes that appeared glued to the floor. As she had since childhood, Mariam gave the *mukhabarat* officers silent nicknames to calm her fear.

Cauliflower and the Mouse, she pronounced them.

Her heart rate slowed when Cauliflower asked if Razan was at home, and could everyone please show identification. The Mouse collected the state ID cards and Cauliflower, understanding this to be the home of a well-respected colonel in the SSRC, said they would not be long but had to ask Ms. Razan a few questions about her arrest. They offered identification as well, which Mariam thought was polite and decent, since the *mukhabarat* would sometimes just show up in the leather jackets and demand to have a conversation with you. Cauliflower was a colonel. The Mouse a lieutenant.

“Can we do this another time?” Daoud said in annoyance.

The Mouse kept eyeballing the floor, but Cauliflower held firm. “We’ve been asked by General Qudsiyah to have a private chat with Ms. Razan. A follow-up, I’m sure you understand. These must occur frequently, given the, hmmm, I would say unusual terms of her release.” The Mouse coughed. He looked at a lamp.

Qudsiyah was the director of Political Security. He was untouchable, and the mere mention of his name was the end of the argument.

“Last week it was Military Intelligence,” Razan said. “The week before, State Security.” How many of these will there be? Mariam saw her nostrils flare, her voice was pinched and throaty.

Cauliflower looked at Daoud, then back to Razan. “You committed offenses punishable by—”

“Stop,” Daoud said. “Stop, Colonel, it is unnecessary. Razan, speak to these men. How long do you need?”

Razan’s cheeks flushed. She folded her arms across her chest. Stay quiet, girl, Mariam thought, just talk to them and get it over with.

“Ten, fifteen minutes,” Cauliflower said.

MARIAM AND DAOUD SMOKED CIGARETTES on his balcony. He still tended a small garden of potted plants and flowers, as Mona had liked: white jasmine now in summer bloom, damask rose, towering hibiscus flanking the sliding doors. She remembered planting jasmine with Aunt Mona, Razan toddling around, Daoud cooking something inside and laughing with Papa.

There was no laughter inside now. Mariam knew that the visit happening in the kitchen between Cauliflower, the Mouse, and Razan was both civil and debasing, bureaucratic and savage. It was not the knock-down-the-door-and-snatch-you-up varietal. There was no violence, no assault. That had already happened. This was a reminder that you were owned.

The men would ask what Razan had been doing, had anyone from the Coordination Committees contacted her, how are the doctor’s visits? They would write it up into a report that Qudsiyah would probably never read. Then it would go into a file. Military Intelligence had one, so did State Security, and the Security Office probably did, too. They would not share the reports. Paper would sit in filing cabinets in basements. Representatives of the *mukhabarat* would continue to visit Razan for the next few decades. They would come into her home uninvited. Watch her children play, if she ever got around to having them. Some would coyly demand bribes. Others would accuse, probe, and threaten. They would ask the same questions, already knowing the answers.

This time, the conversation took twelve minutes. Cauliflower thanked Razan for cooperating and apologized again to Daoud for the intrusion. He nodded at Mariam and then left with the Mouse in tow.

"Were they decent to you?" Mariam asked.

"Yes. But I can't take any more talk tonight. Papa, can I sleep here? I need to lie down."

"Of course, *habibti,* but don't you want to finish dinner?"

"I'm not hungry."

Razan hugged her father and Mariam and padded back to her childhood bedroom, closing the door.

"I need a whiskey," Daoud said.

HE POURED A FAT FINGER of Johnnie Walker Blue Label—she recognized it as the bottle her father had given Daoud for his last birthday—into two glasses and met Mariam on the balcony. Mariam had always liked this place. The balcony looked directly into another family's apartment and on weekends you could hear the din of Bab Touma's nightlife: partygoers, couples out on dates, women in tight jeans and some in hijabs all dancing in the Old City's bars and restaurants. Now it was eerily quiet and the apartment across the street was black. Daoud drank half his whiskey in the first gulp.

Mariam remembered what he'd said at the engagement party: *The regime broke its end of the deal. Look what happened to Razan. And we have no recourse. We are trapped.*

She looked at her dear uncle's ballooning waistline and his sallow cheeks. A spark in his eyes ignited some nightmare and he rubbed his forehead and scratched at his neck. She glanced at an open sore under his shirt collar where he'd dug in the fingernail. He picked at it and finished the whiskey. He leaned back in his chair to close his eyes and smell the flowers.

Mariam thought she would have to press for information, but as it turned out only one simple question would be required. "What's wrong, Uncle?" she asked.

"We ran a test," he mumbled with his eyes still closed.

"Don't you always?"

"Yes, but this test was on people."

Mariam set down her whiskey. Her hands felt cold.

He opened his eyes and looked at her, again scratching at the sore on his neck. "And it was successful." Then he poured himself another glass. "They are preparing the sarin for war."

MARIAM SNUGGLED INTO BED NEXT to Razan two hours later but did not sleep. She sensed her cousin's warm body and the fluttering of her chest, its gentle ups and downs. Mariam pulled the covers over herself and turned to face her cousin. The patch. Tissues were stuffed under the pillow.

Mariam had asked many questions. Too many, she feared. But Daoud had crossed a line. Several, in fact. The words he'd spoken did not seem real. They made her want to shut down. They kept her from sleep.

In the morning she snuck out early and went to her apartment, where she sat in the closet and wrote a short note, folding it up the way Sam had taught her in France. Satisfied it would fit inside a can, she stuffed it into the bottom of her shoe, put on athletic pants and a long-sleeve white T-shirt, and started out for the mountain.

When she returned to her apartment, she found Razan in the kitchen drinking coffee and reading a magazine. She had snuck out early from her father's place.

"Want to talk about last night?" Mariam asked.

"Not really."

"Have it your way," she said, and went back to her bedroom, sweating out the last of the whiskey as she ran through her Krav movements.

When she finished, she pulled down the window blinds about halfway.

24

DAMASCUS STATION SUBMITTED MARIAM'S INFORMATION to NE Division for immediate processing and publication in cable traffic. The Deputy Chief of Syria Reports at Langley, Louise Boolatte, released the report, muttering to herself that those Syrians are butchers, savages, and monsters. Boolatte, like Damascus Station, wondered if the flagrant violation of POTUS's red line would compel a response from the White House. She doubted it, but what the hell did she know? At this point she was just hustling for the overtime pay. An Exceptional Performance Award wouldn't hurt, either, even if the paper-pushers in DO Finance had recently replaced the cash bonuses with restaurant gift cards.

Boolatte had flagged the report for the Director's evening read book by late afternoon. The Director read it, cursed the Syrian regime, and called the National Security Adviser, who did likewise and said he would convene the Syria Working Group at the White House that evening to discuss, once again, the lethal authorities against Ali Hassan and the chemical weapons plotting coming out of Damascus. The Director, already late for dinner with the Saudi ambassador, explained that Ed Bradley would represent the Agency at the Small Group. In the Situation Room, Bradley sat through a three-hour argument about whether to enforce the President's red line. In the end, the National Security

Adviser presented three options for POTUS: destroy the regime, bomb the Jableh facility, send a covert message.

"Make it clean, Ed," the President had said as he chose the third option. "Just the general. No innocent bystanders."

THE NEXT DAY PROCTER SUMMONED Sam into her office for a videoconference with Bradley, who was apparently still awake, at home in the Box, and probably a few beers in as Damascus Station came online. His pixelated image emerged on-screen.

"Hey, guys," Bradley said. "I'll keep this quick. Last night POTUS considered bombing Damascus in retaliation for the sarin test ATHENA reported in her intel. He decided against, but still wants to send the Syrians a don't-fuck-with-us kind of message. Office of Legal Counsel at Justice thinks they can interpret the Val and KOMODO murders, coupled with Ali Hassan's surveillance operations in Damascus, as an ongoing threat to America and her interests. Which is why I am now holding in my hand a piece of paper, signed by POTUS forty-five minutes ago, declaring that an operation to eliminate Brigadier General Ali Hassan is, and I'm quoting from Title 50 of the U.S. Code here, 'necessary to support identifiable foreign policy objectives of the United States.' This is not an assassination. It has been certified as national self-defense."

"Very classy. Nightgown-like elegance," Procter said. "That's why everybody loves lawyers."

"What are the conditions?" Sam asked.

"And how much is on paper?" Procter asked.

"Procter, I am going to assume from your tone that you are really asking if we can run this like the drone operations in AfPak. And the answer is no. Only Ali dies. There can be no collateral damage. That is the only restriction on paper."

"Any others not on paper?" asked Sam.

"Yes, one, from me," Bradley said. "The President agrees. Call it commander's guidance. We need our facial recognition experts to confirm it is Hassan before we pull the trigger. I don't want us flubbing and killing the wrong Syrian general. We'll need video footage in real time to confirm it is him." Bradley's eyes narrowed and he seemed to stare into Sam from the screen. "This is a rare opportunity to avenge one of our own. We all want Ali Hassan dead for what he did to Val. But let's be smart. Nothing crazy."

"Of course," Sam said. His heartbeat picked up. CIA usually had to look the other way when one of its officers was killed. Now he could avenge Val. He could pay Ali back for that thin line he'd traced on her forehead.

Procter removed her tweed blazer and stood facing the screen, staring back at Bradley. Sam could see the *IN HONOR* stars visible on her lats above her black top. What the hell were they for?

"Is this your way of hinting that this Station isn't pulling its weight?" she said.

"No," Bradley said. "This is my way of telling you explicitly—no hints here—that you all are under the damn gun. Expectations are high and increasing because of your great work. Is your door closed?"

She looked at the closed door.

"No, it's wide open, along with the door to the chancery. There is actually a Syrian in the room here with us, Ed, he's off-camera and has been acting as notetaker. Mahmud, Mahmud, come join us on-camera and smile for Ed." Procter waved wildly toward the door.

She turned back to the screen and gave Bradley a smug smile.

He laughed. "I forgot how much of a pain in the ass you are, Procter. I should have sent you to Europe Division so you could terrorize someone else. I'm getting the same shitty treatment you offered the Pakistani Taliban and Qaeda."

"At least you're still alive," she said.

INSIDE THE AMBASSADOR'S SECURE CONFERENCE room in the American Embassy, Yusuf kicked his heels up on the table and took another bite of pizza. The box claimed it was "Authentic Syrian Pizza" from a place called Café Costa, and Sam could barely look at it. "Stop the tape here, Rami," Yusuf said in response to a question from Procter.

He sat up. The screen showed Ali Hassan's car weaving through the concrete berms into the Security Office building. They'd been watching the BANDITOs' surveillance footage.

"See how low that Lexus is riding?" Yusuf said. "It's armored, so we'd need something fairly heavy. "Also, take a look at this." He slid the surveillance log across the table.

Sam opened the file. The BANDITOs had marked Ali's arrival and departure times. It varied every day, sometimes by hours.

"Does he mix up the route, too?" Sam asked.

"Yes, unfortunately. He rolls up from different directions," Elias said as he pulled another slice off the pie. "We haven't found a pattern."

"Gatehouse attack?" Procter asked, casting a sideways glance at the pizza. "Run-and-gun while he shows the badge?"

"Typically, one guy works the gate, between four and seven guys outside passing the time smoking and bullshitting with each other," Rami said. "Not particularly professional, but you'd have a shoot-out on your hands."

Procter stood up. "I said I'd take his balls, I meant it. You got any actual ideas?"

"One," said Yusuf.

He removed a pack of Marlboro cigarettes from his breast pocket and placed them on the table.

"No, thanks, Yusuf," Procter said, giving a wise-ass grin. "The ventilation in this tin box is not so great."

"No. Watch." Yusuf fast-forwarded until he reached footage taped at 9:55 p.m., one week earlier. The camera focused on Ali Hassan as he emerged from the Security Office building and walked along the street, winding through the cars parked on the sidewalk, just as Sam had seen other pedestrians do when he'd watched the building.

"I was filming this one," Yusuf said. "Watch closely." The camera zoomed in on Ali. He stopped next to a parked car and pulled the distinctive red Marlboro package from his shirt pocket. He paused to remove a cigarette, light it, and then began walking again. He moved slowly, as if he were deep in thought.

"Now watch this one," Yusuf said. He fast-forwarded the tape again, to the next day's footage. The time stamp read 10:02 p.m. Ali walked the same route, smoking his Marlboros.

"Guy does it a lot. One week he walked the route four times."

Sam picked up the cigarettes from the table and turned the package over in his hands. He nodded to Procter, who nodded back.

25

JAMIL ATIYAH WAS BOUTHAINA'S PEER. THEORETICALLY, anyway. But the old man had been deputy director of Military Intelligence, he'd helped smooth Bashar's ascension to the presidency, he was in charge of the Iran file. He had more *wasta* than Bouthaina. And he had a penis. He told Bouthaina what to do.

So Bouthaina was apoplectic but not surprised when she received another curt summons to brief Atiyah on Mariam's efforts to peel oppositionists away from the National Council. "I will handle the pedophile in the meeting," Bouthaina said. "But I'd like you to come in case he asks for details. We can share the reports you drafted in France. Of course, he doesn't give a shit about the actual work, this is about our war. Another battle in his effort to destroy us." Mariam unconsciously lifted a finger to her mouth as she thought of the three bodies in her Villefranche hotel room, her shaky fingers attaching the DO NOT DISTURB sign as she closed the door behind.

Around the time of the brush pass, Mariam started biting the skin around her fingernails. She would not notice at first but by the second or third finger she would catch herself. But Bouthaina, poor self-absorbed Bouthaina, seemed not to notice.

Mariam placed her hands on Bouthaina's office table and noticed a drop of blood peeking from the nail bed of her right thumb. Bouthaina's phone rang and she stepped into the washroom. Mariam fiddled with reports on the table, mulling over her boss's horrendous communications security as Bouthaina spoke with Rustum. She was gnawing at the left middle finger when she realized it and bit her lip in disgust.

Bouthaina hung up and emerged from the washroom. "Let's go see that old creep."

Mariam smoothed her dark blue skirt and picked up her reports to follow. Atiyah sat at his desk reading and did not look up to acknowledge them. Today he wore a fine-cut black suit with thick pinstripes that made him look like a gangster.

Bouthaina and Mariam sat at the table. Atiyah finished reading his report, then looked up. He sipped tea but did not offer any. Instead, he drank in Mariam for a beat and did not hide it.

"She's a little old for you," Bouthaina snapped.

Atiyah did not even acknowledge her comment. Instead he spoke to Mariam. "I forgot to ask the last time we saw each other. How was France?" She caught an edge in his voice. The rage was about to break through. His eyebrows quivered for a second, but then, in an instant, they stopped and he raised them, smiled, and said, "Eventful?"

"The meetings with Fatimah did not succeed," Mariam said. "Not yet. Though as you can see in these reports we've taken active measures to shift her opinions on the matter."

Mariam slid the paper toward Atiyah.

Atiyah made a flapping motion with his hand as if shooing her away. He said: "I already know that Fatimah's mother has been arrested. I don't need these reports. What I want to know is why, Bouthaina, your office keeps failing. Fatimah is still on the council, lounging in Europe and mocking us."

Bouthaina glanced longingly at a letter opener propped on the desk. Instead, she looked down for a moment and brushed lint off her left pant leg with an air of indifference. She, too, knew her war with Atiyah required composure. "My office is traveling to squeeze the life from the opposition, and you're traveling to Thailand to squeeze teenage flesh. We all have our priorities."

Atiyah snickered, but he locked his eyes on Mariam. She folded her hands in her lap to keep from biting her fingers and glanced at the letter opener herself. It would be fitting payback for the hotel incident in Nice.

"You keep using the same weapons, Bouthaina," he said. "It is not working. Try something else. If you do not solve this problem, you will lose the file. Then I will take it and succeed where you and Mariam have failed." He held up Mariam's reports as he stared at her blouse. "I may actually read these, Mariam, and when I'm done maybe you'll provide me with a proper briefing." The word *proper* spoken as if it would be anything but.

Overpowering the Botox, Bouthaina's forehead wrinkled. She looked like she was about to speak, then, in silence, she stood up, turned for the door, and left. Mariam tried to follow, but she felt a hand gripping her shoulder and hot breath on her neck as she reached the door.

"I'm glad you've returned safely from your French vacation," he said.

She turned and brushed his hand from her shoulder. "It would have been a shame to lose you, but please understand—it is nothing personal. Bouthaina started a war with me." She dropped the reports and pulled free, slightly off balance because of the heels.

Surprise registered in his eyes. "Be vigilant, Mariam. There is much to fear. I will summon you for a full report once I've read these files." He looked at the papers on the floor and laughed. He closed his office door.

Mariam quickly gathered up the scattered papers and walked back to Bouthaina's office, holding eye contact with a portrait of the President as she marched past.

BOUTHAINA WAS ALREADY BACK AT her desk, typing furiously with her eyes locked on the screen. Mariam only knew Bouthaina was aware of her return when she said, "I think that went well, don't you?"

She went to the table, where she began rifling through paper, muttering. This was a proper Syrian bureaucratic war, Mariam thought, fought with papers, files, and meetings, the subordinates as cannon fodder.

"Here it is," Bouthaina said. She smacked an Iranian intercept of Fatimah's travel itinerary in front of Mariam. "Atiyah wants to tell the President that we have failed. He thinks it will give him leverage, and he's correct." She pointed to the report. "Fatimah is going to be at her family's home in Tuscany for a few days starting on July sixth. You will go see her. You will bring her home, plaintive, muzzled, gift-wrapped. We will have Ali arrest a few more family members to soften her up. You, Mariam, will succeed this time."

"Of course, Bouthaina. I will handle her." She raised a fingernail to her mouth but caught herself and put her hand down, balling it up like a fist.

ON THE WALK HOME MARIAM nibbled at crackers she'd bought to settle her stomach. Atiyah's threat ran through her mind, as did the forbidden thought of Sam joining her in Italy. He would calm her down, help her think. She crossed the street and entered the bustling Souq Al-Hamadiya. Some of the shopkeepers called out as she passed, asking if they could show her a nice dress, or perhaps some sunglasses. But she was in Èze, on top of Sam, taking her pleasure when the club cracked open the head of the thick assailant in the Pink Floyd T-shirt. She was in the backseat of the car, guiding him inside, when the second man's blood sprayed onto the hotel room mirror. She was next to Sam in the bed, fingers tracing the muscles on his chest, when the back of the third attacker's head collapsed onto the freshly made sheets. Mariam nearly tripped on a raised paving stone and stopped to rummage through her purse for another cracker. Removing one from the foil, she held it between her lips as she felt again to be sure the marker was still in her purse. She grasped it for a moment to reassure herself. She slung the bag over her shoulder and quickly closed her eyes to recall the image of the graffiti they'd practiced on napkins in Èze.

“This is the emergency signal,” Sam had said as the napkin whipped in the Mediterranean breeze. “Someone will check for it every day. If we see it, we service the drop site right after.”

Mariam stopped at an alleyway three blocks from her apartment. “What do I do if someone sees me?” she had asked him. “Don’t let them,” he had replied.

She checked to be sure she was alone. She went into the alley and left the mark on the wall.

26

SAM AND PROCTER READ MARIAM'S MESSAGE IN THE Station. "Woof," Procter said. "A face-to-face with a newly minted asset in this slaughterhouse? I hate it."

"I don't like it, either," Sam said, then read the message again:

BOUTHAINA. AND I MET WITH ATIYAH. PALACE TURF WAR ONGOING. ATIYAH USING MY FAILURE WITH FATIMAH TO SQUEEZE BOUTHAINA. PHYSICAL THREAT MADE AGAINST ME AT END OF MEETING, INCLUDING HINTS AT ATTACK IN FRANCE. ATIYAH SAID: "BE VIGILANT. THERE IS MUCH TO FEAR."

BOUTHAINA SENDING ME TO MONTALCINO, ITALY, ON 6 JULY TO MEET AGAIN WITH FATIMAH. WILL HAVE TIME TO MEET IN PERSON.

The period after the first word indicated Mariam had not planted the message under duress. Procter was reading the message over his shoulder. "Woof," she said again, shaking her head. "Badness, Jaggers."

"But we really have no choice, do we?" he said. "They already tried to kidnap her in France."

"You have an idea of how to help her out?"

Sam tapped a pen on the table. "Why do you keep that Mossberg there, Chief? Not like the armory is far."

"I find the presence of guns comforting."

He tapped the pen again, then doodled *ATHENA* into a notepad. He had nothing but an idea he remembered hearing from Bradley over beers in Cairo Station. It was insane, but Bradley insisted it had saved his asset's life. What the hell, it was worth a shot. He had to protect her.

"All right, crazy thought, but I remember Bradley telling me about an op he ran back in Algiers to protect an asset in a similar situation."

"No shit?"

"Yeah, but full disclosure: it involves a subminiature camera and a necklace."

"Damn. Usually you have to pay double for that one."

PROCTER LIKED THE IDEA AND raised hell in cable traffic. (The words "dogshit bureaucratic red tape" were used in a cable read by most of NE Division and Science and Technology leadership.) Forty-eight hours later they sat in her office, well past midnight, as a very tired-looking techie from the CIA's Office of Technical Services on the secure video teleconference, the SVTC screen, held up a sapphire necklace matching one from a Paris surveillance photo snapped by the BANDITOs before Mariam's recruitment. Sam remembered it glittering as she drank a glass of wine on the terrace in Èze. Then, it had been the only thing she wore.

Procter was feeling loose at this late hour and now swilled a can of Coors Light—likely smuggled into Syria by a friend in Diplomatic Security—as she pointed at the techie dangling a necklace on the SVTC screen. "It's like fucking QVC in here. How many minutes left to order, Jaggers?"

The techie took an admirable swing, running his hand along the necklace and explaining that she had twenty minutes and it could be Procter's for "ten installments of *just* nineteen ninety-five." Sam laughed.

Procter mumbled something unintelligible and the techie ran his hand along the necklace again. "Explain how it works, man," the Chief said.

The techie showed the single power button and how the asset would stick a needle or a hairpin inside to turn it on or off. He said it could be dunked in water, dead-dropped, no problem, it was all-weather. "A plastic bag around it wouldn't hurt, though." The techie saw Procter raise an eyebrow, but before she could say anything he blurted out that its memory could hold about thirty hours of footage, a minor miracle he called it. Then he gave a technical explanation of the camera's strontium power source.

"Now, hold on," Procter said raising her hand. "Our asset here is a chick, and she is going to wear this thing around her neck, like right on the skin, man." Procter pointed to her chest in case the techie had problems with the anatomical vocabulary. "We have a breast cancer risk here, with some voodoo radioactive battery?"

Sam could not tell if the techie wanted to laugh or cry. Probably both. His face had been vacuumed of color.

"No, no risk. No risk to the asset," the techie said. "Completely harmless."

"How soon can you get it here?" Sam asked.

"We can pouch it overnight," the techie said, relieved the call appeared to be ending.

Procter hung up.

SAM WAS THE FIRST TO arrive at the safe house, which was tucked into a quiet side street of the Christian Quarter. He was bone-tired. The SDR had required twelve exhausting hours, though he'd been certain he was black by hour six.

The safe house had a small kitchen with a fully stocked refrigerator and pantry. It led into a sitting area stacked with modern furniture. The walls were bare. A bedroom and bathroom lay beyond the sitting room. A tech from the Station had swept the room for listening devices earlier in the day.

Sam started the coffee and pulled the trays of catered mezze from the fridge. As Sam opened pantry drawers and foraged through the crispers and freezer, he felt rising guilt. There was a food shortage across Syria, not to mention skyrocketing inflation happening outside the bubble of central Damascus. The starvation was so bad in Douma that people were eating grass to survive, according to the intelligence reports. What little food they had was hoarded by the rebel commanders. The regime called it "Kneel or Starve." He picked out a bottle of olive oil (prewar per liter price: two hundred Syrian pounds; now: eleven hundred) and set it on the counter.

He surveyed the food and saw the spread of olives, makdous, tabbouleh, and yalanji stuffed grape leaves. He started the warmer and put four skewers of lamb kebab inside. He went back to the fridge and found cousa, a southern Syrian dish of small zucchinis, their insides scooped out and filled with lamb and rice seasoned with cumin, mint, coriander, and baharat.

He poured himself a cup of coffee. He had thirty minutes until she arrived. He had to do something to cut the nerves, to stop thinking about Mariam running an SDR, now, in Damascus. He drank the coffee alone in the sitting room, looking uneasily into the inviting bedroom. He had not seen Mariam since the brush pass in the spice market, and even then it had not been more than a passing glance. He wondered if she would look different. If he would be able to control himself. If Washington would bomb and the Station would evacuate and he would never see her again.

Damascus was on edge, like someone about to jump off a building. There was the sarin test and the reports about a regime counterattack, but even more vivid was the daily grind of life itself: the suicide bombings, the mortar volleys, the bread lines, the power outages, the bare grocery shelves. The journalists and UN officials holed up at the Four Seasons reminded him of places like Mogadishu or civil war Beirut: so hopelessly smashed that foreigners lounge at one safe watering hole, working their sources and stringers poolside, not because they wanted luxury but because it was too dangerous to go anywhere else.

Damascus did not feel safe. And not just for him, for his tribe: Procter, the Station. And, of course, Mariam. He dared to imagine Mariam outside Syria. The possibility of an actual, human relationship. What had started as a physical magnetism had matured into something more complete, somehow without losing any of the spark. Mariam was street-smart, playful, courageous, hopeful. He knew how he felt. Could not bring himself to say it, though, even to himself.

He got up to pour himself more coffee and leaned against the counter.

The door clicked and Mariam walked in. She wore dark jeans, a blue blazer that slimmed into her wide hips, and a clingy gray T-shirt. She entered the kitchen and he pulled her in for a hug. She pressed her head into his shoulder and said, "Hello, *habibi*, I have missed you so much." Sam, in his suit and white dress shirt, thought the scene probably looked like any couple greeting each other after separate days at the office. He kissed her, closing his eyes to inhale the lavender.

"How much time do you have?" he asked. The first question for any asset.

"Two hours."

He'd planned to start with the operation against Atiyah, but then they were kissing again in the kitchen and her hands were in his hair and he was leading her into the bedroom. She bit his chin and pushed him onto a small sofa. He started unbuttoning his shirt. They smiled at each other and she giggled and stood and glanced toward the bed. His world narrowed to Mariam, now playfully kicking her ankle-slung jeans across the marbled calligraphy on the floor. They unbuttoned and unsnapped and slid off and pulled down until they reached the bed's edge and fell in.

AFTERWARD, HE LOOKED AT THE trail on the floor. Shoes at the beginning, near the couch. Her jeans, then his slacks, her gray shirt, a black bra, his white collared shirt, the black lacy underwear, ending with his boxers. A slow-motion rapture into the bed.

Rising, they scrunched into the single sink bathroom to reassemble for the outside world. He fixed his hair and she hip-checked him as she dawdled with her jewelry.

She leaned into the counter. The flush on her cheeks had subsided. Her hair was combed back and drawn up, her lipstick reapplied. This close, he could catch the slight tinge of sweat and the lavender.

"I wanted this because I didn't know if we'd ever have the chance again," she said. "Maybe never. But here we are, and who knows how many times we have left? Maybe we end up like so many Syrians. Alive one minute, gone the next. Maybe you go home again and I never see you. We grow old separately. I know there are rules, I'll do my job, but there is something between us. It matters to me."

He put his hands on her hips. "It means something to me, too, Mariam. I care for you."

He loved her, but he hated himself because he but could not, would not, say it.

They kissed, and she pulled back and nodded to him. "I know how you feel. It's how I feel, too."

THEY TOOK PLATES INTO THE living room and she walked him through the meeting with Atiyah. He asked for every word, every detail. When she finished, he told her about his plan and showed her the necklace.

She gave a wan smile. "How did you re-create it perfectly? Kind of creepy, no?"

He coughed. "Some pictures from Paris."

Thankfully, she let it go. She tried it on. He'd brought an aluminum can and she practiced dropping the necklace inside, as she would on the mountain after she took the video of Atiyah's office.

"Do you think anyone is following you?" he asked as they refilled their plates in the kitchen.

She shook her head. "I've been careful. I do not believe he is following me. Now—"

That was when a mortar landed on the roof of the building across the street. The safe house rattled and groaned. Mariam, accustomed to the sounds, put her plate down on the table and went to the window, brushing aside the drapes. He knew this was the last place in the apartment they should stand but his curiosity briefly overpowered the training. The windows on the building's top floor had fractured outward, and Sam could see chunks of limestone and plaster and glass fragments on the street below. Sirens bayed in the distance.

Another mortar struck a building a few blocks south. Then a third, a fourth, a fifth, a sixth in staccato succession. The walls rumbled with each impact.

They stepped back from the window.

"They like to shell the Christian Quarter, if they can," she said. "Filled with Christians and *mukhabarat* buildings. If they miss the *mukhabarat* they might kill a few of us as a bonus."

Sam scanned the apartment to find the space farthest from the window. They couldn't leave now, especially with police and fire and probably *mukhabarat* arriving to investigate.

They stepped back into the bedroom. Standing next to the bed, she smoothed her hand over the rumpled sheets. "Will we be alone in Italy, *habibi*?"

"Procter will join us. We'll have the same surveillance team follow you to make sure Atiyah doesn't try anything while you're out of Syria."

She put her hands on her hips. "Hmm," she said. "A crowd."

He sat down on the bed and ran his hands through his hair. He was in deep, and he had no plan to get out. If he told Procter, CIA would fire him. And if he stopped seeing Mariam? He wasn't sure he could.

She pushed him back onto the sheets and climbed on top to straddle him. The sirens wailed outside.

27

GRATITUDE FOR HIS WIFE'S BARREN WOMB WAS A strange thought upon reviewing the dead wrapped in *kaffan*, the burial shrouds, like a hundred cotton cocoons. Strange, but not rare, for this gratitude had become a frequent companion since Abu Qasim had started fighting Assad's siege works in Aleppo.

Last Friday: the boy bringing water to the trench, killed by shellfire.

On Saturday: the jaundiced girl who died of typhus in her mother's ruined apartment, then serving as a sniper nest.

On Sunday: a boy, sixteen, poking his head out from behind a street corner, AK-47 clattering wildly, missing everything downrange as a bullet tore into his throat.

On Monday: a barrel bomb dropped on the field hospital, killing a ten-year-old with leukemia and two girls on the street outside.

And now, in this village called Houla, hours away from Aleppo's rubble, the gratitude had returned as one of the elders, weeping, explained what had transpired. As he reviewed the dead, heads pointed toward Mecca, Abu Qasim looked down at the body of a small child wrapped in the *kaffan*, noticing that the head appeared to be missing. He drew his wife, Sarya, close and prayed over her stomach, thanking Allah for her fallow womb as he always did when he saw dead children. Giving thanks that Abu Qasim was only his *kunya*, his nom de guerre, and that there had never been a child, nor would there ever be.

The old man did not notice. He was hysterical.

Abu Qasim told him he would appreciate a full report, and could he please take a few moments to compose himself? "Yes, yes, Commander, of course," the elder said. He wiped his eyes. "I will fetch tea and return."

Abu Qasim stared out into the shrubland, away from the line of bodies, as Sarya stretched and doffed her hijab, using the elder's absence to rearrange her long hair, once oily black but now striated with grays and whites. Her belly fat, once peeking gently over her jeans, had been replaced with lean muscle, and her face was now creased where it had once been smooth. Her breasts had shrunk from the hunger and she walked and sat with a slight stoop, as if hunched over a gun, which she often was.

Despite it all, she was still beautiful. The smile remained wide, her long hair was thick, her eyes still alive, her appetite for him undiminished. He felt his own face, now gaunt and sallow, and thought of his wispy hair, his bony legs and arms, his left hand with its four fingers. He'd lost twenty-five pounds since he went to war.

They had to keep moving. They'd received reports of the massacre yesterday and detoured on impulse. The trip from Aleppo would have required four hours before the war. Instead it took four days winding through a maze of highways, checkpoints, and back roads. At government checkpoints, they'd used doctored ID cards stolen from dead Alawis to pose as military couriers. At those stops Sarya wore fatigues and spoke directly to the government men.

At rebel checkpoints, it had varied. They always used their true ID cards, but at some checkpoints Sarya donned a niqab in the back of the van, while at others the hijab sufficed. She never spoke at the rebel checkpoints. When they had passed through, she always let out her frustration, for she had killed more soldiers with her sniper rifle than the young men running the checkpoints. Why should she answer to them? She was up to one hundred and forty-two kills. The rifle, a Russian-made SV-98, had been acquired when Sarya killed its owner and upgraded from her Dragunov, another Russian weapon, which she'd taken from an earlier victim on the Aleppo front lines. The SV-98 was stashed in the false bottom of the van's trunk. They would need it in Damascus.

The old man returned with tea no one drank. "We have one hundred and two dead now," he said. "All yesterday. Five or six more are likely to die today. The doctor is not optimistic. More than fifty are from a single clan." He rubbed his eyes. "My own clan lost eighteen."

Abu Qasim said nothing. He needed the man to speak. He could mourn when they had left. The old man got the message, apologized, and regained his composure. "The men of the village had gathered for a demonstration in the morning. Then the shelling started and continued for two or three hours. The men could not get back to their homes. Several tried, and they are dead now. In the afternoon, the mortars stopped. Some military, some *mukhabarat*, some *shabiha* militia gathered near the water plant, they kept us pinned down. The *shabiha* came from the Alawi villages."

The old man jabbed his finger toward the villages and his chin quivered.

"They had guns but also cleavers, machetes, meat hooks," he said. "They started the slaughter. Forty-seven children, many of them babies, toddlers. Shot, stabbed, throats slit. Thirty-four women, too." Now he was yelling, standing and pointing outside toward the lines of the dead in the burial shrouds. Abu Qasim now saw that many were just bedsheets. They'd apparently run out of cloth.

Abu Qasim took pictures of the dead, ritual washing and burial preparation under way, and sent those to his commander. They loaded into the van for the voyage to Douma, which the rebels had already liberated but was now choking under siege.

They did not speak of the massacre on the drive. They'd seen the same in Aleppo and there was nothing to say anymore.

THEY ENTERED DOUMA THROUGH ONE of the pedestrian tunnels after nightfall.

Zahran Alloush, Douma's warlord, greeted them in a command headquarters, which was bunkered under an abandoned electronics store and was thick with the smell of sewage. The floor was covered in crusted carpets. Beads of moisture collected on the ceiling, and pipes and electrical cords snaked up the walls. Flat-screen television monitors showing the tunnel network, Al Jazeera, and several Saudi satellite stations sat cluttered on a row of card tables. The room, usually bustling with activity, had been emptied for the meeting.

Though the food shortages now forced inhabitants of his fiefdom to eat weeds and old leather, Alloush had prepared a meal of bread and chicken for his visitor. Abu Qasim stared at the glistening skewers and licked his lips without realizing it. He could not remember the last time he'd eaten meat that was not from a rat. He wished he could share the meal with Sarya, but Alloush would not allow a woman's presence at his war table.

Alloush gestured Abu Qasim to sit. They ate quickly and in silence. When he'd eaten his fill, Abu Qasim sat savoring the feeling of a full belly. Finally he broke the silence. "We have an offer for you."

Alloush scratched at his pant leg and smiled. "The emir said this, but what does it mean? My battalions are more than capable of carrying out a mission in Damascus. I cannot understand why you've been sent here. Give me the information and my men will handle it."

"My sources have provided information that requires a particular set of talents," Abu Qasim said.

Alloush leaned forward and pointed at Abu Qasim. "I already have commanders who can run missions into the city."

"Once you have a sniper with one hundred and forty-two confirmed kills, perhaps the emir will not need to send his own," Abu Qasim said. "Or a bomb-maker with so much . . . experience." He looked down at his nine fingers.

"Ah yes, I forgot, the Black Death," Alloush said. He looked around the dank room, grinning, at the mention of Sarya's nickname, given for the black hijab she wore while killing the regime's foot soldiers and militia.

Abu Qasim ignored him and Alloush called for tea. They sat again in silence until the tea boy arrived, leaving two steaming cups behind. "What's the offer, then?" Alloush said as he took a sip.

"First let me explain what we need," Abu Qasim said. "We've brought the sniper rifle and some ammunition, but would like more. We also need small arms for basic security. Standard AKs will be fine, but we'll need several crates of ammo. For the bomb, I need access to your explosives factory and its material stores. Maybe I spend two days there."

Alloush furrowed his eyebrows and leaned back in his chair. "That's it?"

"No. One more thing: I need several of your Republican Guard defectors."

"Why?"

"They are your best."

"I know, that's why I don't want you to have them."

Abu Qasim pulled a letter from his pocket and placed it on the table. "It's a personal request from the emir for these men."

Alloush looked at the paper and passed it back without reading. "The emir and I were brothers in Saydnaya. I don't need to read it. What do I receive in exchange for this shopping list?"

"You take credit for the operation. You go on television afterward. You use it to raise more capital in the Gulf."

Alloush ignored the bait. "What is the operation?"

Abu Qasim smiled.

28

PAULINA JACKSON SAT ON HER WORKBENCH LISTENING to Bone Thugs-N-Harmony's "I Tried" on repeat through her headphones. The glory days were long past, but she was from Cleveland and loved this stuff. Focusing as the song played for the twentieth time that day, Jackson molded the sheet of Semtex with a government-issue steel tube that was, in effect, a glorified rolling pin. They wouldn't use this one for the test today, but she still mumbled to herself not to mess this up. It's gotta be perfect when those white-shoes from Langley show up for the demo. Pasted above her workbench was a picture of Ali Hassan walking on the street smoking a cigarette, snapped by one of the spooks in Damascus. They'd built a mock-up of the same road for practice, like they'd done before the SEAL raid to kill Bin Laden. Then, she had not really been involved, had only been able to steal a few glances at the Teams as they trained. Now it was her show.

The copy of the lethal finding POTUS had signed had made it clear that there was no room for error. And so the suits inside the Special Activities Division had mandated a strict set of technical requirements for the bomb, all of which she knew by memory. After all, she'd already built and tested thirty-one of these damn things. She knew the design so well she'd given it her own nickname: the Frisbee. Fabricated to fit inside a Mitsubishi Pajero's passenger seat stereo speaker, the explosion had to punch outward in a controlled burst to manage the blast force and dispersion.

The first few tests had not gone well. The explosions had been too powerful and Rodney, her boss, had muttered about shrapnel going through the wall and killing babies. "The wall," he would say as he pointed at the mock-up cinder-block wall. "Is it gonna go through that wall, Paulina? Gotta make sure it glances off, just a smooch, like you're kissing your brother." She had quickly reduced the Semtex to just under a quarter pound.

She examined the Semtex plastic she had rolled out into the shape of a disc. She stood and walked over to the Pajero, parked behind her workbench in the hangar. She opened the front passenger door to see if the Frisbee fit inside the gap where the speaker had been. It did. The Frisbee's shape, when detonated, would direct the explosion outward in a tight blast radius, reducing the potential for collateral damage.

Music still blaring in her ears, Paulina returned to her workbench and began wiring the circuits that would link a passive infrared (PIR) sensor to a satellite phone. The CIA would call the sat phone to arm the circuit. When Ali crossed the plane of the PIR sensor, the circuit would close, allowing power to flow from the battery into a blasting cap snuggled into the Semtex, detonating the charge. "The team in Syria," Rodney had said on the first day, wearing those weird Coke-bottle glasses and reading directly from the ops proposal, "proposes that the bigwigs at Langley verify the target's identity, then a spotter in Damascus arms the PIR while maintaining visual contact with the target until he crosses the infrared plane and blows the charge." The cable had been drafted by some case officer with a weird funny name. GOLDJAGGER, she remembered it was. Rodney took off his glasses. "Seems easy enough."

Finished linking the PIR and satellite phone to a nine-volt battery, she then wired the device to a Turkish-made blasting cap and set it on the workbench to inspect her handiwork, packing a lipper of Grizz chewing tobacco into her mouth as she did so. Satisfied, she bound the device together with electrical tape, spat into an empty coffee cup, and placed the Thuraya satellite phone and the PIR inside the door next to the Frisbee. She would connect the blasting cap to the Semtex once she had positioned the vehicle on the proving grounds. She closed the compartment. This one, she thought as she gently closed the Pajero's door, was the best Frisbee yet. She drove the Pajero outside, through the hangar doors, past the blackened remains of the first Pajero—not her best bomb—and onto the proving ground's parking lot next to the other three, which she assumed represented the vast majority of Pajeros available in the Western hemisphere. Even though Semtex is a stable explosive, she still avoided the potholes, because you never really could be sure.

She checked her watch as she turned off the music, and rubbed her ears. The white-shoe from Langley would arrive in a few hours for the test. Where was the guy with the cadavers?

ABU QASIM, HAD HE KNOWN, would have been jealous of Paulina's professional operation, particularly her access to Semtex. For at the exact moment that Paulina was fabricating her Frisbee, Abu Qasim was clothed in a grimy smock in an underground workshop grumbling about the steep price he had paid for two kilos. Unlike Paulina Jackson and the CIA, though, Abu Qasim had no specific vendetta against the man, at least not relative to any of the other monsters inside the regime. He was targeting Ali Hassan for the simple fact that he was an important general. And he had a source who could plant the bomb at one of his meetings.

Abu Qasim scanned the pictures of the tea cart and kicked at the shoddy plastic mock-up they'd stolen from one of Douma's storage rooms. He reviewed the shelves and inspected a drawer filled with blasting caps. The bomb had to fit inside a box, on the lower rack of a tea cart. He examined the caps carefully, shaking his head gravely whenever he spotted one with rusty wires.

Abu Qasim found a workable number-eight-type blasting cap. Two grams of a mixture of mercury fulminate and potassium chlorate packed into a metallic cylinder the size of a large pen, the fuse wires protruding from one end. The wires would receive electric current—he would use a prepaid cell phone for the trigger—detonating the cap and finally igniting the Semtex. Abu Qasim smiled as he turned it over in his fingers. In Aleppo he'd not had the luxury of prefabricated blasting caps. In the early days, he'd been trying to synthesize mercury fulminate when it exploded, taking his left ring finger with it.

Abu Qasim cut the orange Semtex from its plastic wrapping, picked up an aluminum tube from the floor—sufficiently thin to fragment when the Semtex exploded—and eyeballed how much length could fit on the tea cart. He drew a line with a black permanent marker and rummaged through a toolbox for a hacksaw. Finding one, he cut off the end. Then he rolled the Semtex into a tube as if it were modeling clay, periodically stopping to measure the diameter to ensure it could comfortably fit inside the aluminum tube. Opening a box of the 4.7-millimeter ball bearings he had requested from Alloush's men, Abu Qasim individually pressed them into the plastic until the Semtex's burnt-orange hue was replaced by a chromy metallic shine. He paused for a minute to wipe his sweaty hands on his smock and imagined one of the ball bearings tearing through Ali Hassan's skull. Then he collected a spool of copper wire from one of the cabinets and unwrapped a nine-volt battery and two prepaid Nokia cell phones. Abu Qasim checked to ensure the phones were charged, then used each phone to call the other. Both worked. Using a red marker, he drew a large circle on the phone that he would implant in the device. He saved that phone's number into the contacts of the other phone, which he colored with a green marker. He also wrote the number he would dial on a piece of tape and put it on the back of the green phone. To be safe, he removed the red phone's battery. Then, using the wire, Abu Qasim began creating the circuit that, when completed, would set off the device. When he dialed the phone, an electrical current would flow from its circuit board into the blasting cap, detonating the Semtex.

The fans shut off as the electricity flickered. Beads of sweat dripped on the workshop table as he fiddled with the wiring. When he was done with the circuit, he connected the phone and the nine-volt to the blasting cap, which would eventually be inserted into the Semtex. Finished, Abu Qasim squatted on all fours searching through a bin under the workshop table. He pulled out two strips of Velcro to attach the phone and battery to the tube, and stepped back to examine his work. It weighed less than five kilos and would fit nicely into a large cardboard box filled with tea and sugar. The walls rumbled with impacts aboveground, maybe barrel bombs. It was hard to tell so deep down. The electricity wobbled again. Abu Qasim looked up, then back to the bomb. One of his more straightforward creations, thanks to the Semtex Alloush's militia had pilfered from the regime's stockpiles.

Still, he wished he could test it.

RODNEY BROUGHT ED BRADLEY TO Paulina's workbench to introduce the Chief to the bomb maker before the test. "Chief, good to meet you," Paulina said, offering her right hand. She appreciated that Bradley didn't balk at the missing finger or the leathery skin.

"We're getting everything set up now," Rodney told Bradley as they left the hangar for the mock-up of the road in Damascus. Out on the proving ground, Paulina put on her aviators and a Cleveland Indians baseball cap and joined them in the raised observation stand. The group baked behind two feet of plexiglass in the July sun. Lyle, one of the techs, drove the Pajero onto the mock-up curb and parked.

Bradley turned to Rodney. "We running a flesh test?" he asked.

"Yes sir," Rodney said.

"Always a little weird," Bradley mumbled as he put on his own sunglasses and rolled up his sleeves.

The most reliable bellwether of an explosion's impact is actual human bone, muscle, and skin. There were no lab rats in bomb testing, but there were people who'd already died, and Paulina's team could always get a few for high-profile tests like this one. Four technicians wheeled cadavers on Rollerblades out of the hangar toward the street mock-up, their body weight suspended on what Paulina always assumed were IV poles. Lyle positioned the Ali cadaver ten yards behind the Pajero's trunk and then connected the IV pole to a long length of rope that would be pulled during the test to simulate a human walking. Then he arranged the other three around Ali as if they were innocent passersby. When signing the delivery forms, Paulina had learned that the cadaver playing the part of Ali was actually a sixty-year-old male named Darryl who'd died of a heart attack. She felt a little bad for Darryl.

Lyle strung sensor packets on each cadaver that would measure the explosion's "K factor," or kilopascals—the pressure that would rupture air-filled voids in the human body such as lungs or eardrums. He then draped what looked like a large sheet over the mock-up version of the cinder-block wall. The sheet was a type of carbonless copy paper coated with a micro-encapsulated dye that would release when pressure was applied, displaying where fragments lodged. Lyle and the technicians wheeled similar sheets strung up on what looked like whiteboards to form a ring around the Pajero and the cadavers.

"How long from dial to activation?" Bradley asked Paulina.

"We tested calls using multiple satellite assets to pass the signal," she said. "Half a second in all cases. Ali emerges from his office, Damascus team arms device from the safe house, Langley has time to validate the target's identity, then as Ali crosses the plane of the car he goes boom. Gives us time to abort if pedestrians get in the way."

Bradley nodded. "Anything on this device U.S.-made?"

Jackson shook her head. "All foreign. If they investigate, it will look like a terrorist made it. We didn't buy American on this project."

Bradley smiled.

"Device in the door speaker?" he asked.

"That's right.

Bradley turned to the mock-up. "Let's see it."

Lyle gave a thumbs-up and hustled up the stairs into the viewing tower. He opened a laptop connected to the sensors and stared at the screen for a moment. "We're ready."

Jackson dialed the sat phone to arm the device. Then signaled down to Lyle, who began pulling the rope. The Ali cadaver slid along the sidewalk supported by the IV pole.

There was a whump when the cadaver broke the infrared plane. The

Pajero kicked slightly off the curb. Darryl's head vanished and his shoulders and chest shredded into ropes of flesh. The IV pole listed, then Darryl fell toward the wall.

The other three cadavers stood tall. "K23 on the others," Lyle said. "Twenty-three kilopascals means they'd be safer than a breacher during an assault. Downright gentle." The team left the observation post and toured the mock-up grounds for a few minutes to review the damage. There were minimal signs of fragmentation on the other cadavers. Lyle estimated based on the overpressure readings that even if pedestrians had stood exactly where the cadavers did, the worst-case scenario would have been a ruptured eardrum.

Bradley walked the mock-up grounds for ten more minutes, Rodney following. Paulina excused herself for the glorious air-conditioning of the hangar. She packed in another fat lipper of Grizz to relax and sat with her feet up on the workbench staring at the picture of Ali Hassan. She opened one of the drawers and removed the photo of the dead case officer, the poor white girl who'd started this whole thing by getting herself kidnapped and killed in some godforsaken country. Paulina pinned the picture over the image of Ali Hassan and spit into her coffee cup.

THOUGH ABU QASIM DID NOT have the resources of the U.S. government to support his bomb-making efforts, he was able to score one small victory: he put his weapon into position first.

Abu Qasim, Sarya, and his team of four Republican Guard defectors—lent by Alloush—had entered central Damascus hidden in the back of a delivery van accompanied by ammunition, AK-47s, Sarya's sniper rifle, and the crate that gave him heart palpitations every time they hit a bump.

The safe house felt like a refugee camp: makeshift beds, garbage cans jammed to the rim, the fetid stink of sweat. Inside, they waited for two men to arrive. Sarya sat in the bedroom oiling the rifle's bolt action and keeping her distance from the defectors.

Abu Qasim heard the knock. He picked up his AK-47 and pointed it toward the door. The defectors scrambled from their mats and did the same.

There was a knock, then another. Then another. It was them.

Abu Qasim opened the door and saw an old cleric and a young man wearing a blindfold. The cleric looked past Qasim into the safe house living room, at the troupe pointing AK-47s at the door. "Relax, brothers," the cleric said. He was Umar, Abu Qasim's agent in Damascus. He ran the network of sources who'd provided information on senior figures in the government. He had procured the safe house. He had discovered the time and place of Ali Hassan's meeting. He had recruited this young man.

Abu Qasim pulled them into the room and closed the door. Sarya emerged from the bedroom.

Abu Qasim shook the young man's hand. The grip was limp, his hand slick. "What is your name?"

"Jibril."

"It is an honor, Jibril. Now, sit, we have much to discuss."

In the living room they sat on pillows and went through each step of the plan. Abu Qasim pointed Jibril toward the crate holding the bomb. "You put it on the bottom shelf of the tea cart," he explained.

Jibril was quiet. He nodded.

Jibril cringed as Abu Qasim opened the crate. "You need to do just two things before the meeting," he said. "Put the battery in the phone and turn it on. The battery is fully charged and should last for at least fifteen hours. But to be safe, turn it on no more than ten hours before the meeting starts. You understand that you wait to place this until they have all gathered for Ali Hassan's meeting?"

"Yes, Commander."

"It is still scheduled for July eighteenth?"

"Yes."

Abu Qasim slid one of Umar's intelligence reports from his pocket and handed it to Jibril. "Do you still expect all of these men to join?"

Jibril read the list. "The defense minister comes rarely, so maybe not.

And this list is missing Ali's brother, Rustum, commander of the Republican Guard."

Abu Qasim's pulse jolted with excitement. "You are sure?"

"Yes, he now comes to every meeting. Rumor has it that Ali initially did not invite him, but Rustum intervened with the President to secure a spot. The two brothers despise each other. Rustum makes a point of coming because it bothers his younger brother."

"That is excellent news," Abu Qasim murmured. "Jibril, what type of screening will happen outside the building?"

"Very little," Jibril said. "There are no dogs and the metal detectors usually do not function. I bring in boxes this size each week loaded with tea supplies. They will not search me."

Abu Qasim nodded and stood to place the crate inside a box.

"Qasim, you know that even if we succeed, they will just promote more men to take these positions," Umar said. "This will not be enough to topple them."

"We may never overthrow this government," Abu Qasim said as he closed the crate. "And I've never intended this bomb for that purpose." He slid it toward Jibril.

"The goal is simple. It is that they suffer."

THAT NIGHT, JIBRIL LUGGED THE box into his third-floor apartment. Though the package was not particularly heavy and the air-conditioning was blasting, he was still sweating profusely as he climbed the stairs. Inside his apartment, he packed more tea and sugar packets into the cardboard box, covering the wooden crate that made him want to vomit. He placed it in his closet, shut the door, then opened the closet again. He stared at the box, briefly imagining throwing it out and fleeing to Turkey as his brother had done. But then he remembered his father's limp and his arms. "What are the little circles, Papa?" he had asked one day. His mother tried to shoo him away. His father had smiled. An eerie, knowing smile. "The disease of Saydnaya, my son." Noting the black irony, Jibril lit a cigarette to calm himself down and again closed the closet door.

THE ORANGE DIPLOMATIC POUCH HOLDING Paulina Jackson's bomb arrived at Amman Station accompanied by a gruff CIA mechanic named Yates who had no idea what was in the Pajero door and did not want to know.

Inside the emptied embassy motor pool Yates removed the front passenger door from a 2012 Mitsubishi Pajero. He took out the car battery and disconnected the fuses for the power windows and locks. He opened the door, hammered out the door pins, and pulled back the harness covering the wires. He cut them, being careful to leave enough length to attach them to the new door. He unbolted the hinges, and let the door fall to the concrete floor. No point in pussyfooting around. This vehicle was never coming back from Syria.

He took a cigarette break outside in the blazing desert heat of the compound. More like a fortress, but holy shit, the heat. He tossed the butt aside before he burned into the filter because it was too hot to even smoke. His shirt was splotched with sweat stains by the time he returned to the motor pool. He took the new door from the orange pouch. He held it aloft for a moment, feeling its weight. Then he picked up the old door. The paint matched. Same weight. Whatever this door was, it wasn't reinforced with armor, he knew that for damn sure. He went to work connecting the wires from the door to the car, and found the wire marked with yellow tape that he'd read about in the cable traffic. He made sure to wire this one into the door's power system so that whatever they'd put in here would get a charge when the car was running. As he worked, he noticed that the feed for the sound system was absent. Out of habit, he pulled closer to see what the deal was and then caught himself. If they cared enough about a door to ship it to Jordan and replace a perfectly good door with it, they had a good reason.

The wrench slid around in his hand, and he had to put it down a few times to wipe the sweat off his palms on his pants. When the bolts were tight, he put the battery back in. He looked at his watch. Forty-five minutes, smoke break included. Not bad for a free night at the Four Seasons. Though he didn't care about the room itself, the bar was the kicker. He'd never seen people drink like that anywhere, let alone in a Muslim country or whatever this was, and no way he was gonna miss out on that, especially since he had about $150 of Uncle Sam's per diem to spend. He gathered up his tools, then closed the door on the vehicle real careful, just to be sure.

RAMI KNEW BETTER THAN TO ask Sam what was in the car he'd just driven into Damascus from Amman. He'd brought the vehicle to his family's dealership, removed the plates as instructed, and pulled a new, identical Pajero alongside. He scanned the two. They matched, thank god. He smoked and ate pizza in his office while he waited. The man who arrived at ten p.m. was squat, surly, and in possession of a permanently furrowed brow. Tariq was another Damascus Station support asset. He was polygraphed, trustworthy, and a stellar mechanic who did not ask questions. A rare combination anywhere in the world, let alone Damascus.

Rami pointed to the door on the car he'd driven in from Jordan. "That one, to that one."

Tariq nodded and followed the same procedure as Yates had in Amman. He finished in an hour and left. Rami looked at the Pajero: Syrian plates and registration, CIA door. He drove it to the edge of the Kassab Motors lot, careful to avoid any bumps, and placed a SOLD sign on the windshield

Then he signaled Sam.

29

THE BOMB NOW IN THE HANDS OF ALLAH, ABU QASIM and Sarya sat in the safe house bedroom, arranging another man's death as they pored over the intelligence reports collected by their network in Damascus. The information had been purchased at tremendous cost for very little money. Three of the volunteer informants had disappeared into Saydnaya and at least one had died under torture, according to one of the emir's spies inside the prison. Much of the information, though, was an unstructured collection of random observations by an untrained intelligence apparatus: there was a log of Ali Hassan's activity from a Monday through Wednesday, but then a gap for several weeks. The intelligence describing the meeting at which Jibril served tea had been notable for its specificity. As was the map of the route Riyad Shalish, the chief of the SSRC's Branch 450, would take across the city the next day. It was the reason they'd brought Sarya and her rifle into Damascus.

She tossed the papers on the floor. "I am done studying," she said. "We are ready. As ready as we will be."

"There is something . . ." he began saying before he trailed off at the look of her darkening face. The anticipation of killing always made her quiet. Planning done, she would stop talking and did not want to hear his voice, either. He'd always been chatty before operations, talking to work out the nerves. This she could not abide. "My needs become animalistic, more basic," she had told him once. "Before the hunt I want to eat, lie with my husband, sleep, and pray. The killing must happen, but once I know what to do, I do not want to discuss it anymore." Abu Qasim had killed dozens—perhaps hundreds—of men, women, and children with his bombs, but he could not picture the faces. He found that comforting. Sarya, however, had looked into the eyes of her one hundred and forty-two victims just before they died. The intimacy, oddly, offered certainty that the men she killed were deserving of death: they were soldiers of the Republican Guard or *shabiha* or Persian mercenaries. "If I do not kill them, who will?" she would ask. This, he knew, gave her great peace. And so, again, she now sat in silence.

He brought stale bread and lentils from the kitchen and they ate facing each other on the mattress. His faith, he thought, was weaker than hers. It must be, because he did not know if after tonight he would ever see her again, in this world or the next. Thoughts of another life danced through his mind, one where they grew old, children shrieking at play. And yet I am here. Life had run its course: businessman, outlaw, rebel commander, assassin, mass murderer. He wondered how Allah would judge. The thought took him back to Aleppo, to the birth of the uprising before the war. Before the massacres, before the bombs, before he'd lost his soul.

ALEPPO INITIALLY STUCK UP ITS nose at the rabble inconveniencing them with demands for the President's ouster, for the protesters were worse than disloyal. They were poor.

Many were university students. Others, in the provincial countryside, were underclass *felaheen*, hicks, who covered their women, wore long beards, and did not hide their gruesome teeth or filthy smells. Many had lived a half century of shattering humiliation and predation at the hands of the House of Assad. They had accounts to settle.

In the beginning, none were like Abu Qasim's family. His father, owner of a successful textile manufacturing operation, had sneered that the demonstrations were bad for business. "These idiots are going to cost us," he'd said. He'd been right, of course. He just hadn't known his son would instigate it all.

Upper-class Sunni families like Abu Qasim's stayed on the sidelines when the protests started. At the time he worked for his father and traveled frequently to Turkey on business. There he kept a mistress, drank, and smoked. Sarya primarily socialized back in Aleppo. She did not wear the hijab then. They did not pray, he attended mosque infrequently. He had resented her: the quasi-arranged marriage, her barren womb.

As with many others' entrance into the rebellion, his invitation had been delivered by a *mukhabarat* club. He did not feel the blow himself; that had been borne by a university friend during a protest at their alma mater. Abu Qasim had not been there himself. But he had seen the corpse: a body so swollen, bruised, and bloodied that he did not recognize his friend.

The next Friday, he attended a protest organized by the *tansiqiyas*, the local committees then fueling the resistance. They chanted in a carnival atmosphere, banners fluttering in the wind, dancing, cheering, savoring freedom. More than ten thousand marched. The size of the crowd convinced him that the protest movement would grow, the streets and squares would fill, and Assad would eventually step down like Mubarak of Egypt or Ben Ali of Tunisia. The next week he brought Sarya and saw in this new world a chance at redemption, at meaning, at something more than the life his father had given him. That week, he and Sarya secretly joined the *tansiqiya*.

An informant gave him up. The *mukhabarat* visited. It went poorly. Ten men decamped to his father's factory to deliver a warning to stop protesting or there would be consequences. They arrived during a party as one hundred employees gathered around listening to his father applaud a retiree. The squad leader interrupted, demanding Abu Qasim and his father join him for a private conversation.

His father's cheeks reddened with rage. Then someone threw a hammer at one of the *mukhabarat*, striking his forehead. The room fell silent, the man convulsing and frothing on the floor until he died. *Ya allah*, Abu Qasim's father yelled. My god.

A retaliatory shot into the crowd killed one of the ladies who swept the floor, and initiated the fateful melee. In the end, the workers killed six of the *mukhabarat*. The *mukhabarat* tossed his father from his second-floor office, butchered thirty-one employees, and set the factory ablaze. Abu Qasim had managed to escape, but that night he and Sarya fled Aleppo to find the emir, a man Abu Qasim had known at Aleppo University and who had just been released from prison. He would protect them.

They discovered Sarya's remarkable gift by accident on the shooting ranges of the emir's encampment. Instead of giving babies to the world, the emir said, this woman has been sent to harvest the *kuffar*'s children. And harvest she would, under the banners of jihad. One month later they returned to Aleppo, Abu Qasim now in the emir's army, to take the countryside's fight to the great city, to settle the old accounts. There, in the pulverizing trench warfare, he established the bomb works, lost his finger, redeemed his marriage, absorbed two nails from a barrel bomb, nearly died from typhus, skinned rats for sustenance, stood watch for the Black Death's plague, and, in the end, lost all hope.

HE SET DOWN THE EMPTIED bowl and wiped his hands on the side of the mattress. Sarya looked toward the closed door, then the sheets. He smiled thinly and stood. As he slipped from his pants, stiff and well grown, he watched Sarya slide from hers and they fell together onto the mattress, making love silently as each one's mouth captured the other's noise. She fell asleep splayed out above the sheets to escape the sticky heat. But he lay awake until dawn broke outside, watching her stomach move up and down as she breathed. He felt gratitude once more for her barren womb. That no children would spring from their love to live through this hell.

HE'D JUST DRIFTED OFF WHEN he awoke to Sarya's fluttering recitation of the suras describing the first battle ever fought by the armies of Islam. Then, the Prophet himself had commanded.

"Remember thy Lord inspired the angels with this message," Sarya whispered, her eyes closed. "I am with you: give firmness to the Believers: I will instill fear into the hearts of the Unbelievers. Therefore, strike off their heads and strike off every fingertip."

"Allahu Akbar. Allahu Akbar," said Abu Qasim. He slid his hand onto Sarya's belly. She squeezed his fingers.

"This is because they acted adversely to Allah and His Messenger," she continued. "And whoever acts adversely to Allah and His Messenger—then surely Allah is severe in requiting evil."

"Allahu Akbar. Allahu Akbar."

"Thus it will be said: so taste it, for those who resist Allah receive the penalty of the Fire."

He kissed her forehead. She kissed his cheek, then stood to put on her shirt.

THEY NEEDED THE STRANGER'S APARTMENT, but Abu Qasim had still felt a tinge of regret at killing the old man. Fahd, one of the defectors, had knocked on the door wearing his Republican Guard uniform. An old man answered. "A fellow soldier? Come in. Come in," he said. Instead, Fahd put his Makarov pistol to the old man's head and explained he would die if there was noise. The old man gave a thin, knowing smile and waved them inside. Abu Qasim and Sarya shuffled in behind Fahd. Abu Qasim closed the door and Fahd backed the man into his living room. A parakeet chirped from a cage hanging above a chair. Abu Qasim raised his Makarov.

"Do it quickly, boy," the old man said as he sat. "I've got no secrets for you, and no money."

Abu Qasim's eyes darted around the cramped apartment. "Are you alone?" Fahd disappeared to search the bedroom.

"I am," the old man said. "In fact, I have been for some time." He ran a hand through his thinning hair. "I always knew it would end this way, you know? I was in Air Force Intelligence for almost thirty years. I've done my share. Now it's my turn." The parakeet squawked. Abu Qasim shot him in the forehead as the old man looked up toward the bird.

Now the body lay at rest in the chair. Sarya sat next to the dead man behind a table, using the open balcony door as her keyhole onto the street below. She pulled off the hijab to take advantage of some air in the sweltering heat. The Russian rifle balanced on the table, peeking through the window out toward the jammed boulevard below.

Abu Qasim scanned the road approaching the Security Office through his binoculars. The wind picked up from the north. Sand clipped through the air, flicking against the windowpanes. Sarya looked back. "The gusts are erratic," she said.

Abu Qasim's cell phone buzzed. "Commander, he's left the building. Vehicle description and license plate match the intelligence reports."

"Understood." He hung up.

"Twenty minutes," he told Sarya.

She nodded and looked again at the anemometer, a Kestrel she'd taken from a dead Russian, who'd himself probably taken it from a dead rebel. "Ten clicks," she said, shaking her head. What she really wanted to know, however, was the wind speed at point of impact. She glassed the intersection and spotted laundry, hung on a nearby building, flapping in the breeze. "About six clicks down there," she said. She then consulted the ballistic chart on her phone to calculate the bullet drop based on the distance, wind, and elevation. Sand and dust whipped about. She tested the bolt action, pretended to press the trigger, then popped the bolt open and closed. She withdrew from her scabbard a mixture of bore cleaner and oil and lapped it through the bolt for several minutes.

Then the Black Death of Aleppo, reaper of one hundred and forty-two souls, put the hijab over her head. She began to pray for the one hundred and forty-third.

ABU QASIM'S PHONE BUZZED AGAIN as he watched the anemometer tally another gust.

"Commander, they just passed my position. The window tinting is quite severe, but I think there are four in the car. Driver included. I cannot tell which is the target." Abu Qasim swore.

Sarya pulled back the hijab and wiped her watering eyes. "We will need two clean shots to have certainty. One into each front-seat occupant through the seats into the back passengers."

Abu Qasim looked for the car through the binoculars. Still praying, beseeching Allah for vengeance for the souls of fallen martyrs, Sarya clicked a full magazine into the rifle—though they expected she would have time for three shots at most—and increased the scope magnification to see farther down the road. Her tongue fluttered with singsong praises for Aleppo's dead and curses on the *kafir,* the infidel, as she adjusted the cheek plate. She glanced at the anemometer and the laundry. Abu Qasim joined in the prayers, not knowing where they traveled but understanding their gravity in this moment.

She dialed down the magnification as the car approached.

A gust of wind clipped through as the car turned into view, still more than a kilometer away. A jet-black Lexus sedan, license plate 9760112. The yellow stripes on the plate identified it as a government vehicle.

"It is them," he said. Abu Qasim watched her back's movement slow as Sarya regulated her breathing in advance of the shot, taking full breaths then exhaling to find the natural pause as her lungs emptied.

She beseeched Allah for the end of the regime. He prayed the wind would die.

It did.

The prayers ended. The car slowed to a stop at an intersection five hundred yards away.

Sarya slowly expelled the air from her lungs. She pressed the trigger.

DAOUD HADDAD HEARD GLASS SHATTER and then warm liquid sprayed the left side of his face and neck. His eyes were on fire and he put his hands on his face and slumped into the window. He could not see. He heard a gurgle from his boss, Shalish, in the backseat, then something heavy and hot gulped the pressure from his left ear. Then the horn was blaring. He tried to get out but only crumpled to the floor in pain. Then he reached up—where was the door handle? There it is, but why won't it move? He pawed at it and then realized that his hands were too slippery. Glass shattered again and sprinkled down on him. He heard the driver's body slump between the front seats.

The horn stopped.

He tried to open his eyes but could not. He thought of Razan as a little girl in a yellow dress. He could not picture Mona.

SARYA SLID THE BOLT ACTION to expel the third round and thanked Allah for the harvest. She sat up cross-legged. She folded up the rifle's rear leg into the stock, the bipod into the rifle's forearm, and unclipped the scope and ejected the magazine, placing them into the scabbard with the rifle. She removed her hijab and also put it inside. A head covering would draw attention in this neighborhood.

"One hundred and forty-five," Sarya said. He nodded.

Abu Qasim stopped himself as he was closing the front door behind them.

"What is it?" Sarya hissed. "We've got to go."

He walked back into the living room and closed the old man's eyes as the sirens picked up in the distance.

30

UNCLE DAOUD WAS IN STABLE CONDITION BY THE TIME Mariam arrived at Tishreen Military Hospital to visit. He had his own antiseptic room soaked in harsh artificial light. The lone window opened into an alleyway teeming with feral cats. Razan sat in a flimsy folding chair next to the bed, reading a novel while Daoud slept. A nurse fiddled with the IV drip, smiling at Mariam as she stood in the doorway. Razan had been the first to call Mariam with the news, her voice so wobbly that Mariam could hardly understand what had happened. The second call, more measured, came after the doctors were certain Daoud's injuries were not life-threatening.

"How is he?" Mariam asked Razan as she entered the room.

Razan stood and hugged her, clasping tight. "Good. Just tired. They removed the last of the glass this afternoon. He was lucky, they say. No bullets." She tried to smile.

Mariam sat in a chair next to Razan and watched Uncle Daoud's chest move up and down with each breath. She dragged the chair next to Razan and put her head on her cousin's shoulder. "Do they know who is responsible?" Mariam asked.

"I don't know."

"Have you apologized to him yet, Razan?" Mariam asked. "For the silent treatment." A tear welled in Razan's good eye and she pushed Mariam's head aside to sit up straight. She sniffled.

"Not now, please, Mariam," Razan said.

Mariam nodded and stood to look out the filthy window. A dumpster, cats, peeling macadam, more cats. When she turned around Daoud's eyes were open. He had bandages wrapped around his cheeks and neck and head and hands like a mummy. Still, he smiled and said: "Mariam."

She kissed the lone unbandaged spot on his forehead and pulled her chair up to the right side of the bed. Razan held his left hand.

He spoke quietly, taking breaths between words. "They say I will be fine," Daoud wheezed. "The surgeries were successful. A lot of glass. Shalish, though . . ." He trailed off, staring into the glow of the ceiling's fluorescent lights.

Mariam had collected a few details from inside the Palace after receiving Razan's panicked calls: Daoud, his boss Riyad Shalish, and another SSRC official had been traveling to the Security Office for a meeting when their chauffeured car took sniper fire. Uncle Daoud was the sole survivor. With Shalish dead, her uncle would be the likely choice to lead Branch 450. Sam and CIA, she knew, would welcome the promotion as an opportunity to learn more about the SSRC. Looking at her dear uncle, post-op and bandaged, Mariam agreed a promotion would be helpful, then swelled with shame at the thought.

"How do you feel, Uncle?" Mariam asked.

"Fine. They have me on a nice medication." He nudged his chin in the direction of the IV bag. He closed his eyes.

"Do they have any leads?" Mariam asked.

Daoud's eyes opened, searching for Razan. "Rebels, of course. *The opposition.*" Mariam could feel Razan's face heat up at the word, the insinuation that Razan's friends in the *tansiqiya* bore some cosmic responsibility for his injuries. Of course, he knew as well as Mariam that the protest groups had not done this to him.

Razan grimaced but said nothing and held tightly to his hand.

Mariam gave her a grateful look for the silence. "Which rebels?" she asked.

"They do not know for sure," Daoud said. "But we have picked up chatter recently that Zahran Alloush's Douma militia has sent teams into the city center to kill government officials and incite mayhem." Daoud closed his eyes again and sucked in a heavy, raspy breath.

Douma. The word transported Mariam to that night with Umm Abiha. Now, looking at her beloved uncle, Mariam knew the gap between them had become an unbridgeable chasm. It was the demonic thing about this conflict. Flocks of decent people who had gotten along before the war were now murdering each other. The old woman and her husband had looked after Mariam and Razan in Douma, though they had not deserved the kindness. Now a rebel hit squad from Douma had almost murdered her uncle in the street, though surely he— She broke off at the thought, remembering his visit to the tunnel. Instead, she thought of Fatimah, and the ache returned because she knew she was involved, perpetuating the cycle. It would have taken millions of idealists like Razan to overcome the forces now binding families and sects and ethnicities together in opposition to everyone else. Mariam looked at Razan's eye patch and Daoud's bandaged face and wanted to cry.

She kissed her uncle's forehead and hugged Razan tight and they both cried as Daoud lapsed back to sleep. Mariam held Razan and let the tears roll down onto her cousin's back and she heard nothing but their sniffling and shuddering and the reassuring beep of the EKG in the far corner of the room.

BACK AT HOME, HAIRPIN IN hand, Mariam stood in her closet and reached into her jewelry drawer. She removed the necklace Sam had given her in the safe house and gazed at the sapphire. She found the little hole on the back that Sam had shown her and stuck the pin inside until she heard a click. Mariam put on the necklace and stood for a moment, eyes closed, breath deep, ballooning air into her lungs. She put on a sensible black dress with three-quarter-length sleeves that smothered her bust, necklace sitting atop the acetate fabric on the cleft of her breasts. Atiyah had made good on his threat for a follow-up meeting. She did not want him to gaze at the necklace, though she suspected he would. She left her apartment and scanned for the signal graffiti, a daily ritual. There wasn't any today, and she walked on to her office, running the moves from France to determine if they were watching and wondering if—and when—Atiyah would decide, again, that she should die.

AS MARIAM APPROACHED HIS OFFICE, she fought the terror by imagining the pedophile's death by her hand. His brain splattering from her club. If she and Sam succeeded, though, Atiyah's demise would occur off-screen, in the hideous basements of the Security Office before a quick trip to the hangman to finish it off.

Now, though: a one-on-one with Atiyah to review her work against the National Council. Her chance to scan his entire office with the necklace camera, as Sam had said. Today Atiyah wore a jet-black suit—Italian manufacture, she thought—white shirt tight against his muscular frame, and a lime-green tie that she knew Sam would describe as douchey. She fought back a smile.

Atiyah waved her in, eyes locked on her chest. Undeterred by this ritual of retinal undressing, Mariam merely smiled. If her curves distracted him, it meant that the little camera got some nice footage of him, his desk, and his sitting area. She had never really studied his office until this moment, but now she realized it was quite minimalistic. There were few natural hiding spots. The desk—no drawers—a couch with thin cushions, a table and three chairs, and a bookshelf, which looked promising.

As she approached his desk, Mariam noticed an elegant black briefcase at his feet. Atiyah waved her toward one of the chairs and joined her at the table. He grabbed one of the binders and began flipping through the pages in silence. Mariam started to speak, but he put his hand in the air for her to stop and kept reading. She imagined kicking him in the groin, then driving her knee into his face before tossing him into the bookshelf. As he lay in a pile, she could strangle him with the necklace, surely the world's most expensive garrote. Assuming it didn't break... in which case, sorry, Sam—collateral damage. She smiled pleasantly and scanned the room as he read. She shifted her body position slightly to capture the right side of his desk, where he kept a small wooden cigar box. But Mariam really wanted a clear shot of the document bag. Atiyah's eyes focused as he read, and she nudged her pen to slide off the table onto the floor toward his desk. She stood up to fetch it and as she knelt down, she tilted the dangling necklace toward the bag, holding it there for a beat. When she stood up, she kept her body pointed toward the bag. She could feel the heat of his eyes on her backside and swung around to return to her chair. Gazing at her, he set down the documents. He leaned back in the chair, rubbing his eyes as though he were trying to wake up.

"I am still puzzled, Mariam. I cannot figure out how you killed all three of them. And where are the bodies? Not a trace. They simply vanished. Remarkable." Atiyah whistled and clapped his hands together.

She kept painting the smile, wondering if she should deny the charge. She let the silence hang, though every instinct in her now said run, run far away.

"They were not the most skilled," he continued. "But there were three, and I imagine they maintained the advantage of surprise. Perhaps someone was with you in Villefranche?" Atiyah stared through her now, into the wall, as if considering the possibilities.

She imagined saying: *I was with my CIA lover and we murdered them before the Americans disposed of the bodies.*

Instead she folded up her notebook. "I do not know what you are talking about," she said. She stood to leave—getting another nice angle on the document bag—but he clutched her arm. She looked at his hand, and instinct drew her eyes to the clump of nerves between the thumb and forefinger. She could sever the grip in an instant. But instead she stood silently.

"I have eyes everywhere, Mariam. Everywhere. Eventually, all will be known. You tell Bouthaina, too. Be a good girl and tell her for me." He released Mariam and smacked her on the bottom as she turned to walk away. It took all of her mental strength to not hit him, to instead focus on the little camera and a few wide-angle shots of the office on the way out. As she walked, she imagined the camera one day capturing Atiyah's body as it swung from the gallows, his feet twisting in a late summer breeze.

31

BRIAN HANLEY CHUGGED HIS DUNKIN' DONUTS COFFEE and grimaced as he saw the message hit his Lotus Notes in-box. Fricking Lotus Notes. What is this, 1995? FDT, the CIA team that released information to foreign intelligence services, had been a pain in the ass for the past few days, stripping and editing the talking points and published intelligence reports that would be passed to the Israeli Mossad during the regular liaison exchange on Syria. The "REL ISR" stamp they would bestow was a necessary but maddening hurdle to climb, even though the Israelis were NE Division's closest regional partner.

But Hanley was pleased to see that the FDT trolls had come around in the end. They'd cleared for hard-copy passage the imagery of the SSRC activity at Jableh, and an interesting report on a small-scale sarin test. Mossad's Syria reporting was usually quite good—better than CIA's, in fact—but the Israelis had recently lost some of their primo SIGINT access. They would like this. He printed the Jableh imagery in color, which he thought was a nice touch. Copies made and placed into his black lock bag, Hanley spent the rest of the morning reading articles recapping the baseball All-Star game before driving to an unlabeled annex in Tysons Corner, distinguishable only by the carbine-wielding security guards checking for blue badges outside. The CIA preferred to keep the Israelis off-campus. There had been an unpleasant incident a few years back, when a Mossad liaison officer snuck around headquarters unsupervised for a day.

DANNY DAYAN, MOSSAD'S OWLISH WASHINGTON Deputy Chief of Station, led the Israeli delegation that week. Dayan listened carefully as the CIA officers prattled on, reviewing the hard-copy material between bites of a gigantic scone from Corner Bakery. After more than sixty liaison meetings with the Americans, he'd come to wonder if the restaurant was actually owned by the CIA. No matter, he thought midbite, he could see that the girls and boys at Langley had some interesting cases cooking right now. After the briefing, on his way to the parking garage, he pulled the Hanley kid aside.

"Great stuff this month. My best to the team in Damascus," Dayan said.

"Joseph will be pleased to hear it, he's got the kick-ass case out there," Hanley said, before his face flushed at the indiscretion. Dayan nodded and half smiled as the young officer ducked into his Toyota Prius and sped off.

In his apartment that evening, Dayan drank three glasses of wine as he jotted down notes and took pictures of the CIA documents using a subminiature camera. He removed the film and placed the tiny roll in a sealed dime bag like a drug dealer. He folded up his notes and did the same. They had given him a leather messenger bag with a hidden compartment but he despised the clunky thing, so Dayan stuffed the bags into his underwear. He put on a Washington Nationals baseball cap and set out for Rock Creek Park.

Yekaterina waited for him on their bench. Dayan grinned and she frowned as he pulled the bags from his underwear, shoved them in her lap, and sat.

"Your gambling habits got you in trouble in Moscow, Danny," she said. "Why do you insist on gambling with your life here?"

He refused to take the bait. An argument might prevent him from catching the last few innings of the Nats game. "You'll see some interesting hard-copy reporting in there," he said. "Syria-related. SSRC, chemical weapons. All gold."

"General Volkov will be pleased," Yekaterina said, referring to the head of SVR's Middle East Department and Dayan's recruiting officer in Moscow.

Dayan nodded. "There is something else. After the exchange, I spoke with one of their junior officers. Apparently someone named Joseph is running the case that generated these hard-copy reports. He's in Damascus."

"Joseph what?" Yekaterina asked.

"Not sure, but I actually think it was his last name," Dayan said. "Traces should pick him up."

Dayan pulled the cap snug on his head, stood, and left.

32

RUSTUM SET ASIDE THE SVR REPORTS AND RAN A HAND over his mustache as he finished his tea. Following his own strict security protocols for document handling, he put the stolen CIA satellite imagery of his Jableh complex and the rest of the SVR reporting into the safe. How had the Americans found it? No one had left the Jableh compound in months. They'd produced two hundred tons of sarin, and now they had to evacuate. Who had told CIA? Another fucking spy inside the SSRC, like Marwan Ghazali? His little brother apparently could not do his job. Thinking he had the rage under control, Rustum put his hand on the doorknob to leave his office and join Bouthaina for lunch. Then he remembered Shalish. Deeply involved in the chemical operation, ultimately replaceable, but, still, a man in a role. Rustum required Branch 450's sarin expertise for his attack. Shalish had managed that portfolio and now he was dead, shot by a sniper in central Damascus. Now who to elevate? Rustum paused and took a long, slow breath during which he realized he was not yet ready for the outside world. It had been a bad few days.

He could not remember picking it up, but when his mind returned to the present Rustum was slicing a letter opener deep into one of the couch cushions. He'd gutted the two cushions and three of the pillows by the time his aide arrived asking what is wrong, Commander? The aide looked around. Tufts of stuffing floated through the office while the commander of Syria's Republican Guard knelt on the floor eviscerating a faux-silk pillow. Rustum cursed, for he did not know he'd been yelling. "What was I saying?" he whispered to the aide.

"The same story, Commander." He paused. "Hama."

Rustum stood, picked a piece of stuffing from his linen shirt, and shooed the aide out. Bouthaina said he sometimes told the story while he slept, similar to what the psychologist said Basil would do.

He had retreated to his villa in the mountains near Lebanon for a few days of cooler weather and nubile frolicking with Bouthaina. He stepped outside. The terrace was nestled into a copse of almond trees just above Bloudan, a mountain getaway for the Syrian elite. A place in which, as a child, he could only have dreamed of waiting tables. Now he was its lord. Rustum saw Bouthaina sunbathing, a half-drunk bottle of white wine chilling in a bucket nearby. She was bug-eyed in her gigantic Chanel sunglasses, soaking in the sun. She smiled when she saw him. He could still hear the beating in his chest and wondered if a fuck might calm him down. Then his phone rang. He looked down at the screen with a strange mixture of annoyance, rage, and anxiety. It was the President.

THE SVR REPORTS HAD VINDICATED Ali's instincts about the American, Samuel Joseph. He had concrete information that, if leveraged properly, would lead to a spy's capture. He reread the SVR's commentary again, just to be sure:

SVR ASSET ELICITED NAME OF CIA OPERATIONS OFFICER HANDLING SYRIA CASE RELATED TO JABLEH AND ALLEGED CHEMICAL WEAPONS USE IN EFREH. SUBSOURCE DESCRIBED HIM AS "JOSEPH." SVR TRACES INDICATE OFFICER IN QUESTION MAY BE US EMBASSY DAMASCUS COMMS OFFICIAL SAMUEL JOSEPH.

Then there was the sarin test and the Jableh complex. Ali lit a cigarette and went to the window. His brother was not just a savage, he was insane. And he had no way to fight him. He'd been losing fights to Rustum for forty years, so Ali knew when he was beaten. Whatever this program was, the President had approved of it. But gas, really? And in such large quantities? What were they planning? Anytime the regime went on the offensive, the rebels punched right back. He saw no way out of the war, but also no way to win. And there was no safety net if they lost. So he would focus on the investigation. It was something he could control.

Ali pulled his memo on the Samuel Joseph investigation from his desk drawer. He'd drafted it in an inspired spell after the SVR reports arrived. He wanted paper in front of Assad to have the upper hand over Rustum. He had addressed it to His Excellency Bashar al-Assad, President of the Syrian Arab Republic. He'd also sent a copy to Rustum. They would discuss it at the Palace in thirty minutes.

Ali reread the memo. He thought it could work. Then he wondered to what end. An irritating, useless thought. He pushed it aside.

Kanaan swung open the door. "Can I get you more coffee before we go?"

Ali smiled as he stuffed extra copies into his briefcase. "Why do you ask?"

"You look tired."

"As would you if Rustum was your brother."

THERE ARE TWO PALACES IN Damascus. One, the People's Palace, is a gargantuan sandstone structure set on Mount Mezzeh, overlooking the city like a feudal castle. President Assad barely visits unless he needs it for sterile handshake photo ops with visiting dignitaries. The second, Malki, is Assad's family residence, and it is tucked into a leafy district of central Damascus. It is more bungalow than palace. The rooms are well kept but cozy, and certainly not grand. Assad's toddlers' toys are scattered on the floors. Unlike Saddam Hussein and the House of Saud, Bashar al-Assad—like his father—does not display his wealth with innumerable mansions, gold toilets, faux–Roman bathhouses, and walls plastered with gaudy erotic paintings. Even amid the civil war, the House of Assad sees itself as an expression of the popular will. A dynasty with an earthy image to protect.

Ali arrived first, and was ushered into Malki's sitting room and served tea. The meeting would occur in Assad's modest personal study amid cracking leather sofas, muted televisions, a treadmill, and stacks of files and paper. He had just finished his cup of tea when Assad's secretary emerged from his office. "The President is there," the secretary said. "But we are still waiting on the commander. You can go on up, though, General."

Ali knocked twice at the door and heard a lispy, "Come in, come in." Bashar al-Assad, President of the Syrian Arab Republic, had forgone his usual jeans and dress shirt for a black suit and metallic blue tie, the one he usually wore for interviews with European TV stations. Assad was seated in front of his Mac as Ali opened the door. Three leather sofas formed a U shape around a mother-of-pearl-inlaid coffee table scattered with magazines. Behind the couch was a desk stacked high with manila folders and newspapers. A television broadcasting Al Jazeera hung on the wall.

Assad was tall and slender, but there was something very awkward about his appearance, like he was constructed of random body parts that did not belong together. Some of the rebel graffiti, Ali knew from the intelligence reports, called Assad "the Giraffe." He had a long neck that stretched into a weak jaw, topped with a faint boyish mustache. His ears, Ali had always thought, looked more elfin than human. But all of his weaknesses—his appearance, his lisp, the cerebral medical background (he had trained in London as an ophthalmologist)—played in his favor. For they all led observers and enemies to underestimate him. It was always a costly mistake. The President, like all of them, was a murderer.

Ali took a seat on one of the couches and Assad sat down next to him. A copy of the memo, marked up with red ink, sat on the coffee table. "Inspired work here, Ali," Assad said.

Assad asked Ali about Layla and the twins. Ali did the same for Asma and the President's children. Ali did not ask about the mistresses and girlfriends. The President, despite his awkward appearance—or perhaps because of it—used sexual conquest as a way to demonstrate his virility and power to the Syrian elite. Ali purposely kept Layla out of his sight whenever possible.

The President checked his gold wristwatch.

Rustum arrived suited in his full military attire, replete with black shoulder boards and the red cap of the Republican Guard. Ali's jaw clenched when he saw Basil, also in his uniform, following at Rustum's heels. These killers were all cleaned up. They almost looked respectable wearing those pressed uniforms, shaking the President's hand, and politely providing tea orders to the assistant. One could almost forget the stories from the previous troubles, in the eighties, when Basil first earned the nickname Comanche.

The President, who had been watching an Al Jazeera report on Saudi funding for Syrian rebel groups, cursed the House of Saud and turned off the television and gestured for Rustum and Basil to take a seat. "Now," he said. "We have a breach. We need him rolled up quickly. Ali, what is the plan?"

"Certainly, Mr. President. Has everyone read the memo?" Rustum grunted. Ali knew that he was furious that he had not been invited to shape its message. Basil shook his head no and licked his mustache.

"I've laid out three paths to capture the traitor," Ali continued, ignoring Basil. "All should be pursued simultaneously for maximum effect."

Assad put his right elbow on the coffee table and rested his chin in his hand as he scanned the memo again. He began questioning. "In this first path, you think your agent can get a CIA device?"

"It is possible. The agent may also be able to elicit information for us on the CIA's operations here in Damascus. I think this Samuel Joseph will bite with the right bait placed in front of him."

"And the Iranians are confident that they can exploit a device?" Assad asked.

"Yes," Ali said. "Assuming the CIA provides an actual device connected to a satellite and does not use a website as in the Ghazali case." He stopped and set his jaw. "The Iranians are confident they can exploit it."

"Do you have an idea of who you would run against this Samuel Joseph?" Assad said.

"We have a few ideas, including one who has met him before. I believe we can work quickly. And that we have nothing to lose by trying."

Ali grew silent as Assad's secretary entered the room with a tray of pastries and steaming teacups. He placed it on the table and left.

"I think this first approach is too elegant, in fact," Rustum said. "And the payoff is uncertain."

Assad waved off Rustum. "I doubt it. Ali is correct: we have nothing to lose and everything to gain. Make sure to bring the Iranians in if it bears fruit as you predict. Their technical teams can assist in quickly exploiting the device."

"Of course, Mr. President."

Ali continued. "The second approach is to feed unique information to the list of people who knew about Jableh. Each one gets something different. The information has to be sufficiently important that it would be passed to the Americans. It also should be connected to our chemical weapons program. The SVR comments, and the markings on the CIA documents, suggest to me that their source is Israeli and the exchange is focused on chemical weapons. Then we see what comes back."

Rustum had picked up a teacup and now sniffed at the steam. "It's correct," he said taking a sip, "that the list of suspects has narrowed now that they've found the facility. Too damn sweet, by the way, this palace stuff."

Assad gave a high-pitched chuckle.

Ali continued: "We know three things about their source. One, he knows about a compartmented Republican Guard effort inside the SSRC. Two, he knows about a chemical weapons test in Efreh. Three, he knows the location of the Jableh facility. Who has this information?"

"There are maybe four living," Rustum said. "Shalish, but he is dead. The commander at Jableh and his deputy. Jamil Atiyah and the SSRC director. Rumors of the compartment and even the test could have percolated through the Palace, the SSRC, or the Guard, but the specific location of this facility narrows the list substantially."

"You are confident in the lockdown at Jableh?" Assad asked.

"I am. It is a prison camp."

"You're forgetting one name, though, big brother," Ali said.

Rustum smirked. "Who?"

"Bouthaina. I have my little birds inside this government, and I know you used her cutouts to procure some of the material. And who knows what other information she may have come across in the course of her duties, official or . . . unofficial?"

Assad smiled, enjoying the fratricide.

Rustum waved in the air, staring at Ali with rising anger. "Fine. We test her."

"Good," Assad said, waving his hand to end the debate. "The Jableh commanders, Atiyah, the SSRC director, Bouthaina."

"What do you recommend we pass to them, Ali?" the President asked.

Ali ran fingers over his mustache. "The location of another facility. We say there is a backup. The Americans would want the information. And the story only has to hold up long enough for someone to report the information to the CIA. It should be a place where we will know if something happens. That way we have two avenues for information to come back to us. One, the SVR reporting. Two, if the Americans bomb it."

"Supply depots," Rustum said, knuckles whitening as he gripped his teacup.

"Yes, perfect," Assad said. "Warehouses large enough to hide production equipment. Sufficient for storage."

Ali paused, looking at his brother's clenched hands. An irresistible thought formed, an opportunity to dish something back to Rustum. "And you know, big brother, that you will need to pass this information to each person. I, of course, have no knowledge of the program."

"Of course," Rustum said through clenched teeth.

"And I would appreciate if you could write down the names of the suspects paired with the facility location you've given them. This way I can verify that everything is consistent."

Rustum's eyes flashed. He scribbled the list and passed it to Ali. Ali caught the last two names and locations before he slipped it in his pocket. He would scan the others later.

Jamil Atiyah—Khan Abu Shamat
Bouthaina Najjar—Wadi Barada

"Thank you, big brother," Ali said.

"Excellent," Assad said. "Now, the third approach?"

"We know the CIA officer running the spy. We beat him on the street by convincing him that he is free of surveillance, when he in fact he will be covered. He will lead us to his agent."

"And I assume your agent may also be able to determine when he is readying for an operation?" Assad asked.

"It is possible, Mr. President, but it is not certain. The CIA typically compartments such information between its assets. But we will try."

Rustum now pointed to Ali's memo, mashing his finger into the paper for emphasis. "Are you sure the Russian team is necessary?"

"Yes. They have operated extensively against the Americans for decades."

Assad again waved off Rustum without looking at him. "I will call Putin this afternoon. This is approved."

Basil whispered something to Rustum in that burry voice. Now Rustum swung back. "Mr. President, this plan is very thorough, but why do we not just arrest the CIA officer and interrogate him for the name?"

Assad leaned back, amused, and skimmed over Ali's face for a reaction. The President enjoyed watching his lieutenants squabble. Better he be the hub, each adviser a unitary spoke at war with the others. The President sipped more tea.

"What do you think, Ali?" Assad said, knowing the answer.

Ali rubbed his scar. Rustum smiled. The damn thing always knew when it was in the presence of its creator.

RUSTUM HAD IN FACT FAILED to kill Ali. Twice.

When Rustum was eight he pieced together that his mother had died birthing Ali and decided he didn't like the exchange of his beloved mother for the colicky toddler commanding his father and stepmother's attention.

So he led Ali, who had just started walking, toward the stairs and pushed him down. Rustum lied to his parents and claimed young Ali walked off the top step.

Ali had no memory of this. Rustum explained it during his second attempt, the night their father and stepmother were murdered. The day Ali made the fateful decision.

The decision, as an impetuous ten-year old, had been to demand his father make good on a promise to take him for a tractor ride.

The Hassans had owned grocery stores and a distribution business. They'd just opened a new node in Homs, the country's third-largest city, then—as now—roiled by rebellion. It was 1980, and the Ikhwan, the Muslim Brotherhood, was contesting Assad's rule. Ali's father said that the Ikhwan wanted two things: Sharia law and the Alawis dead or holed up in the mountains. Preferably both.

In those days the Alawi presence in Homs was new. Ali's father liked to say that the Alawis' success—our ingenuity, my son—had brought them out of the impoverished mountain villages into the prosperous cities. The Ikhwan terrorists fought the tide, killing two of his father's employees outside one of the stores in the middle of a sunny spring day. They opened the new distribution center soon after. The Hassans lived near the coast, in Latakia, but their parents brought the brothers to Homs for the grand opening and rented an apartment in the city. "We need to stay here for a few months to keep an eye on things," said Ali's father. Ali's grandfather also came down from the coast and stayed with the family.

Ali and Rustum had walked the aisles of the new building. Freshly painted walls filled the room with distinct chemical smells. The place was stuffed: dry goods, machine parts, furniture, farming equipment. And the centerpiece of Ali's affections: a Soviet tractor, inexplicably painted aquamarine, in which he sat every day. After much begging on Ali's part, his father promised him a ride before it sold, or at least before they went back home.

By June the tractor had not sold and it was time to return to Latakia. Ali saw Rustum loading bags into the car and ran to his father, wailing because they had not ridden the tractor yet. He'd promised. Shut up, Rustum had told him, but his father waved his older son off and, looking at the boys' stepmother, said they could all stay in town tonight and make an appearance at the governor's party. She hated those events, Ali knew. Then he would take Ali on the tractor the next morning, and they would actually leave. Ali sniffed. That was okay.

His father and stepmother went to the party that night in a black chauffeured Mercedes. The tint had been so dark that to this day Ali sometimes wondered if his father saw him wave goodbye.

The driver had survived to explain the chronology to Ali's grandfather. While Ali sobbed in his bed, Rustum eavesdropped outside the kitchen. The driver recalled how he had turned onto the street toward home and a man wearing a uniform appeared in the road holding out his hand, motioning for a stop. There were traffic cones scattered haphazardly in the street. The man declared himself to be captain something or other from the police and did you know there had been a shooting two blocks over? He showed a badge. We are taking the necessary precautions. ID cards, please.

ID cards were checked and rechecked and there was a long wait, for apparently someone at headquarters was not responding on his radio. There was a solo crack and then two more and then a rattling volley that swept through the car's back doors. Hands reached in through the window and yanked the driver out and sat him on the ground, dazed.

You watch, you watch, the captain said angrily, pointing at the car.

Two other men pulled Ali's father and stepmother from the car, tossing the bodies to the ground before leaning them against the car facing the driver. The two men stuffed their IDs into their open mouths. Their native Alawi villages, printed on the blood-splattered cards, would be enough for people to understand the message.

A car pulled up and the men got in, all except the captain. He told the driver to pass this message from the Ikhwan. You tell the others, he said. Tell them everything.

In the kitchen, the driver put his hands over his eyes and wept. At this Rustum snatched a knife from a drawer and kicked open the door to the room he shared with Ali. Rustum straddled him in the bed and shoved the knife toward his neck. Ali pushed at his brother's arms to keep the blade away. Rustum sank the tip of the knife into Ali's neck and tried to slide it across his throat. Ali jabbed at Rustum's arms and the blade slid into his jawbone and up the bottom of his cheek. Saliva dribbled from Rustum's mouth as he screamed that Ali should have died on those stairs and he would die now. "Now I am vengeance," Rustum screamed, "for my mother and father and stepmother."

Then Rustum and the blade fell away, and Ali realized that his grandfather had knocked Rustum from the bed. He saw through his tears as his grandfather's strong fists rained down on Rustum. When it was finished, Ali's grandfather had him taken to a local doctor to sew up his wound, Ali covered in his own blood, his grandfather wearing Rustum's on his hands and his once-white linen shirt.

THE TWO BROTHERS HAD NEVER discussed that night. Never had, Ali thought, and never will. What was there to say? Their parents were gone, Ali had inadvertently helped usher in their deaths, and Rustum, his brother Rustum, had died along with his parents. Now he was something else. Ali's rival. Ali's tormentor.

Ali set down the teacup. He looked toward the President. "If we arrest and interrogate the American, we embark on a dangerous journey with an uncertain outcome. One CIA officer has already disappeared in Syria. Their tolerance for losing another, I expect, is low. The CIA will know we've jailed him and the Americans will immediately apply pressure for his release. We will have a limited time to squeeze out the name. We may not succeed. I expect the Americans, working with Zion, will then attempt to kill everyone in this room, you excluded, Mr. President. We should attempt the strategy outlined in my memo before taking such risks."

Assad's eyes flitted between the brothers.

Ali took a chance and continued. "What this spy has passed to the Americans, if true, is very sensitive. If I may ask, though, what is the operational timeline for the compartment mentioned in the CIA report? How much time do we have?"

"How much time do you need, Rustum?" Assad asked.

Rustum simmered. "A month would be ideal. The exposure of Jableh has shut down production. It is now just a matter of logistics. I cannot understand, though, Mr. President, why we do not just snatch the American and throttle the information from his head."

Ali interjected, "It would be out of bounds," instantly regretting the words as they left his mouth.

"Out of bounds?" Rustum's voice quavered and he now shouted. "Are you insane? The CIA is shipping weapons to the *irhabiun*, the terrorists, that kill my soldiers every day. You sit in your office and play cop while my men are slaughtered. Your wife and your twin boys are safe in their apartment because I don't play by the rules, I kill these savages however I can, whenever I can, wherever I can!" He was screaming now, spittle flying toward Ali. "I kill their elderly and their children and their livestock, and those that I let live are forced to eat grass to survive. I drop barrel bombs on them, launch missiles, and will gas them. Our government is still standing because I do what is necessary to live!"

Basil, expressionless during the monologue, stared at Ali's scalp with the dispassionate interest of a livestock inspector.

"Enough," Assad yelled. "Ali, you have a month to find the spy. If we don't have the traitor by then, we arrest the American. I approve everything else in your memo." Assad stood. The meeting was over.

"Mr. President, may I ask for more details on the operation?" Ali asked, risking the President's irritation as he had already stood. "It will help my hunt for the spy."

Rustum's jaw was clenched in rage.

"The Americans have said that there will be consequences if gas is used," Ali continued. "Obviously, none of us know what this foolishness really means. In fact, I bet the American President does not, either. If the SVR report is accurate, we've already crossed this red line without trouble, but . . ." He trailed off.

Rustum smiled and exhaled through his nose. Assad nodded at him.

"Little brother," he said, emphasizing the first word. "We are going to conduct a counterattack against the rebels. We will gas their villages, their neighborhoods, their tunnel systems. We will win the war in a few months. It will be our salvation."

Salvation. At that word the Palace walls crumbled in an avalanche around him and he was young again, a police investigator in Latakia, the twins in Layla's belly.

And the phone has rung for you and you find the three crosses fashioned on telephone poles, three Alawi men crucified, hands and feet split open with railroad spikes in a mimicry of the Christian Bible. Blood at the base of each pole. And when you found the killer, he said he wanted to set Syria on fire, to turn the squares into butcher's blocks and the buildings into burning coffins, to usher in the end of our world. That will be our salvation, he said.

"And Ali," the President said, interrupting the memory as he furrowed his brows. "Your brother is correct that your plan to entrap the spy is very elegant. Just be careful, particularly with your operation against the American. There is potential for blowback and subterfuge, as you well know. I will call Putin and ask for his men."

"Certainly, Mr. President," Ali said.

Rustum huffed out, Basil behind, dishwater eyes reviewing Ali once more as he left. Ali touched his neck, scar throbbing. Before entering his car, he lit a Marlboro. He noticed with approval that his hands were not shaking.

33

BOUTHAINA WAS TEN YEARS YOUNGER THAN RUSTUM and, like him, lubricated by power. The regime's gladiatorial combat was the couple's primary topic of conversation and thunderclap aphrodisiac. They both typically enjoyed discussing their enemies, but Rustum that night had been too embarrassed to even discuss the meeting with Ali and the President. So he'd let Bouthaina go on the warpath about Jamil Atiyah, explaining how she planned to squeeze the old man by the balls. Rustum offered to have Basil surveil Atiyah to see what additional misdeeds could be discovered. This had frustrated Bouthaina. She wanted to overcome Atiyah herself and, further, did not want to take the risk. "Two sadists prowling around each other, one a pedophile, the other nicknamed for his scalp harvesting? No, *habibi*, no, thank you. Keep your Basil on his leash. I will handle Atiyah."

An angry monologue ensued that aroused him, and when she got up to open a second bottle of wine, he had actually picked her up and thrown her onto the bed. It had been a pleasant distraction from Ali's victory at the Palace earlier in the day.

Rustum was not introspective, but even he, in the comedown of morning, could examine his expansive gut, could finger the hair that had sprouted in his ears, and wonder how Bouthaina could tolerate such sloppiness. He scratched his hairy chest and ran his eyes over

Bouthaina's body, her stomach still flat and her face taut and bronzed. Rustum had paid for the plastic surgery. It had been a good investment.

He got up from bed, put on a robe, and walked into his office. The palatial room had for its throne a walnut desk fabricated from fragments of an ancient *noria,* a water wheel, from the Orontes River in Hama. He sat down and began reviewing reports from the *mukhabarat* guards at the U.S. Embassy. When he had finished the first few pages, he leaned back and looked at the desk as he sipped his tea. The inscription on the piece of wood fashioned into the right leg indicated that this *noria* had been built in 1361 to supply water to the city's Grand Mosque. There was a small groove nearby that reminded him of the violent winter of 1982, during the last civil war, when he had been a young lieutenant. That day a rebel detachment, the Muslim Brothers, the Ikhwan, had holed up in an apartment directly behind the *noria*. Their sniper fire claimed ten soldiers before his commander, the old President's brother, had ordered Rustum's platoon to take the building. They fought through the morning, inching closer, until both sides volleyed through the wheel, fragments splintering through the air.

By the time they reached the apartment, Rustum had already killed seventeen Ikhwan. Inside, he notched six more, including the women and children, inexplicably still huddling with the fighters. When they had taken the apartment, he and Basil smoked cigarettes before harvesting the *noria*'s wreckage from the pool of shell casings. Then they took one Ikhwan scalp for each of their thirty-two dead comrades, cutting and bagging deep into the night. That night Rustum had regained a brother in Basil. A replacement for the one who'd murdered his father and two mothers.

Rustum put his right hand on the top of the desk and gently ran his fingers over the wood. Finally, he found the name he wanted on the fifth page of the report, the one with the pictures of every U.S. official working in the embassy.

He picked up the phone.

"Get me Basil," Rustum said to another aide.

Rustum soon heard Basil's familiar scratch, the voice of a man whose trachea had been ripped by shell fragments in Hama, three days after they'd gathered the *noria* wood.

"I have a job for some of your boys. Not the Guard. The Defense Committees, the militia. Keep it unofficial. I want to send a message to the Americans. A mob to cause chaos at their embassy for a few hours. No violence."

Basil grunted affirmingly.

Remembering Basil's eyes as he scalped one of the Ikhwan alive in that apartment, Rustum decided to be more specific with his blood brother.

"No Americans die, Basil. No accidents. Understood?"

"Yes, Commander."

"Use your best men."

"How soon?"

"As soon as possible."

SAM WAS WALKING INTO PROCTER'S office when one of the State Diplomatic Security officers called the Chief and said there was a demonstration outside. A couple hundred people, all waving pro-Assad banners and the presidential portrait like zealots. "Did you say buses?" Procter said. "What are the *mukhabarat* goons outside doing? Nothing? Figured. Okay, I'm coming up." She emerged from her office and began barking at the Station officers. "We're in Destruction Phase One. We have exactly two minutes to shred all the paper."

Phase 1 was based on the time it would take for a team of hostiles to breach the perimeter and reach the Station. Sam thought it would be more like three minutes here, but Procter was a stickler.

Procter snapped at the Station support officer to turn on the acid-boosted shredders, capable of crunching through hard drives and up to fifty pages of classified material in a single bite. A commo tech hustled over with a large stack of technical manuals—inexplicably printed—and began tossing them into the shredders as if feeding a wood chipper.

"We're not in Destruction Phase Two"—electronic media—"but remove all your hard drives and put them in the safe as a precaution."

The Station kept a small armory of M4 carbines, tactical shotguns, and Beretta pistols in case, as Procter liked to say, things got spicy (Destruction Phase 3—personnel exfil and officer self-defense). "I'm headed upstairs and will be back in a sec—no one touch the fucking weapons!"

"Should you take one, Chief?" Zelda asked.

"Oh, Z," Procter said, shaking her head. "Sweet, sweet Z." She blew the analyst a kiss and marched off.

Sam and Zelda removed their hard drives and put them in the safe. Then he motioned toward the door. She nodded.

Sam closed the Station's vault door behind them. As they climbed the steps to the chancery's second floor, he began to register the chants and screams of the mob outside.

Zelda did not look well. Sam pulled alongside her and explained: "No guns in a situation like this. If we killed anyone, the mob would go nuts. And even with our weapons we'd eventually be overrun. We'd have another Tehran on our hands."

At the second floor they punched the code and entered. The offices and cubicles for the State officers had emptied. Everyone was at the windows, scanning the scene in the circle below.

The mob began hurling garbage onto the compound. A tomato slumped into the glass. One of the State Political officers jumped back from the window, startled. A brownish head of lettuce was next. Soon a volley of old fruit and vegetables pummeled the windows like a hailstorm. A rancid smell wafted through the chancery.

The ambassador grimaced at the window. He had recently drawn the regime's ire by making an unauthorized trip to join a protest in Hama. The ambassador, like Sam and Procter, spoke Arabic fluently, so he knew that the mob had begun a chant calling him a dog. Procter smiled.

One of the Diplomatic Security officers pointed to the fence around the embassy. "That is a *climb-resistant* fence. Top-of-the-line."

"So it just *resists* the climbing, puts up a good fight? Perfect," Procter said, her head bobbing around the sludge-flocked window for a clean view of the street.

Sam saw two men start climbing the fence. Several Marines spilled into the courtyard, urging the climbers to stop. They kept coming. Then another jumped onto the fence. Then another.

Sam noticed that one of the climbers carried a Syrian flag. Zelda shuffled toward him. "They aren't going to come in the building, are they?"

Sam shook his head. "Don't think so. See that flag? They're just sending in a few people to take down ours. If they wanted to storm the embassy they'd send more in."

All four men were in the courtyard. They began making obscene gestures toward the Americans upstairs.

"The fence didn't resist very well," Procter said.

No one else tried to climb and the Marines lost the argument and shuffled inside. A crowbar was catapulted over the fence to one of the men. They began climbing the chancery building.

One reached the roof and shimmied up the flagpole, pulling the American flag down and replacing it with that of the Syrian Arab Republic. He held up the stars and stripes, victorious, to a crescendo of supportive hoots from the mob. Then he shoved it down his pants.

"The guy with the crowbar is up on the roof now," one of the State Department political officers said.

The Syrian's position on the roof allowed him to look at the Americans across a narrow courtyard. He made more obscene gestures, then started smashing the air conditioner, stopping once or twice to whoop toward the mob in the street. Sam heard the fans shut off.

"That *shabiha* shithead," Procter said. "It's a hundred and five degrees out."

PART IV

Hunted

34

ALI WATCHED THE HEAT RISE OFF THE TARMAC asphalt at Mezzeh Military Airport on the western outskirts of Damascus. He smoked a Marlboro, but the heat had burned away any of the pleasure of it. He checked his watch. The band was soaked in sweat. Half past twelve. The Russian team should be arriving any moment. Kanaan removed his suit jacket and slung it over his shoulder. "Maybe we wait inside, boss?" Kanaan said.

Ali shook his head and scanned the sky. "No. We greet them personally." He pulled his sunglasses lower on his nose for an unobstructed view as a metal glint appeared in the sky.

Ali stubbed out the cigarette as the cargo plane cut through the clouds, and lit another as it landed. "Here we go," he said to Kanaan. The taxiing plane carried a team of twelve officers of the SVR and the Federal Security Service, the FSB, Russia's internal security service. All had experience operating against the CIA in either Moscow or Washington. The Russians, under the command of an SVR general named Volkov, would partner with Ali to track and entrap CIA officer Samuel Joseph. Ali held a hand over his face to shield the sun as the plane's turboprops stopped whirring and the cargo bay opened.

Volkov—Ali recognized him from the *mukhabarat* files—was the first to descend the ramp into the stifling heat. His men shuffled behind, dragging large crates of equipment from the belly of the plane. Volkov wore aviator glasses and a brown bomber jacket. Ali, who had quickly wiped his sweaty hand on his pants when he saw the man approach, now extended it and shook Volkov's mallet hand. "Welcome to Syria, General," Ali said in English.

"It is a pleasure to be here on such important business," Volkov replied, then turned and gestured toward his men, who were wheeling boxes and crates from the aircraft.

"Only half is vodka," Volkov said. He laughed, as did Ali.

A surveillance van drove down out of the plane onto the tarmac. Then more crates, followed by two more surveillance vans.

"We are going to up-fuck this American," Volkov said, relishing his loose command of vulgar English. "I've done two tours in Washington working against them. This will be a great honor."

"We will track him together," Ali said, already liking this Russian.

Another van emerged from the plane.

"Where are we going to put all of this stuff?" Kanaan asked Ali in Arabic.

KANAAN TOOK THE LOSS OF his offices better than Ali expected. By late afternoon, the Russian surveillance gurus had settled in and had wasted no time in getting to work.

They established a command center decked out with maps, real-time video and audio feeds, pictures of Samuel Joseph and his known or suspected CIA associates.

"It looks like we're going to get drunk and kill the American," Ali had joked to Volkov, pointing to the crates of vodka and the omnipresent photos of the CIA officer. "Not a bad idea, General," the Russian said without any hint of jest. "Not a bad idea."

Together, the teams traced Samuel's known routes through Damascus. The Russians walked them with Ali and his men to understand how Samuel Joseph thought about the street. Though the rest of his team opted for short sleeves, Volkov continued to wear his leather jacket in the midsummer heat.

They monitored Samuel's phone and Skype calls and one of Kanaan's men broke into his apartment to implant listening devices. The report said that the apartment was sparsely furnished except for the refrigerator, which was stocked with an ample supply of smuggled Coors Light.

They organized into seven teams—four Russian, three Syrian—that could operate in cars, on foot, in fixed positions.

The Russians coached them on the particulars of CIA denied-area operations: how the Americans operated in Moscow, how they behaved on the street, the mechanics of CIA SDRs. ("They are long, General, up to fifteen hours in some cases. Exhausting to watch.")

The Russians showed surveillance footage from Moscow. They ran the Syrians through the surveillance detection and countersurveillance training provided to fresh SVR and FSB recruits. Kanaan took notes like the over-eager student he was.

They drilled. One of the Russians, an SVR operations officer, role-played as Samuel in these simulations. They watched as he tried to shake them through Damascus or convince them he was, as the CIA said, "black." In the beginning, he won. But soon they were sticking him, making the correct assessments, watching him role-play at a safe house, video feeds running, monitoring the exits and entrances to spot his asset when the fake meeting ended.

They followed Samuel every moment of the day. Volkov knew how to keep watch while stretching the distance between the target and their teams. He had an inspired taste for where to place the fixed positions. His attention to detail never seemed to flag—despite the fact that he drank vodka like water.

Over cigarettes and vodka—Ali was trying to cultivate a taste, or at the very least a stomach for the stuff—Ali told Volkov about the plan he had proposed to Assad to entrap Samuel Joseph and find another spy.

"Inspired, Ali," the Russian said. "Risky, but inspired." They toasted. Volkov refilled their paper cups.

ALI WAS STARING AT THE portrait of Assad over his door when a knock broke the presidential gaze. It was very late, but as soon as Kanaan entered the room Ali could tell the man had bad news for him. He motioned him toward the table and offered a cigarette. "Tell me. It's late."

Kanaan sat and accepted the cigarette. "We are placing a lot of trust in her, boss. Maybe too much." He lit it and leaned back in his chair.

Ali arched an eyebrow. "You have concerns?"

"We are also asking a lot of her."

"She will be rewarded. I made this clear. And we are not asking for this to drag on. She is not a trained intelligence officer, I have no intention of running her for more than a month. Once we have the device, her work is done." Ali stole another glance at the Assad portrait and stubbed out his cigarette. "What did she say? Did something happen?"

Kanaan thrust out his lower lip and blew a wall of smoke overhead. "Nothing happened, but I think we should be more certain we have her under control."

Ali stood and put his hands on the chair's backrest. Bending down, he stretched his back. He went to the bookshelf, opened one of the agricultural books left by the previous occupant, and ran his fingers along the dusty jacket. He trusted Kanaan's instincts. He put it back on the shelf. "Do you have a proposal?"

Kanaan nodded. "The usual methods, boss. We just arrested five of Fatimah Wael's relatives to assist Bouthaina Najjar's work against the opposition. We should do the same here. We won't treat anyone badly, of course. We just need to send the message: we are in control." He put out his cigarette. "The cousin, for example, has publicly called for the President to step down."

Ali grunted. "Get the paperwork ready." He lit another cigarette.

35

MARIAM WORKED HER HAND IN THE COMFORTABLE motion she'd taught herself as a teenager, her mind floating along the French Riviera as she thought of guiding Sam inside. Savoring the swell as it ran through her body, she applied pressure until she glimpsed a ruined nailbed on her right hand, cruelly drawing her back to Damascus before she could shudder out the tension. She'd been holding her breath, and now gasped for air and cursed as she turned on the light and sat up to look at her finger. She sat on the edge of the bed and saw her bedroom window blinds—all the way down, no signal tonight—and felt nausea replace the pleasure. It was all too much. She had needed that damn release. She was torn in so many directions: working with CIA, squeezing Fatimah Wael, protecting herself against Jamil Atiyah and Ali Hassan. The work with Sam was the only thing that made her feel free. The rest made her feel like a villain.

She dressed and called Razan. "You coming, *habibti*?" she asked, hearing the now-familiar beeps of Uncle Daoud's hospital room in the background. She would leave for Italy in the morning and needed her cousin before she left. Razan had not often left Uncle Daoud's hospital room, but Mariam knew her cousin could use a break. She wanted one, too. To drink a little too much, smoke cigarettes, fall asleep watching an American movie with Razan on the couch. "Be there in twenty minutes, *habibti*."

Razan had brought Belvedere vodka instead of the cheap stuff they used to drink in college. “We need this, girl,” she said, presenting the bottle as she brushed past Mariam to enter the apartment. In the kitchen they each downed two shots and went onto the cramped balcony to smoke, bringing the bottle with them. They left the shot glasses behind.

“Uncle was okay today?” Mariam asked as they leaned on the railing.

“Yes. Better every day,” Razan said. “Doctors think he’ll be out in a few days. You heard about the promotion?” Her face darkened.

Uncle Daoud had been tapped to lead Branch 450, replacing his slain boss, Shalish.

“I did.” Sam and CIA would be ecstatic. Razan hated it. Mariam just wanted him out of the hospital.

“So, Italy?” Razan said, changing the subject.

“Yes. Palace business.”

Razan dragged on her cigarette and unconsciously fiddled with the eye patch. Mariam usually forgot it was there, but sometimes it was impossible not to notice.

“How does it feel?” she asked her cousin.

“Fine. Except my eye doesn’t work anymore.”

Mariam gripped the railing. The booze, thankfully, was kicking in. She took a pull from the bottle and handed it to Razan, who took her own pull and handed it back. As Mariam took another drink, she realized that though she’d always loved Razan, she now finally understood her cousin. She, too, was free. In that moment, Mariam wanted to tell her everything.

“You know I love you, don’t you?” Mariam said. “That I love you more than the Palace?”

“We are sisters. Of course I do.”

“Have you contacted the rebel committees again, Razan?”

Razan smirked and took another drink of vodka. “And if I had?”

Mariam kissed her cousin’s cheek and whispered into her ear. “Then I would say I love you even more.”

Surprised, Razan opened her mouth slightly, but Mariam put her hand over it and kissed her forehead. "I have something for you," she said.

It was a black dress with ruffle sleeves she had bought in Paris. Mariam had never found the right time to give it to her. Tonight, it made sense. Inside the apartment, Razan slipped from her clothes and slid into the dress, smoothing the hem while Mariam zipped it up. Razan twirled. "It's beautiful, *habibti*. I love it." Mariam took another sip of vodka, then handed the bottle to Razan, who watched her hands as she passed it over. They stood facing each other in the living room for a heavy second. Razan kept her eye on Mariam as she drank. "You know that I love you more than the rebel committees, *okhti*?" Razan asked.

Mariam nodded.

"Do you know this, *okhti*?" Razan repeated.

A tear rolled from Mariam's eye. She wiped it away. "I do, *habibti*. I do."

Razan took another drink and set the bottle down on the coffee table. She stepped toward Mariam and took her right hand. "So, then tell me why you are doing this?" She ran a finger over a scab.

Mariam could really feel the vodka now, and she had to fight the urge to blurt everything out. But she stayed quiet, watching Razan's fingers delicately run along her own. Another tear escaped.

"Maybe some more vodka would help?" Razan said. She picked up the bottle, took a drink, and began handing it to Mariam.

Then there was a loud knock.

The knock. Mariam knew it and apparently Razan did, too, because she dropped the bottle on the floor and took a step away from the door. "Jesus, Jesus," she muttered. Mariam watched the door, wondering if maybe this was a dream and the knocker would disappear. A mistake! We have the wrong apartment, Ms. Haddad. This is a terrible mix-up.

There was another knock. "Security Office, open up. Now."

"Jesus, Jesus, Jesus," Razan said, taking another step back from the door.

Mariam opened the door to find Ali Hassan and his lieutenant, Kanaan, the one who'd first called her to ask questions about Sam after she'd returned from France. Before they started pressuring her, before they had dug in their talons, before they owned her. She noticed both men looking past her toward Razan. "Good evening, Ms. Haddad," Ali said. "May we come in?"

She let them in. Ali appeared relaxed, but Kanaan had his eyes locked on Razan, who kept backing away. Ali removed a piece of paper from his breast pocket and began reading aloud. Mariam understood the first few words—*"By presidential decree under the powers vested by the Emergency Law of 1963, the Supreme State Security Court finds Razan Haddad guilty of weakening national sentiment . . ."*—but then she could no longer hear Ali, just a scream and the sound of her cousin's skinny legs sliding against the silk fabric of the dress as she ran for the door to the balcony. Razan was fiddling with the door, fingers not working so well because of the fear and the booze, and Mariam realized then what Razan was trying to do. The door began to slide open. Then Mariam was running at her, screaming Razan's name like she'd done at the protest, though now protecting her cousin would mean giving her over to the *mukhabarat* instead of saving her from them. She could hear Ali and Kanaan moving, too, but she had a step on them and made it through the balcony door just behind Razan.

The dress tore as Razan hoisted her right leg onto the railing, and she was starting to jump when Mariam caught her by the shoulder and yanked her back. They both fell, Razan's back pressed into Mariam's chest, until Mariam's head struck the carpet just inside the door. She could not see straight, but she felt Razan trying to free herself and pulled her in tight. Razan shrieked and began sobbing.

"Please, Mariam, please, I can't go with them. Let me go, let me jump, it will be so quick. I won't feel anything."

Razan tried to pull free. Mariam held her.

"We can do it together," Razan said. "Please, please, *habibti,* don't make me go with them."

Mariam cried, feeling the silk dress as she held her cousin tight. Razan went limp as her fight gave out and her breathing slowed. She looked up. "The sky is so clear tonight, *okhti,*" Razan said at last, slurring her words from the vodka. "I can actually see a few stars."

Ali gently pulled Razan up and the men handcuffed her and reread the charges. Razan was silent now. Kanaan led her out of the apartment. Ali lingered. Mariam sat on the floor and thought about killing him.

"Why, General?" Mariam gritted out.

Ali did not answer the question. He turned for the door, on his way righting the bottle of vodka. "Do your job in Italy and your cousin will be fine. Her fate is in your hands."

36

OUTBURSTS FROM CIA CHIEFS OF STATION WERE NOT uncommon. Some of the old-timers even encouraged the behavior, believing it was critical to a Station's operational discipline. The rage blackouts usually occurred in the Chief's office—a safe space, for the Chief at least—burned hot, and subsided quickly. Sam's Chief in Baghdad had once punched a case officer in the back of the head during a staff meeting because he had flubbed the distro list for a cable. In Cairo, Bradley had sometimes let the case officers have it for the dumbest mistakes. Sam considered Ed a near-father figure, but he'd still reamed him out in front of the entire Station for drafting a few crappy assessment cables.

Artemis Aphrodite Procter belonged to the same school.

"The Jableh complex..." Zelda paused and coughed, knowing the rest of the sentence would not be met warmly by Procter. "The Jableh complex has been evacuated."

Procter picked up a mug, currently doubling as a pencil holder, and smashed it into the wall. "Holy fucking hell! Those vadges in D.C. fiddle-fucked around for weeks," she screamed. "They signed a goddamn finding and did nothing about the goddamn fucking sarin. They should have dropped a few JDAMs on it when they had the chance." She rummaged around for candy but found nothing and slammed her desk drawer. "Fuck," she said softly.

Sam, observing the outburst from the Chief's table, saw Zelda picking shards of ceramic from her skirt and blouse. Her face was expressionless, and he marveled that the analyst had become either acclimated or numb to Procter's unconventional weather patterns.

Sam looked at the report. The commentary box below the report's banner included the analyst's judgment that the jam-packed loading aprons, abundant forklifts, and general disarray visible in the VIP parking lot suggested the Republican Guard and SSRC had evacuated Jableh, taking the sarin with it. "To where, we cannot assess," it concluded.

Sam tossed it down on the table and stepped over the mug fragments to take a seat. The faint smell of rotting fruit still lingered in the room, as it did throughout the embassy compound. Embassy contractors had quickly repaired the minor damage to the signs and removed the graffiti, but the smell persisted. Sam pinched his nose and took in a deep breath through his mouth. "The evacuation happened too quickly, Chief," Sam said. "Someone told them we knew."

"I know," Procter said. "How many people in D.C. touched that report, do you think? Ten thousand. Probably. Ten thousand goddamn suspects. Now we're going to have to produce *actionable* intelligence, actionable, Jaggers, as in bomb-droppable, telling POTUS where they took all the stuff when they closed Jableh. Dreamy."

Sam reminded Procter they had to talk to Bradley and the Chief of Counterintelligence, Samantha Crezbo, about ATHENA's covcom. "A meeting?" The Chief said. "Goddammit."

THE SVTC BEGAN WITH PROCTER'S opening statement as the pixilated screen illuminated to show Bradley's Langley office: "The meetings, Ed, fuck, we have so many fucking meetings. This country is burning to the ground, and I'm in meetings jabbering on and answering pointless emails from your assistant about when I can meet for more meetings. How are we supposed to run ops out here with all these goddamn tribal meetings? I mean, fuck."

"This is standard operating procedure, Artemis," Bradley shouted, matching her volume.

"SOP for whom? Ed, I'm like a Sioux Indian chieftess—is that the right word for a lady chief?—with all these powwows."

Sam bit the inside of his mouth. Zelda looked at the floor of Procter's office.

The meeting's opening depth charge from the technically subordinate Procter had blown Crezbo's mouth open wide, and it was still partially agape when Bradley responded.

"Shut up, Artemis. If we're going to give ATHENA a state-of-the-art covcom system, we're going to make sure Counterintelligence agrees. We don't hand a system out willy-nilly, especially with the queue for access to the platform."

"Can we start with the information corroborating her recent intel?" Crezbo asked. "Rather than flay ourselves? I've read the agent assessments. Everything there looks fine."

"Yes ma'am," Procter said, recovering and waving her hand toward the analyst. "Zelda here has scrubbed the databases for corroborating intel. We have good stuff."

Zelda coughed and shuffled her papers. "In addition to the Jableh facility, there are four SIGINT reports that corroborate ATHENA's information," Zelda said. "NSA tasked the phones for several of the brokers identified during the Bouthaina op. Three of these reports show the same transactions we saw on Bouthaina's computer." She coughed and took a drink of water from a mug emblazoned with a cartoon of Bashar. Sam looked at the shards of the other mug on the floor.

"Noted," Crezbo said. "Ed, I think the case meets muster. It jibes with the bar we've set in other Divisions."

"Fine. Look, team," Bradley said. "I'm going to bump a couple agents in the queue to get you this thing. We're giving ATHENA one of these because the reporting stream so far has been compelling and because of this corroboration. "We'll pouch it to Rome Station. You can give it to her in Tuscany."

37

MARIAM THOUGHT FATIMAH'S EYES HAD DIMMED, though the Tuscan sun glimmered through the windows of her palatial villa. The resilience had vanished, replaced by hatred for her.

Ali had arrested Fatimah's mother, an aunt and uncle, and two cousins. Mariam was pointing toward the bottom of the list, at the next relative that would be arrested, as she fought the red-raw ache that accompanied her to meetings with this woman.

"Everyone is being treated well, Fatimah, you have my assurances. But we will keep moving down the list until you comply. If we get to the bottom and you have not cooperated, I cannot promise they will be treated well." Mariam slid the paper across the table to the fiery woman, who had not offered tea or refreshment and who now clenched the armrest of her velvety sofa.

"The price is still the same?" Fatimah said icily.

"Yes."

"And you will release them when I say the lies you desire and come home."

"Yes." She held Fatimah's eyes to see how she reacted to what came next. "And they will remain free as long as you stay silent."

Fatimah rubbed her eyes and looked out the window, almost longingly, Mariam thought, as though she might dive through it. She sat for a beat, lost in her thoughts. "I will do it, Mariam. But you are now with the devil, yes? You have lost everything else."

Mariam did not allow her face to react, but she felt the force of Fatimah's condemnation in her stomach. Because she knew that it was, at least partially, true. "As soon as you've resigned from the National Council, printed your denunciations, and come home, they will be released. That is the Palace's word," Mariam said.

Fatimah gave a single glacial nod.

As Mariam stood to leave, Fatimah followed and began to walk her to the door.

"For their sake, do not delay," Mariam said, then turned and walked outside.

"There is one more thing," Fatimah called, and Mariam turned around and took a step back toward the door.

"Yes?"

"I'm sorry the rebel snipers were not able to kill your uncle," Fatimah snarled. "I hear the monster will live."

Then Fatimah spit in her face. The saliva flocked Mariam's forehead and dribbled into her eyes.

THAT EVENING MARIAM JOGGED THROUGH Montalcino, up its steep cobbled streets toward a cozy, stone-pillared church. It was empty and darkening as dusk fell, its doors flung open. She went inside and sat in a pew. Thick marble columns flanked the room. Windows carved into the dome above the altarpiece illuminated ornate sculptures of two angels watching over Christ and the Madonna. The Haddads were Christian, but they did not go to church. The last time she'd been inside one had been six years earlier for a nephew's baptism. She sat in the silence and put her head in her hands.

Mariam shut her eyes for a less heavenly landscape.

She saw herself surrounded by a group of men: Jamil Atiyah, the *mukhabarat* officer who had struck Razan, Ali Hassan. Then they came at her, all at once. She reached for a weapon: A club, a knife, a gun. Anything. She picked up a club. She swung at Ali Hassan. And there was Fatimah in front of her, arms above her head, saying, *okhti*, sister, please stop, please stop, please stop until her voice faded away.

Mariam opened her eyes in the empty church and sobbed. For her family. For herself. For Sam. She thought of him and put her head on her knees and curled into herself, shuddering. She was alone. So alone.

38

THE SAFE HOUSE, ODDLY CODE-NAMED TAQUERIA, CONsisted of a small cluster of medieval houses renovated in Tuscan country style, with mahogany furniture, red carpets, and sketches of agricultural scenes covering the walls. The houses were nestled into an isolated hilltop surrounded by vineyards, shadowed by an unoccupied castle owned by an obscure descendant of Italian nobility. He made his home available to CIA so he could pay for its upkeep.

CIA officers in real life typically do not drive exotic sports cars. In fact, Sam had learned while discussing the rental with a very old-sounding woman in Global Deployment, Agency regs dictated that he could only choose from the "economy" class at Hertz. But as Sam drove the rental up a gravel drive lined with cypress trees and saw the villas, the swimming pool, and the abandoned castle, he silently cursed Procter. Nobody driving a Rav4 could afford to stay in this place. Though Procter had chosen the car, she rode shotgun. Crammed in the back was an apparel expert from the Office of Technical Services named Iona Banks. She would outfit Mariam with the materials necessary to take down Atiyah.

Mariam would be joining Sam and Procter at the safe house that evening for dinner. She would spend the night. The BANDITOs had run a constant countersurveillance operation on her since she had arrived in Italy. They were confident that she was not being watched. "This place reminds me of Afghanistan," Procter said as Sam pulled the car into a small, dusty parking lot surrounded by vineyards, now cooling in the cypress shadows of dusk. She jumped out and began to twist her torso and stretch her short legs. "Minus the grinding poverty and the terror, of course."

SAM WAS READING IN HIS room in the early evening when he heard a car crunching on the gravel in the parking lot. She was right on time. He walked up the drive to meet her.

"Hey," he said as she opened the car door—a BMW hatchback—but she did not smile back. She had a forlorn, glassy distance in her eyes. Something was off. "How was the meeting with Fatimah?" he said.

"Terrible. Can we talk about it later?"

"Sure." He stepped back from the car as she opened the door.

She opened the trunk and Sam yanked out her suitcase. A brisk wind whipped the hilltop, bending the cypresses.

He wheeled the suitcase into Mariam's room and said they would eat on the pool veranda, behind which Iona had discovered a fully equipped working kitchen. She'd gone shopping in Montalcino and spent the last few hours cooking. "That sounds lovely," Mariam said. "Could I have a few minutes to get ready?"

He ducked out of the room and went to the veranda, where he discovered a feast of fried olives, freshly baked focaccia bread, and lasagna. Procter was pouring the wine while Iona finished setting the table. Iona was thin, with pale skin, dirty blond hair shaved close on the left side, and a sleeve of tattoos on her right arm. From what Sam could see, most were horses.

Procter poured the wine and rings formed on the tablecloth around the bottom of each glass. Mariam arrived, hugged Procter, shook Iona's hand, and they sat, Iona explaining that the lasagna was not the marinara garbage you find in the States, it was real Bolognese sauce mixed with bechamel and fresh parmesan. "Six layers," she said proudly. As they settled into the meal, Sam asked about Daoud.

"He will be fine," Mariam said. "He is still in the hospital, but the doctors expect a full recovery."

"Any leads on the perps?" Procter asked in English.

"Perps?" Mariam said.

"Who did it," Sam said.

"Oh, nothing specific. Rebels, certainly, but no one has been arrested." She put down her fork. "I'm sorry. Could we talk about something else?"

Sam assumed Procter's duties and refilled everyone's glasses. Procter glowered at him. Now, as he sipped his third glass, he stole a glance at Mariam. Ever since Cairo and, frankly, the tables in Vegas, he'd taken pride in his intuition and ability to shift his strategy—or fold—as the situation warranted. And now, as she looked up and met his gaze, he knew something had happened.

Sam nodded to Iona, who plopped onto the table a plastic bag containing a black leather Ferragamo briefcase. Iona had purchased it in Florence for nearly five thousand euros.

"We studied the video of your meeting with Atiyah. Besides being creepy, it was also helpful," Sam said.

"What were you wearing when you met with him, by the way?" Procter asked.

"I think it was a black dress. Why?"

"A sexy one?"

Mariam coughed and wiped her mouth. "I suppose."

"Figured," Procter said. "When we watched the video, it seemed like he knew there was a camera there because sometimes he just stared at it. Makes sense, with a tight dress and your chesty heft."

Mariam blushed and Procter winked indiscreetly and there was a general silence. Iona took a big sip of wine.

"Now," Sam said, pressing on, "we used your video to create large, high-res images of the bag here in Rome," Sam said.

"It was easy to identify the brand and the specific type, of course," Iona said. "But then we studied every millimeter of the outside to create a replica. For example, in the video you can see a scuff mark just below the stitching connecting the handle to the bag." She pointed to the case. "We've re-created that here."

The bag had just one pocket. It was simple, elegant, a briefcase meant only for documents. There were no inner compartments. Sam had timed himself removing a stack of papers and placing them in the new bag. He could do it in two seconds. He figured she needed to be alone in his office for fifteen seconds, maximum, to make the switch. He explained the logic to Mariam, who nodded, picking at uneaten lasagna with a glassy stare.

When they had finished eating, Mariam picked up the briefcase, still covered in plastic, and examined it as if she were shopping. "We've put everything inside and sewn up the bottom, using the bag's original materials, of course, so that Atiyah would never find it unless he destroyed the briefcase," Iona said. "It deploys with a small spring lock mechanism embedded inside. But we did add one feature a trained *mukhabarat* team should spot if they look closely: we pulled away some of the stitching around this lock."

"That way," Sam said, "when they dump out the documents and scan the bag, they'll see a couple frayed stitches inside and pull the rest to pieces. Then they'll find the device and the documents we've hidden inside. We'll also make sure he receives texts and emails from strange sources."

"The key here," said Procter, wiping bechamel sauce from her mouth, "is that in the tip you provide, you mention *nothing* about the briefcase. It should be innocuous, but enough to cast suspicion and get an investigation started. Then, as they pull the threads, they find the bag, and boom. He's done." She made a slicing motion across her neck.

Iona nervously asked if she should open another bottle of wine. None of the palpable anxiety registered with Procter, who continued. "I'd suggest you tell Bouthaina you saw him typing into a strange device. That should be enough."

THEY ENDED THE EVENING PROFESSIONALLY: finalizing operational details, cleaning up the meal, and turning in early. Sam lay awake in his bed, turning the case over in his mind, Mariam maddeningly in the next room. By the time sleep came, he'd still not found an explanation for her coldness. In the morning, Iona took a large telephoto camera to visit a Cistercian abbey outside Siena. Mariam said she needed to run. "I'll join you," he offered. "Alone, *habibi,*" she rebuffed him, gently, with a kiss on the cheek. As Sam watched her run off, he realized that the flakes of guilt after France had either disappeared or been buried deep as the case had progressed and his feelings for her deepened, the two things bound together in one package. His relationship with Mariam—forbidden by CIA—to him seemed blindingly normal, natural, the way things should be. He did not understand her coldness now. He also had no plan for how to manage the CIA fallout if it came to light.

He drank coffee on the veranda overlooking the Tuscan countryside. On his second cup, Procter joined him. She wore a red pullover, unzipped just far enough to see the top of a banana-yellow sports bra peeking through. "They have hills in Minnesota?" Procter asked. "Or is it just a bunch of cornfields?"

"Not like this," Sam said. A bird chirped from one of the cypress trees. He took another sip of coffee and noticed Procter was looking at him. He turned his head and they stared at each other for a half second. Her green eyes narrowed. She was rooting through his mind, punching through holes in his poker face to find out what the hell was going on in there. He wished he knew.

"What is going on with our girl?" she said abruptly.

"She's off, Chief," he said.

"I think so, too," Procter said.

"But I don't know why."

Procter's phone rang. "I gotta take this. Grab me in thirty minutes?"

Sam nodded and exhaled in relief.

"And wear your swimsuit," she said.

Sam smiled. "What?" Procter tilted her head sideways like a scientist examining an alien specimen.

"Because it's a pool party, Jaggers."

SAM KNOCKED ON PROCTER'S DOOR thirty minutes later. He had not brought swimming trunks to Italy, and instead was wearing a pair of running shorts that were stupidly short and flimsy. He was profoundly uncomfortable.

Procter answered wearing a gigantic fluffy white robe, edges brushing the floor as if she were a wizard. She walked outside without a word and marched toward the pool. Sam followed at her heels.

The idea of being half-naked and alone in front of Procter was not a pleasant one. Not that he thought she was into him. Or men—and maybe also women—for that matter. He hadn't liked her sideways glance on the veranda and did not want to get into the details of the case with the Chief before talking to Mariam first. He threw his towel on a chair and watched as Procter fiddled around with the stereo system, stopping on a station blaring something terrible. "EDM, perfect," she said.

Then she removed her robe. She wore a black two-piece swimsuit that matched her hair and was actually kind of normal, unlike everything else in her wardrobe.

Sam instinctively looked away—they didn't prepare you for half-naked Chiefs at the Farm—but she walked straight past him along the edge of the pool, toward the steps. Realizing there was no way out of this, Sam grabbed two Peronis from the stocked wet bar.

He handed her a beer, which she had half emptied before he dipped into the water. She leaned her head back, closed her eyes, and took in the EDM. Sam had never seen her this relaxed. Or, for that matter, relaxed at all.

"I need to talk to her tonight," Sam said after a minute.

Procter put her empty bottle on the ledge, leaned back, and dunked her hair underwater. She came to the surface and slicked it back. "You have counterintelligence concerns?"

Sam continued, barely able to hear himself over the thundering music. "No. She gave us paydirt intel on the sarin program, which we've corroborated through multiple channels. Not something the Syrians would offer if she was a dangle, I think.

"But there is something off," Sam said. "Last night did not sit right.

There was something about her face. Something bad has happened. I know her. But I can't tell if she doesn't like the mission against Fatimah, the Atiyah op, or if something else is going on. I just know she's off."

Procter looked as if she wanted to ask him something, but instead she said: "Well, take her to dinner tonight and figure out what's going on. Tomorrow we review the covcom."

SAVORING THE VIEWS, SAM AND Mariam drove in silence to San Angelo in Colle, a sleepy hilltop town of steep, stony streets, chipped-tile-roof homes, and a single square with two restaurants. Three old women held hands strolling through the square as Sam and Mariam took a seat on the patio at one of the restaurants. Dusk was settling, and the murmurs of café conversations were broken occasionally by the bass notes of a local jazz band rehearsing in a basement nearby.

She wore jeans and a white T-shirt underneath an olive drab Barbour coat. She'd curled her hair slightly and wore it down, but it did not hide the large gold hoop earrings dangling in the breeze. Sam was sporting a long-sleeve gray T-shirt and jeans with a pair of driving shoes, and he realized they looked like many of the other vacationing couples that had descended upon the square. He ordered Tuscan ragù with boar, Mariam cacio e pepe. "Just like in Èze," she said as she handed the dinner menu back to the waitress. Sam smiled back at her, thinking of that first night, hearing her earrings jangling as they'd moved together. He wondered if they were the same ones she had on now.

Sam let Mariam handle the wine order and, as the waitress scurried off, he put his hand on hers across the table. She smiled. "This makes me happy," she said, seeming to relax for the first time since she'd arrived. The sound of brass rang from the band's rehearsal, escaping the basement into the night air. A warbler called from the bank of hillside cypress trees. Sam dunked a piece of bread in olive oil and took Mariam in. He'd seen those eyes on other assets and, sometimes, across the poker table when a guy was over his skis and had too much money in the pot. He'd also seen it on Mariam once before, right after the attack in Villefranche.

The waitress poured the wine. They drank in silence, holding hands on the table. He had to calm Mariam down. He had to assess ATHENA.

"What are you afraid of?" Sam asked. He could have offered a half dozen legitimate hobgoblins but let it sit, letting her fill the space.

"I am afraid," she said, "of so many things." She attempted a smile and gestured toward another couple, about their age, on the other side of the patio.

"Look at them. They've been holding hands and kissing. And here I am, wondering if Atiyah or the *mukhabarat* are watching. Or thinking about what happens if you are expelled from Syria. Or worse. Things inside Damascus feel shaky, like we are all heading off a cliff. What happens then? What happens to my family, my cousin? I'm afraid of . . ."

She sniffled into a napkin and set her jaw, trying to stop the tears from trickling down her cheeks.

"What are you afraid of?"

"I'm afraid for my family if I am caught," she said through tears. "Not for myself. For them."

Sam shifted across the table into the chair beside her. He wrapped his arm around her, and when he did, she pressed her head onto his shoulder. He wasn't sure how long they sat in silence. He waved off the waitress as she tried to collect the barely touched plates. The band had stopped playing. A few musicians trickled out toward cars parked near the hill's green edges.

"Did something happen?" he asked.

She shook her head.

"I will always protect you, Mariam. Always," he whispered into her ear. "The work we've chosen is dangerous, but it led us to each other. And we'll finish this together in Damascus. I promise." He kissed her forehead and then her mouth, savoring the feel of her hair as he caressed her neck.

"There is something about us," she said. "It gives me power. I can't do this without you, Sam."

He was beginning to think the same thing. But Sam pushed aside the realization that he'd become a massive fuckup, instead holding three thoughts in his mind, each at war with the others, and all, he was certain, completely true. One, he wanted to run off that night with Mariam. Two, everything she had said was true, but she still held something back. Three, Mariam was loyal. To him, to the CIA.

The chef and bartender had already left, so the waitress finally tiptoed to the table with the bill, avoiding eye contact with the weeping Arab woman and her handsome boyfriend. Whatever they'd been fighting about, it was apparently over, because they were now kissing. The waitress smiled. So touching.

Sam paid the bill and they kissed walking down the hill to the car. An elderly couple sat on their front step drinking wine ten feet from the parked car, yelling at each other. Sam couldn't understand what they were saying, but it was loud and angry enough that he had to consider a Plan B. He saw that Iona had left a blanket in the backseat after she'd taken the car to the abbey. "There's a vineyard on the way back," Sam said.

"Perfect, *habibi,*" Mariam said. "Just drive."

THE DRIVE TO THE BOSCARELLO winery was fast and efficient despite the narrow, winding roads. Sam had learned how to drive in treacherous terrain when he'd finished second in his defensive driving course at the Farm a decade earlier. Now, though, the distraction was not an opponent smashing into his car, but the Syrian in the front seat.

Reaching the winery, Sam pulled the car to the side of the road. A shallow ditch and a stone fence separated them from the vineyard. He opened the trunk and pulled out the blanket.

They hopped the fence and walked deep into the neat rows of vines. Fifty yards in, Sam unfolded the blanket. The moon was incandescent.

They lay down together, kissing, tossing away clothes until there was nothing but warm skin and the feel of her around him. She groaned and kicked her knees toward the vines, pressing her mouth to his ear. "You promise, *habibi?*"

He ran a hand through her hair. "I promise, *habibti*. I promise."

He felt her nails digging into his shoulders as she laid her head back onto the blanket to see the sky. He moved slowly, locking onto her eyes, that glassy look gleaming in the moonlight, bothering him even as her eyelids fluttered and her muscles quivered in the shadow of the old vines.

SAM, MARIAM, AND PROCTER COVERED the covcom device over breakfast. Mariam picked at a piece of toast while Sam demonstrated how the PLATYPUS system functioned. "It will work just like your iPad," he said. "Because it is one. Or was one. The one difference is that it lets you communicate with us. I'll show you. The device communicates with a satellite through a burst transmission. It is very hard to intercept."

"Very hard, or impossible?" Mariam asked.

Procter caught the hand grenade before he could respond. "We won't bullshit you and say it's impossible. But the opposition has to know exactly where the device is, where the transmission is headed, and at what time it's headed there. If they don't have all three, it's impossible to intercept."

"The longer the message, the longer the burst, and the easier it is to detect," Sam said. "So this platform restricts character count and won't let you send a stream of messages all at once from the same location. This platform will allow you to send short messages to us, and we can send them back. We don't need to use the drop site to schedule meetings."

"Well, that's good," Mariam said.

"Exactly," Sam said. "Let me show you how to talk to us. We'll create a distinct swiping motion over the screen as your passcode. For now, it's programmed for me, so I'll open it."

He swung around the table and sat next to her. He could feel Procter's eyes on him, as he had on the safe house veranda. She could sense something was up.

Sam made a series of squiggly swipes over the screen to open a program resembling Gmail. "The platform creates a fake in-box, behind a firewall, in case anyone comes up behind you and sees the screen while you're typing. You then type us an email, just like you would in Gmail, and hit send. You can enter any address, any subject line, it doesn't matter. It can only go one place." He pointed to the sky. "To us."

"This part of the device is completely firewalled from the rest," Procter said. "The phony email program does not even live on the iPad permanently, meaning that if the *mukhabarat* gets it and tries to find what's here, they won't, because it's not."

"Your swipe brings up the program, you type, hit send—that initiates the burst—then you put the iPad to sleep. Boom. It's done. Next time you open it normally, and all your apps, movies, songs will all be there."

Sam reached into his bag and took out a small black sphere with cords dangling from its top and bottom. Each cord linked to a USB connector. One was red, the other green. A single button, like a navel, was implanted in the sphere's midsection.

"This will transfer everything from your old iPad in just a few minutes. Then we put the new one in your old case and we take the old one with us," Sam said.

Mariam was staring at the PLATYPUS. "It makes me nervous," she said without looking up. "I am not sure I want it."

It was classic covcom paranoia. Sam knew there was a fair chance Mariam would be uncomfortable with the device. He'd run a Saudi general who'd refused one even though his tradecraft was sloppy and the methods he preferred—moving car drops, brush passes, dead drops, chalk marks—were more vulnerable to detection. Sam told him all this and emphasized the consequences, but it didn't matter. The man wanted what he knew. Other agents did not like the devices because they were a constant reminder of treason. A device sat in your bedroom, taunting you.

He shot an all-but-imperceptible glance at Procter, who took the baton. "Can you tell us why?" Procter asked.

"I know that these systems have been compromised in other places," she said. "China. Iran. There is an Iranian contingent in Syria now, as you know, helping the *mukhabarat* target the opposition. Having a device like this, in my home. It makes me feel . . . vulnerable."

Sam nodded. "I get it. But no one has ever hacked into one of these. Ever. The compromise in Iran happened on a temporary, web-based system. The Iranians found agents who visited particular sites. The Chinese went a step further, they actually used that system to break through a firewall into another one, and then found those agents as well. But no one has been able to get into one of these."

"I'm sure that's what the CIA told their agents in China, too." Procter opened her mouth, presumably to counter, but Mariam didn't give her the chance. "I do not want to pass much information over this device," Mariam said. "I'd prefer to meet in person if we have a lot to cover."

"So do we," Procter said. "We can use this to arrange meetings, work out logistics, and you can pass us any urgent intel on it. Just the highlights. Then we talk about all of it when we meet in person."

Mariam stared at the cords and iPad and asked Sam to transfer everything into the PLATYPUS. Ten minutes later she said she should be going. "I have to call Bouthaina in thirty minutes."

Iona appeared at the breakfast table holding the briefcase, now in its original cloth Ferragamo bag with the tags attached. She handed Mariam the receipt. "In case anyone asks," Iona said. "A souvenir from Italy, for someone you love." Sam saw her wince and her jaw set, as it had at dinner the night before.

Mariam hugged everyone, then slipped the new briefcase into her suitcase and asked if Sam and Procter could walk her to the car. In the parking lot, Mariam looked sad again. "I love you both," she said. Then she closed the door, started the engine, and left.

Procter and Sam watched the car throw up a cloud of dust along the ridgeline before it vanished behind a wall of cypresses and vines and descended into the valley.

"You get an answer last night?" Procter said, turning to Sam.

"She's afraid. And something's going on with her family."

"She tell you that?"

"She might as well have."

39

THE BANDITOS HAD GONE THROUGH THE SAME MOTIONS four times in as many days: drive the bomb-laden Pajero to the road outside the Security Office, park it on the curb, and load the safe house with the video equipment Langley would use to confirm the target was indeed Ali Hassan. Each time, something different had caused the abort: the encrypted video link did not function, Sam was bumper-locked, Ali did not take a walk (twice).

"We try again tomorrow," Procter said as they watched Ali walk past the car next to a woman pushing a baby stroller. "Like every day."

SAM AND PROCTER SPENT SIX hours designing the SDR. The lethal finding stipulated that a CIA officer have physical eyes on the target before they pulled the trigger. The BANDITOs could support the op, but Sam would have to direct it from the safe house alone. He had to get black.

The Chief's office was littered with cans of Diet Coke and chewing gum wrappers. She did not appear fatigued. The opposite, in fact, and Sam was also wired. He was occupying himself with the Mossberg, aiming it at one of the cans while Procter played the plan back aloud.

They were debating Sam just disappearing, kicking active surveillance as if he were in Moscow or a denied-area operating environment.

"Not yet," Procter said. "It would confirm you as Agency, piss them off, and who knows what they do? Maybe beat the hell out of you for fun. Russkies would pull that crap in Moscow when we got black aggressively. Or maybe they catch you and kill you like Val. You read the SIGINT on the Russian team that arrived from Moscow?"

He had. The report was the passenger manifest from a Moscow-Damascus cargo flight that had arrived before he went to Italy. The name traces indicated it contained seven FSB and five SVR officers. No one knew why they'd come. "The composition of the Russian team is odd," he said, lowering the Mossberg for a moment. "It's like someone asked for help against us."

She nodded. "Look, the Russians put some of their best people on us in Moscow, so the request could have been for Russian help, and they sent the A-team. But yes, yes, yes, of course it's unsettling," she said, her chin swinging up and down.

"It's like the Syrians know we're running a big fish," he said. He pointed the Mossberg at the trash can and pretended to pull the trigger.

THE NEXT MORNING SAM SAT in his kitchen drinking coffee, reviewing his mental map of the SDR. He poured a second cup and Skyped his mom. He told her he was going shopping today and asked what she wanted. They talked about furniture and jewelry and she finally settled on a rug. She said there'd been a deluge of newspaper articles arguing for U.S. military intervention in Syria. Sam shrugged it off and said he was safe in Damascus. They said they loved each other and then hung up.

He closed the laptop, picked up his phone, and padded to the bathroom. He texted Stapp, the Station techie, to confirm drinks in the Old City. He showered and shaved and took stock. Dressed in jeans, dark blue tennis shoes, and a wrinkled white linen shirt, he set out from his apartment into the Malki neighborhood carrying a small shoulder-slung satchel with a digital camera. The routine at the apartment, the camera, the attire—all of it was designed to fit his pattern of life and lull an active surveillance team into thinking he was preparing for a normal weekend day in Damascus: shopping, seeing friends, wandering the tourist sites.

The streets already teemed with pedestrians and the AK-laden soldiers and the stray cats scratching in the alleys. He walked to a store to buy water. He drank it walking down Jawaher Lal Nahro Street along the hypotenuse of Tishreen Park. The fixed surveillance he spotted matched his mental map. The solo surveillance operator riding his tail had also become commonplace. The stocky *mukhabarat* foot soldier was not trying to hide his presence. He followed about forty yards back. Sam hailed a cab in the blender bowl of the traffic on Umayyad Square and asked to go to Abbassin.

The cabbie shot into the chaos of Damascene traffic. Driving here was the worst. The drivers ignored everything save for the nose of their own vehicle. They honked like crazy, frequently bumped into each other, and irregularly stopped for pedestrians.

Sam snuck a glance in the car's rearview mirror and saw the solo tail pull a radio from his pocket. Sam knew they wouldn't let him off the hook this easily. The call was almost certainly to a mobile team that would follow the cab. It was also extremely obvious.

The SDR would occur in the pocket of central Damascus, but he and Procter had developed a new route and extended the duration beyond the Station baseline of ten hours. It started on the eastern rim of the Old City and worked westward in a zigzag pattern until he reached the Kafr Sousa safe house, down the street from the Security Office.

It was now eight a.m. He snapped pictures as he decamped from the cab. Mobile teams had picked him up again. A black sedan and a yellow vehicle that looked like it had once been a cab idled outside a parking lot.

He walked toward Abbassin. The surveillance cars eventually disappeared but the solo operator was back, strolling behind. They could shovel resources at him all day. The key was to draw this out for hours.

Make it so unbearably boring for the surveillance team that they would decide to surge resources elsewhere. Sam finished logging the people around him and pulled the tightness into his chest.

ALI AND VOLKOV SAT IN the Russian command center. A faint body odor hung in the air. Discarded cigarette butts clotted the ashtrays. A bank of television monitors illuminated live footage of the American arriving at a restaurant, courtesy of a car parked outside. The Syrian and Russian surveillance teams had arrived at the restaurant with Samuel Joseph.

Kanaan and two of the Russians were hunched over a detailed map of the Christian Quarter, debating the American's next move.

"What do you think, General?" Volkov asked Ali. "Is today the day?"

STAPP GREETED SAM OUTSIDE AT noon, grinning and explaining that the trendy Abu George Café served booze earlier than any other establishment in Damascus.

The place was empty. Stapp shook hands with the bartender and ordered two pints of Stella. They sat at a table near the window so Sam could see the street. Stapp had no idea Sam was operational and spoke without interruption. He was explaining that someone had been stealing his booze from the fridge at the office when Sam saw the same solo tail walk past the front of the café and stare conspicuously into the window, puffed up like a gorilla wearing a white shirt and cheap black slacks. He logged others. A guy in blue jeans, scuffed brown shoes, and an Adidas shirt: Seems tense, a possible tail. Keep the profile. Another one in gray slacks and a plain black T-shirt giggling into a phone: Head and shoulders relaxed, laughter genuine, unlikely surveillant. Discard.

Sam kept updating the catalog as Stapp droned on. They finished their beers—Stapp ordered another for himself, Sam declined—and the tech started crushing shelled pistachios. One-thirty. Time to cut across the Old City.

SAM BEGGED OUT OF THE restaurant, telling Stapp that he had to do some shopping for his mother. "Whatever, man," the tech said, slapping his back as he glugged down more beer.

Sam walked westward down the Street Called Straight, the ancient east-west Roman road bisecting the Old City. He neared a cluster of merchant houses selling custom furniture and hand-woven rugs. He strolled for thirty minutes, stopping to take pictures, to look up at a fighter jet soaring overhead, to send his mother a text message. Pedestrian traffic on the street was thin.

The solo tail had disappeared. Had they backed off? He had not observed the subtle, snap movements of a surveillance team trying to operate clandestinely: no quick duck-backs into side streets, no repeat sightings from earlier in the day, no pedestrians maintaining a steady, consistent distance. It was promising.

Sam went into a store and ducked into a back room rimmed with stacks of rugs. There was a patch of concrete in the middle where the merchant would display the rugs. The proprietor, a gregarious character named Amin, barked at a prepubescent teenage boy to fetch tea and began showing product to Sam with gusto. His mom did genuinely want a carpet, so he took thirty minutes to evaluate the inventory and finally settled on a Baluchi rug, muddy red and embroidered with lively birds and floral patterns. He haggled with Amin, but not as much as he should have—it was time to leave. Sam snapped a picture of another rug and left his digital camera and satchel on one of the stacks of carpet. He departed westward again toward Souq Midhat Basha.

Ten minutes later, he felt confident the solo tail was gone. Time for a reversal. He made a show of patting at his sides, where the camera bag would have been, and then abruptly turned back down the street in the direction of the rug shop. He kept his head pointed forward while his eyes swiveled to take everything in: the heat, the people, the movement, the energy. He started to feel clean. He pushed his gut back down and listened to his body for the tingle. His heart thumped and his blood coursed hot.

Sam retrieved the camera and satchel from Amin and set off eastward, back toward Abu George.

Four o'clock. Time to stair-step back across town: multiple changes of direction, reversals, a half dozen stops. He would use the Old City's hairpin switchbacks. A street pro had dozens of opportunities to test a surveillance team by losing them, however briefly and with good reason, in the medieval warren. Stretch them out, force the hostiles to reestablish their perimeter, where even solid teams would make mistakes.

He snaked past the Mariamite Cathedral, past Naranj—examining the posted menu and snapping a picture—then cut to a pharmacy. The large Band-Aid he bought for his blistered foot was not part of the plan, but he needed the relief and an extra stop could only help draw out the opposition. He slithered into crowds and then out again, alternating the density to lure the opposition into the open. The masses grew as he approached the Umayyad Mosque, but instead of joining them he crossed the old Roman road toward Bab Al Saghir.

Seven o'clock. The air felt charged, though whether it was the war or his own tension, he did not know. He felt black. Sam stopped at a souvenir stall hawking pro-Assad swag. Then he heard his stomach and realized he needed to eat.

HE WAS MIDWAY THROUGH A cup of booza, an elastic Levantine ice cream, and nursing a bottle of water when the mind games started. He'd executed the tradecraft perfectly, he thought. Or had he? Had the woman buying ice cream been the same woman from the jewelry store? Had the quick peripheral movement outside the pharmacy actually been a teenager kicking a soccer ball? As he marched on to the train station, his fatigue surged, his calves ached, and he tugged at his dampened shirt.

He thought of Benson, who'd seen ghosts during every role-play SDR, washed out of the Farm, and eventually left the service after ten months, riding a desk into the sunset.

Trust the tradecraft, he told himself. Almost there. It felt quiet, but the air crackled. Mortar fire began somewhere east. The sun's sugary pinks and reds fired their last volleys. He reached the square in front of the Hijaz train station and stopped. He took a picture. Then he saw a darting motion in the southwestern corner of the square. In the eerie silence a crackle, maybe a radio, maybe a footfall on crumpled foil. His spine tingled and he considered how a team could have evaded detection for almost twelve hours. He sat down on a bench.

He felt hunted.

The word dredged up a memory. An officer, a guy named Sanders, was going to meet with a Russian asset in Ankara. He'd executed the SDR and had the meet. The next day the Russian was sent home, put against a wall in the Lubyanka, and shot. The postmortem found that Sanders had been *hunted* by a multi-team, combo fixed/mobile SVR squad, who suspected he was running Russian assets based on his use of the language at a diplomatic event three weeks earlier. They also suspected a leak in Turkey. Sanders was a thread to pull. The Russians had bubbled him, staying far enough back to evade notice, but keeping him in sight at all times. He'd never seen it coming. Bradley, then Chief of Station Cairo, had forced every Station officer to read the post-mortem. Sam knew that he would have done exactly as Sanders did, and the report scared the shit out of him.

And now there was a Russian team here, in Damascus, doing god knows what. He thought back to that report. One of the authors, an old-timer from Russia House, had written that the only way to guarantee you're not in a bubble is to travel quickly in a direction perpendicular to your existing route, busting the bubble and forcing hostile redeployment. Was it possible that all of his moves earlier had happened inside the bubble?

A moped puttered through the square cutting toward the river. Sam could not see the driver's face, but the woman's clothes seemed familiar, maybe. A ghost?

There was no way he was going to be the one to fuck up the op to kill Ali Hassan. The bastard had killed Val, he had to pay. Sam had to be sure he was black before he entered the safe house. He did not know if a team was out there surrounding him, but he had to find out. He had to break the bubble. Sam stood up and began to walk north at a quick clip. The sunset call to prayer rang from the muezzins around the Old City. He wasn't listening, though. The tradecraft had taken over, he was running hot and feeling the street.

He walked north on Port Said and hailed a cab bound in the same direction.

"Where to?" the cabbie said in English.

Sam tried to think of a good stop. "Head north," he replied in Arabic. He closed his eyes. His heart was racing, and he was sweating. He began to breath very slowly. He had spent hours memorizing maps of the city, and after a minute of slow breathing, eyes still closed, he managed to call them to mind. Dahdah Cemetery. It was directly north, and made no sense based on his route's currents. But it was a tourist stop. He could explain it. Inside the cab he told the driver to head into the circle near the city hall, then turn east on Baghdad Street.

The cemetery was rimmed by a thin pine grove. Sam entered as the sun began to dip below the horizon. He walked between the tombstones, taking slipshod pictures along the way. He was twelve hours in. A wave of fatigue roiled him. Nearing the cemetery's opposite end, he heard the screech of car brakes, then the antsy, hushed voices of two men and one woman.

Two mortars soared overhead. He didn't hear them land. He saw, heard, felt no one in the cemetery.

He walked toward the voices. A young woman walked past. She had the same height and build as the Hijaz Square moped driver. Her shoes, now black flats, were different from the leather riding boots. Then two young men strolled past, holding hands like family. Sam glanced at the shorter one's shoes. Brown, scuffed. The same pair had been outside Abu George during his drink with Stapp. He was positive. Then, the young man had worn an Adidas T-shirt. Now, he wore a gray blazer and matching slacks. Sam was covered in ticks.

He took a seat on a bench outside the cemetery. The sun had set. He sat for thirty minutes, replaying everything, questioning every decision, until he decided he had enough to face Procter. He could sense the hunters out there, probably wondering now if they'd been made or if he was waiting for his agent. He just sat, drawing it out for them, pissing them off, agitating their commanders with each passing minute. They'd wasted more than twelve hours of his time. He would try to return the favor.

ALI AND VOLKOV WATCHED A live video feed of CIA officer Samuel Joseph sitting on the bench outside the cemetery. Ali sensed they'd been spotted somewhere around the train station, but he wanted to learn more about Joseph's behavior, and he stood glued to the feed with Volkov. He hated to admit it, but he was impressed.

Ali lit a cigarette for Volkov, then one for himself. They'd been on full war tilt since lunchtime. Ali had argued on a hunch that Samuel Joseph was operational. *The day seems too casual,* he'd told Volkov, when the Russian asked if today was the day. *It feels wrong.* Volkov said why the hell not, let's trap him. They'd surrounded him with the seven teams and bubbled him into his route across the Old City. The fixed positions had been perfect, Ali thought, a credit to Volkov. Watchers embedded artfully around the American, each sending word to the mobiles as he moved farther downroute. A Syrian team, one of Ali's, had nudged the American a bit too close near the train station. Then they'd panicked and shown themselves at the cemetery. And the damn American had just kept walking around town with his wits up.

The video feed went out. The team in the Security Office command center listened to the radio chatter updating them on the operation.

"This is Team Three, he's gotten into a cab, so we've taken down the televideo. We're following."

When Team Five reported that the cab stopped at Samuel's apartment, Volkov smashed a stapler onto the floor.

Ali nodded to Volkov and went to his office, closing the door behind. He looked at his watch: ten-thirty. He had not seen Layla and the boys in five days.

He lit a cigarette and started writing the report.

40

THE MORNING WAS HOT AND HUMID. EVEN WORSE than the heat, thought Rami, was being stuck in traffic driving a Mitsubishi Pajero with a busted passenger-side speaker and what he suspected was a hidden cache of military-grade explosives. He did not want to know, he kept telling himself.

Twenty minutes later he found a parking spot halfway on the sidewalk down the road from the Security Office along Ali's smoking path. He parked the car directly parallel to the concrete wall. He exited the vehicle, walking away from the Security Office and its surveillance cameras.

AT THE SAME TIME, HIS brother Yusuf sat inside the safe house arranging the video equipment. He needed to witness two events to send the message to Sam. One, his brother had to park the Pajero. Two, he needed to observe Ali entering the Security Office.

He sat waiting for the second event. The last month sitting in the damn safe house had been soul-crushing.

One hour later he saw Ali's car drive through the gate, even caught a glimpse of him on video entering the building. He sent an encrypted text to Sam: *Here.*

"DENIED-AREA RULES," PROCTER HAD DECREED as she slammed down yet another cable from Langley asking for a status update on the operation to kill Ali Hassan. "As of now."

Denied-area rules: You got black, you disappeared, then you'd reappear. You'd do it aggressively if you had to, Sam knew. Just up and vanish in front of the watchers. The *mukhabarat* would eventually retaliate, but Sam had no choice. The pressure from Washington had increased, and the Station couldn't be passive. They had to take out Ali.

Wrapping the morning meeting in Procter's office, he went to his computer to check the ATHENA traffic. The in-box was still empty. He clicked violently on the computer mouse as he closed the database. It had been more than a week of silence. What was going on? Had they found her? The host government typically didn't tell you when they'd rolled up one of your assets. Hell, it had taken more than a month for CIA to learn that Val had died in custody. Maybe Atiyah had caught her with the bag. Maybe they'd found the program on the iPad. Maybe her father had died in Aleppo. Or maybe she was just anxious around the device. Locking his computer, he went into the bathroom and sat for minute on the toilet, fully dressed, head in his hands. Then he went outside the Station to the cell phone cubbies to check for a message from the BANDITOs, his new daily ritual. He opened his burner phone and saw: *Here.*

Sam texted back: *Vacate.*

Procter fist-bumped him on the way out and told him she'd send a NIACT—night action—cable to Langley. They'd call in Bradley, the other suits on the Seventh Floor, the facial recognition experts, and OGC, the Office of General Counsel.

Everything, again, depended on him getting black in a city turning sideways on Damascus Station.

SAM WENT TO HIS APARTMENT, showered, and changed into dark jeans, a checkered blue dress shirt, and a powder-blue linen sport coat, which he hated. He sent Zelda a text message from his phone confirming drinks at ten in Sha'alan. He mentioned he was going to do some shopping beforehand.

Sam left the apartment carrying his messenger bag loaded with a phone and a variety of disguises. He noticed immediately the surveillance van and the man smoking on the sidewalk, looking right at him. It would not matter. He just needed a few seconds in the gap.

He walked toward Umayyad then north toward the embassy as the distance widened with the trailing *mukhabarat*. He saw the street, his pulse quickened, and he cut right, scanning for a fixed position. Nothing. Then he ran. He made another right, then a left, sprinting.

The road was empty, save for one car: a black BMW 5 Series, engine running, trunk ajar, Elias at the wheel. He dashed for it, swung the trunk open, scanned the alleyway for witnesses—none—and hopped inside the trunk. Scrunched in the compartment, he felt the vehicle accelerate smoothly and then bank right. He managed to remove the sport coat and his dress shirt, and fumbled around in the bag to find the fake gut and a fresh T-shirt. He got his arm twisted in the T-shirt. Elias hit a bump and it felt like the arm would snap off. Then he inserted the fake foam stomach under the T-shirt. He placed a shaggy brown wig over his head along with an itchy mustache. Elias hit another bump and he swore. He rearranged the mustache.

Sam lay back and prayed they wouldn't hit any surprise checkpoints. If the militia stopped Elias and found a tall American inside, wig on his head and a glorified pillow jammed up his shirt, they would all be royally fucked.

IT WAS KANAAN WHO TOOK the call from the winded corporal and made out, through the labored breathing and cursing, that they had lost Samuel.

When he was finished yelling at the man, Kanaan walked to Ali's office to deliver the news. His heart dropped when he saw General Volkov, drinking vodka out of a coffee cup, and realized he'd have to confess their failure in front of this master. “What do you mean, lost?” Ali said, nearly choking on the words. As Kanaan relayed the colonel’s pitiful explanation, Ali saw Volkov’s face go strangely blank, except for his eyebrows, which lifted ever so slightly.

“The bastard burned us,” Volkov said to Ali, as soon as Kanaan had finished.

Ali nodded. “They know we almost had them last time. Do you think he’ll meet his colleague for drinks later, as the text message said?”

Volkov took another drink and looked at the map. He shrugged. “It’s been fifteen minutes. He has four hours. Plenty of time for an op and then a nightcap with his lady friend.”

“Kanaan, I assume the street team has no idea what the car looks like?” Ali said.

“None. They never saw one.”

“We could get lucky,” Volkov said. “Maybe a checkpoint picks them up.”

“Maybe,” said Ali. He lit a cigarette and opened his shirt another button. The room had suddenly become unbearably hot. “Maybe I meet him for drinks.”

“An excellent idea,” Volkov said. “You know, sometimes when they’d go black in Moscow we’d just snatch them up afterward and beat the shit out of them.”

THE CAR MADE A SERIES of turns before weaving back into the city toward the safe house. Ninety minutes later Elias opened the trunk and grinned at his passenger, now scratching his mustache.

Sam walked the lamplit streets through Kafr Sousa and neighboring Al-Lawan, incorporating a series of bubble-busting techniques, but it was all unnecessary. He was black. At eight p.m., he arrived at the safe house to find it empty. The BANDITOS were already gone. He stood the video camera on a tripod facing the Pajero below. He checked to make sure the encrypted satellite link was active. Then he removed his phone from his pocket and called a very long, very strange phone number.

"Hey, Sam, can you hear us?" It was Bradley.

"I can. Do you have video?"

"We do. We're looking at an empty street and a lonely Pajero."

"Copy that; me, too. Procter, you here?"

"Yes. Damascus Station online."

"We have the facial recognition team here with us in the Director's conference room as well," Bradley said. "Both MOLLY, the AI program, and the real person. Her name is Susan Crawley, by the way."

"Hi, Susan," everyone said.

"All right, team," Bradley said. "The Director's given me button-pushing authority on this one. Once Ali leaves the office, Susan and the AI program will independently render judgment. When that's done, I'll arm the device and enable the infrared sensor. Sam will maintain visual on the target and blast zone throughout, and we'll abort if any pedestrians get in the way. Everyone understand?"

"Yes."

"Now we wait."

Sam sat watching the video feed, wondering what Ali was doing inside and in what room of this godforsaken place they'd taken Val's scalp.

DOWN THE STREET, ALI HAD followed Volkov to the Russian's makeshift command center, where he assessed the hunt for Samuel Joseph to be progressing poorly. No sign of the American anywhere.

His plan was beginning to bear fruit, but he was running out of time. Still, he had enough leash from Assad to give the American one warning. Then, on to Rustum's plan to bring him in for an interrogation. He did not want the investigation deteriorating into such thuggery. But he was running out of options. The Americans were running operations, thumbing their noses at him, as he tried to play the game civilly.

At any rate, there was no news about Rustum's operation to provide false information on the backup production site to Bouthaina and the others. If the information didn't come through in the next batch of SVR reporting, his window would expire and they'd arrest Samuel Joseph to extract the name from him. Given the young man's street antics, Ali was beginning to sympathize with that view. But not quite yet.

He needed to clear his head. He grabbed his cigarettes and went out for a walk.

FROM THE SAFE HOUSE, SAM saw a familiar figure weave through the concrete berms outside the Security Office. Sam turned the video feed toward the figure and zoomed in.

"It's him. It's Ali."

He just had to walk on the right side of the road. Surveillance logs said he almost always did, but there was still a chance he'd change up the routine. "Come on, you bastard. Right side," Sam muttered under his breath.

Ali stood talking with the guards, burning down his cigarette and laughing. Sam remembered that Ali had a wife and twin boys. He felt a momentary pang of sadness, some distant sense of Ali's humanity. He forced himself to remember Val, her mother, the Memorial Ceremony.

All the while, Ali kept on joking with the guards.

ONE OF THE RUSSIANS, LISTENING to an FSB team on the radio, heard excitement crackling, then screamed to Volkov: "We found someone matching Sam's description. Kafr Sousa. An apartment. He's close."

Volkov threw an empty Styrofoam cup toward a garbage can, missing completely. "Show me. Where?"

The lieutenant walked to the map and asked the mobile team again for the address. He pointed.

"It's just down the block," Volkov said. He turned to Kanaan, currently hustling the Syrian teams in place so they could arrest the American and whoever he was meeting.

"Colonel, where is Ali?"

"He went out for a walk, down the block."

Volkov rolled his eyes. This Levantine. Soft, probably from the sun. "I'll go get him and we'll proceed together on foot. Understand?"

Kanaan nodded and put the phone back to his mouth, barking at his teams to speed toward the Kafr Sousa apartment.

"HE'S WALKING NOW," SAM SAID. "Right side. Our side. I've enabled the Frisbee." The team had adopted the nickname. "Focusing feed for facial recognition."

Ali walked slowly for twenty yards, then stopped to put out his cigarette. Still about a hundred yards from the Pajero. The sidewalk around the car was clear.

Back at Langley, the facial recognition expert was reviewing the live video feed, comparing it to the footage from the BANDITOs' surveillance operation. Simultaneously, an algorithm called MOLLY sorted through the same information. If MOLLY and Susan agreed it was Ali, they were a go.

Ali kept walking. Slowly.

Sam coughed. Thought of the flour mill, for some reason. Then the Tuscan vineyard with Mariam. The SDR where the Russians almost burned him. Then Vegas, getting cleared out. All of it, weirdly, him. He wondered if this made him a murderer. Even if he wasn't detonating the blast, he would arm the infrared sensor, after all.

"We've got confirmation here at Langley," an unknown voice said. "This is Paul Gartner, by the way. Chief, OGC. "Susan and MOLLY agree. It's Ali."

"Copy," Bradley said. "Sam, go ahead and arm it."

Sam dialed the satellite phone, illuminating the PIR sensor and arming the bomb. "Fifty yards," Sam said.

AS ALI STROLLED HE LIT another cigarette and sucked smoke into his lungs, wondering why he was doing this. Pushing the thought out of his mind, he checked his watch. He had wanted to see Layla and the boys, but now it was too late. He closed his eyes and wished, for a moment, that he was wrestling with the twins instead of playing cop for his animal of a brother and this ridiculous President. He stopped and flicked his cigarette. Then he lit another and kept walking.

"TWENTY-FIVE YARDS," SAM SAID.

"Does this guy have mental problems?" Procter asked. "Because he's walking like a special."

"Shut up," Bradley said.

"Fifteen yards. Sidewalk still clear. Just Ali."

"Ten yards, five."

"Should be about two seconds," Bradley said.

ALI HEARD HEAVY STEPS BEHIND him on the sidewalk.

"General," Volkov yelled. "We've found him. Come back."

Ali spun around and saw the Russian sprinting toward him. As Ali turned, he lost his footing, wobbling toward the street, catching himself on the trunk of a parked Pajero. He stood up, embarrassed.

"What's happened?" he said.

"One of the mobile teams spotted him. Here in Kafr Sousa, an apartment just up the block. Kanaan has sent teams to make an arrest. Start running. We'll catch up."

Ali started running.

SAM HAD FLIPPED OFF THE INFRARED SENSOR when he saw the man running toward Ali. He now sat in silence watching the chaos unfolding on the video feed.

Bradley broke it. "Okay, folks, Sam has disabled the sensor. Susan, can you make out what that guy said to Ali? He didn't look Syrian to me. Sam, get out."

Sam packed up the equipment and reattached his mustache. He noticed he'd run the whole op wearing the fake gut and wig.

Susan's voice cut through. "The guy with Ali said, 'We've found him.'"

"Sam, you hear that?" Bradley said. "Don't move, obviously, you don't have any assets there with you. Hang tight and stay on the line."

Mariam, his world, his presence here, it had all hung by a thread that Ali Hassan was now cutting. If they caught him in the safe house, the Syrians would kick him out of the country or kill him. He wouldn't be able to protect Mariam, to feel her skin on his, to hear her laugh. He would never see her again. He cursed and kicked a hole in the wall and sat down in the conference room, debating how to destroy the video equipment.

ALI AND VOLKOV ARRIVED OUTSIDE the white stone building, which was indistinguishable from the others on the block. They approached a Security Office captain, who was smiling ear to ear. "How'd you find him?" Ali asked.

"We got lucky, saw him walk inside. I followed him up the stairs, saw him go in one of the apartments."

"Did you see anyone enter with him?"

"No."

"Take me there."

They rode the elevator in silence, Ali's pulse accelerating with each floor.

They reached the apartment. The captain tried the lock. He shook his head.

Ali knocked on the door. "This is the Security Office. Open the door. Now." Silence.

"You have three seconds to open the door." Still more silence

Ali nodded and drew his weapon. The captain kicked in the door. Ali ran in.

THE LIVING ROOM WAS EMPTY, as was the kitchen. Ali entered the bedroom and saw an attractive young Syrian woman smoking on the bed, nude and serene. She was well groomed, he saw as she stood unashamedly to put out her cigarette. Picking up her bra, she nodded toward the closet.

As it turned out, the man the team had identified as Sam was in fact Clement Lacroix from the French Embassy, a young man who bore a striking resemblance to the CIA officer and who was bedding a Syrian hairdresser with an apartment in Kafr Sousa.

Clement hid in the closet at the sound of the knocks. His girlfriend, the brains of the operation as in most Syrian relationships, had enjoyed a smoke as she waited for the *mukhabarat* to realize this was one big horrible mistake.

SAM HAD WAITED PATIENTLY FOR Ali to kick down the door. After thirty minutes Bradley and Procter agreed he should depart. He'd not been followed and had no idea where Ali and the Russian had gone. He left the video equipment inside and slowly discarded the disguise on the outbound SDR. By the time he arrived at his apartment, the bag was empty and he resembled himself again.

He was exhausted but needed to attend the dinner with Zelda on the chance the Syrians did not know he'd been operational that evening. Given the text messages, which they were surely reading, they'd expect it. The *mukhabarat* foot soldier watching his apartment entrance appeared shocked to see him enter. Same guy for the last five days, poor bastard, Sam thought, and considered waving but decided it would be offensive, a professional slight. That was the kind of thing that would invite them to break into his apartment for a search—or just to have some fun ransacking the place.

Zelda had made a reservation at Three Tables, a trendy restaurant in Sha'alan. The district was normally packed, overrun with families, young couples on dates, and strollers on the sidewalk. That was before the war. Now the luxury boutiques and upscale liquor stores were quiet, the restaurants open unevenly.

Zelda had arrived first. She sat uncomfortably at a table with a view out the window. Most of the tables were empty.

Ali Hassan sat beside her.

He smiled and waved at Sam, beckoning him to the table. As Sam approached, Ali stood to shake his hand. He motioned to one of the empty chairs facing inside the restaurant.

"Samuel, please have a seat," he said in English.

Zelda had ordered wine, presumably before the Syrian had arrived. The waiter now brought the bottle.

Ali smiled as the waiter poured it into his glass for the wine ritual and Ali turned it about and sniffed. "Domaine de Bargylus, an excellent choice." Ali took a sip and nodded at the waiter, who filled everyone's glasses. "You know, this is the only Syrian wine considered suitable for export. The rest is garbage produced in state-owned vineyards. A pair of Lebanese own this one, even though it is in Latakia, near my ancestral home. Rebels occasionally shell the vineyard, I hear."

Sam noticed the sweaty imprint on the tablecloth when Zelda removed her hands to place them on her chair.

"Shame on you for drinking," Sam said in Arabic, winking at Val's killer though he wanted to drive his knife through the man's heart. He sensed Ali was at ease, in control.

Ali laughed and took another sip. "I am an Alawi, Mr. Joseph, we are all heretics anyhow." The Syrian smiled at Zelda and she looked down at the sweat marks on the table.

The waiter arrived with bread, and Ali nodded at him to serve them. Ali turned to Zelda and said, "Allow me," as he drizzled her bread with olive oil. Then he seasoned his own bread, but his focus remained on her. "Are you enjoying your stay in Syria?"

"I am." She now looked him in the eyes. "It was a beautiful country."

Ali's English was apparently not sufficiently fluent to notice Zelda's derogatory use of the past tense. "It's too bad you cannot travel up to the coast, or to Aleppo," Ali said. "Although I'm afraid the latter is not presentable these days. It is a shame."

"My father was born there, I visited once when I was young," Zelda said.

"Ah, very good, so you know its former glory. And you are half Syrian? Incredible. America truly is a melting pot, as they say." He tore off another piece of bread and took a bite. His eyes narrowed at Sam. "Let's take a walk, Mr. Joseph."

As they left, Zelda remained at the table, taking a long and grateful gulp of her wine.

Ali lit a cigarette as they walked and offered one to Sam, who declined. The Syrian led them toward a park. "Is a team covering us?" Sam asked.

"Not from my agency, but you never know. Another group might be running an op." He laughed at his own remark and ashed the cigarette.

"How are your twins?" Sam asked.

"They are fine, thank you. I've always wondered what my CIA file looks like. Do you have all the juicy stuff?"

"We've only found six of your mistresses." Ali laughed again, and Sam noticed a red-rope scar on his neck.

"Ah, you've missed the remaining four. They are the ones I've hidden most carefully . . . maybe even the CIA cannot find them?" He grinned, then motioned to a small convenience store and patted at his breast pocket. "We have much to say, but I am out of cigarettes."

Sam followed him inside and held out a few bills. "I'm happy to have the American government pay me back for all the inconvenience," Ali snickered in Arabic. The cashier appeared visibly discomfited by the presence of a *mukhabarat* official and an American chatting in his establishment. Sam smiled at him and asked, in Arabic, "How is your night going?"

"Fine, sir," he said, though his eyes begged them to leave.

Ali led them out of the store and they walked in silence until they arrived at the park. Curiously, Ali had not opened his fresh pack. He gestured to a bench and they sat down.

Ali tapped the pack against his wrist, packing the cigarettes, and then pulled one out and lit it. He waited for a couple to walk by, then turned to Sam. "Mr. Joseph, you are permitted to live and work in this country by the grace of my government. We monitor you for your own protection. Disappearances are not tolerable."

"I understand," Sam said.

Ali continued: "And you must not confuse my geniality for weakness," he said. "If you break the rules again, there will be punishment. And as you well know, there are dark forces at work now in this country. Rule-breaking will give them cause to lash out."

"I understand," Sam said again.

"Good," Ali said. He finished the cigarette and tossed it to the ground and stamped the embers with his shoe. He stood to leave.

Sam wanted to get the guy talking. He really wanted to ask why they'd butchered Val, see the look in Ali's eyes at the mention of her name. But any mention would spook Ali and endanger the op. So instead he tried to elicit something. "You have a wife, children. You read all of the security reports," Sam said. "I suspect you do not approve of your government's response to the unrest. Am I correct?"

"The government has made mistakes, certainly."

"And do you believe this government is your best chance to keep your family safe?"

He lit another cigarette and handed the pack back to Sam before leaving. "Mr. Joseph," he said. "Let me spare you the breath. I am the only one keeping my wife and boys alive. I suggest you spend less time worrying about my safety and devote more to your own. You will need it."

WHEN SAM ARRIVED AT HIS apartment, he did not need to wave at the *mukhabarat* guy. The man was looking right at him, smiling. Sam was not surprised to find that his apartment door was already unlocked. Nor was he surprised to find his shelves overturned, books spilled out and torn to shreds, laptop crushed with a hammer, kitchen knives scattered in the living room where they had been used to carve up the couch. He opened his front hall closet. He did not have to touch his coats to know they were slick with piss. Following a burning smell into the kitchen, he found his garbage disposal had been stuffed with silverware and run to mechanical failure, and his kitchen chairs splintered to kindling. The oven was off, but he opened it anyway out of morbid curiosity. Inside, he found the ashen remains of his books. He smiled. The air conditioner—too precious to destroy—had been carted off. Smart. And when he got to the bathroom, he was actually impressed. They had smashed the tub into bits, filled his sink with urine, and stuffed his pillow into the toilet.

One flourish, though, exceeded expectations: the superhuman pile of human excrement mounded in the middle of the bed. A grainy surveillance photo of Sam and Ali leaving the restaurant jutted from the top like a candle on a birthday cake.

41

ALI HAD TRIED HIS BEST TO AVOID INVOLVING THE President. He'd called Rustum twice, he'd sent an official eyes-only memo with the list of names and the false locations Rustum had agreed to deliver. He had received nothing in return. When he had sent Kanaan to Republican Guard headquarters, one of Rustum's aides had kept him waiting for three hours before informing the lieutenant that Rustum was at the villa in Bloudan. In Bloudan, they told Kanaan that Rustum was in Damascus. So, finally, Ali had hovered outside the office of the President's secretary waiting until he could be squeezed in for a five-minute appointment.

"Your brother assures me he has already had the discussions," Assad said, distracted as he surfed on the internet. Ali stood in front of his desk. He had not been invited to sit. "I know that he has at least told Atiyah, because the man asked me about the site during a meeting earlier this week." Assad clicked his mouse, then clicked again in rapid succession. "Those two men, as is probably apparent, despise each other." Assad chuckled. "I honestly worry that Rustum may order Basil to kill Atiyah someday." He laughed again. Ali could not tell if he was serious.

"He has had all but one conversation, Mr. President," Ali said. "The surveillance operation against the American is proceeding, but we still need to test the officials that had knowledge of—"

"I heard your team lost the American," Assad said, continuing to stare at his computer screen. The President looked up and shifted the conversation back on topic. "You are talking about Bouthaina, though, yes? Your brother does not think it is necessary to test her, Ali."

"Do you agree, Mr. President?" Ali asked.

The President put his hands behind his head and leaned back in the chair. He rubbed his thin mustache. "What do you need?"

ALI CARRIED THE CLASSIFIED PRESIDENTIAL decree into Rustum's home office, brushing past an aide who insisted Rustum was in the middle of a meeting. When Ali opened the door he found Rustum sitting at that awful *noria* desk, reading reports. "Get the hell out—"

"Do you think your girlfriend is spying for the CIA?" Ali asked.

"Fuck you, little brother. I do not."

"Then why have you not passed to her the false information on the backup facility at Wadi Barada?"

"How do you know I have not? And for god's sake, we both know the spy is that rapist Atiyah."

Ali slammed the presidential decree down on the desk. "Read this."

Rustum picked up the paper and read, his face reddening as he finished. He set it neatly back on the desk, upside down.

"You have until tonight to pass her the information," Ali said. He turned and left.

MARIAM SLOWLY ATE AN ORANGE, glancing sideways at the gigantic purse she'd used to smuggle the document bag into the Palace. She'd eaten three oranges in the past hour, her fingers were discolored, and the juice was stinging her exposed nailbeds. She worked part of the peel off and kept looking at the bag, as if she could will it into Atiyah's office without needing to make the journey herself. It was ironic that this monster had sent men with guns and clubs to kill her in France, but if she succeeded, his end would come from a simple briefcase.

As she ate a section of orange, Bouthaina stopped outside her door. "Night, Mariam."

"Night." Mariam smiled at her boss. The fewer people on this floor, the better. She did not want a crowd around as she switched the bags. Bouthaina disappeared and Mariam's eyes turned back to the purse. She lifted another section of orange to her lips and the smell suddenly reminded her of Ali's henchman Kanaan. He had been eating an orange during one of the rounds of questioning after Italy. He'd sat silently, working away the skin as his boss again asked the same questions and Mariam answered.

Q: *The device you provided. It connects to a satellite?*

A: *Yes, that is what Samuel Joseph said. I've already told you, General.*

Q: *Why did he give it to you?*

A: *I gave him the information we agreed upon. I said I needed a way to talk to CIA from Damascus. I needed a device. I have said—*

Q: *What else did you tell them?*

A: *Nothing.*

[Shuffling paper]

Q: *Which of these people is the CIA Chief of Station?*

A: *This woman.*

Q: *Name?*

A: *She told me her name was Artemis.*

Q: *Is that a real American name, Kanaan? It sounds like a pseudonym.*

[Inaudible]

Q: *Really? Okay. Did they provide other safe houses here in Damascus?*

A: *Just the one I've shown you, General.*

Q: *Did he promise you anything in exchange for your cooperation?*

A: *Money.*

Q: *What did you have for dinner in San Angelo?*

A: *Pasta*

Q: *What kind of pasta?*

A: *Cacio e pepe. Spaghetti with cheese and pepper.*

Q: *What did Samuel Joseph eat?*

A: *I have told you four times—*

Q: *What did Samuel Joseph eat?*

A: *Pasta. Tuscan ragù. With boar.*

[Muffled conversation, the click of a cigarette lighter]

Q: *We can take a short break. Would you like to see your cousin now?*

A: *When will you release her?*

Q: *When your job is done.*

A: *When will that be, General?*

Q: *When it is done. Anything else?*

A: *May I use the bathroom first?*

She'd vomited, then scrunched herself next to the toilet and hyperventilated into her hands. In the moment, she'd been unaware that she'd latched her teeth onto her pointer finger. She cursed as she broke the skin. Dabbing the blood with the toilet paper, she looked at herself in the mirror. She remembered Sam's promise in the vineyard and felt like a whore. "You look worse than I do, *okhti,*" Razan had said as Mariam was led into her cell for a brief visit. "And I'm the one in prison."

Mariam finished the orange. She picked up the pieces of the peel and walked them to the trash. It was 8:45. Fifteen minutes. She went to the bathroom and washed the residue off her hands. Returning to her office, she turned off the lights and closed the door as if she were not there. She sat under her desk, holding the giant purse containing the document bag, and listened to her heart beat. She heard footsteps outside and checked her watch, which she could barely read in the darkness. It was 8:58. "He's a prompt pervert," Bouthaina liked to say.

She heard Atiyah's footsteps pass her office on the way to visit Hasan Turkmani, another adviser to Assad. Mariam had waited for a very specific date for this operation. She needed Atiyah to meet with Turkmani, preferably late at night, when Bouthaina was gone. With those conditions met, she could hustle down the hall into Atiyah's office, replace the bag, then return without Bouthaina wondering why she was walking into that part of the corridor. Bouthaina was as suspicious as Atiyah, and she would probably interpret Mariam's presence near his office as evidence of treachery.

Mariam sprang into action when she heard Turkmani's door open, then click shut. Picking up the purse, she walked quickly down the hallway, past Bouthaina's office, then turned left into the corridor housing Atiyah's team. She picked up her pace until she reached his office, which was thankfully open.

Walking inside, remembering him smacking her bottom right in the doorway, she pulled the new document bag—loaded with U.S. passports for Atiyah and his unfortunate wife, cash, and a device preloaded with a message asking for exfil—from the purse and set it on the floor next to Atiyah's original. "How do you think the *mukhabarat* will react?" Sam had asked. "I think they will kill him," she had said. "Good." He had nodded coldly. "We'll also arrange for his phone to receive a few strange text messages from American numbers. Just to be sure."

Mariam pulled the papers from Atiyah's bag. She closely examined the inside compartment before making the switch. "There is one caveat," Iona had said. "We obviously cannot see the inside of the bag from your video. We've subjected our bag to a couple months of wear and tear on the inside. I personally crammed papers in and lifted them out more than one hundred times. But there could be a stain, there could be rips or scuffs we cannot see. When you make the switch, again, you check and abort if the bags don't match."

Her eyes frantically moved from bag to bag, searching for any differences. It was more terrifying that she found none, because it meant she should keep going. She shoved the papers into the new bag and set it back where the old one had been. She put the old bag in her purse and quickly left the office. She hadn't experienced any physical tics during the operation, she'd been so focused, but now she felt sweat on her back and noticed how heavy the purse felt over her shoulder. She winced at each loud footstep as she turned the corridor, almost running now, trying to clear Bouthaina's office and reach her own.

Turkmani's door began to open. She heard Atiyah's voice. She made a snap, instinctive decision and ducked into Bouthaina's office. She stood by the desk, breathing heavily, as Atiyah approached. She imagined him asking what was in the bag. *Such a nice purse. Show me what's inside, dear,* he might say as he reached in. She backed farther into the office and watched as his passing footsteps briefly blotted out the light seeping through the crack in the bottom of the door. After a minute, Mariam took a single step forward, then another, moving toward the door.

She had her hand on the knob when she heard two familiar voices in the hallway, though, unlike most of the conversations on which she had eavesdropped, the current subject was not sexual. Mariam pulled her hand off the knob, backed into the office, and closed herself in Bouthaina's washroom. She'd tried to get out of sight, but as Bouthaina's office door opened she kicked herself for not just leaving the office and making up a story for Bouthaina about why she had been inside. As Mariam sat on the closed toilet in the darkness, she heard Rustum and Bouthaina bickering as they entered. Someone turned on the light. Should have said I was bringing a document into her office and forgot it. Should have said I sleepwalked here. Should have done anything but hide. Her whole world was on fire and now she'd probably doomed herself by stupidly wandering into Bouthaina's washroom. She stood still, feeling her heartbeat in the darkness. Why were they here? If it was for sex, she was completely out of luck, because they'd open the washroom door and find a CIA spy sitting on the toilet, sweating, holding a purse containing a stolen document bag.

"What couldn't wait?" Bouthaina said. "And had to happen here? I was halfway home."

"We had a problem at Jableh. You remember the shipments?"

"Of course. What problem?"

"The Americans found it. We had to evacuate and move all of the sarin to a new facility. A backup. At Wadi Barada. I wanted to make sure you knew, in case you were sending anything else to Jableh."

"I see. Is the attack still moving forward?"

"Yes. We've made enough. But please keep this between us, *habibti*."

From behind the door, Mariam could imagine the glare she must have given him. Bouthaina didn't even respond.

SHE LISTENED TO THEM SCREW for at least thirty minutes, Mariam's discomfort overpowered by the relief that the animal noises coming from the couch would easily drown out any sounds inadvertently made in the washroom. She heard fabric tearing out there, probably Bouthaina's panties, and the sound brought Mariam back to her apartment when Razan had her leg up on the balcony, dress ripping, ready to kill herself. Then they were on the floor, crying, screaming, gazing up at a rare starry sky. She'd saved her cousin, for what? The dungeon. She'd failed everyone she loved. Razan. Sam. Uncle Daoud. And now she was locked in a washroom. What was she doing? What had she done? She closed her eyes and tried to blot out the noise.

She had betrayed Sam to Ali Hassan, a man she hated, to save her cousin. In the darkness she saw Razan in her black ruffle dress, though it was not ripped. She twirled. Then she heard Razan say: *Why are you helping these monsters for my sake? I'm already free, okhti. You need to free the others: Fatimah, Uncle Daoud. Yourself. And who is going to help you? Ali Hassan? Please, girl. Sam is the only one you can trust. And you've screwed it all up.*

She'd selfishly tried to protect her cousin, and now, finally, she realized that Razan never would have approved. Razan would tell her to keep fighting. Mariam had been trying to save Razan, first from joining the rebellion, then from the clutches of Ali Hassan. But now she knew that to save her cousin she had to free herself.

She opened her eyes.

Mariam stayed put for another half hour after they left, just to be sure. Sweaty and edgy, she emerged from Bouthaina's office and hugged the wall for support as she returned to her own. Mariam lay down, pressing her cheek onto the cold floor. She had to tell Sam, but Ali had the device and the drop site would take too long. A mortar landed outside, close enough to shake her windows.

She checked the time. Sam might still be at the embassy. She gathered the purse and left.

She would do it tonight. She would atone for her mistake. She would collect his promise.

42

THE FUCK ON THE COUCH HAD HELPED CLEAR HIS MIND. In his office rereading Ali's reports on the Samuel Joseph surveillance disasters, Rustum felt a moment of extreme clarity. The evaporation of the CIA officer into the night. The mix-up with the Frenchman. The ransacking of the apartment. The shit all over the bed was a nice touch, but it did not compensate for the fact that Ali had failed. And his little brother had the gall to rub his nose in it by having the President write a decree forcing him to pass that silly message to Bouthaina. Rustum felt himself descending into anger, his jaw clenched tightly. He was a boy again, pushing Ali down the stairs, jumping on him in bed with a kitchen knife to slit his throat. He was vengeance. He was Syria's salvation.

He would have to clean up the mess.

He had to arrest Samuel Joseph. The President would understand once it came to light, even if Ali still had time for his silly operations. It would only take a few hours for Basil to cut the traitor's name from the American. Then, sure in the knowledge that no spies lurked inside his army, Rustum could unleash his attack to end the war. The Americans had dropped atomic bombs to defeat the Japanese and end the Second World War. Why could he not kill the terrorists with gas?

He picked up the phone and barked Basil's name. An aide patched him through.

"I have a job for your boys," Rustum said

"Certainly." Rustum heard the scratchy sounds of Basil cradling the phone between his head and shoulder. "What is it?"

"There is an American, a CIA officer, here in Damascus. Samuel Joseph. I will send you his file. He's running a traitor. I want him brought in."

"Understood. Militia?"

"Yes. No paperwork." Rustum thought again of the dishwater eyes, Hama, the scalps. "And no wet work on this one, so make sure the boys you use are clean. No heroin. I need him talking, not dead or in the hospital. Understood?"

"Will your brother be watching him with the Russians?"

"I will call them now and order them to back off, give you some space to work."

"Yes, Commander. How soon?"

"Now."

Rustum hung up, dialed Ali's office, and was patched through to the assistant. "Get me Ali," he growled, but instead of Ali he heard the assistant stammer that Ali is not here. "Then get me the Russian," Rustum growled.

A moment later, Rustum was greeted by a thick Slavic accent. "Yes, Commander."

"Back the surveillance teams off the American for the rest of the night. I need them elsewhere."

43

THE EMBASSY'S CONTRACTOR CLEANING CREW WAS still at his apartment—"Never seen anything like this, Mr. Joseph, never seen anything like this," one of the men had mumbled on repeat as they toured the ruined apartment—so Sam stayed at the Station later than usual and used the time to check for messages on the ATHENA database. It was empty, like every day since Italy. Exhausted and worried, he put on his suit coat to leave. Inside the pocket, he felt the Marlboros he'd purchased for Ali. Even though Vegas was one of the last places in America you could smoke in public, he'd never taken to it. He'd always preferred dip. But this was better than nothing.

Outside the chancery building, he bummed a light from one of the Marine Guards and felt obligated to bullshit with him about the deteriorating security situation. The young Marine, Sam thought, looked genuinely excited about the prospect of the collapse of law and order in the capital. "Mind if I borrow this?" Sam said, holding up the box of matches, and the jarhead said go right ahead. Facing up toward the sheer cliff of climb-resistant fencing, he debated when the *mukhabarat* would toss him from the country. The excitement he'd felt during the first days of his tour had vanished, replaced by the ominous feeling that his work in Damascus was collapsing.

Procter had charged him with two jobs: kill Ali Hassan, run ATHENA. He had failed at both.

First, Ali. They'd come close. Sam still did not understand why the Russian had run after him on the street, or where they'd gone, but he knew from the words on the Slav's lips ("We've found him") that they'd been hunting him. Ali's warning and the trashing of his apartment meant he was on thin ice. Stick another thumb in Ali's eye, and you may not be able to gouge it out. He'll just bite it off. PNG you. Maybe worse, like he'd done to Val.

Two, ATHENA. Mariam. She had hidden something from him in Tuscany. They hadn't heard anything from her on the device for more than a week. Something was very wrong. Sam lit another cigarette and gazed at the American flag, flapping against the mortar-streaked sky. He thought of the protester who had climbed the roof to tear it down. He thought of Mariam's fearful eyes in Italy. He remembered his promise.

His time in Damascus had run its course. He had no clue what would happen to his career after this night. It might be over. But he knew what he had to do.

Sam stubbed out the cigarette. He punched the code to enter the chancery building and walked down the steps toward the Station. Entering another code, he swung open the metallic vault door, collected his bag from his desk, and walked into Procter's office. She was yelling at someone on the phone, but when she saw Sam, she hung up. The embassy walls shook as a regime artillery barrage picked up. He leaned in the doorway.

"I know I'm on thin ice here, Chief. Maybe we talk to Bradley in the morning and figure out what to do next?"

She stared at him and did not answer the question. "Take care of your agent and get the intel," Procter said. "It's all that matters."

Sam nodded. He exited the Station, strolled into the motor pool, back through the metal detectors, and left the embassy compound. Tonight he would keep his promise.

FROM A BENCH ON THE other side of the circle, Mariam watched Sam leave the embassy. She had to speak to him without watchers, without surveillance. Tricky, because she thought he would be followed by a *mukhabarat* tail. Maybe she could swing up alongside and give the message quickly, pretend like she was passing him on the street. It might work. She knew he would not be startled by her presence, he would play it smart. She was also fairly certain she was clear of the Security Office team. She'd run the moves from France upon leaving the Palace.

Sam walked along the river toward Adnan al-Malki, the broad, tree-lined avenue funneling cars and pedestrians into Umayyad Square and the Sheraton. The streets were emptier than usual, the fighting and the mortars keeping everyone inside. Mariam wished there had been thick crowds, the kind of crowds the area used to draw. She felt naked by herself, trying to trail a CIA officer. As Sam cut onto a remote sidewalk along the river, it registered that she did not see a *mukhabarat* tail. Odd. He was fifty yards ahead, still along the river, walking at a brisk pace. Mariam quickened her stride, cursing her heels and her stupidity. The street was poorly lit and empty, the bustle of the embassy a distant memory.

Then she saw them. Three men emerged from behind a dumpster to block Sam's path. It was not a checkpoint. She knew what it was. She pulled a nail file from her purse, clutched it into her wrist so they would not see until it was too late, and dumped the bag on the ground. Thankfully, she'd already trashed Atiyah's old briefcase.

She kicked off her heels and ran.

SAM STOPPED IN HIS TRACKS as the three men appeared on the crumbling sidewalk. They did not have proper uniforms. A burly guy in an I ♥ NY T-shirt held a club. The other two held AK-47s, one in flip-flops, the other wearing camo fatigues. The guns were not pointed at him—yet. He couldn't figure out the vibe. Militia? Criminals? Rebels? The lines had blurred in Damascus. Not that it mattered. Then he saw the handcuffs on NY's belt. Whoever they were, they wanted to abduct him.

"Good evening," Sam said in Arabic. "What do you want?"

"Mr. Joseph," NY said. "We need you to come with us."

Well, shit, Sam thought. They knew his name. Good news was they wanted him alive, otherwise why bring cuffs, so maybe he had some leverage. Just a little.

"Who are you?" Sam said, still in Arabic.

"Military."

Sam glanced down at the other man's flip-flops, then up to the gun, then again met NY's eyes.

NY looked past him. Sam heard the steps, the sound of bare feet on pavement behind him. He braced himself.

RETZEV, BENI HAD SAID IN Paris, was one of the core principles of Krav Maga. A seamless explosion of violence. She picked up speed, feet burning on the pavement as confused looks formed on the faces of each militiaman.

Three men, two guns drawn. She needed to take the weapons out of play.

They kept staring, uncertain how to handle the barefoot, fashionably dressed, wild-eyed woman running toward them.

At twenty feet out, the one with the club and the New York T-shirt yelled stop. She ran faster.

Then she was on them as the nail file flashed and she drove it into the scrotum of one of the men holding an AK, the one wearing flip-flops. He wailed as blood soaked his pants. She swung her right arm down onto the gun, clattering it to the pavement. He collapsed, clutching the file in his groin as he sank to the sidewalk.

SAM HAD BARELY REGISTERED THAT it was Mariam who'd leapt into the fray when he stepped toward the guy in camo fatigues, currently staring in horror at the castration of his friend.

Sam drove his fist toward the man's sternum, but the bag around his shoulder caught his arm as he swung, and the blow missed by an inch. Camo stumbled a step back, then started to lift the gun. Sam kicked the man's shin, then turned his hand into a claw and jabbed into his face, searching for a cavity. He lodged his middle finger in Camo's left eye and began twisting, his fingertips slickening as the man shrieked, still clutching the gun and trying to steady it at Sam.

Sam's right shoulder exploded in pain. He lost purchase on Camo's eye socket and stumbled. The club came down on his right kidney, then again. He tried to get up and NY hit him again, this time on his shin, bellowing something in deep bass notes that Sam could not understand as he crumpled to the street.

MARIAM, KNEELING, PICKED UP THE rifle from the sidewalk and pointed it at the man in the I ♥ NY T-shirt beating Sam with the club. She compressed the trigger and heard the AK's distinctive rattle and saw the bullets tear into his pelvis and thighs and knee. He fell.

The man in camouflage clutching his eye stumbled toward the short limestone wall between the sidewalk and the fifteen-foot plunge down to the riverbank. She fired a volley into him but started too low, rounds skittering on the sidewalk. She corrected upward, the bullets ripping through his butt, back, and neck, until a round found the base of his skull and he sandbagged onto the wall. Mariam kept her finger on the trigger as she watched the body seesaw for a moment and then disappear over the side onto the riverbank below.

Mariam scanned the scene. Miraculously, the sidewalk remained clear of pedestrians. There was a dead camo-clad man on the riverbank, another in flip-flops moaning on the ground with a nail file jammed into his groin. The man in the I ♥ NY T-shirt was trying to crawl away and doing a bad job. Sam managed to stand, grasping his right side.

She felt the spent shell casings underfoot as she walked over to the man in flip-flops clutching his groin. He had dislodged the nail file, but his pants were soaked through with blood. "Who sent you?" she asked, towering over him, the barrel pointed at his head. She wanted him to tell her they were rebels or robbers. Fine. Still a mess, but they wouldn't know Sam was CIA and wouldn't be able to connect her to the Americans.

Flip-flops did not want to fight. "Basil Mahkluf. We're militia." He winced, pulling in oxygen to finish his sentence. "Here to arrest the American."

She looked away. Then she held down the trigger and felt the matter splash across her feet.

"They're official militia," she said in English to Sam. She noticed now her teeth chattered, though the night was muggy. She clenched her jaw then pointed the gun at NY crawling away. She pressed the trigger until he stopped moving.

There was a volley of car horns back toward the embassy, but Mariam did not hear them.

BY ANY MEASURE, THE SCENE was bad: three dead Syrian militiamen, a wounded CIA officer, and an asset who'd inexplicably appeared during the holdup. Miraculously, the sidewalk remained pedestrian- and police-free, but that would not hold for long, given the gunfire. Sam had no idea why Mariam had come. It broke every security rule they'd discussed in France.

Mariam ran back for her bag and shoes. Sam wiped prints from the gun and snatched the nail file. He looked at the dead man lying in a heap by the river. Sam checked his own bag and confirmed he had one of the burner phones inside. He texted Elias an address. The message ended with four periods, indicating it was an emergency.

Mariam pulled a wipe from her purse and he scrubbed speckled blood from her face and neck. She tucked her blouse back in and pulled her hair back. She rubbed her eyes, which were twitching. Sam gave her the address.

His phone vibrated. The message said: *Ok. 10 minutes.*

"We can't go together," he said. "You go toward Rawdah. Shortest SDR in the world, our pickup is ten minutes."

"Where are we going?" she asked.

"Someplace where we can talk."

THE FUNDS ALLOCATED TO THE BANDITOs had purchased a spartan apartment on the northern tip of Malki, nestled into the feet of Mount Qasioun. There was one bedroom with a mattress splayed on the floor, although there were no sheets; a small kitchen, stocked with canned soup; and, in the entryway, a card table with a single metal chair. The overhead lights flickered. It smelled like ammonium disinfectant and mothballs. Anticipating blackouts, the BANDITOs had set several battery-powered camping lanterns along the wall of the bedroom.

Elias would text again in two hours and would ferry Mariam most of the way home, far enough to get her through checkpoints but not all the way to her front door. In spite of the squalor, Sam would have loved nothing more than to spend time with Mariam here. But even two hours was pushing it. And if Mariam was being watched—as he knew she was—a prolonged absence would generate questions from the people keeping track of her.

They sat on the mattress facing each other. The lights shivered again and went out. He heard artillery overhead. Sam turned on one of the lanterns.

"Why were you there?" he asked.

"I had to tell you something."

He almost screamed at her, *Why didn't you use the device we gave you?* But he already knew why—it was why he felt both betrayed and assured of her loyalty—though it did nothing to cool his frustration. No longer trusting his own judgment, he remembered Procter ("Collect the intelligence"). His eyes were narrowed at her. "What is it?"

"I heard Rustum tell Bouthaina the location of a backup facility for the sarin."

"Where is it?"

"Wadi Barada."

"How did you find out?"

"I overheard. I was in her washroom. I'd just put the bag in Atiyah's office. I—" She started crying.

By now the Syrians would have learned of the shoot-out and connected Sam to the murders. They might kill him if they found him. Or they might arrest him and put him on trial and *then* kill him. He would have to get the information to Langley tonight.

"Who has the device, Mariam?"

She looked directly at him, eyes aflame. "I'm so sorry, *habibi,* I'm so so sorry." She sobbed, pressing her hands into her eyes. "Forgive me, please forgive me."

"Who has it?"

She sobbed. "I'm sorry, *habibi,* I'm sorry, I'm sorry."

"Where is it?"

She looked up, face wet and flushed red. "Ali Hassan has it. They took Razan, Sam, they came into my apartment and arrested her the night before I left for Italy. Ali Hassan used me against you, *habibi,* I'm so sorry, I'm so sorry."

He had expected it, and thought he'd be angry when she confessed. Instead he was sad. Sad that she had not told him in Italy, when he and Procter could have helped her. They could have gotten her out. Now they were trapped in Damascus and he wondered whether they would get out of this mess alive.

"Do you know what they wanted from the device, or from me?" Sam asked. She was shaking now, wiping streaks of makeup with her hands, wetting spots of dried blood from the fight missed in the harried cleanup. Now, in the stillness of this squalid apartment, he actually saw her for the first time since Italy. Her face was sallow, broken. Dark rings hung under her eyes. She bit at red-raw finger skin.

"They were not specific with me, Ali only said that they knew you were meeting with a traitor and had to find him. I wondered if it is me they want."

He gently placed his hand on her fingers and lifted them away from her mouth and held her hands in his.

"What did you give them other than the device?"

"Background information, mostly. I told them about Procter." She bit her lip. "And the safe house here in Damascus. They told me to make contact with you. They knew that I had met you at the party in Paris. Ali wanted me to operate against you. He wanted the device."

Sam ran the inventory: A top-of-the-line covcom device and primo safe house burned, a crown jewel Syrian asset the leak. Counterintelligence would go berserk.

Sam began pacing the room. More artillery fire on the mountain. The electricity came on. Within seconds the apartment darkened again.

"Why did you follow me tonight?"

"I heard the information and knew you needed it. And I had no way to contact you."

"Did you run the Atiyah op? Is the bag switched?" Station had heard nothing since the return from Italy.

"Yes. But I didn't tell you because I didn't have the device."

"Did you tell Ali about the Atiyah op, or Bouthaina's computer?"

"No. I am loyal. We fight together."

"I know you are, *habibti*, I know." He sat down. Her head slumped onto his shoulder and she wept. She had betrayed the CIA, betrayed their agreement in France, betrayed him. But Sam knew she was telling the truth. She'd risked everything by killing the militiamen. In another life, in another world, they would have settled down somewhere. But instead they were in Damascus with front-row tickets to the city's descent into hell. He would put the anger and the sadness and the shame aside. He would focus on the one thing he could control right now. He would protect her.

"Did they release Razan?" he asked.

She shook her head, setting her jaw and staring at the lantern. "Not yet," she said. "Ali Hassan is a liar."

Sam's mind worked quickly now, considering responsibilities and potential moves. Protect your agent. Keep your promise.

"Then the only way to protect you," he said, "is to give Ali exactly what he wants."

THEY BUILT THE PLAN FACING each other on the mattress.

"In case something breaks we'll need a way to talk, even if just for a few seconds," he said finally. "I'll have Elias give you a throwaway phone on the drive home." He texted the BANDITOs. He gave her his burner number.

He didn't need to check his watch, he already knew: they had twenty-five minutes until Elias arrived to collect Mariam.

Sam stepped into the kitchen out of earshot and called Procter. He explained the attack but did not tell her where he was.

"Time for exfil, man. This party is over," she said.

He honestly had no idea how to explain his next move, so he just said: "You need to pass this tonight, Chief. ATHENA intel: the sarin is at Wadi Barada. Confirmed subsource."

He hung up and took a deep breath. Even if he pulled this off, he wasn't sure that facing Procter and the CIA brass would be that much better than a Syrian trial. In the end, the only difference would be whether he got a star on the wall.

Mariam was on the mattress when he returned. He lay down next to her. Please forgive me, *habibi,* she said again and again until he pressed his forehead into hers. They sat entwined in silence for several minutes until they were breathing in rhythm. He kissed her.

Mariam wiped her eyes and held his gaze as she unbuttoned his shirt. He cringed as the sleeve pulled on his shoulder.

"This might actually be the last time, *habibi,*" she said.

"I know," he said. "But we're usually wrong."

44

RUSTUM MANAGED A LITANY OF VENDETTAS AS HE walked into the National Security Bureau headquarters on the balmy, sun-drenched morning of July 18.

The list would balloon as the day wore on.

These damn meetings were tiresome. The President had established a group, chaired by his little brother, to centralize the counterintelligence effort during the war. The one amusing aspect of the meetings was that they had to gather outside of the Security Office because Ali's run-down headquarters did not have a conference room large enough to seat everyone. But, jab at his brother aside, Rustum found the meetings exhausting because so many of his comrades were doughy bureaucrats. They were nothing but talk.

"Commander, I need a moment," he heard a familiar voice say as he entered the building. Basil stood in the lobby, awaiting his arrival. Rustum pulled him aside.

"Do you have him?" Rustum whispered. The NSB headquarters was not the place to have this conversation.

"There was an incident last night with the militia."

"An incident? Speak plainly, Basil," he said, drawing the gaze of a passerby.

"The men sent to arrest the CIA officer are dead," Basil said. "He killed them and escaped."

Rustum stood dumbstruck. Someone saluted him. He ignored it.

"We found the bodies early this morning," Basil continued. Shot up near the river. One stabbed in the penis. Another tossed onto the embankment with his eye gouged out."

"Stabbed in the penis?"

"Yes."

"*Haywaan,*" Rustum growled. Animal. He felt his blood pressure rising. "Find him."

"We are searching everywhere, Commander." A pause. "And if we find him?"

"Alive. If possible."

ENRAGED, ALI WALKED INTO THE conference room and took his seat at the head of the table. He had prepared an agenda for this meeting, but it was now useless because the only thing on which he could focus was the violent anger he felt toward his sadistic brother and Basil, his imp of a henchman. Volkov, usually stoic, had been equally apoplectic to learn that Ali had not approved or been aware of Rustum's surveillance call-off the previous evening. Hearing the news, the Russian had thrown a ceramic mug against the wall of the Security Office command center, the liquid mess confirming his anger by the fact that it had been at least half full of Zhuravli, his vodka of choice for the early morning hours. Ali had burned down two cigarettes watching one of the Russians sweep up the mess.

The manhunt for Samuel Joseph had then commenced as every security agency—all seventeen—had been informed and instructed to prioritize the search. Ali had personally led the raid on the American's apartment. They had searched the safe house he had provided to Mariam Haddad. Ali had summoned Mariam for an interview. The border guards had been put on alert. The Americans had been officially informed in a tense meeting that, Ali had heard, ended with the Syrian deputy foreign minister cursing at the U.S. ambassador. And still they could not find Samuel Joseph.

Ali waved over the boy serving tea as he shuffled through papers. He could never remember his name. The boy walked around the table pushing a creaky cart. He tried to fill the cup but instead spilled much of it along the sides and onto the serving tray. "I'm sorry . . . I'm sorry, General," he stammered, wiping down the sides of the cup.

"It's fine," Ali said, taking the tea. "Just give me a napkin . . . remind me of your name, again."

"Jibril, General."

"Well, Jibril, hand me that napkin." But the boy did not hear. He was staring toward the door with his mouth open. Ali turned.

President Assad walked in. He was always invited to this meeting but had not once come. Ali stood to shake his hand and stepped aside, giving up his center seat for the President, who was now greeting each of the officials around the table.

Rustum took his seat at Assad's right and ignored Ali, who leaned closer to his big brother. "I know you tried to kill the American last night. Do you have him in custody, or did your men really screw up so badly?"

"You think I killed three militia to throw you off the scent, little brother? Make you think he'd escaped when I in fact have him?"

"I would not put it past you, big brother."

Rustum smiled. "Fuck you, little brother, I don't know what happened to him or where he is." The President reached Rustum and shook his hand before sitting down. He smoothed his tie and nodded to Ali to start the meeting.

"Our focus today is on finding the American Samuel Joseph," Ali said to the group, his eyes darting toward the rickety tea cart as Jibril finished serving the interior minister and moved closer. Assad waved Jibril over and the cart squeaked loudly as he rolled it to a stop between Ali and the President. Ali stopped talking because every eye in the room was locked on the distracting tea cart. Jibril tried pouring, but he spilled and hot tea ran down the sides of the President's cup onto the table. "Damn it," the President said, sliding the liquid away from him in a vain effort to keep it from rolling onto his pants. He stared at Jibril, who frantically searched the tray for a napkin. This kid was having a very bad morning. He looked sick.

"Don't you have one in that cart, boy?" The President pointed to the bottom of the cart, which was draped by a tablecloth.

"I . . . I . . . need to go get one, Mr. President." Jibril began to walk away, leaving the cart between Ali and the President.

"Boy," Rustum snarled, "take the tea cart to the other end of the table so it's out of the way."

Jibril looked at the President, then at Ali, who could see sweat forming on the boy's brow. Ali started his briefing again as the tea cart squeaked away. The boy parked it between the defense minister and Turkmani at the other end of the table. Ali saw that Jibril stared at him as he left the room. Something felt strange. Ali had stopped talking, and he now looked down at his papers, struggling to focus.

"General Hassan," the President said. "Please try to continue. My ears are ringing from that damn cart, too." Assad stuck a finger in his ear and moved it around, laughing.

Ali heard a faint ring. Then came the heat, his body covered in a hot light that blotted out the room. Then the sensation of spinning, weightless, in the depths of a pool as his arms and face seared and smoke caked his nostrils. A severed leg tore through his field of vision in slow motion as he somersaulted again. Then, spinning again, he glimpsed a fuming, jagged hole in the floor—or maybe the ceiling—and as the world stilled, the edges focusing, the rotations slowing, all he could hear were grunts, shrieks, whimpers, and desperate, heavy breathing.

Finally, he heard the President offer a struggled gasp: "*Ya allah.* My god."

Ali discovered himself now sitting upright against the wall, several feet behind his chair. The President lay behind his own chair, head up and moving. Ali looked down and saw his legs, still there, intact. He felt one with a finger. He could sense the pressure. He tried moving a toe. He could.

He looked around the smoky room, hacking phlegm. Chunks of blackened flesh littered the floor. The far side of the table had vanished. The ceiling tiles had disintegrated, leaving a gaping hole above. He could not see to the other side of the table, but to his right lay Rustum, slithering toward him on his elbows.

Assad stood, wild-eyed, then collapsed again, wheezing in the haze. Ali found he could stand. He hobbled to Assad and helped him up. Rustum also stood, and held the wall for support. Ali looked around and the defense minister's eyes looked back furtively, as if asking where the bottom of his head had gone.

AN HOUR LATER ALI SAT with Rustum and Assad at the Palace. The President wore a bandage over his right eye and dressings for the burns on his arms and chest. The doctor had insisted Rustum wear a foam bandage around his neck. Ali miraculously had suffered only minor cuts on his face. He had not yet called Layla. He did not know what to say. He wondered if he was in shock.

They watched a report on Al Jazeera waiting for Jibril's audience with the President. The boy had been caught trying to flee the building after the bombing. On the television, Zahran Alloush, Douma's warlord, claimed responsibility for the bombing and said it was the start of an offensive to take the capital. Assad threw the remote into the television, cracking the screen and killing the picture. Ali put his head in his hands. They all sat in silence.

Then the head of presidential security swung open the office door. The manacled tea boy Jibril marched in front, sweaty and bruised, his eyes wide with shock, probably because both he and the President were still alive.

Ali wanted nothing more than to go home to Layla and his boys, but here he was, stuck in the Palace, watching yet more misery unfold. He hated this. He hated himself. Jibril stared at the floor.

"Look at me, boy," Assad said. Jibril shuddered. The President took a step closer. "I said look at me, boy." Jibril looked up. The President spat into his eyes. Then he slapped him across the face. Jibril began crying. Ali looked away.

"My father did not spend three decades constructing Syria to have traitorous filth like you destroy it during my reign," Assad said. "This country must be governed by the boot, the sword, the gun, you understand? There can be no freedom in Suriya al-Assad, precisely because of creatures like you. You, boy, are the chaos my family has held back for decades. You are the reason why I fight, why my government will never surrender. Syria is mine, boy, not yours."

Assad motioned to his head of security, who dragged the boy out.

"Start it now," Assad said to Rustum.

Rustum nodded and left, ripping off the neck brace as he walked down the stairs out of Assad's office.

"Find the American," the President said to Ali.

KANAAN DROVE ALI BACK TO the Security Office, and as they rode through traffic—six checkpoints—he watched the Syrian MiGs overhead and the tense Republican Guard officers and wondered if this was it. He called Layla.

"*Habibti,* are you and the boys at home?"

"Yes. What's going on?"

"There was an attempt on the President during our meeting. I am fine. Others are not. The Guard is preparing an offensive."

"What should we do?" Her voice was shaky. He could hear Sami yelling in the background.

Ali considered the options:

Run. Bad idea, rebel checkpoints are popping up all around the city and Rustum is no doubt shuttering the airport.

Hide. Also bad. You die if either side finds you.

Fight. The best option now. A chance at survival.

"Stay put. The city center is still safe, *habibti.* I am going to the office. I will come home soon."

Reaching his building, Ali walked past the Russian command center on the way to his office. He spotted Volkov, a triumphant look beaming from his meaty face. He held a new mug filled with vodka and a single piece of paper.

"General, I've been instructed by President Putin himself to provide you with this information. It is, as the Americans say, hot off the pressures," Volkov said as they sat.

Ali was about to correct the phrase but stopped himself. Who knew how much vodka the man had in him?

Volkov continued. "We've had some luck in Washington. One of our most highly placed sources received an interesting piece of information late last night."

Volkov slid the paper across the table.

It had markings like the other information—(TS//HCS//OC REL ISR)—and was very concise. Just five lines of text including the source description. The text did not matter, just the title:

"LOCATION OF REPUBLICAN GUARD SARIN STOCKPILE AT WADI BARADA DEPOT."

Ali thought he might laugh or cry, he was not sure. Wadi Barada. The facility provided to Bouthaina.

ALI FOUND HIS BROTHER IN his office, six aides standing around slack-jawed as Rustum screamed at someone over the phone to ready the missile and rocket forces nationwide. As Ali entered the room, Rustum turned his entire body to look at him because he could not move his neck. His brother's eyes were feral, and Ali saw that his mustache was singed. He had not noticed at the palace.

Ignoring Ali, Rustum continued yelling into the phone and went to a map, pointing at coordinates inside Douma. He slammed down the phone and made a crazed gesture with his right arm toward Ali, beckoning him to sit and wincing in pain as he did so. He shooed the aides out of the room.

"Why are you here?" Rustum asked.

Ali slid the Russian report across the table. "The SVR delivered a copy to you, but I assumed you'd be too busy to read."

His big brother gazed at the report for several significant seconds, as if imagining the title might change. Then Rustum breathed deep and sank his head. He set the paper down on the desk.

"I will handle this. I alone."

Ali had initially considered arresting Bouthaina, but he knew that he could not have his way, not this time. She was done.

"Yes. You will, big brother."

45

THE RUSSIAN PAPER OPENED A WORMHOLE IN RUSTUM'S brain. Hama. February 1982. He had boarded an attack helicopter in Damascus and flew, scanning the rebellious scrublands below, wind whipping through his hair, tactical shotgun in hand, preparing to reclaim the city house by house. Back in Damascus they'd joked about *kus* and played cards, but now he and his boys were silent, flying low, observing farmers pointing at their choppers, probably readying to inform the Ikhwan terrorists of the government's arrival. In Hama they'd stormed the apartment, running forward into the maelstrom. Tossing grenades, taking cover to return fire, rage rising with each comrade destroyed. In the apartment, they'd turned their tactical shotguns on the family huddled inside before taking the scalps.

Rustum emerged from the wormhole in the bathroom of his villa in Bloudan, helicopter whirring outside, Russian combat shotgun pointed at Bouthaina, SVR report tossed at her lithe frame soaking in the gaudy bathtub, the one with the gold bear paws for feet. The paper fluttered into the suds. She picked it up, shaking. The Hama apartment then had been ratty, pockmarked with bullet holes, thick with the stench of death. This room felt clean, peaceful, refined. He steadied his vision and saw Bouthaina trying to read the paper, now soggy and illegible.

"What is this, *habibi*?" she stammered. She slid back in the tub. Away.

They always tried to scoot back. Anything to get away. Rustum now saw his villa, his girlfriend bathing, apparently ignorant of the chaos choking the capital. He gripped the shotgun and watched the SVR report sink into the bubbles.

"It is your death warrant," he said.

He leveled the gun at her head. Bouthaina screamed. Then Rustum pulled the trigger.

RUSTUM RETURNED TO DAMASCUS, A bit jittery from the murder, to find Daoud Haddad seated in his office, as he thought he remembered requesting. "Daoud, sit," Rustum said to the already seated Daoud. Rustum then explained his need for Branch 450 expertise in general terms, often referring to the Republican Guard as the Defense Companies, the Guard's predecessor, a now-defunct military unit to which Rustum had belonged in the 1980s when he had been a young lieutenant.

Rustum explained that gas, Daoud, is the only way. The only treatment for vermin in tunnels, the only terror sharp enough to make them put down their swords. "We launch as fast as we can," Rustum said. The Ikhwan, those terrorists in their rat holes, we'll smoke them out.

Rustum fished into his desk drawer and produced a large knife, which he drove into the map on the wall. Directly into Douma. He spat at the map and slime snaked down the M5 highway from Aleppo to Homs.

Rustum turned around. "Now, Daoud," he said, yanking himself from the graveyard of his imagination. "We have the matter of Branch 450's expertise. We've received orders from the President to initiate a retaliatory strike on the terrorists using our chemical stockpile. My men are preparing ballistic missiles at the sites on this order, which I am issuing to you as the newly promoted head of Branch 450." He slid the piece of paper across the table.

"You will see on this order the air bases at which we will mix and load," Rustum said.

"We don't have a sufficient quantity in our stockpile, Commander," Daoud said, reading the report. "Not for an operation of this magnitude."

"We've produced several hundred tons of sarin at a place called Jableh, all moved to a nearby bunker once the site was discovered by the Americans and Zionists. My men have made rough allocations of the binary components and sent them to the launch sites on the order I just handed to you. I would like you to personally oversee the preparations."

"What is the timeline?"

"Tomorrow morning."

"Yes, Commander." Daoud stood and turned to leave. He was picking at his neck.

"Oh, and Daoud. Though you have a rebellious daughter currently in our custody, I consider you a loyal servant. Do not let me down. For her sake."

46

LIKE MANY SYRIANS THAT DAY, MARIAM WONDERED IF this was the end. Militia checkpoints had proliferated, looters roamed the streets, and the rebels gave interviews on Al Jazeera proclaiming the last days of the regime. She heard artillery fire and sirens constantly.

By the midafternoon, Zahran Alloush's militia broke through Rustum's siege and sent raiding parties into the city center. An entire Republican Guard battalion defected, according to a Reuters report she read online.

Bouthaina had gone to Rustum's pleasure palace in Bloudan, which left Mariam in charge at the Palace. She'd sent the team home after the explosion and said sit tight, for now.

Her cell phone rang, and she saw the name of Amina, one of Bouthaina's assistants. "Mariam, she's dead, she's dead," Amina shrieked as soon as Mariam answered.

"Who is dead? What happened?"

"Bouthaina, Mariam. In the tub. The tub, Mariam." More screaming, the sound of helicopter blades whirring. Amina yelled something incomprehensible into the background. "Shot by Rustum," Mariam heard her say, at last. Then whimpering.

"Rustum?"

"Yes. He arrived on a helicopter, walked inside, shot her, and left. I was in the office. I found the body. Oh, Mariam, it was—her face is gone, the tub is covered . . ." Amina was yelling again, and Mariam could not understand what she said. The young girl stammered and whimpered and mentioned something about a paper she'd found in the tub. "A paper?" Mariam asked.

"Yes I could see English words on it but I couldn't read much of the rest there were strange markings and it was very wet and my English is not as good as yours and—"

Mariam cut her off, suddenly feeling very cold. "You stay there, the roads are not safe. And destroy the paper. Understand?"

"What if he comes back, what if the monster comes back?" Amina asked. Mariam thought of the information she had passed to Sam. Wadi Barada. A single site, yet it had come from Rustum's lips, to Bouthaina. Mariam had given it to CIA. Then Rustum had killed Bouthaina. Coincidences did not exist in Syria anymore. She could not suck in enough air to breathe. She felt light-headed. Maybe she was going to throw up.

"You will be fine," she told Amina. "He will not come back. His business is done. But, Amina?"

The girl whimpered.

"Amina?" Mariam raised her voice.

"Y-ye-yes, Mariam?" she stammered.

"Do not tell any of the soldiers that you saw who murdered Bouthaina, understand?"

The young woman hung up, muttering. Mariam went to the bathroom and threw up.

NOW SHE SAT ON HER bed waiting to set the plan into motion. Or for Ali Hassan to take her away. Or for Jamil Atiyah to murder her. Or to die during a mortar volley. Whichever came first.

She heard the rattle of gunfire outside her window. Looking down, she saw a man in a mask sprinting through the street with a box slung over his shoulder. The looting had begun. The Security Office minder that had been posted outside her apartment was gone. Coward. She closed the window blinds. She ripped at a piece of finger skin with her teeth.

She jumped at the knock on the door. Opening it, she was greeted by Uncle Daoud's ruinous figure. He no longer wore the bandages from the shooting, but he somehow looked more broken than ever. She beckoned him in. They sat in her living room listening to the shriek of jet engines and the thump of mortar fire, and she served lemon tea as if this were a normal social call.

Daoud's uniform was damp, the armpits drenched. There was perspiration collecting on the tip of his nose, and it dripped into his teacup, which shook as he sipped.

"What is the matter, Uncle?" she said.

"I would have called your father," Daoud said. "But I have not been able to reach him." He grimaced, and her chest compressed with a dull pain, like a hand had pressed against her lungs. She nodded.

"I am going to an air base for work, maybe as early as tonight. I am not sure how to say this, other than I expect I may not return."

She wanted to laugh and say: *Are you joking?* But she knew he was not. "What is happening?" was all she could say.

Daoud set the cup down and ran a hand through his hair, taking several strands with it. He rubbed them into his pants.

"I said something to you at your cousin's engagement party, a lifetime ago it seems. I said that you were always a member of the war councils."

"I remember, Uncle. I was honored. Am honored."

"I cannot tell you why I may never come home, but I need two things from you, as a member of the council. I am sorry to ask like this."

Mariam saw his frantic eyes. She did not want to hear what he had to say, but she said, "Tell me, Uncle."

"I need you to promise me you will care for Razan and see that she is freed. If I do not return, there may be . . ." He stopped and scratched at the sore on his neck.

He finished: "Questions. Uncomfortable questions."

"I promise," she said. "Of course, Uncle." His face rose, just a little. "What is the second thing, Uncle?"

Daoud took a piece of paper from his pocket, wet and eroded and shaking with his hands. "There is something happening that you should know about. Something so evil I am ashamed to mention it. But if I give you this paper, you will be *involved*. You will have choices to make."

"Why are you telling me this, Uncle?"

"You are on the war council, no? And what is this, if not a great war? Do you want the paper?"

I did nothing.

She nodded. He slid it toward her, placing it under her teacup, and stood to leave. "I have written everything I can on it. Everything I know."

At the door he hugged her, and she found herself crying. When he saw her cry, he, too, began to shed tears. "Your father," he said, "would be proud of you. Whatever part my information plays in this, please, when the time is right, tell Razan that her own father stood up to be counted. That in the end, in some way, I avenged her. Tell her this, please, Mariam?"

She could not speak, just nodded and said yes with dark, frightened eyes.

He turned to leave, then wheeled around. "There are five locations on the paper I gave you. It would be best if they were destroyed tonight or tomorrow morning."

"But Uncle, how—"

He put his hand up and smiled, his face lighter. He had tossed a weight from his body. "There is no need, Mariam. I am telling you for me, for my soul."

SHE CLOSED THE DOOR.

She read the paper.

She vomited again.

She wished she had a better way to reach him.

She called Sam's burner phone.

She told him everything, quickly.

She felt an unseen grip release from her chest.

And yet there was everything left to do.

47

SAM THOUGHT IT HAD TO BE ONE OF THE MOST CALAMitous messages sent from an asset to the CIA. He wanted to run to the Station. But he and Mariam had more work to do. He picked up the burner phone and called the embassy. One of the consular officers answered.

"Tell the people downstairs to call this number on a throwaway. Do it now. Understand?" Sam said.

The man did. Sam hung up. He paced the room and accidentally knocked over a stack of soup cans. Five minutes later, the phone rang. He answered.

"Fucking hell, man, where are you?"

He'd never been so happy to hear Procter's voice.

"Laying low. I'm sorry, but I don't have a choice. I'm going to read something to you. It's from ATHENA's subsource. We need to toss this in a restricted-handling compartment so about three people can read it. Ready?"

"Go." She complied, but he could hear the rage in her voice.

He read it. She was silent for a moment. "I'm going to send it and call Bradley. I will call you back." Click.

The phone rang again ten minutes later. "It's out. Now, tell me where you are, otherwise you'll be in chains when you return to the United States."

PROCTER'S BLACK ENERGY FILLED THE safe house upon her arrival. Grunting, she pushed past her case officer and smacked her bag down, buckles clanking against the table. Sam eyed the black leather purse. He'd never seen the Chief so enraged.

Her eyes narrowed. She continued to glare at him until his eyes turned to the bag. "My knife and a pistol from the Station," she said, anticipating the question. "City's gone nuts. Fall-of-Rome kind of shit. Visigoths wetting themselves at the gates, thirsty for blood and goddamn plunder."

Procter retrieved a rubber band from her bag and tied her frazzle into a crooked ponytail. "You wanna tell me what the fuck is going on?"

She barged on without waiting for Sam to speak. "Let me paint the picture, and you tell me why I shouldn't knock you the fuck out, dump you in a car, and drive you across the border to Amman myself, okay?"

Sam was silent. Procter leaned against the table, he against the wall, facing her.

She continued, voice tense, gritty, seething. "I have a case officer, brilliant recruiter, but with one of his assets I am now suspecting his dick is the primary assessment tool. This person is attacked by government militia, said asset in tow, for reasons I cannot even begin to fathom. They retreat to this pleasure palace"—Procter gesticulated around the shabby room toward the bed—"after committing a triple homicide, and then pass uncorroborated intelligence on a backup production facility, which I duly report to Langley in the hastiest of fucking manners."

Sam opened his mouth to speak, but Procter cut him off. "This case officer then refuses to come to safety, forcing me to run a death-wish SDR through checkpoints and falling mortars."

He tried to speak again, but she put a finger over her mouth. "Ssh. Ssh. Ssh. You will shut. The. Fuck. Up and let me finish. This asset's subsource then provides us with the information necessary to stop Assad's sarin party. The intrepid Chief of Station passes said intelligence to

Langley, guaranteeing that POTUS issues an order to bomb the sites in the next day. Endangering everyone at the embassy if the Syrians decide to respond."

She glanced toward the door as someone screamed down the apartment hallway.

"And meanwhile said case officer sits in this safe house commanding his own Station. Running ops, refusing to tell me where the fuck he is. And why is that?"

"Bec—"

"I'll tell you why. Because you knew I'd come here, grab you by the sack, and drag you back to the embassy. So now you need to explain a few things to me. Right now. You are ATHENA's handler. Tell me what's wrong with her. Tell me why she was at the scene of the crime."

Procter stopped talking and folded her arms across her chest.

"Ali got to Mariam. *Mukhabarat* reported our conversation in Paris. He arrested her cousin as leverage. They sent her to Italy to acquire a device, not knowing we'd already recruited her. She wasn't read into the op but pieced together that Ali was on a mole hunt."

Procter sighed loudly. "She told you this?"

"Yes."

"What else did she say she gave them?"

"Background info on me. The safe house we used with her."

"She give a particular reason why they wanted the device?"

"No. She doesn't know. And she hasn't had the device since she got back to Damascus from Italy, hence the comms blackout."

"So that's why she ran to meet you?" Procter said. "To pass intel without using the device because she had a change of heart."

"Yeah. She overheard Bouthaina mention Wadi Barada, knew we needed that information, and came running. Then I got jumped. Oh, and Bouthaina is dead," he added. "Shot at Rustum's villa. Happened this morning."

"Fuck. You sure?"

"Mariam told me."

"So maybe not."

"She was borderline hysterical when she called. Asked what we did with the intel she passed on Wadi Barada."

"Girl's clearly an actress."

"No, she's not, Chief, I could read her in Italy. I knew—and I told you, if you remember—that something was wrong."

"She could be playing us man, playing you. Have you thought it through? Maybe the Syrians wanted us to think they were moving the goods to Wadi Barada?"

"Makes no sense, Chief. Think about it. Two big things are true. One, Mariam stalks me outside the embassy to provide the Wadi Barada intel in person. Two, she kills three militiamen, saving my life."

"And you're just holding your wang through all this, Jaggers?" Procter asked, clearly not expecting a response. The Chief looked again toward the bedroom, and Sam could tell she was rummaging through her imagination for details on what had transpired there. Her left eyelid shut halfway. She nodded at him to continue.

"If Mariam is really turned, she doesn't act like this," Sam continued. "And if Ali is smart, which he is, he doesn't run the op this way. First, they wouldn't send Mariam in person with the Wadi Barada intel. That would, and has, raised massive red flags. No, they would send the info via covcom. Simple and easy. Second, if Mariam is bad, she doesn't murder the militiamen. She lets them make the arrest."

Procter ignored the logic, meaning she agreed, and instead went back to fighting: "So why the fuck is Bouthaina dead?"

"I bet Ali is trying to flush out the mole. They must have narrowed down the list of suspects to a manageable number. And they don't know that Mariam passed us the original intel on the sarin test. Ali provided them with something he knew would come back to Damascus. We got our hands on Bouthaina's bait. Somehow the Syrians saw it. Now she's dead."

"Bullshit," said without conviction.

"Is it, though? We passed the information on Jableh, and within days the Republican Guard started evacuating. Very few people inside the regime knew about that site. They got intel—from somewhere, how many people in D.C. read our stuff anyways, thousands?—then moved the sarin. The leak narrowed the list of suspects, so they passed false information. One of those people had to have been Bouthaina. Someone told Bouthaina about Wadi Barada, Mariam overheard, told me, I told you, it got distributed in D.C., funneled to a faceless mole, then somehow got back to Ali. I'd bet Rustum killed her. Not Ali's style, I think. Mariam had no idea the intel was fake, she just knew it seemed important, so she passed it to me, risking everything to fucking do so."

Procter was with him now. "Her info on the five deployment sites is probably accurate, then, if they think Bouthaina was the mole. With her out of the picture, the Syrians would feel free to move forward with the sarin attack. Mole is gone."

He'd reached the top of the climb with Procter. It was time to jump. If he won the argument, he would again be in mortal danger. If he lost, Mariam would probably die. He stood tall and straight for the coup de grâce.

"Yes," he said. "Unless we bomb the sites, of course. Then Ali takes stock. He'll know Bouthaina wasn't the mole. Even if he suspects satellite imagery tipped us off, they'll dig deep to be sure. Ali will do two things, guaranteed. They will bring Mariam in. Ali will know that someone passed the Wadi Barada site, and that it probably wasn't Bouthaina, because lo and behold the attack failed hours after her death, posthumously exonerating her. Ali will shift his gaze to the woman in Bouthaina's office, who may have heard about the Wadi Barada site, whose loyalty was apparently sufficiently suspect that they arrested her cousin as leverage. They will torture her until she breaks."

Procter had pulled the knife from her bag, unsheathed it, and was now twirling its point into the table, lost in thought, as it cut a pinpoint divot. "What is the ops proposal?" she said at last.

"I think I know how to protect our agent and keep her in place. I give Ali what he wants, personally."

"Tell me how."

PROCTER'S FURY AT BAY, SHE continued spinning the knife and listened without interruption. When he'd finished, she sheathed it and walked toward the bedroom, scanning inside, poring over the mattress lumps. The walls rumbled. Plaster flaked off the walls in dusty clouds. They heard the screech of a jet overhead. Procter was close now, looking up at him from her standing perch a full foot below his head. A political Chief of Station or a self-serving bureaucrat would have rejected the plan outright, maybe would have hustled the embassy Marines to the safe house to haul him back for exfil. But not Procter, though she had everything to lose. If the Langley mandarins demanded heads, hers would be the first piled into the basket under the guillotine. But Artemis Aphrodite Procter played the game according to only two rules: Collect the intelligence and protect your agent. Nothing else mattered. Sam had offered a way to satisfy both. It was a weighty trade, though.

"You thought about what happens if they aren't satisfied with the name?" she said. "If the White House doesn't go to the mats? If the Syrians just keep turning the crank? If they treat you like Val?"

"Then we end up where are now. Mariam on the chopping block. But if we try my way, we get a shot at keeping her safe, in harness."

The Chief nodded, then Procter's eyes shot to the bedroom before landing on him.

She spat on the floor and said nothing.

She knew.

Bradley in Cairo, a lifetime ago: You are permitted one fuckup, Mr. Joseph, provided that you come clean. The hiding, the lies, these are worse than the fuckups, by the way. Fuckups happen to good officers. Deception does not. You can lie to your wife, your girlfriend, your kids. But not to CIA.

Sam looked at the Chief. It occurred to him that months earlier he would have considered the professional repercussions of his plan and confession. Now he did not care. Protect your agent. It's all that matters. And he couldn't lie to Procter. They were operationally wed, and he'd forsaken his vows. He wanted forgiveness.

He had locked eyes with her, but he didn't see her. He saw his body talking to her from a roost on top of the refrigerator, like an observer. It made the confession easier. "I'm in love with her, Chief," he said.

Procter's eyes narrowed. She took a step toward Sam.

Then she hit him, a solid hook from below that landed with a pop on the underside of his jaw. He fell, and Procter stood over him, just a wild spray of blurry black hair because he couldn't see straight. She knelt down, eyes at his level. He tried to move his jaw. He winced and put his hand over the bone.

"I could say you're a fuckup," she said. "And I'd be right on some accounts. Wrong on others. But you have a job to do now, one that transcends your dick-fueled indiscretion. You and I will have our reckoning later, on the other side of this horror show."

She pulled him up from the floor and propped him against the counter. Then she turned around and pulled her gray blouse up over her shoulders, revealing her back: the seven-starred tattoo, the straps of a weird orange bra speckled with palm trees. Sam wondered if he was hallucinating from the force of the blow. Then she tucked in the blouse and turned to face him.

"Seven stars. One for each officer killed in the attack on Khost Base back in '09. I got the tattoos when we finished killing the responsible parties. I led the hit squad, I was the Angel of Death. And nothing has been more joyful. Probably nothing ever will. This is my tribe. I've picked my side, and you, for now, are on it. But know this: If you fail, I will hold you personally responsible. If I have to put a star on my back for you, I'll hunt you even on the other side of this life."

Procter put the knife in her purse and zipped it inside. She swung the bag over her shoulder and looked back at Sam. "I'll put the mark down and send the message in the next hour. Then you tell her we're a go."

Procter left amid the din of another mortar volley without so much as a glance back.

48

ALI FELT HIS PHONE BUZZ IN HIS POCKET. IT WAS MARIAM.

"What do you have?"

"He's signaled. Emergency meeting. The safe house."

"When?"

"The marking was for an emergency, but the time was not specific. I'm sure they've sent something to the device, too."

"Thank you. I assure you that your cousin will be free soon." He hung up.

The gamble of running Mariam at the Americans had borne fruit. She had performed, Ali had to admit. She'd secured the device and provided the safe house. She had done her part, and her cousin was in his Security Office prison, unharmed and well fed. Mariam was untested. Ali had required leverage. Harmless leverage. It had worked.

Ali walked to the iPad and opened it with the flourish Mariam had demonstrated. Sure enough, the Americans had tried to contact her:

1. REQUEST EMERGENCY MEETING AT REGULAR LOCATION ASAP. PRESENT BY 10PM.

2. NEED TO MODIFY EXFIL GIVEN VIOLENCE IN CAPITAL.

3. BRING PASSPORT AND HANDBAG.

4. EXFIL WILL PROCEED DIRECTLY FROM MEETING.

Ali looked at his watch: eight-thirty p.m. He walked downstairs to the Russian command center and found Volkov, sipping at his cup.

"He's signaled for a meeting with Mariam."

Volkov's face remained placid. "Exfil? It's shit out there."

"Yes. They need to modify the route and want to talk through details in person, then get her out tonight."

Volkov grunted. "We've had a countersurveillance team watching the house in the Christian Quarter for the past day. They've seen nothing. It is clean."

"Good. Tonight, we end this madness."

49

ON SAM'S SDR TO THE SAFE HOUSE HE DODGED MAIN thoroughfares to avoid checkpoints, he zigzagged closer and closer to the Christian Quarter, he checked for repeat faces and cars, he thinned crowds as best he could. None of it mattered now, but he did it on instinct and because if they were watching his trip, he had to appear as they would expect: a CIA officer heading to meet a prized asset in the heart of war-torn Syria.

He climbed the stairs inside the white stone building. When he reached the top landing, he paused and closed his eyes and thought of his last time here with Mariam, before Italy. He sighed. To anyone watching on a video feed, likely tucked into the hallway lights or the smoke detectors, it would have been almost imperceptible.

But in that moment, between the short sigh and the opening of his eyes, he saw his kid brother, he saw Val, the lives his mistakes had interrupted. He saw Mariam in that red dress from Paris.

He opened the door to the safe house and heard the muffled steps on the stairs behind: hurried, growing louder with each footfall. Sam had expected them.

Ali stood in the kitchen, smoking. Unsmiling, he gazed at Sam.

"Nice kitchen here, my friend." He tossed the butt on the marble floor and stubbed it out with his shoe.

Then, from behind, over the top of Sam's head: The rush of displaced air. Darkness.

50

PRESIDENT ASSAD, ARMS AND CHEST STILL WRAPPED in bandages, summoned Rustum and Ali to the Palace early the next morning. The Russian President had an urgent message, and Assad wanted the brothers to listen to the call.

Now, seated on the presidential couches, earpieces inserted, Ali heard the wobbly English of the Russian President say good morning to the President of the Syrian Arab Republic, offering his sincere concern for Assad's safety following the attack and his hope that the Syrian security forces would defeat the scourge of terrorism wherever it be found. Rustum pressed his palms into his forehead as if willing the English words into his brain.

Then Ali heard the fateful, heavily accented words: "We have received credible intelligence from Washington just this hour, from a well-placed SVR source, indicating the Americans plan to bomb you. Our source received this directly from a senior CIA official who participated in deliberations yesterday at the White House." There was a pause for dramatic effect. "Our sources indicate the intelligence comes from the highly placed asset the Americans recently recruited."

Putin continued. "We expect the Americans to leverage the USS *Abraham Lincoln* and Carrier Strike Group Twelve, now in the eastern Mediterranean. We have tasked imagery and SIGINT resources for more information, as well as worldwide SVR *rezidentura*. We of course will provide more details as they come available."

"Did your source indicate the timing?" Assad asked.

"Imminently," said the czar. "It is my assessment that the American strike is designed to prevent the use of what they allege to be chemical weapons, not to unseat your government. Even so, it has been my experience dealing with the Americans that they only respond to force. A bombing, even a set of one-off strikes, must be met with a stiff-necked response."

Assad murmured his agreement, trumpeting his father's adages about resistance. Putin appropriately and resolutely concurred.

Closing pleasantries, vague offers of mutual assistance, and vows of brotherly affection exchanged, Assad clicked the secure phone back into the receiver on his desk. *Ya allah. Al-Amyrikan Al-Malaeen Al Sharameet! Haywanaat! Hameer! Shayateen!* American fucking bitches, animals, donkeys, demons, he screamed to the Hassan brothers. It had been a rough twenty-four hours for the President, Ali thought, now recovering from an assassination attempt, contemplating the widespread use of sarin gas against his own people, and wrangling with the possibility of a retaliatory American strike. A lot to handle, for anyone.

"Rustum, how much longer until you can begin?" Assad asked, calming himself.

"We started mixing the product and loading munitions yesterday evening. We can begin now with some of it, if you wish."

"Do it."

Assad pushed a button on his desk and barked at his personal secretary for tea, wincing from the burns as he yelled. Ali glanced toward the ceiling, wondering if the American strike package would include the presidential residence.

"Now," the President said, "the mole. I thought that Bouthaina had been identified as such."

"It is possible they have another," Rustum countered, vocal volume oddly high, uncalibrated, like a radio dial cranked up. Rustum did not look well. His hair was mussed, eyes hounded and bloodshot, uniform rumpled. Ali saw blood splatter on one of his brother's socks, as if he'd begun changing clothes after Bouthaina's murder, become distracted, then given up.

"I suppose so," Assad said. "But even so, we must assume the worst. Ali, have you managed to exploit the device your agent procured?"

"We are reading the traffic but have not yet been able to positively identify any spies yet. It will take time. The messages are cryptic. But the Iranians believe they will be able to help."

"You have the American in custody now, correct?"

"Yes, Mr. President, we entrapped him last night on his way to meet with our agent. He is in custody."

"Put him under interrogation today. I want to be sure we find the Americans' spies. He has killed three Syrians, the Americans are going to bomb, any violence done to him will be easily explained or lost in the shuffle. Just get the information quickly."

"Yes, Mr. President," Ali said. "I will interrogate him personally, until we have names."

"Now, Rustum." Assad turned to Ali's older brother, a smile settling on his face. "The Russian President is correct that if the Americans bomb we must deliver a strong response. What is your recommendation?"

Rustum ran his hands through his hair, furrowed his brows, and wiped something translucent from his mustache. "We've played with the CIA presence in this country for the past few months like a cat batting a toy mouse. We have run elegant operations to capture a device, to entrap their officers. All wise in their time. But now they are coming for us on the morning of our greatest victory, after their terrorist allies attempted to murder us all, Mr. President. No, once the bombs drop, the teasing must end. If they bomb as the Russians say, I suggest we send the militia to overrun the embassy and take hostages. In their patriotic fervor they swept into the embassy, we will say, to protest the American-Zionist bombing of humble Syria."

Rustum coughed up phlegm into his hands and wiped it on his uniform. "And in so doing," he continued, "we cut off their ability to spy on us in the future. They will close the embassy, their CIA Station. We send Basil and his militia, to send them a message."

Assad picked at the top of his head and fussed with his bandages. Then he asked Ali what he thought.

"If we do that, the Americans will apply yet more pressure. More bombings, targeted killings, who can say? It will spiral the conflict further downward."

Assad regarded him, considering the options, and Ali knew he'd lost. "You would have been right, Ali, under the old rules. But now I am afraid your brother is correct. The Americans must be taught a lesson."

The President pointed to his bandages. "They do not play by the rules. Neither shall we."

PART V

Freedom

51

SAM LAY BOUND IN THE CELL SHIVERING IN THE COLD, stony gloom. They had taken his clothes after a light beating. Nothing serious, just a few blows to the ribs and face. He was sore, but it was manageable. No one had offered food or water. He had spent long hours awake as unidentifiable music—sounds, really—blared through unseen speakers. Not that he would have slept anyhow: there was much to do.

Sam had toiled for hours, arranging his mind for the coming assault, putting items in appropriate cranial boxes, rooms, and safes. He did not know what methods Ali would employ, but the pattern and flow would be similar to his long-ago training at the Farm: a climb toward the summit of pain. At the base camp Ali would expect stonewalling, lies, and half-truths. As they climbed—onward to electricity, perhaps—the Syrian would expect breakage: more truth, some inconsistency, fewer lies. At the summit he would expect a name. Then he would verify everything.

If Ali was to walk away certain that he had captured his spy, Sam would have to make the Syrian think he had won. Sam's eventual breakage could not appear rushed and he could not be compliant. Ali would view both outcomes as evidence of subterfuge and continue onward, toward the summit, even after Sam had provided the name.

If this happened, the plan would come apart. Ali would climb up the mountain, dragging Sam, until he drilled—maybe literally—into the safe hidden in his head. That safe held a name: Mariam. It had been the first item Sam packed away, deep in the mazework of his mind.

Now, alone in the darkness, he rummaged through his mental organization to sort the rest of the material.

A few items he classified as already burned or expendable: his CIA affiliation, the safe house, knowledge of the Republican Guard operation at Jableh and the second site, Wadi Barada. He thought of a package of defunct or lightly used drop, signal, and brush pass sites that CIA could replace. All of this he would reveal, over time and under extreme duress, after the denials of the base camp. These targeted revelations would build credibility with Ali, luring the Syrian into the mistaken belief his path toward the summit was bearing fruit.

The gift-wrapped, bow-tied box set on the table for Ali contained a single name: Jamil Atiyah. With that, Sam had to convince Ali they'd arrived at the summit. The end. They would toss Sam back in the cell while they tore Atiyah's world apart looking for proof. They would find the device, the money, the American passports under a false name. A search of his computer and phone would reveal the strange emails and phone calls.

The cell door opened and blinding bars of light burst in. Two men grabbed him by the shoulders and dragged him to another dank room. The walls were covered in rusted pipes that snaked through rough-cut holes in the ceiling. A flimsy, floodlit table ringed by four chairs sat in the room's center. Brown tile covered the floor and there was a drain under the table.

The two men sat him down in one of the chairs and left. The floodlight bore down. He sank his head and closed his eyes for relief. Base camp. The initial discussion. He examined his mental organization again and tucked the safe with Mariam's name deep away. The one containing his knowledge of her true loyalties: the operation against Bouthaina's computer and the Republican Guard sites he imagined would soon be destroyed by U.S. warplanes.

He waited for what felt like an hour. A metal door creaked open, bathing a section of corroded piping in light. It shut again.

Ali Hassan sat down across from Sam and lit a cigarette. The Syrian rubbed his scar, put his hands down on the table, folded them, and began.

"You did not heed my warning," Ali said in Arabic. "You killed three Syrians. You went into hiding. Then you attempted to exfiltrate one of your spies. Mariam is in custody now, of course. In this very prison, actually. It is how we found you at your safe house last night." He dragged on the cigarette, looking at Sam.

Sam eyed the table and stayed quiet.

"There is an outstanding matter, one of grave importance to my government. The name of a remaining spy. We know she was not your only contact."

He tried not to wince or move. He decided to mention her name, just to test. He suspected Ali would use his arrest outside the safe house as bait, would tell him they'd caught Mariam and try to use it as leverage or to throw him off. "I thought you said you already captured Mariam," Sam said.

Ali scratched his head and removed a cigarette pack from his shirt pocket. Tapping it on the table, he ashed the lit cigarette with his other hand. He shook his head.

"The lies will not go so well for you, Samuel. I know there is another. I require the name, and the specific information he passed to you regarding our military plans. Now."

Sam squinted into the floodlights so the Syrian could see him staring back. "I don't know what you are talking about, Ali."

ALI LEFT THE ROOM AND the two men returned. One stood Sam up while the other worked on his ribs with haymaker blows, alternating sides in rapid succession. No one said anything, but the room echoed with muffled grunts and gasps until they threw him facedown onto the floor. One sat on his back as the other swung something down on his right foot, working the back of his ankle in a precise fashion. His neck muscles tensing to failure, arc lights dancing across his vision, he heard a crunch. He screamed.

They rolled Sam over, then split the work between his face and the phalanges and metatarsals of his ruined foot. The man who had been on his back now straddled him, holding tufts of his hair to stabilize the skull while he jabbed at his jaw, taking over where Procter had left off the previous evening.

The head work, Sam thought as he lolled off, a classic mistake. Unconsciousness is a gift.

"FOR GOD'S SAKE, COLONEL, YOU don't knock the subject out," Ali barked once a sheepish Kanaan and his brother had returned from putting the American into the refrigerated cell and dousing him in water to wake him up. "We've got to keep him talking."

"Gen—"

"Not a word." Ali scratched his scar. "Call me as soon as he wakes up. And wire him up with electricity for the next round."

Ali ran upstairs to his office, past the Russians now twiddling their thumbs waiting for orders to return to the Rodina. Ali shut the door, sat down, and looked out his window, toward the east. Fighters and a few attack helicopters operated over Douma. He had hunted this American for months, but he had failed to find all of his spies. Now he wondered why he even cared, when Rustum's attack would begin, when the Americans would bomb, what Layla and the kids were doing.

He heard a gigantic explosion in the distance. The building wobbled. Rustum must have begun. He lit a cigarette and went to the window, where he saw a tower of smoke over the SSRC's headquarters in Barzeh.

Then he saw a plane, not a MiG—not Syrian or Russian—soaring over Qasioun. He recognized it from one of the briefings the Russians had provided. It was an American F-35. It dropped several bombs on the Shaab Palace, conjuring a fiery flash, then a puffy, wafting cloud. The plane left his field of vision. *The Americans.* He craned his neck to see where the plane had gone. Nothing. He could hear his own breath; his stomach heaved. Then the plane, or maybe it was a different one, reappeared, banking south from the mountain toward Kafr Sousa and the Security Office.

Ali remembered Layla and the twins, and felt sick that he didn't have time to say goodbye. How he was a coward. The plane closed the gap in two seconds. It flew low, seemingly at eye level. He stepped back, turned away, and ducked, all instinctive and yet useless if the plane dropped a bomb on the building. At the last moment the plane knifed upward, easily clearing the building while shattering every pane of glass on its northern side.

The shards rained down on Ali's back as he huddled on the floor. The screech of the engines faded and he stood, dusting himself off. He was shaking. He could feel a weak trickle on the back of his head. He heard screaming down the hall. He stumbled to his desk and called Layla.

"Are you okay, *habibti?*" He was shouting, trying to overcome the ringing in his ears. He could hear the twins shrieking in the background.

Layla was crying. "My god, what is happening, I heard a couple big explosions and the boys are hysterical and the electricity is out and someone in a ski mask showed up outside the apartment and fired a gun in the air. Did you hear me?"

He'd heard a lot of what she said. But my, the ringing.

"We're holed up here waiting to die," Layla screamed. "And what were those planes, the Israelis? And I'm in the bedroom now looking into the street and militia are outside. Someone ran down the street this morning carrying a television, Ali, the city has gone insane. Get home, okay? When can you get home? When can you get home? When? Can you hear me? Ali? Ali?"

The ringing swelled now. The building rumbled as another American bomb fell. Hot summer wind whipped through the open windows, kicking dust into his eyes.

Layla screamed, Sami said, "Daddy, daddy, daddy," in the background. He heard another explosion in the distance. Then ambulance sirens and the air raid horns, ironically delayed.

But mostly he heard ringing, dear god, the ringing.

"Stay there, Layla," he yelled. "Hide in the bedroom closet with the boys. I will come now. I love you. Tell the boys."

Ali hung up. He was walking toward his door when it swung open wildly, slamming into the wall.

His big brother Rustum, commander of the Republican Guard, hero of Hama, stood in the doorway. His face was contorted, and specks of blood dabbed his collar, which clung to his bruised neck.

He clutched Mariam's right arm, manacled to her left behind her back. Her face was red, and her eyes were exhausted.

He coughed something ruddy and wiped it on his arm.

"Today is the day, little brother."

SAM AWOKE IN A MEAT locker, his skin soaked and frigid. Someone said he's up in Arabic, and then a pair of rough hands grabbed him by the shoulders and led him to the table. They attached electrodes to his fingers and testicles and then he was alone under the floodlights.

Sam looked down at his stillborn foot. He could not move it.

The door flung open and three shapes walked through. He could not make out their faces, but the second seemed to be pushing the first one. The third one, trailing behind, closed the door. The second man led the prisoner to a chair facing Sam. He squinted into the bright floodlights and saw the prisoner's outline.

Time for the ascent.

THEY HAD PLANNED FOR THIS in the safe house. Before the lovemaking on the mattress, their bodies begging each other for forgiveness. She, for her betrayal; he, for getting her involved in the first place.

Mariam still felt sick knowing their crimes had not been equal. She had wanted to work with Sam, with the CIA, against a government she despised, against a life she did not control. She had betrayed him in Italy, it was true. She took the device. She might have told Sam and Artemis about Ali Hassan's threats instead. Then they could have built a way out.

"They might bring you to me," Sam had said on the mattress that night. "Ali believes that I think you are a loyal CIA agent. He might use it as leverage. They might put you in the same room, or a cell next to mine. It's important you keep up the act, that you play by Ali's rules, follow his lead."

When the knock came, she'd expected to see Ali, to be brought into a plan to break the American spy. Instead, it had been his brother Rustum, Bouthaina's blood dried on his uniform, eerie smile frozen on his face, his neck discolored by bruises.

"Yes?" she had said.

Then he slapped her, hard. Two men poured into the apartment behind him. She swung a knee into the groin of the first, but the second man barreled her to the floor, muscling her arms behind her back, pressing her neck into the marble. They bound and hustled her into a car, speeding for the Security Office as American planes soared overhead. Rustum brayed and squealed with each explosion. He had mumbled the same words during the drive: My Bouthaina, my Bouthaina, my Bouthaina.

Now, eyes locked on Sam's battered face, Mariam imagined driving her nail file through the neck of each brother, these sadists masquerading as policemen. But first she had to hold it together.

"Why am I here?" she said to Ali, wriggling against the cords.

No one answered.

A PHONE RANG.

Sam's head slowly seesawed as he registered that it was Rustum Hassan answering.

"Are you sure?" Silence, screaming through the phone. "*Ya allah.*" He slammed the phone onto the table. Sam could smell Rustum creeping closer. Breath stale and hot. Rustum pressed a hand into his shoulder and slid a chair beside him, breathing heavily. Rustum bent over to examine Sam's foot. Then he pressed his boot into the top. Sam yelled as black dots littered his vision.

Rustum removed his foot and stood. "Seems you survived the easy stuff," he said. Then he looked at the wall, then the floor. He pointed several feet to Sam's right and leaned in close. "Your friend Valerie died right about there, on the concrete. Ironic, isn't it?" He mussed Sam's hair.

"Who is the spy?" Ali said suddenly. Sam saw that Ali was leaning over a small black box. He pushed a button without warning.

He saw nothing but felt everything.

The pain was pure and saturating. He had trained for this, but simulations are just that. Simulations. He did not realize that it would feel like boiling water running through the muscles and veins and bones, a stream of it running from his feet to his brain, now expanding like an overfilled balloon ready to burst. Then it stopped, just like that, and the room returned in a tide of light and noise and he saw his chest ripple and he vomited on the floor.

He heard Mariam cursing.

"Who is the spy?" Ali said again.

In the memory palace he'd built in his mind, Sam caught a glance of the hidden safe containing Mariam's name and her loyalty. He blinked to erase the memory, tried to forget what room it was in, but it was still there, beckoning. Sam blinked again. He thought of the first set of boxes and offered them in a rapid stutter.

"I'm CIA," he said. "I don't know who you want, but I do know Damascus sites. Safe houses at the foot of the mountain. Dark, demon lights, got hit by the Chief, the Proctologist—"

"Stop using code names," Ali said.

"Brush pass, by the mosque." Even if he had wanted to, he could not string the words together for a full sentence. "Map. I show."

"We don't care about this," Rustum said.

Ali pushed the button again and the world dropped away. Time an infinite, searing loop, the arc lights dancing across his mind as he considered the safe and its contents. He smelled a Minnesota pine forest, heard his mom weeping. Then he collapsed back into the chair. Was this the summit? How long had it been?

Mariam yelled. Sam coughed and blood dribbled down his chin. He heard the two brothers bickering, but he could not make out the discussion. He heard Mariam's hoarse voice again and his mind struggled to process the Arabic. "Why am I here?" she said.

"How did you know about Jableh and Wadi Barada?" Ali asked.

Sam's head tilted back. Rustum pawed it forward.

The peak. Now. Do it now. "Overheard Wadi in Palace," Sam yelled. "The hall."

"What? Who overheard? What hall?" Ali said.

Sam did not know how many times Ali pushed the button. Time had stopped, and in the blackness he saw the safe holding Mariam's name. During one of the loops he placed his hand on its top, ran fingers along the bumpy metal, heard clicks as he spun the dial.

The electricity started again. He tried for memories but could not hold them. They rolled by without stopping, each darkened, edges stained like old photographs: the corn hedges of Shermans Corner, Mom reading him a book, the mill, Vegas, the Bradleys' humid kitchen in Cairo. Then Mariam: her silhouette in starlight, the laugh, the moon-drenched vineyard. He grasped at them, tried to pull them in tight like a shield from the wild currents thrumming his bones, but as his fingers reached the memories they vanished. He cried for help into the void, but the only answer was pain.

Then he remembered the box wrapped for Ali. Play the hand now.

He gagged bile onto the floor as the world again appeared. "Atiyah," he gasped. "Atiyah, Atiyah."

"Jamil Atiyah?" Ali said. As the world focused, Sam could see the Syrian smoking, finger tapping on the table next to the torturer's button. Ali appeared to be considering the name.

Sam nodded. His eyes rolled back, then his head. Rustum jerked him forward.

"Heard Wadi Barada. Bouthaina. Setup," he stammered out.

Something in the blackness bellowed at him. Then he heard cement scraping metal and felt himself sliding closer to someone, screeching across the floor. He saw Mariam's shape appear on the horizon. The scraping stopped. They were facing each other now, knees inches apart, and he could smell her hair. He looked into her eyes.

Then Sam felt the heat on his neck. A metallic spray dashed his tongue, and the heat carved upward, along the mangled jawbone, into his face. He heard names shouted. Bouthaina, Atiyah. He saw the safe again and reached his hand toward it.

ALI HAD TURNED HIS BACK to the interrogation for exactly fifteen seconds. In that time he called Kanaan with orders to turn Jamil Atiyah's world inside out, immediately. Ransack his office, his villa, get the computers, the phones. Everything.

When he turned around, he saw his brother carving a jagged ivy line into the CIA officer's neck. Rustum screamed and said, "This is for my sweet Bouthaina." Ali touched his own scar and watched as Rustum removed the knife from Samuel's cheek and turned to Mariam.

MARIAM SCREAMED FOR HELP AND rattled her bound hands and arms against the chair as Rustum cut Sam.

"Do you know I killed her?" he slobbered, spittle flocking Sam's dimming face. "You made me do it, you framed her."

He yanked the knife away. Mariam saw the blood beading along its path. Sam spit something from his mouth. Stay with me, *habibi*. Stay here.

Rustum cupped his hand around Sam's chin and bent over to focus his eyes. "I never liked the setup with this *sharmoota*." He used the knife to point at Mariam. "I wonder what she told you in Italy. She worked with Bouthaina. Maybe she overheard about Wadi Barada. Maybe Bouthaina let too much slip."

Rustum shuffled around the chairs to Mariam's right side and said softly into her ear: "Did you kill my Bouthaina?"

"Who is the spy?" a voice boomed. She could not tell if it was Ali or Rustum or God himself.

She shuddered, looked at Ali, the rage escaping from its bag. She thought of those militia boys and Villefranche, and the image flashed through her mind of doing the same to the Hassans, standing above each brother and pulling the trigger until the magazine emptied. "You bastard, Ali, I've done nothing but cooperate. I got you what you wanted, and this is how I am repaid? Damn you both, I—"

The knife slid into her side, wriggling deeper as Rustum whispered the same question again and again: Did you kill my Bouthaina? It hit a rib, but he forced it through with a grunt.

She wanted to look him in the eye and yell, *Yes, I did kill her, you monster*, but instead she looked down at the blade, now hidden inside her body. She could only see its slick handle. Sam now yelled, his eyes berserk. She tried to hold on to them, like she did when they made love, but things were wobbly now and something slippery ran down her leg as Rustum removed the knife.

THE BOY ALI LAY UPRIGHT on his bedroom floor, Rustum straddled atop, trying to bring the knife down into his throat, to finish the work undone, to avenge his father and both mothers.

Then his grandfather knocked Rustum aside and pummeled the boy. The old man had been strong. Choking, gasping for air from the struggle, his grandfather sat against the bed and held Ali in his arms while he sobbed. Rustum, unconscious, was sprawled out next to him.

"Whose fault is it, Grandpa?" Ali had said, the words shaky and tight. "Whose fault is it, then?"

Not yours, my boy. Not yours.

Rustum withdrew the knife from Mariam's side and brought it up to her neck.

Ali barreled into him. The blade clanked to the floor as Rustum stumbled back. Ali stepped forward again and drove a palm into his brother's gut, then swung across his head, striking the ear with a crunch.

Rustum fell. He tried to get up. Ali picked up the knife and kicked his chest, sending him back to the icy concrete. Then Ali sat on him, ramming the butt of the knife into his nose. Blood spurted out now, lots of it, and Ali repeated it again, this time hearing a damp crunch and Rustum's shriek. He swung again, splatter misting his face.

His brother's hungry eyes looked back, his hands grabbing upward for the knife, for an eye, for anything. Ali held him down and glared at him, holding his eyes. Then Ali sank the blade deep into Rustum's neck, severing the carotid and tearing through sheets of muscle until Rustum's eyes dimmed, his legs stopped flailing, and his breath ceased.

Ali rolled off his brother onto the floor and sat upright.

Mariam was quiet now, head slumped over, Samuel shouting that she needed help. Samuel's chair collapsed, and he tried to inch closer to Mariam by wriggling on the floor. Ali walked to the table, almost collapsing into it. The American was yelling and scooting on the floor toward Mariam, who was ashy white and still.

One of Kanaan's men flung the door open, hands on his head, surveying the carnage. He stared at Rustum's body and ran his hands over his face.

Ali fumbled to light a cigarette. "Get a doctor here. Now."

SAM SCRAPED TOWARD MARIAM, YELLING for her to stay awake, each breath like glass in his lungs. Though he could barely move his neck as he scooted toward Mariam, he could make out Rustum's corpse splayed out on the floor, Ali compressing Mariam's side with his shirt, and a man wheeling something into the room through hazy light.

Mariam's head was hanging lifelessly. The flicker in her eyes was gone. "Mariam! Mariam! Mariam!" he yelled.

Someone picked him up, and he felt his entire body scream as he landed on a cart. The prison room disappeared. He felt wind on his face, bright lights above. He saw the safe, unopened, in his room. For a moment he saw Mariam on a gurney beside him. Someone, far over the horizon, yelled. She was on her side, wound tilted up. The shouting person held a bag of fluid. Tubes protruded from her body.

He stared into the eyes for something, anything.

Then they wheeled him away.

52

ALI RETURNED TO HIS OFFICE SHELL-SHOCKED AND short his white collared shirt, which had found a second life as Mariam's shoddy tourniquet. The unflappable Volkov had actually gaped as Ali passed the Russian command center. In his office, Ali brushed glass fragments from his chair—residue from the American plane's flyby that morning—and proceeded to smoke six cigarettes in quick succession. When his hands had stilled, he donned a spare shirt he kept in his desk drawer.

He called Layla. "Where are you?" she screamed. "Where are you, Ali? Get home now!" He could hear the twins crying in the background.

"Are you safe?" Ali asked

"Yes, for now. We're in the closet. Come home."

"Rustum is dead."

"Dead? How? The bombs?"

"Something happened. In the office. He lost his mind. He's gone."

"Lost his mind?"

"I will explain later." Tremors rippled in his right wrist. He tried to slide another cigarette from the pack, but it fell on the floor. He picked it up. "You are safe, Layla? You and the boys?"

"Yes, but come home."

"I will. I have to do something first."

"Come home," she screamed.

"I love you." He hung up and lit the cigarette.

When he hit the filter, he stood and looked out the shattered window at the smoke pillars rising from Damascus, listening to the wail of sirens. He took stock of the mess.

He had killed his brother, the commander of the Republican Guard.

His agent, Mariam, lay dying in a makeshift hospital room several floors below.

He had brutally, maybe even successfully, tortured a CIA officer for information. He still held the man in captivity.

Basil's mob was now overrunning the American Embassy.

His phone buzzed. Kanaan.

"What is it?"

"We're in Atiyah's office. We found a document bag with a hidden compartment. Inside were false-name U.S. passports, quite official by the look of them, wads of cash, and a device. I don't know what's on it, but I've never seen anything like it."

"What about the computer, the phone?"

"Strange texts from American and European numbers on the phone. Likely code. Same thing with his email account."

"Make the arrest. Bring him here and put him in lockup. I'll call the Palace with the news."

Ali went downstairs. He noticed the Russians boring into his face with wary, questioning eyes. He did not care. He had no time.

"Volkov, turn on Al Jazeera."

The Russian flipped on one of the televisions.

The images switched—*Breaking News*—to the American President addressing reporters from the White House. He said that the United States had received credible intelligence indicating the Syrian government planned to use chemical weapons. As a result, the President explained in a muscular tone, the United States had bombed targets around Syria to stop the assault and send a message to the barbarous Assad that such cruelty would not be tolerated. The President said that the U.S. believed it had prevented the chemical assault. The President opened the floor for questions. A reporter, noting that the civil war's death toll now measured in the hundreds of thousands, asked why the U.S. had intervened to stop a sarin attack but not the earlier conventional slaughter. The President fidgeted behind the podium. Ali turned off the television.

Volkov looked like he had questions. Lots of them. Instead, Ali wheeled around and left, again retreating to his office. He had to get home. At his desk, wind bristling his back through the shattered windows, he considered defecting. Driving to Jordan with the family. The roads would be riddled with checkpoints now, after the strikes. The airport, too. He had official documents, it might work. Might not. Running might make him look like a murderer, which he guessed he was. The *mukhabarat* would arrest and interrogate Layla's parents and brother. Maybe threaten violence to lure Ali back. This was how they lashed you to the throne.

He went downstairs and found the filing cabinet. Sliding open the top drawer, he found the folder labeled "Lake Assad Water Level, Reports and Analysis, 1988–1992," and removed a videotape and photos of two corpses. Valerie Owens and her asset, Marwan Ghazali. Taking a pen from his pocket, he wrote down a number and a short phrase on a scrap of paper and slid it inside the folder. He looked briefly into the lifeless eyes in each photo. He called the doctor as he walked upstairs. "Is the American conscious?" Ali asked.

"Yes. In bad shape but able to talk. I wouldn't put him under an interrogation, though."

"I understand. I'm coming to see him."

THE DOCTORS SCURRIED FROM THE room when Ali arrived, leaving him alone with Samuel. A row of stitches ran up the American's neck and cheek, his jaw had been bandaged, and he wore a fresh cast over his destroyed foot.

The American lay on his back. He blinked at Ali. "Is Mariam dead?" he asked

"I don't know. I'm here with you."

Ali wanted to smoke, but the room was cramped, and he was not sure if the American's lungs could manage. He rubbed his own scar.

"You and I will now share a similar mark," he said. Samuel held the ceiling's gaze, blinking again.

"A number of strange events have occurred today, Samuel. I have never had a morning quite like this. I want to go home to my family. I'm sure you do as well. So I have a proposition."

The American tried to turn his head to face Ali. He grimaced and lay back facing the ceiling, listening.

"I could keep you here indefinitely, of course," Ali said. "Wait until you heal, then run you through the electricity again to verify everything. Our friends in Hizballah have experience interrogating Americans for long periods. They held your Beirut Station Chief William Buckley for years, just to be sure they'd gotten everything. And to send a message, of course. I would learn more with you back under the knife."

Samuel did not speak.

"My men are arresting Jamil Atiyah as we speak."

More silence from the American.

"This morning, your government bombed Syria, stopping an alleged chemical attack in the process. Several bases were hit, and our attack did not succeed."

Samuel tried to speak, grunting at the effort. "Why are you telling me this?"

"Do you know what I've come to realize? I do not care about this government. But I do care for my family. It is all I care about. And do you know what this regime has done? Do you understand it, even a little? It takes people like me and binds them to it. The fate of my family is intertwined with the government. In your system, you have choices, how do you say, agen—, agen—"

"Agency."

"Precisely. Agency. You have been a free man for a long time. You take it for granted. Probably assume I have the same leeway here in Syria. Of course, I do not. I am a slave, like the others. A higher-ranking one, but a slave nonetheless. But I do not want my family to perish. And I do not want the American government hunting me anymore. So I want to offer two things."

Ali put the folder down on the bed. "The first."

"What is it?"

"It is a videotape of the interrogation of Valerie Owens and her asset, Marwan Ghazali. Both, as I assume you know, are dead. In the tape, you will see that I intervened in an attempt to save her life during the interrogation. I was not successful. My brother, Rustum, held me back while one of his men cut off the top of her head. They forced me to write the report afterward, to fabricate some nonsense about Valerie overdosing on pain pills."

Ali removed the photo of Valerie Owens from the folder and put it in Samuel's hands. The American stared at it knowingly, like he'd seen it before.

"How do I know this isn't fake?" Samuel asked.

"It would be a fairly elaborate plan on my part, no? To make a tape like this today and give it to you? I am sure that somewhere inside the CIA's or Mossad's files you have pictures or intercepts of him talking. You can use that to corroborate this tape, ensure it is the man I say."

"Name?"

"General Basil Mahkluf."

Ali stood and walked closer to Samuel, hovering directly over the American. He put his hands on the bed's railing. "I know you do not speak for your government, certainly not now, but I want your personal assurances that when you return you will convey to your superiors that I have provided this information in good faith. I would like it to be considered when future bombing targets are chosen, or should I contact you in the last days of this government, asking for help. Do we understand each other?"

Samuel did not answer. "What are you going to say happened to your brother?"

"The truth. He brought my agent, Mariam, into the interrogation to provide leverage against you, he lost control, and I killed him before he could murder her."

Samuel nodded. "Two things," he said. "You said you would offer two things before releasing me. The Basil tape is one. What is the other?"

53

ON THE GREEK ISLE OF HYDRA, AN OLD FORTUNE-teller had shown then-nine-year-old Artemis Aphrodite Procter her own death.

"And it was a lot more fucking violent than this," Procter said to the entire Station as she heard the second volley of rocket-propelled grenades slam into the chancery building upstairs. The *shabiha* buses had arrived in the circle thirty minutes earlier heralding another demonstration, vandalism, and maybe a few token trespassers on the embassy compound. Instead, Procter thought, they'd sent a goddamn raiding party over the walls and shot a couple Marines inside the western entrance and breached the doors with Semtex or a land mine or some shit. She had not seen it, just heard the whiny call from the Dip Security guy whose name she could never remember. Then: Invasion. A bunch of militia maniacs swarming the compound like insects.

Procter barked for the Station to initiate Destruction Phase 3 (personnel exfil and officer self-defense). They shredded the papers, they dissolved the hard drives and commo equipment in the acid-boosted shredders. As the shredders chewed through everything, Procter called Bradley: "Ed, we need a goddamn regiment here with horses and choppers and shit, cuz these lunatics are coming in to fuck us up." She lifted the phone so he could hear the gunfire and explosions. Then she hung up.

Procter went to the bank of monitors near the support officer's desk. They beamed closed-circuit footage of the compound. She saw Marines shooting militia in the motor pool, militia running toward the ambassador's office through a blown-out door in the chancery, a crew of State Department personnel and Marines scampering to the third-floor crow's nest to huddle up and wait out the attack. A Syrian in the uniform of a Republican Guard general was marauding around the second floor with a combat shotgun and a goddamn knife. Total chaos.

"Caught us with our twats flapping in the breeze," Procter said to the entire Station. She looked around, counting her officers.

"Where the fuck's Zelda?" Procter said. Another grenade volley struck the chancery and the Station walls shook.

Someone said that Zelda had been upstairs briefing the ambassador in the SCIF.

"Fuck," Procter shouted. Everyone held a weapon. They huddled around Procter as she watched the screens. "Why is there a fuckin' Republican Guard general running around in here?" she said to everyone. She watched the man unsheathe a knife and enter an office. On the screens Procter could see two militia descend the stairwell into the hallway outside the Station. They walked slowly, AK-47s drawn, peering around.

"Fuck this," Procter said as she picked up her Mossberg shotgun, opened the vault door, and jumped into the hallway. She sent two shots into the men and pivoted back inside the Station. She heard moaning and yelled in Arabic that she would offer a quick death if they told her who was in charge. There was more moaning. Procter repeated the offer.

"General Basil Mahkluf," was the reply. "He shot guard. We did . . . did . . . did not mean f-f-for—" A gurgle, another groan, then silence.

"Goddammit," Procter said.

"Chief, Zelda is making a run for it," someone said.

Procter turned back to the monitors. Zelda ran from the SCIF and Procter saw the Republican Guard guy, this Basil, emerge from the ambassador's office. He fired his shotgun at the fleeing analyst. Another camera captured her collapse down a flight of stairs into the landing. Basil ran toward her.

Procter saw that Basil carried a ruddy-white scalp. Then the long-ago explosion at Khost Base in Afghanistan filled Procter's skull. She reloaded the Mossberg and went for Zelda.

She turned the corner and ran right into a militiaman. She raised the gun at his gigantic fucking eyes and blew his head off, clean, with a single shot. Zelda lay facedown at the bottom of the stairs.

"I'm just gonna drag you tits-down, okay, Z? You tell me if you're gonna pass out from the pain."

Procter sent another volley at a shape up the stairs and grabbed Zelda by a shoulder, dragging her down the hall into the Station as beads of shot sprayed the walls around her. Procter heard a weird bass voice declare that these Ikwhan women are indecent without their head coverings. The voice called for backup. What was this Ikhwan shit?

Procter looked down at the analyst's whitening face. Her legs were pretty fucking messed up.

"Z, you there?" Procter shouted. She heard a crunch in the hall, swung around, and fired, sloughing half a leg from a man pointing a rocket-propelled grenade launcher into the Station. He fell.

"They're getting the big stuff now," she yelled. She looked down at Zelda. The analyst was motionless. "Someone compress her, get a tourniquet or some shit." One of the support officers began wrapping Zelda's shredded legs.

"Hold on, Z, hold on." Procter again swiveled around the corner and slapped a burst from the shotgun into another man coming down the hall. He fell in front of the door, then looked up, shrieking. Procter shoved the Mossberg into his temple, squeezed the trigger, and dove back into the Station.

Now she heard the weird voice again, this Basil, and she ducked into a crouch and rolled back into the hallway, where she saw him holding a scalp. She fired, and he fell onto his stomach, then tried to shimmy back toward the stairwell for cover. As he crawled, Procter fired again and heard the *thwap* of shot lodging in his right haunch. He gave a satisfying scream and she felt the heavy heat of rounds flying past her face. She remembered what that old Grecian seer had foretold about her end, the specific location and the time of day and the fucking wildness, and considered running up the hall because she knew she was invincible right now. But she couldn't leave Zelda.

"I got him in the ass, Z," Procter said as she edged back into the Station. "Right in the butt. You hold on, dear."

A rocket-propelled grenade slammed into the ruined bathroom outside the Station. Procter turned away from the heat, then stood tall, all five feet of her.

In Arabic she yelled that she had seen her own demise, and this was not it.

That she, Artemis Aphrodite Procter, was the Angel of Death.

54

SAM DID NOT REMEMBER MUCH OF THE DRIVE TO THE embassy except that Ali sat next to him in the backseat barking orders to his men over a radio. Sam could no longer feel his foot, and his vision was still wobbly and blurred: shapes and colors flocked in orbiting dots, occasionally punctured by fleeting moments of clarity soon obscured as the fog rolled back in.

He realized something was wrong when they reached the embassy: shouts in the distance, the choking fumes, Ali's admonition to wait in the car. Sam couldn't walk anyway. There was more crackling from the radio and Ali gave orders to a group of his commandos outside the vehicle. In the Security Office basement, Ali had explained that his second display of goodwill would be safe passage to the embassy. And that it would be unwise for anyone but Ali to accompany him.

Now Sam tried to sit up and look out the window into the sunshine. Which entrance was this? The circle. He saw buses. A crowd. He heard the clatter of machine gun fire inside the embassy compound. Then a shot from a handgun. Nearby, in the circle. More yelling. Is this how it ends? Picked apart by a mob outside the embassy. He tried to sit up, but he couldn't move his foot, couldn't get the leverage. Another shot from a handgun, closer this time.

A raised voice. Gunfire. More shouting.

Ali opened the door. Sam felt pressure on his shoulder, then multiple hands underneath his arms, lifting him out of his seat. Someone—maybe the doctor? Sam whiffed the familiar smell of ammonia—jabbed a needle into his side. Sharp at first, then nice and warm in his veins. He was moving, they were carrying him inside. He could see the ground underneath, stones and gravel and pavement in motion. Then wood-patterned floors raced by. He craned his head to the left and saw Ali. Sam had the sensation of falling through an abyss, like in a fever dream. He wanted the warm sun on his face. He wanted Mariam here.

He closed his eyes to imagine hers. When he opened them, a shape stood over him. Gradually, he made out the black frazzle of hair jutting out wildly, the shape clutching a stick or a gun or something. He tried to move but could not.

The shape knelt down and spoke to him.

"Jaggers. About time you showed."

55

SIX WEEKS LATER

The night-vision camera slowly focused on a Pajero parked up on the sidewalk. The street was empty, save for a young couple out for an evening stroll.

The man operating the camera coughed, rocking the lens. He turned it back to the dirty stone building. Four guards doused in harsh sodium light milled around a gatehouse, laughing. "Wonder if he's spending the night," someone said. Another cough from the quiet camera operator.

A beep. "This is Gartner from the Office of General Counsel. Still waiting?"

"Yep. Slumber party in there," Procter said.

"Shut up, Procter," said Bradley.

"We've just checked MOLLY again using the video collection from last week and the photo library. Algorithm working now. Don't know why she was glitchy earlier."

"Copy."

The camera focused on the Security Office's entrance.

"Someone's coming out," the camera operator said. The video feed focused on a figure emerging from the entrance.

THE WEEKS SINCE THE DESTRUCTION of the U.S. Embassy had sent Langley into full crisis tilt. The Director established a Syria task force and pulled in, Sam had heard, more than two hundred analysts, operators, techies, linguists, and targeters. The loss of the Station in Damascus midwifed the creation of a Syria-focused CIA cell in Amman with Procter in command. While recuperating from the operation on his foot in Germany, Sam had heard through the CIA rumor mill that Procter's team had been charged with finding the parties responsible for the mayhem in Damascus. Bradley provided the grim accounting to Sam during a clipped phone call. Fourteen Americans were dead, including six Marines, the Defense attaché, and seven State Department officials. Twelve Syrian Foreign Service Nationals had also perished. Another twenty-six Americans were hospitalized across Landstuhl, including four CIA officers, Zelda among them. It was, Sam realized as he did the mental math, the deadliest day for America's overseas presence since the bombing of the Marine barracks in Beirut back in '83. "Do we know yet who led the attack?" Sam had asked.

Bradley, he could tell, did not want to talk. Sam heard the phone shift between Bradley's ears. The old operator coughed. Sam let the silence sit.

"The psychopathic fuck who killed Val," Bradley finally said. "General Basil Mahkluf. He scalped a few of our people during the embassy overrun. Procter says he was also the one who shot Zelda. We're working to find the bastard. All I can say for now, you get it."

Bradley coughed again. And it was then, in that strained second of silence before Bradley graciously changed the subject, that Sam's brain finally began to process the deep hole he was now in.

In the end, they gave him a week to stew in the hospital at Landstuhl before the bureaucratic onslaught began. Bradley greeted him fresh off the air bridge, offering a furnished apartment in Tysons Corner for the next few months. He also explained that Sam had been placed on administrative leave, all accesses temporarily forfeited. Ed was not angry, just sad, as if he had to put down a beloved dog who'd bitten the neighbor kid.

The investigators built an exhaustive case file for the Peer Review

Board hearing—unscheduled, looming—at which a panel of Agency brass would decide his fate. Best-case: cleared of counterintelligence concerns and strapped to a desk at Langley for six to twenty-four months. Worst-case: severed from the service, blue badge confiscated, security clearance forfeited, pack your box and prepare for the crushing boredom of civilian life.

The weeks at Langley were unpleasant. Four psychological exams. Daily check-ins with the OMS medical team. Three formal physicals. A raucous three-day interview with a rotating team of increasingly rabid interrogators bent on constructing an exhaustive chronology of his last week in Damascus. He surrendered every communications device he owned, personal and professional. They questioned him about every SDR. They offered a deep-tissue massage of every cable and asset assessment he'd drafted since Cairo.

The polygraphs were extensions of the myriad "interviews" and interrogations. They were aggressive, loud, coercive. But to each gaggle of cement-eyed security investigators he offered the same story: the truth. The polygraphers framed each question so he could answer with a simple yes or no. They asked for intimate, graphic, chronological detail about his romantic liaisons with Mariam. He told them everything. ("*Did you have a sexual relationship with your asset, Mariam Haddad, in France, Damascus, and Italy?*") They asked for the circumstances of his release from Ali's custody and subsequent appearance at the shattered embassy. ("*Did you provide classified information to General Ali Hassan beyond the name, drop sites, and safe houses already specified?*") They asked about the triple homicide. ("*Did Mariam Haddad tell you that she arrived outside the embassy to provide you with intelligence outside her channel with Ali Hassan?*" "*Did Mariam Haddad kill the three militia?*")

Two weeks in, Zelda died.

She'd been on life support in Landstuhl. CIA airlifted her back to D.C. for the funeral and Counterintelligence graciously paused the bureaucratic beatings to let Sam attend. Bradley and Procter were there. Sam remembered the analyst hopping into the Chief's car at Damascus International, full of energy, ready to unroll the Palace procurement network. Nausea lingered as he thought of the cable in which he and Procter had prolonged Zelda's TDY. "STATION REQUESTS THREE-MONTH EXTENSION TO SUPPORT ONGOING, CRITICAL INTELLIGENCE OPERATIONS." Antiseptic garbage. He had helped kill her. And Val.

He tried to catch Procter after the service, but the Chief left before he could pull her aside.

That night, Bradley invited Sam to dinner at his farmhouse. "First dinner at home in three weeks and I'm choosing to spend it with you, like a jackass," Bradley said. Angela helped him out of Ed's car, gave him a teary bear hug, grilled burgers, and left them with a six-pack of Coors on the porch. They watched late summer light streak across the Blue Ridge Mountains and finished the first round in silence.

Bradley cracked open his second beer and took a sip. Sam thought Ed looked about four years older than he had before Damascus. "This conversation did not happen, understand? Security will toast my ass if they find out."

Sam gulped down the remnant of his first beer and nodded.

"No word from ATHENA. Not a peep since Ali's basement. There is, however, growing agreement that ATHENA did not play us, at least not for long. Story on her cousin was corroborated by some stolen documents. They let her out, by the way."

Sam gave a thin smile at the news, then turned to Bradley, the father he had failed. Or betrayed. He didn't know how to think about it, exactly, but it didn't matter. He was ashamed. "I'm sorry, Ed. I screwed up with her. I hope you'll forgive me."

Bradley nodded. "I can. I have. I'm not going to flog you for it. You've made your confession. You've owned the mistake."

Sam reached down into the cooler for his second beer. He winced, gasping lightly, and sat back up as he cracked it open.

They again drank in silence as the sun dipped below the ridgeline.

"The covcom system we provided ATHENA continues to puzzle," Bradley said. "NRO scrubbed the satellite platform and found something odd, like malware. Details are sketchy, but we've transitioned all assets and are watching it closely. It's possible Ali and the Iranian techies stole a few weeks of covcom traffic. Counterintelligence is red-teaming the information to figure out if they'll be able to determine anyone's identity from the traffic. We may need to exfil a few if we think they've been burned."

"How many assets on the platform?"

"Four. Not including ATHENA."

"A mess," Sam mumbled.

"Yep. I wish she had told you in Italy. We could have gotten her out."

Sam set down the can and placed his forehead in his hands. Bradley put a hand on his back. They again sat in silence. After a few minutes Sam lifted his head to stare at the mountains. Bradley held his shoulder and took another sip of beer.

"PRB probably scheduled around the holidays. Polys have gone well, but there will be more. All I can say about that piece, you get it. I think they'll drop the counterintelligence angle. They don't think you are lying, which bodes well for your ability to remain in the service. I've seen enough PRB proceedings to know that there is always a ledger. On the one hand, they have your romantic indiscretion with an asset and her subsequent decision to provide a covcom device to a hostile service. On the other, they have her confession, subsequent truthfulness and cooperation, and your collective actions in Damascus on the eighteenth and nineteenth of July."

Bradley polished off his beer and tossed the can. "Here is how I see it, by the way. Your management of the ATHENA case led to a U.S. military operation that stopped a devastating attack. You two saved thousands of lives. That's going to be crystal clear to the PRB. Black-and-white. A jewel in your crown. No, the controversy will be the decision to turn yourself in. And of course your relationship with her. Did that put you and our assets in *more danger* and create counterintelligence headaches because maybe you don't remember everything you said to Ali?"

"If I'd fled and Mariam had turned in Atiyah, Ali never would have bought her story about the Wadi Barada intel. They would have dug and tortured until she admitted everything."

Bradley nodded. "I hear you. I have no idea how the PRB is going to go, though."

"You've seen a lot of these, though. What's your gut?"

"Two-year probationary period at Headquarters. But I'm probably fifty-fifty on that."

"What's the other side of the coin?"

"They fire you."

Sam nodded, finished his second beer in a long gulp, and registered that he did not care, as long as Mariam made it out alive.

"There is one more thing. Wait here." Bradley walked inside, padding downstairs to the Box. He returned with a scrap of paper and sat. Bradley cracked open another beer, rubbed a bristly chin, and started to speak before abruptly stopping, as if reconsidering the wisdom of what he was about to say. Or saying anything at all.

"You're on administrative leave, so this is of course not kosher," he said. "But fuck it. I need your help." He held out his hand, offering a folded piece of paper.

Sam took the paper, turned it over, and inhaled the scent of smoke and ash. He'd been on a thick sedative drip in Ali's basement prison the last time he'd seen it. It made him sick to see it again.

Bradley's mouth upturned in a wry smile. "You may not remember, but Ali slipped this into the videotape he passed you before he returned you to the embassy. The video, by the way, confirms his story. General Basil Mahkluf, under the watchful eye of the recently deceased Rustum Hassan, murdered Val and Marwan Ghazali during an interrogation." Bradley grimaced and stared at his shoes.

"What was Ali doing while it happened?"

"That's the odd thing. Tape's not conclusive, but it looks like he tried to stop Basil. His brother, Rustum, got in his way, let Basil slice off Val's fucking scalp."

Sam nodded. "What do you want me to do?" He opened the paper and saw the numbers, recognized it as a Syrian phone number. There was a phrase scrawled in Arabic. He folded it up.

"We do not yet have a lethal finding to kill Basil, but I expect we will within the week," Bradley said. "He's drenched in blood. He's responsible for the deaths of fifteen Americans, including Zelda and Val. But here's the problem. I can't find him."

"POTUS doesn't want to bomb Damascus again?"

"Basil's gone dark. No comms, no visits to the office, abandoned his villa. He's a ghost. We wouldn't even know where to bomb."

"I would hide, too, if I'd murdered a bunch of Americans," Sam said.

"Look, at this point you know Ali better than anyone in the U.S. government."

"And you want to know if I think he'll help us find Basil."

"Yes. What's your take? You said Ali was ambivalent about the regime. Hell, he passed you a videotape that put a giant target on Basil's back."

Sam grunted. "Ali told me he wanted consideration from our government when future bombing targets are chosen."

"Do you think he would help us to get that consideration? If you make the ask?"

Ali. Sam looked down at his limp foot, thought of the electricity frying him as Ali dug for a name. Then he remembered Ali's smile that night with Zelda at the restaurant. Decent, halfway kind. Sam recalled Ali's words about the regime before releasing him, the hate flushing his eyes as he had spoken Basil Mahkluf's name. "Ali's a complicated guy," was all Sam could mumble.

"That he is," Ed said with a glance at Sam's foot. Mosquitoes dive-bombed the porchlights while Bradley waited for him to continue.

"Did you trace the number on this paper?" Sam asked.

"Yes. It's Ali's office."

"What about my admin leave? My access is gone."

"I want you to work the op with Procter, administrative leave be damned. Procter is fine with it. We won't tell anyone else. I'll handle restoring your access. Temporarily, of course. You'd start from Langley, then close it out in Procter's new shop in Amman. That is, assuming POTUS signs a new finding." Bradley's eyes veered back to the foot.

"Ed, I appreciate that and all, but please, for god's sake, stop looking at the damn hoof. I'll be fine. I would love nothing more than to finish this one. I'm in." Sam finished his third beer, crushed the can, and threw Bradley a stony stare. He wanted the op, but doubted it would help him find Mariam. The woman he loved more than anything had disappeared into the heart of Damascus: Dead, captured, or silent. Last seen on a gurney with a knife in her ribs. And, as always when this image floated through his mind, a vacuum followed behind, wrenching him from his own body.

He let it pass. "When do I start?" he asked.

SAM AND PROCTER SETTLED INTO the operational planning like an old married couple after a fight: they ignored his indiscretions, assumed their old roles, and marched on, chins up. Sam brought up Mariam once, but Procter, reading his hangdog expression even over the videoconference from Amman, had thrust a tiny pixilated hand toward the screen. As she lowered it, Sam saw the angry eyes and redirected their collective attention to a recent run of satellite imagery of the Security Office, noting that the number of cars parked on the adjacent street had increased considerably in recent weeks. Procter nodded and took a generous bite of what appeared to be a Payday bar (king-sized). "Next photo," she said.

So he let it drop.

The most pressing operational challenge was the White House and Seventh Floor's continued insistence that the CIA authenticate the target's identity with MOLLY, the algorithm, and Susan, the facial recognition specialist. The CIA had no one left in Damascus. Who to run the cameras? On this front there was spirited debate among the operational team, culminating in a volley of cable traffic in which Procter lobbed a response to Sam's half-serious suggestion that they test the MOLLY software on board a surveillance drone. Procter cabled back a one-paragraph response judging Sam's idea to be operational dogshit. Sam interpreted the vulgarity as Procter's twisted form of forgiveness. For her enemies, she offered only silence.

In the end, Sam led the charge for the cleanest approach: use the

BANDITOs. They had been polygraphed. They were in the game. They are our only shot, Sam argued. The approvals were thorny, the lawyers nervous about foreign nationals directly involved in a lethal op. But Bradley and Procter heaved their weight behind it and soon all held a copy of the revised finding for CIA lethal authorities targeting General Basil Mahkluf. Sam locked it in the safe under his desk. Other than a scattering of empty Dunkin' Donuts cups, his temporary workspace in the Langley cube farm was bare.

There was just one piece remaining. The most important step. They had to find him. Sam wouldn't sleep for two nights.

It began at lunchtime on a Wednesday. Sam appeared outside a basement room at Langley marked with the bland nameplate: GLOBAL TECHNOLOGY SOLUTIONS. He carried the piece of paper Ali had placed inside the folder in Damascus. An NSA tech opened the door and showed Sam into a darkened room with a bullpen of sterile cubicles at its center and a bank of television monitors covering each wall, all displaying cable news. The tech led Sam into a side room. Procter's face was already splashed on a screen and one of the CIA linguists, Abdallah, a native Syrian, sat at the table. There was a single telephone and a set of computers stacked against the wall. The tech sat at the computer and motioned for Sam to sit.

"As discussed, if the MOIS or the Russians or anyone tries to trace this call, it will look like it bounced from a tower in the Mezzeh suburb," the tech said, pointing to a satellite image of Damascus's western rim with the cell towers marked by blue dots.

"We've been over this like twenty times, Jason, for fuck's sake," Procter said to the tech, whose name was not Jason. "Everyone put on the goddamn headsets and let's get this moving. Sam, it's your show."

Sam reviewed the plan with Abdallah once more. Then he unfolded the paper and dialed the number. It was eight o'clock in Damascus. Ali was probably in his office. The phone rang twice before he answered.

"Hello?"

"Hello, my friend, I am sorry for not calling back last night, but I wanted to let you know that I've sent over the wine," said Abdallah in flawless Levantine Arabic, reading from the paper Ali had passed Sam.

A lingering pause. Sam heard breathing, the phone shuffle between ears, the rustle of a drawer and papers.

"Thank you. How much do I owe you?" Ali said.

Abdallah read out three prices that could be constructed into a phone number.

"Okay, thank you," the man said.

The line went dead. Sam's neck prickled, the hairs strained upward.

He turned to the NSA tech. "You can run the voice-recognition cross-checks, but it's him. It's Ali Hassan." Sam swiveled to Procter. She gave two thumbs up.

"If he calls back, he'll help us find Basil," Sam said.

Procter sliced a thumb across her windpipe and the screen went black.

SAM FOUND IONA BANKS SITTING at her workbench in the OTS spaces, nestled inside a windowless room of the Original Headquarters Building saturated by fluorescent lights. Smiling, she ran a hand through the hair on the unshaved side of her head and waved him over to the table. Pushing aside several black Gucci messenger bags—"all the Chinese intel guys carry these," she said—she removed from a drawer a single manila folder and slid it to Sam.

"I have so many questions I'm not asking," she said.

"Smart."

She put her hand on the folder, pulling it back an inch. "But I have to ask one: What are the odds this gets me fired?"

Leaning over, he rested his forearms on the table and absentmindedly looked at the picture on his badge. He had been so young. "Low."

She smiled and released the folder. Her eyebrows wrinkled at the sight of his blue badge. "When do you lose that, by the way?"

"Soon. I have some business in Amman. Then the PRB process starts." He opened the folder. In it was an envelope bearing French postage. It held several flyers for vacation rentals and hotels. Thumbing through the papers, he stopped when he reached an advertisement for a chateau in Èze.

"How did you get this picture?"

Iona just frowned.

"What did you tell the guys in Documents?"

"I just told them to make it. They didn't ask questions. They love this stuff."

"It will look like it came from Villefranche?" he asked.

Iona smirked. "It will. It is in fact a promotional package delivered by the good people at the Villefranche Office de Tourisme, hoping to entice her to return to the area for another holiday."

"Perfect."

There was a silence. "Is she okay?" Iona asked, her face darkening.

"I don't know." Now the picture of the Èze chateau made his chest feel tight. He closed the folder.

She nodded and kept silent.

He reread the Damascus address on the front five times to be sure it was correct. Tucking the flyer of the Èze chateau back in the envelope, he passed the manila folder to Iona and rapped his knuckles twice on the table.

A FEW DAYS BEFORE HE left for Amman, Sam hobbled to the Global Deployment Center with his black diplomatic passport and Procter's cable approving his TDY. The nameplate on the counter proclaimed the grandmotherly attendant to be Cornelia G. The cane on the floor and the magnifying-glass eyewear suggested an EOD (entrance on duty) date during the waning days of the Eisenhower administration. Sam smiled and introduced himself. Cornelia did not. She stood, shakily reaching for his papers, and began typing his employee identification number into her computer.

After a few minutes she looked up and reread Procter's cable approving his travel. "You forge this, dear?" she said.

Sam laughed. Cornelia's face screwed into a grimace. He erased the smile. "I did not," he said. "You can check the cable database."

Cornelia did. It took a long time to enter the numbers. Finally, she looked up and spoke softly. "How'd you pull this one off, dear, being on administrative leave and all? Never seen this, and I've been here a good while. You shouldn't be able to access this approval cable, much less travel on Agency business."

Cornelia motioned toward his badge. "What color is that, anyway? You got the red one? Escort required? One of these nice people here keeping an eye on you, minding you don't lift classified paper from the vaults?" She motioned toward the people in the line behind Sam, which was now stretching into the hallway.

Sam held up his blue badge. "Still blue for now, Cornelia."

Now she grinned, and her rheumy gaze lingered on his fresh scar. "Well, dear, I want to ask what horrible thing you've done, but I'll spare you. You don't keep a job like this being nosy. Let's get you ready." Unprompted, Cornelia read aloud the provisos of Agency Regulation 41-2 as if it were Holy Scripture. "Any journey must meet or exceed thirteen hours in duration, including layovers, to merit the purchase of an airfare above Basic Economy Class—or its nearest equivalent—on a U.S. carrier (Delta, American, United, etc.)." The et cetera said like Amen.

Sam knew you don't fight with Deployment, so he smiled and nodded and said of course, a middle seat in the back near one of the lavatories would be excellent. She booked the ticket and printed out the papers identifying him as second secretary (Communications) and set to arranging the hotel. "Room has to be above the fourth floor and below the tenth, dear, you know that. No exceptions. Above the fourth to keep you away from the car bombs, below the tenth so the fire truck ladders can reach you. Can't be booking the penthouse for you ops boys willy-nilly." She looked at his ringless left hand and clicked her tongue.

TELEVISION OFF, SAM SHUFFLED BACK to the bed in his room at the Four Seasons Hotel in Amman. He sat on the edge as daybreak traffic swirled and whined in the circle below. He looked down at the carpet, toward the closet. He smoothed the sheets and took a deep, painful breath.

Awkwardly and painfully, he got dressed. He heard four knocks as he walked toward the door. He checked the peephole, unspooled the chain lock, and opened it. "Jaggers. Time to roll. Big day today."

At the Station, late afternoon slid into evening. Procter emerged from her office. An Amman support officer brought in Bennigan's for the ops team, now gathered around a conference table picking at Styrofoam containers of American chain-restaurant fare: burgers, chicken tenders, onion rings, and heaping plates of fries. "Last Bennigan's in the world, I'm told," Procter said. "Right here in the middle of the desert."

Bradley held watch at Langley. Sam would arm the bomb from Amman.

The trigger now sat between Susan, the facial recognition expert, and an untouched platter of fried potato skins. Procter told Sam that she had to pee. "I'm your minder here, so you come with me."

Graciously, she let him wait outside the ladies' room. When she emerged, she pointed to a row of empty desks and took a seat. He slid a chair across from her. She pulled a rubber band from her pocket to tie up her hair.

"You won't get redemption from me, but you'll get forgiveness. Best I can do."

He wanted to hug her. "Thanks, Chief," he said instead.

"And I'm sorry about ATHENA," Procter said. "She was our girl in Damascus. Gilded, primo asset. Plus the not knowing what happened and all that shit. I ran a guy in Kandahar who disappeared on us. Just vanished. Poof. Drove me nuts. Bothers me to this day. And I wasn't even fucking the guy."

Sam was sufficiently attuned to Procter to interpret this as genuine feeling, not a backhanded reminder of his infidelities to CIA. This was empathy.

Sam nodded. Procter's eyes leveled at his. "You do understand that even if she surfaces you'll be about as welcome around the case as a Jew in Mecca, right?"

"Yeah, of course. C'mon, Chief."

Procter nodded and spat into a trash can. She unwound her hair and stretched the rubber band around her fingers. "The night you confessed to me. In that shitty D-town safe house. You said something interesting."

"I said a lot of things."

"You did. But you used an intriguing word, one I did not report to CI or Security when they asked me for the story after you came clean in Landstuhl. You said, 'I'm in love with her, Chief.' Direct quote. Not, *I fucked her, Chief,* or *We've been having sex, Chief.* Love. Ring a bell?"

Sam leaned close to Procter. "Bradley told me once you can lie to anyone except CIA," he said. "So I told you the truth."

She shook her head. "So what's the plan, then?" Procter said. "I'd imagine if it was about the sex you move on, get over it eventually. But love, I've been told by reliable sources, is a stickier fucking feeling to shake."

"There is no plan," he said. "There's nothing to be done."

Procter tied her hair back up. "I suppose. But let me ask you a question, Jaggers. When you joined me in Damascus, you were a gung-ho case officer on his way to a glorious future. Now . . ." She trailed off. "You're a smidge diminished, let's say." She offered a wan smile.

"*Diminished* is a good word," Sam said. "Accurate. So what's the question?"

"Was Mariam worth it?"

Procter's mention of ATHENA's true name, a breach of tradecraft—an intentional one, he suspected—caught Sam off guard. But before he could respond, Susan's voice interrupted from the conference room. "OGC just joined." Sam and Procter walked back into the room to see Elias Kassab training the camera on the Security Office building. Sam sat next to Procter, shifting in his chair, wishing he hadn't neglected his evening dose of Vicodin for the foot.

They watched Ali Hassan emerge and begin walking slowly down the sidewalk.

"Where the hell is Basil?" Procter said. "We aren't trying to kill fucking Ali Hassan anymore."

ALI LIT A CIGARETTE AND walked toward the guardhouse, looking up into a night sky dotted by clouds. The last few weeks had been among the worst of his life. He had not been home in fifteen days. He had stopped looking in the mirror. It no longer mattered.

Ali's title had not changed, nor had his pay, neither unusual for a promotion in Syria. But what had been unusual, and terrifying, was the scope of his new responsibility. "You take your brother's position," Assad had said, flinty-eyed, after Ali explained that he had killed Rustum. The President had not responded to that admission. "The Republican Guard is yours. Do anything you must to smash the rebellion." Ali suspected Assad had set in motion a parallel effort to investigate him, but so far this ghost had kept its distance.

Since then Ali had worried that his own sanity might be bending. He now had a recurring nightmare in which Layla screamed, then disappeared into fire. It repeated itself on a cot in his office, usually just before dawn.

But he had one more distraction tonight before he returned to his work and the nightmares. He stubbed out his cigarette and lit another as he snaked between the cars on the sidewalk.

Ali walked leisurely, inflating his lungs with smoke. He imagined opening Rustum's throat and scratched his scar as he thought of his brother, hoping that it would conjure some feeling. Anger, guilt, loss, joy.

Anything.

But he felt nothing, and the memory burned away into the night as he walked.

SAM WATCHED THE VIDEO FOOTAGE of Ali's walk and scratched at his own scar, which ran from the left side of his neck onto his lower cheek. He traced it with his thumb. Sam felt Procter watching him, and he dropped his hand.

"Anything yet, Jaggers?" Procter asked.

"No. Still nothing." Ali was about fifty yards from the Pajero.

"He's turning around," said Elias. "Very, very slowly."

"Fuckin'-A," said Procter. "Go back inside and bring me Basil."

KANAAN WAITED FOR ALI IN the Security office lobby. "He's finally started talking, boss. I know you're busy, but I think you should have a word." Ali followed Kanaan into the basement toward the same cell they'd used to hold Mariam Haddad's cousin, the skinny girl with the unfortunate eye patch. Kanaan opened the door and Ali entered the freezing room, joining the prisoner on the slab bed and lighting a cigarette for warmth.

"Ibrahim," Ali said. "Or should I say Abu Qasim?" He smiled. "I understand you have confessed to building the bomb that almost killed the President?"

"And you," Abu Qasim grunted. "It almost killed you."

"Yes," Ali murmured.

"And your brother."

"You would have been doing me a favor. As it happened, I had to do it myself." Ali blew smoke in his face.

Abu Qasim turned his head in surprise before shifting his eyes back to the floor.

Ali clicked his tongue. "But I don't want more information about the past. I want to know the future."

"What?"

"Where is the Black Death? Your wife, the sniper. Where is she now? Where is she going?"

Abu Qasim closed his eyes. He wheezed. Then he smiled. "That, General, is the one thing I cannot give."

Ali stood and put out his cigarette on the floor. "You cannot, but you will." He nodded to Kanaan, who brought in a bucket of freezing water and doused the prisoner to prepare for another session. Abu Qasim screamed, then mumbled: Sarya, Sarya, Sarya. The way he said her name reminded Ali of Layla.

ALI HEARD THE DISTINCTIVE VOICE when he returned to his office.

"I'm still not getting the answers I need from Kanaan," Basil said, seated inside. Ali joined him at the table and lit a cigarette.

"I'm surprised you can sit down, Basil, what with the buckshot that insane CIA woman blasted into your ass during your lunatic raid on the embassy." Ali smiled. Basil ignored him.

"You are responsible for disrupting my operation—an approved operation—against the U.S. Embassy," Basil said. "I need answers, and I don't want them from Kanaan. You called me here to your office. So *you* meet with me," he growled. "Don't send me to your underling."

"I am trying to win a war you and my brother nearly lost. It's kept me very busy." Ali nodded toward the door, telling him to leave. Basil spat on the floor. He licked his mustache and lit his own cigarette, blowing the first fumes across the table into Ali's face. He remained seated.

"Get out, Basil."

"You're making—"

"Get out."

Slowly, Basil stood, stubbed out his cigarette on the table, and turned to leave.

Ali normally did not threaten. Nor did he reveal secrets in fits of anger. You did not get to the top of the Syrian *mukhabarat* by running your mouth. But there were accounts to settle. "I saw what you did to those Americans in the embassy, Basil." Basil, the Comanche, stopped walking to the door and turned around slowly, his brows furrowed in confusion. "You did it to Valerie Owens in this basement. You did it in Hama."

Basil began to smile broadly.

"Basil," Ali said, putting out his cigarette in the ashtray. "I had always thought of you as an imp, a demon. But you are merely a rabid dog who wants to be praised for the carcass he brings back to his owner. He stood and approached until he could smell Basil's humid breath, see the spittle-slick mustache. They stood eye to eye. "Your owner is dead, Basil."

Ali delicately sliced a finger across the top of his forehead.

Basil had stopped smiling. He turned and walked out, spitting again on the floor.

Lighting another cigarette, Ali opened a desk drawer and removed a used notepad. He flipped toward the back until he found the page. A trio of prices. A phone number.

He punched them into a cell phone he'd purchased in cash. Then he sent a text message.

SAM'S PHONE BEEPED. THE SOUND was unnecessary; he'd been staring at the damn thing all night anyway. He read the Arabic text: *Leaving.* He showed it to Procter, who nodded and said: "Fuckin' hell, let's do this."

Sam watched as the camera operator focused on the Security Office entrance. Basil walked past the guardhouse onto the sidewalk, weaving between the parked cars.

"Susan?" said Procter.

"Working it, ma'am." Susan watched Elias's livestream video while a second set of videos rolled on another screen beside it. "Damascus, can you zoom in a bit more?"

Elias focused the lens on his face.

"Thanks." Several seconds passed. "Just sent judgment to OGC."

"Copy. I have Susan's and MOLLY's results," said Gartner. "We're a go. It's him. It's Basil."

"Street and sidewalk remain clear," said Elias.

"I'm arming it," Sam said.

"He's walking faster than Ali did with that special stroll," Procter said.

Sam watched as Basil walked past the Pajero's trunk. Procter muttered something to herself, like an incantation.

"Val. Zelda. In honor," Sam said as Basil crossed the passenger-side door.

The blast tore open the Pajero's door, rocketing a barrage of molten plastic and aluminum fragments through Basil's head and body into the concrete wall. The feed showed a puff of smoke trailing away from a small fire that had started inside the car. Elias focused the camera on the blast zone, capturing the gore-soaked wall, a large black shoe, and a bushy pelt.

It looked like the top of his head.

VILLEFRANCHE-SUR-MER TWINKLED IN THE DISTANCE as the woman shimmied into a red dress, hair pulled up to her neck. The windows were open, and the drapes flowed in the night breeze. The muffled revelry of horns and sirens rang from the streets below. He zipped up Mariam's dress and she let her hair fall down her back as he pressed his lips into her neck. He wound a bunch of her long hair in his hand and inhaled.

Maybe when we are old we can live like this.

Sam woke up to the sound of the call to prayer. He felt strange, and it was not until he had picked up the crutches and shuffled back and forth across his room for ten minutes, as the Langley doctors had recommended, that he realized what it was. He was at peace. For the first time since Damascus.

He made some coffee and turned on the television and saw a report on another U.S. missile strike on Damascus and a chyron reading, *U.S. Special Forces operating throughout Syria*. He flicked it off.

Sam stayed in Amman for another day. He slept. He read. He drank more coffee. He wondered when he would feel his foot again.

Mostly, he thought of her.

Procter came to his hotel room at sundown, a single piece of folded paper in her outstretched hand. "I know you've lost your accesses and privileges, Jaggers, but I have a special delivery from a dead drop in our old stomping ground," she said. "BANDITOs still making the rounds.

I smuggled this out of the Station, breaking numerous regulations and laws in the process. But fuck it. It's addressed to you, after all."

Sam eyed her suspiciously.

"Maternal instinct, you could say." She winked as she turned to leave, not quite getting it right.

Sam took the paper to the balcony, unfolding it as a sandstorm kicked up across the reddening southern sky.

56

MARIAM WALKED UP THE MOUNTAIN IN A FOG OF PAIN. She held her right side, gasping for breath, as she looked across her ravaged city. It was her first long walk since the doctors had let her out of the hospital. She had been lucky, they'd said. The blade had found its way between her ribs and punctured a lung. But they'd stopped the bleeding quickly. She would make a full recovery. Now she wanted air. Her doctor had agreed it would do her good.

THAT MORNING RAZAN HAD COME to her room early, well before daybreak. Mariam, sleepless, saw her enter through the shadows. She carried an old backpack. "Come with me, *habibti,*" Razan said. Mariam had known this day would come. Since her release from Ali Hassan's prison and Uncle Daoud's disappearance during the bombing, Razan had been quiet. But it was not the pouty, sulking Razan of the days following the initial *mukhabarat* attack. She was focused. She was preparing. She was ready to be a refugee. Mariam sat up in bed and pulled her cousin in tight. "I cannot go with you, *habibti.* I wish I could." They cried, and Razan ran her hands over Mariam's fingers.

"They look better, *habibti,*" Razan said. They lay on the bed. Mariam ran her hands through Razan's hair and they both slipped in and out of sleep as the clockless hours drifted toward dawn. Once, Mariam got up from the bed and went into her closet. She kept the door open to let in the moonlight. She found a robe and pulled it on. If Ali had installed cameras in her bedroom, she would be able to explain the trip. Sitting on the floor, she pulled a paper-filled box out from underneath a chaotic heap of clothes. It overflowed with old photos, letters, junk mail, magazines she had not bothered to throw away. She found the envelope that had arrived earlier that day, the one with the French postage that had made her stomach twist when she first saw it. She had waited all day. Razan had been shuffling around the apartment and she wanted to be alone when she opened it. Quietly and carefully, she separated paper from glue and began leafing through the flyers. She saw the Èze chateau. She stared at it for a moment until she realized she had stopped breathing. She closed her eyes and took in a long, full breath. He had signaled that he was safe on the other side of Ali's prison. Now it was her turn.

She went back to the bed, curling up into Razan.

"UNCLE VISITED ME BEFORE HE disappeared," Mariam said at last, as the sun rose. Razan sat up, looking confused.

"He gave me a list of the sites the Republican Guard had planned to use during the chemical attack."

Razan looked away from Mariam in disbelief. She stared out the window in silence.

"He wanted me to give the information to some friends."

"Friends?"

"Yes."

"He *asked* you to do this?"

"He did. He insisted. Even though he knew what it would mean for him."

"And you gave it to them?"

"I did."

Razan sat quietly for a moment. "Then the bombs came," she whispered. "And killed Papa."

Mariam lay back down on the bed and cried. Razan snuggled next to her. They lay in silence until two honks came from the street outside. Then a third, longer in duration. Razan pulled a hijab from her backpack and put it on.

"You have arranged everything?" Mariam asked, wiping her eyes. "Papers, passport, money?"

"Yes, *okhti*. I have been careful."

Mariam's legs felt very weak as they hugged. She took in her cousin, trying to capture as many mental photographs as she could: the long hair, the spindly legs, the wicked smile, the fiery eyes—though she imagined the patch gone and both eyes working again. Razan pulled away and slung the backpack over her shoulder.

"I love you, *okhti*," Razan said. "And I understand why you must stay."

"And I know why you must leave, *okhti*," Mariam said. "But I love you more."

Razan had started toward the door. "Wait," Mariam said. "I don't want to know where you are going, but I need something to hold on to. To picture you in your new life in case we do not see each other for . . . for . . . a long time." Mariam clenched her jaw tight to keep from crying. Razan's face was also tight. "How about your new name, the one you will use to escape?" Mariam asked.

Her face brightened. "Umm Abiha," she said.

Then Razan turned and left.

NOW, ON THE MOUNTAIN, EVENING air humming on her skin, Mariam made for the summit. Girl's got the fire, they said after she destroyed sparring opponents in the Paris salad days. Hard blows, tight angles, vicious energy. Vengeance burning in her eyes. Each knock, each strike reclaiming herself, hacking away at the cage.

She pressed on, looking over the city. Syria, her uncle had said, is the heart of the world. Ancient blood flows through this place. Its cities have stood since creation and will stand until the end. And here, he would say, pointing his finger toward the ground, it is here that the world will end.

She saw the lights glowing in central Damascus as towers of smoke rose over the city's embattled suburbs.

The shiny glare from the Palace, where the President managed his chattel.

The black banners of jihad unfurling in the darkness of Douma.

She remembered a protest, her cousin's cry, and felt the hope now dashed, replaced by a war between rival gods.

And I will destroy you both.

She was close now, huffing, sweating, straining for the top with each step. She could not drive Sam from her mind. They were fellow travelers, and her partner was gone. She knew this feeling's name and forced herself, finally, to whisper it aloud for the first time as she marched up the mountain.

Mariam reached the summit as the last fingers of light receded behind Damascus's western horizon. She clutched her side. Keep moving. Keep fighting. Keep going. She sat on a stone wall and looked down at her ancient home. She scanned to make sure she was alone. She removed the note from her shoe.

She spoke to him over the paper, all the things she could not write.

Mariam knelt and put the note in the can. Then she stood up and began to walk down the mountain.

ACKNOWLEDGMENTS

WRITING A NOVEL IS A LONELY TEAM SPORT. MOST DAYS during the writing season I sat in front of a computer, alone, creating a fictional world populated by fictional characters. The writing is, by its nature, a solitary undertaking. But, in the end, a book requires that family, friends, and supporters come alongside to midwife it into the real world. And this novel had them in spades.

I am supremely grateful to my editor at Norton, Star Lawrence, who invested in me and in this story and whose rounds of lively feedback taught me invaluable lessons about writing and storytelling. Thank you for betting on me.

My agent, Rafe Sagalyn, read (very rough) early treatments and chapters, sharpened it all, and encouraged me to keep going. He helped lead this project through the wilderness of the first drafts to the promised land of an actual book deal, and for that I will be forever grateful.

Don Hepburn graciously served as a key adviser and confidant during the writing process. He provided an invaluable fount of expertise, war stories, and operational lessons that litter this novel. All breaches of proper tradecraft are, of course, my own.

Dave Michael, college friend and occasional prank victim, rose to the occasion and, while editing the book, also taught me how to write good. Thank you for giving this novel such a hard time. It is better for it.

My dad, an author in his own right, read multiple versions of the manuscript, provided insightful feedback, and encouraged me onward each step of the way. Thank you, Dad, for always being there.

Kent Woodyard, dear friend and above-average human, offered advice and ideas through the earliest treatments, when the concept was little more than chicken-scratch on a napkin. Years earlier, he also gritted through my first attempt at writing, which was very bad. Thank you for continuing to read things when I send them to you and for occasionally picking up my phone calls.

Alex Holstein offered prescient, farsighted, and candid feedback along with encouragement and humor each step of the way. The moral support and camaraderie made all the difference.

Tim Grimmett made sure I didn't screw up the scenes in Damascus too badly, and saved me from several embarrassing errors.

It is hugely satisfying to watch a team form behind the story. And the team at Norton, ICM, and Curtis Brown rallied in a big way. Nneoma Amadi-obi kept everything moving. Dave Cole saved me from error and made it all better. Rory Walsh had the answers. Stephanie Thwaites and Helen Manders, at Curtis Brown, championed the book around the world. José Prata at Lua de Papel in Portugal offered immensely kind words and was the first foreign publisher to buy the book.

Many other dear friends and former Agency colleagues read early versions of the manuscript and offered help along the way. Hunter and Mary Beth Allen, Elisabeth Jordan, Blake Panzino, Marcus Gibbons, Mike and Jenny Green, Mark Weed, Griffin Foster, Jon Flugstad, Beryl Frishtick, John Wilson, Thomas Kivney, Anna Connolly, Erin Yerger, Sarah G., Becky Friedman, Betsy and Tim Martin, Elle Varnell, Joe L., James D., and Rob and Sahar Sea: all took the time to read and offer their candid thoughts. To each of you, I am abundantly grateful. Brice Wells, though not a reader, gave Norton's Art Department a generous head start by completing a (literal) napkin sketch of the book jacket after several ranch waters at the Reata bar in Fort Worth. In the end, sadly, very little of that gritty concept survived.

Readers living in Damascus—nameless, for their own protection—

also provided invaluable insight and perspective, though any mistakes or creative liberties are my own. While I have tried my best to render Damascus authentically, one creative flourish bears mention: though there are indeed scenic overlooks and a decent restaurant on Mount Qasioun, the running trails that feature prominently as Mariam's dead drop location are a complete fiction. The mountain itself is heavily militarized and, from a tradecraft standpoint, would make an atrocious drop site.

The Syria of this novel, while fictional, does take inspiration from real events that took place in the first two years of the uprising, in 2011–2013. The U.S. Embassy in Damascus, for example, was indeed overrun and vandalized by a pro-Assad mob in July 2011 that, while committing no violence, did leave behind rotten fruit, obscene graffiti, and an inoperable air-conditioning system. The aftermath of the massacre that Abu Qasim and Sarya observe on the road to Damascus did occur, in May 2012, in Taldou, one of several villages in the Houla region of central Syria. Though accounts differ, it is likely that more than a hundred people were killed, most in summary executions, by pro-government forces and militia. More than half of the dead were women and children. Rustum's fictional sarin attack, unfortunately, has all too real precedent on the Syrian battlefield. More than three hundred chemical weapons attacks have occurred during the civil war, the vast preponderance of those carried out by the Syrian regime against rebel-held population centers. The most infamous, the use of sarin in August 2013 in Damascus's Ghouta suburbs—of which Douma is a part—may have killed over a thousand people. The bomb that almost killed Ali, Rustum, and President Assad takes its inspiration from an attack on July 18, 2012, in which—again, though accounts differ—a rebel group likely placed a bomb inside the National Security Bureau's headquarters in central Damascus, detonating it during a high-level meeting of military and intelligence officials. The dead included the Defense Minister, the Deputy Defense Minister—also the President's brother in law—the Interior Minister, the chief of the National Security Bureau, and a Palace adviser and former Defense Minister. The President was not present during the actual attack, and of course the fictional Ali and Rustum were absent as well.

This novel would not have been possible without my past life at the CIA. I have tried to render the Agency—its officers, tradecraft, and operations—as accurately as was both possible and appropriate given the ongoing imperative to protect classified information. Thanks are due to the CIA's Publication Review Board, whose readers sifted through several versions of this manuscript to ensure nothing would endanger sources and methods.

Building the fictional CIA of this novel was quite fun, as was sneaking in the real details that occasionally made life in the secret world so bizarre. Indeed, on the lighter side, there is (or was, at least), a hot dog vending machine inside CIA Headquarters at Langley, the clocks never were quite synchronized, depending on the foreign country it was indeed possible to return to your hotel room and discover human excrement on the bed, and, as Sam laments, it is true that the CIA is both able to track down terrorists in remote mountain passes and yet can sometimes struggle to procure basic office supplies.

And yet, for all its warts and complications, I love and admire the CIA and hope that readers of this novel will come away with a deeper understanding of its Mission and the sacrifices made by its officers to protect America and her way of life. The CIA remains an essential institution for the preservation of our security and the global order. Its case officers, analysts, targeters, support officers, S&Ters, coders, linguists, managers (most of them), janitors, techies, SISers, SOOs, contractors, green jackets, CMOs, and many other cadres make the world a safer and better place. They work tirelessly, and largely in the shadows, for our great republic. We are in their debt.

I also want to thank my two boys, Miles and Leo, who, after each day of writing, served as the joyful—sometimes psychotic—welcoming committee back to the world of reality. Their energy, verve, humor, and unconditional love influenced this book in countless ways. Though you aren't yet old enough to read this (or anything, for that matter), I hope this book someday brings each of you some measure of the joy it has brought me to write it alongside you. And to my daughter, Mabel, just now in the world, I hope this one day makes you proud.

And, finally, and most importantly, all thanks and love to my wife, Abby. She worked out key plotlines and characters and served throughout as the book's foremost champion, co-conspirator, and muse. At each fork in the road, when quitting seemed like a nice idea, she pushed me onward. I could not have a better partner, in writing or in life.